THIS BOOK IS DEDICATED TO KUMA, WHO TAUGHT ME WHAT IT WAS TO BE A CANINE.

FENRIS
FIRAR

DAN COGLAN

Outskirts Press, Inc.
http://www.outskirtspress.com

ISBN: 978-1-4787-3637-0

Library of Congress Control Number: 2014911992

Outskirts Press and the "OP" logo are trademarks belonging to Outskirts Press, Inc.

PRINTED IN THE UNITED STATES OF AMERICA

INTRODUCTION

"What's that? I hear noises," Rita whispered, twisting in Scott's arms.

The horny college student groaned, and tried to calm his nervous date. This was not going the way he wanted it to.

"Baby, relax. We're alone here. All alone. If there's someone out there, it's just another couple, like us. Here to make some magic," he breathed, turning the young woman back to face him. "Make some magic with me, beautiful. Come on, give me some," he coaxed.

"Stop it," Rita said, pushing him away. "I heard something in the trees. Something moving around," she insisted, staring over her new boyfriend's shoulder. She squinted, trying to see into the darkness. "I think there's more than one."

"No shit, Rita," Scott grumbled. "There'd be two of them. You told me that this was the place to go for us to, you know, enjoy ourselves," he said, trying vainly to unbutton her blouse and hold her still at the same time. "It's just some of your friends, that had the same idea we did."

"It's not people. There's something out there, and they're all around us," she whispered again, nervously. She slapped at his hands. "Back off, you jerk. This is so not happening right now." When Scott tried to hold her close, she pushed him away. "Damn it, I said 'no,' Scott!" She snapped, louder than she'd intended.

A branch snapped out in the darkness. Rita jumped and grabbed onto Scott's arm. "See?" The terrified teenager breathed, clinging to her partner.

Scott Thomas felt the soft body of his date press against him and smiled. This was more like it. He slipped his free arm around

1

the girl's shoulders, and decided to play the heroic tough guy.

"Hey, you assholes. Come on out of there, right now. I'm gonna bust you up," he boasted, reveling in his role of the protector. This was going to get him laid, he could feel it. He took a step in the direction that they'd heard the branch break.

"Yeah, I'm talking to you," he taunted. "What are you gonna do about it, huh?" He took another step, dragging Rita with him. The cringing girl resisted but was pulled along by the larger young man.

"What the fuck..." Scott mumbled, peering at the ground several feet in front of them. Rita looked at the spot that her boyfriend seemed to be staring at. She could just make out a shape on the ground. It wasn't human.

Rita squealed. "Oh my God, it's a deer. What happened to it?"

"Shit. It's dead. It's torn to pieces. Damn," he whispered, swallowing hard. "Let's get the fuck outa here," Scott said, his earlier sense of bravado completely gone. Rita felt him tremble.

"I don't like this. Get me out of here, Scott," Rita implored, reaching out to grab his hand. The unnerved young man shook free and stepped away from the deer carcass and his date, intent on fleeing. He took two quick steps but stopped suddenly.

"What? What is it?" Rita asked, bumping into his back in her haste to stay with him. The questions caught in her throat as she looked past him. Not ten feet in front of them was a pair of luminous eyes.

"Oh God," she whimpered. They started backing up, stopping only when they heard the soft growling sounds coming from behind them. Hardly daring to breathe, the two slowly turned. Another pair of malevolent eyes glared back at them.

Rustling sounds came from all around them, and they could just make out huge shapes beginning to encircle them, just out of reach. Whatever had killed the deer was out there, and the young couple was next. Rita closed her eyes, praying that it would all just go away.

She heard a hideous snarl, and felt a sudden rush of movement all around her. Something hot and wet splashed across her face and chest. There was a brief gurgling sound and when she opened her eyes Scott was simply gone.

"Scott..." she called in a very small voice. The park was completely silent for a time, and Rita didn't move. After a few seconds, she heard ripping and tearing sounds to her left. She pivoted slowly, not wanting to see, but unable to keep from looking.

At that moment, the clouds that had been covering the moon parted, and the small clearing was bathed in moonlight. Rita screamed. Savaging the unmoving body of Scott Thomas was a huge wolf, covered in blood.

Shaking, with another scream caught in her throat, Rita felt hot breath on her bare leg and glanced down. A second gigantic wolf stood in front of her, huge jaws parted, fangs bloodied and mere inches from her. A small whimper escaped her lips, and she felt her bladder evacuate.

Giant wolves surrounded her, snapping and growling at one another and at her. She knew she was dead. Again, the young girl closed her eyes. She didn't want to see the end.

A howl split the air, making Rita jump and open her eyes. The biggest wolf, the one on top of Scott, had its muzzle tipped back and was baying at the moon. The others, taking the howl as an invitation, bolted forwards and tore into the remains of Rita's unfortunate date.

The wolves pushed past her, almost knocking her down as they rushed past. For an instant, Rita stood still, unable to comprehend that the wolves hadn't taken her. Then her survival instincts kicked in, and she turned and ran.

Sobbing, the terrified girl blundered through the scrub, heedless of direction, knowing only that she had to get away. Pushing through branches, she reached another clearing and tripped, going down in a heap.

She looked down and saw that she had gotten her feet tangled in what appeared to be a pile of discarded clothing. Other piles were strewn around the clearing. At the far end was a cluster of motorcycles, gleaming in the moonlight.

Rita raced past the bikes, following the path that led out of the park of death. Her heartbeat thundered in her ears, and she couldn't hear if anything was pursuing her or not. At any moment, she expected to feel sharp teeth end her run to freedom.

She reached the entrance to the park and staggered onto the paved road. Shuddering, her adrenalin spent, she slowed to a ragged walk, limping blindly away from the park. All she knew was that she had to keep going, and put more distance between her and the wolves.

Behind her, a chorus of howls rose to meet the full moon that shone down on the deserted highway. Rita flinched but didn't dare look back. She reached up and wiped away some of Scott's blood from her eyes and kept moving.

CHAPTER 1

The phone rang, interrupting the only good dream to visit Robert Parker in months. He tried to ignore the insistent ringing, and recapture the elusive dream, but couldn't. Finally giving in to the inevitable, the sheriff reached over and picked it up.

"Parker," he growled.

"Sheriff, this is Deon. There's an emergency, and Lem told me to call you," replied a hesitant and irritating voice.

"Who? Who the hell are you?" Parker rasped, earning himself a poke in the back from his long-suffering wife. Mary disliked the all too frequent calls in the middle of the night at least as much as he did, but believed that her husband was still too harsh on those poor souls who had the responsibility of making those calls.

"Chief, it's Deon. Deon Lett…the new night dispatcher," stammered the voice on the phone. "You know? I been here for almost two months now."

"Oh. Yeah. Right," Parker grumbled. "Okay, Lett, what's up that couldn't wait until morning? What the hell time is it, anyway?" he said, looking out the window at the darkness.

"Umm, it's almost three-thirty, chief. Sorry. Deputy Lemly picked up a girl wandering down 287, all covered in blood and in shock. He took her to Mercy. He's waitin' for you there, okay?"

"Okay, Lett. Tell Lem I'm on my way. Send Winslow down 287 and see if he can find a car wreck or something. Be there in 20," Parker said, hanging up before Lett could reply.

"What's up, sweetheart?" Mary asked, her voice filled with concern and, not surprisingly, sleep. She was a heavy sleeper, and had never taken being disturbed in the middle of the night lightly.

Parker patted her shoulder and didn't speak. With any luck, she'd be back asleep by the time he was out the door. Quietly, he slipped out of bed and struggled into his clothes, trying to wake up.

He wished that he had time for coffee, but figured the hospital would have something that would at least pass. Emergency room coffee was risky, and didn't always qualify as coffee in his book.

"Robert, you didn't answer me: what's dragging you away in the middle of the night this time?"

"Nothing, dear. Lem picked up a girl wandering down the road and took her to the hospital. I just need to go and see her. Go back to sleep, Mary," he said, gently. As he slipped out of the bedroom he heard her sigh and roll back over.

Once outside, he looked up at the sky. There was a full moon. He hadn't been able to see it from his bedroom window, but it was bright enough to cast shadows in the middle of the night. He permitted himself a small smile: shadows in the dark of night were a portent of evil things to come. At least, that was what he and his friends had believed as kids. Monsters lived in the shadows.

Parker snorted as he got behind the wheel of his Charger. Monsters, indeed. Twenty years of law enforcement had taught him that the only monsters in the world were of the human variety, and what they were capable of was more than enough to make up for any lack of supernatural origin.

Not that this particular situation didn't present itself with some monster scenarios. A young girl walking down a deserted road in Texas, covered in blood? That just screamed Texas Chainsaw Massacre. He remembered sneaking into that movie with his sister and best friend as kids, and later having "chainsaw fights" with him, much to his sister's embarrassment. Girls just didn't get guy stuff.

The memory led to more thoughts about his sister, gone the last three years. She had been the outgoing one, the one with all the personality and zest for living. Even the ridiculous games that James and Robert had come up with, and then embarrassed her with, had been based on ideas of hers.

Not a day went by that he didn't miss her. Almost as much as her still grieving husband and son did, he reminded himself grimly.

Her murder had shattered his best friend's life, and three years later he still hadn't recovered. It hadn't helped Parker much, either; personally or professionally. He shook his head angrily and forced himself to think of other things.

Twenty minutes later, Parker pulled into Mercy Hospital. The emergency lot was mostly empty, and the hospital itself was largely dark. Contrary to popular belief, weekends were much slower for hospitals. All of the clinics closed, and any and all patients that could be sent home, were. Only the emergency room was open for business, and at four am, even that was slow.

Lem met him outside the automatic doors. Ronald "Lem" Lemly was a perfect Texas deputy: tall, lanky, red hair covered by a slouched back cowboy hat, and ever-present toothpick stuck between his teeth. His drawl was more pronounced than anyone else in Iowa Park. The fact that he was from Illinois, and not Texas, mattered not at all.

"Sheriff, we got us here a problem," he said, by way of greeting. The two men walked into the emergency room together as Lemly continued.

"I found this here lil' slip of a girl, wanderin' down the middle a' 287, 'bout an hour ago. She was covered in blood, clothes all mussed, and her hair all tangled, too. Didn't react a bit when I pulled over to check on 'er. Ain't said a word since, neither. I done brought her in here and let the nurse clean her up some, but she still ain't talkin'."

Parker looked at his deputy and friend. "Any ID on her, Lem?"

Lem took off his hat as they reached the ER front desk. "Naw. Nothin'. No purse or anything, Sheriff. Got her clothes in a bag, though. They got blood all over them, but none of it looks to be hers. Her room is this way," he waved, starting to go past the desk with his boss.

Surprisingly, the nurse at the desk stepped in front of them. The young woman scowled at the two lawmen. She held up a hand.

"Where are you gentlemen going?"

Parker was put off. "Where the hell do you think we're going? We're gonna talk to the girl that we brought in," he growled.

"I'm not sure that's necessary just now. The doctor hasn't been in to see her yet, Sheriff, and we have to make sure that she's okay to answer questions. Why don't you wait here, and I'll come get you when it's time?"

"Little lady, it's time when I say it is. I didn't get out of bed and come over here at this ungodly hour just to sit in the damned waiting room," Parker rasped, shaking his head in exasperation at the stupidity of the world in general, and this nurse in particular. "We're going in to talk to this girl and find out what happened to her."

Lem stepped between the two just as the angry nurse was about to retort. "Look here, Amy, is it? Sorry, the Sheriff's a little grumpy without his morning cup of coffee. But see here, we do need to go in and see that girl," he said, turning his hat around in his large freckled hands, seeking to make peace. "We don't know if there's anybody else out there, mebbe hurt and needin' our help. I brought her in, and didn't see no one else, but we don't know, see? We'll be nice, y'know."

"C'mon, nurse Amy, you can go with us," he added, putting his arm around the much shorter woman and ushering her along, keeping himself between his boss and the still upset nurse.

"Fine," she huffed. "But be careful, and hopefully Dr. Simon will be in soon. He's finishing a cast in room one. Your patient is in two. Just a moment," she said, slipping ahead of them to a curtained off room and knocking on the doorway.

"Hello? Hey, it's Nurse Bishop. I'm here with a couple of policemen. They need to see you for a minute. Are you okay?" she asked, peeking around the corner at her patient. Apparently satisfied, she waved for the officers to follow and went in.

Sheriff Parker's first thought was that there was a mistake. Huddled on the bed was a tiny figure, a child really. Dressed in a hospital gown and wrapped in the bed sheet, the young woman that Lem had found looked no older than ten or twelve.

He looked over at his deputy, eyebrows raised. Lem, picking up on his thoughts, simply shrugged. The nurse took up station beside her patient, hovering protectively next to her and fussing over her sheet.

Parker cleared his throat. "Miss? I'm Sheriff Parker. This here is my deputy, Ron Lemly. I guess you already met him," he added. The girl on the bed stared blankly, giving no indication that she even knew that they were in the room. "I need you to answer a couple of questions for me, ma'am, so that we can help you. What's your name, little lady?" he asked, trying again to get her attention, but still not getting even a flicker of response.

Parker moved forwards and crouched down, bringing his face down so that he could look the girl in the eye. This, at least, caused a reaction. The girl shrank back, flinching away and seeming to withdraw even more into herself.

"Okay, that's enough," Nurse Bishop said, putting her arms around the cowering girl, glaring at the Sheriff. "You can go wait outside until the doctor says otherwise."

Parker looked up at the nurse in frustration. She really wasn't helping the situation.

"Nurse, perhaps you should go wait outside. You're making this worse. I need to find out what happened to her. Period. Now back off," he said quietly but with gritted teeth.

"Sheriff, I am not leaving you alone with this patient. For all I know, you could do her serious harm," she all but spat back at him.

Seeing that the nurse was prepared to send them out of the room, Lem stepped in front of his boss for the second time. With a warm smile towards the nurse, he pulled open his wallet and started taking out pictures to show to Rita.

"So, little lady, Ah'll just bet you got people at home wonderin' where y'all are at. I got folks at home, too. This here's my wife, Rhonda," he drawled, showing the girl a photo. So smooth and gentle was his manner, that the nurse let him continue.

"This little rag-a-muffin is our daughter, Emmy. She's five, got no front teeth, looks like an ol' jack-o-lantern, don't she?"

Still no reaction. Lem shuffled his stack of pictures and showed her another. "This one here is Em with Flash, our Shepherd. She's the one with the dress," he chuckled.

The girl's eyes flicked to the photo, and a second later, they widened. 'At last, a reaction,' Parker thought. She pointed at the picture and screamed. And continued to scream. Amy Bishop desperately tried to calm her but she only got worse, thrashing and clawing in an effort to get away from whatever was in her head.

"Jesus Christ, would you calm her down?" Parker rasped. "Maybe give her something?"

"I'm trying to calm her down, you idiot!" Bishop snapped back, struggling with her patient. "If you'd have waited like I told you to, this wouldn't be happening right now. Go get the doctor. Now!"

Parker hesitated, wanting to reply. Deciding that she was right, he turned, shoved his way through the curtain, and slammed into another man who was hustling to get into the room. Both men went down in a heap.

"Damn it, watch where you're going," Parker growled, helping the other man to his feet.

"Just try to stay out of the way, Sheriff," the other man said, stepping around the bulky lawman and taking immediate charge of the room.

"Amy, get me a sedative. Lem, come around to her right, and hold her still. I need her other arm," he said, moving to the girl's left side and gently, but firmly, prying her left arm free.

Amy slapped a syringe into his outstretched right hand as Lem pressed the patient's shoulders down flat on the bed. After slightly depressing the plunger to eliminate any potential air bubbles, Dr. Simon injected the hysterical girl. Within seconds she relaxed, falling silent and slumping into unconsciousness.

While the others were tending to the patient, Parker had picked up Lem's fallen photos. He stared at the picture of Emmy with her dog, trying to figure out what could have led to such a panic.

'Hmm,' he thought. 'Run of the mill photo. Little girl with gap-toothed smile. Not scary. German shepherd with tongue hanging out, being hugged by little girl. Also not scary. What the hell?' Something was off.

"Doc, I want her checked for drugs, okay? And alcohol," he called out, handing the pictures back to his deputy. "There's something not right here."

"Sheriff, we'll run blood work and check for drugs, too. I understand that she was kind of a mess when you brought her in;

do you want a rape kit done, too?" Simon said, taking command of the room again.

"Yeah, go ahead, doc. Thanks," Parker said, exhaling. He turned away, ready to leave.

An orderly appeared. Nurse Bishop saw him in the doorway and motioned him over. She tossed over her shoulder, to the doctor. "We're moving her to the ICU. I'll send her charts and orders with her, doctor," and Simon nodded.

"This is Dusty. He's the best hospital bed driver in the county. You'll be fine," she whispered to her unconscious patient, patting her shoulder as she stacked the paperwork on top of the blanket that she had covered the young girl with.

Dusty swelled with pride at the compliment from the pretty nurse. Grinning at her, he unlocked the wheels and moved out. He caught the corner of the doorframe with the bed solidly, bringing it to a sudden, jarring halt. Charts slid off the bed, scattering across the floor.

Parker bent down and started picking them up, while Bishop hurriedly checked on the patient. Satisfied that she was okay, she bent a withering scowl at the red-faced Dusty. After taking the files from Parker and replacing them on the bed, she stood and watched as the crestfallen orderly carefully maneuvered the bed down the hallway to the elevator.

"What?" she demanded, noticing the look from Parker.

"Nothing. You just do a good job, and you care about your patients," he said defensively.

"And that surprises you? What did you think; that I was an incompetent moron?" Bishop snapped, stalking away without a backward glance.

Doctor Simon stood by the sheriff, looking embarrassed. "I'm sorry, Sheriff. She's new, and young at that. She's a first rate nurse, but has a lot to learn about life. I'll get on those tests for you. Call you as soon as I know anything, okay?"

Parker nodded and prepared to leave. Lem picked up his hat and followed his boss out through the doorway.

Lem looked back at the doctor. "Thanks, doc. You're good people. Y'all give us a call when them tests come back or she starts talking, 'kay?"

Back outside, Parker took a deep breath and let it out, slowly. Then he jumped as his phone went off.

"Yeah," he said, flipping the thing open before it could vibrate a second time.

"Sheriff," came the voice of his new dispatcher, "Deputy Winslow found a car in Pine Cone Park and would like you to come out as soon as is convenient."

"Fine. Lem and I are on our way now. Be there in fifteen. Out," he snapped, shutting the phone and sticking back in his pocket with an oath.

Lem snorted. "Now, Sheriff, let's not be rude 'bout our new dispatcher. He's pretty good at his job. I unnerstand that he makes a mean omelet, too. There's a reason why he's on a desk, ya know."

"Yeah, whatever. Let's go, Lem. I'll follow you out," Parker said, heading for his car. Lem nodded at his back and got into his squad car. Heading out of the parking lot, the deputy slammed on his brakes and stopped as Parker cut him off and led the way out of the lot.

Parker, forgetting that he told Lem to lead, tore off down the road, heading out of town and towards the obscure little park. Behind him, Lem shook his head and smiled. Some things never changed.

CHAPTER 2

Less than twelve minutes later the two cops turned off into the small gravel parking lot. Only two other vehicles were there; a Dodge Charger bearing the logo of the Iowa Park Sheriff's Department, and a red mustang. A short black man stepped out of the Charger as they pulled in.

"Sheriff, I found this here Mustang, 'bout a half hour ago. Ain't seen anybody around, either, while I's waitin' for you."

"Fine. You run the plates, Winslow?" Parker asked, barely glancing at his diminutive deputy.

"Sure did, Sheriff. Car's registered to a Scott Thomas outta Longview. Twenty-one year old college student, looks like."

Parker merely grunted, taking a closer look at the car. Mustang convertible. No older than an '05, since it had the Roush Racing front end that made the muscle car look vaguely like a shark. Top was down, keys still in the ignition. There was a small purse on the floor in front of the passenger seat, tucked up close to the gearshift lever.

"You touch anything in the car yet?" he asked, nodding his head towards the purse.

"No sir. I waited for you guys, just like you wanted, Sheriff. What do you want me to do now? Want me to check it out?" the young and slightly nervous deputy asked.

Parker sighed. He hated new guys, especially the ones that acted all excited and nervous. It reminded him of a little dog, and they drove him nuts.

Lem grinned. He could see his boss was getting fed up again. Robert Parker was a caring and kind man, but he was impatient, taciturn, and had a tendency to make people nervous and defensive around him.

"Jimmy. You done real good. Why don't you let me and the boss check out the car, okay? Maybe you can scout around some, now that we're here, okay? See if you can find out where they went. They might just still be on a bench, making out or something, you know?"

Parker waited for Jimmy to wander off before addressing his deputy. Pine Cone Park was a notorious make out spot for Iowa Park teenagers. The small ten-acre park had two main trails that opened up in a couple of spots to small clearings, and had benches strategically placed along the paths. Since the clearings and the benches weren't visible from the highway, the park was popular with those who didn't have their own rooms to take advantage of.

Having better things to do than attempt to control or even curtail teen-age hormones, the department usually just made a couple runs through the park each night after it closed at ten, then left it alone.

"Was this car here the last time you went through, Lem?" Parker asked, already knowing the answer, but asking anyway.

"Nope. Ran through just before one, I think. Nobody here then, boss," Lem drawled, reaching in to grab the purse. He handed it to the sheriff and then popped open the glove box to look for registration information.

Inside was the usual jumble of flashlights, fuses, manuals, and extra papers, along with an insurance card and the registration. Lemly separated the last two items from the rest of the mess and straightened back up.

"Scott Thomas, 514 Harroun Drive, Longview, Texas. Current tags and insurance from State Farm in Longview for a 2006 Mustang, boss. Nuthin' new here, though, we already knew that. What you got?" the deputy asked, putting the papers down on the front seat and watching Jimmy Winslow wandering over to the left side trail at the edge of the parking lot.

"School ID," Parker muttered, fishing through the tightly packed little purse. He tried to extricate the plastic card and pulled out a small lacy undergarment that had snagged the corner of the

ID. He shook his head and dropped the black bra on the seat with Lem's papers and looked at the card.

"Rita Ibarra, junior at Iowa Park High School. Well, if it's her, she's local," he grunted. "Hard to say from the picture, Lem." He poked in the purse more and came up with a driver's license. "Ah, here we go."Yep. Rita Ibarra, sixteen years old, 5'2", 105 pounds. Sounds like her. Tiny little thing. Lives in town. Call the hospital, Lem, and tell 'em her name, and then have Deon or whatever his name is call her folks. I'm gonna head down the trail on the right and see if anything's down that way," Parker instructed, and walked off.

Lem sketched the Sheriff a salute and pulled out his phone. Parker had just reached the beginning of the trail, when a loud explosion sounded, causing both men to jump.

The explosion settled into a loud, throaty roar that Parker recognized. It was a motorcycle. More joined in. A lot more. Thunder filled the entire park as at least a dozen or so big bikes fired up.

Parker came back and stood next to Lem. The growing roar came from the trail on the left, where Winslow had gone.

Bikers appeared. The first man through was a huge brute, wearing leather pants and a dirty vest. His bearded face was ugly and angry, twisted into an evil scowl as he glared at the two lawmen. As he rolled past he threw up the middle finger of his left hand in salute.

Behind him rode at least twenty others, all similarly dressed. Most wore leather jackets, featuring a wolf's head with bloody fangs. Parker took note of the name on the back- "Fenris Firar." Whatever that meant, he mused. Fenris was a wolf, but the other word made no sense.

'Serious bikers,' he thought. Bedrolls and very few belongings. Most of the women on their own rides. Most not very attractive. With an exception or two, he amended as a blonde rode by on the back of a chopper and winked.

In a couple of minutes, the entire pack had ridden past and pulled out of the parking lot. Forming up into a huge wedge, the bikers headed off towards Iowa Park. The sheriff stared after them for a time, wondering if they had anything to do with his traumatized girl or not.

'Well, if we need them for questioning, they won't be hard to find,' he told himself and turned away. Back to work. He waved Lem towards the recently vacated left path, and inadvertently pointed right at his other deputy.

Jimmy Winslow was running back towards them, waving his hands. "Sheriff, did you see them? All them bikers? They just left!" he shouted, still waving at the exit.

"Of course we saw them. Rode right past us," Parker snapped, indicating by his tone that his rookie deputy was an idiot. Lem turned his face away to hide his grin. The kid was a slow learner.

"They was all parked in the clearing, Sheriff. I started walking up to them, cuz they was all getting' on their bikes like they was gonna leave. I thought you'd want to talk to 'em, and I tried to stop 'em, but they just rode right past me. Thought they was gonna run me over."

"It's okay, Winslow. We got a good look at them. Let's just keep looking around, okay?"

The excitable deputy nodded vigorously. "You bet, Sheriff. You want me to go back the way I came? I'll go back down this here path, and you can take the other one with Lem."

Parker shook his head. "I'll wander down the trail with you, I think. Let's see where those bikers were. Lem can handle the other one by himself, I think."

A short walk took them to the clearing where the bikes had obviously been parked. Tire prints were everywhere, the grass was flattened, and empty food wrappers lay scattered about. Winslow made a show of examining all of the trash, clucking about how rude and sloppy the bikers were, and how much they could be fined. Parker kept walking, ignoring his deputy's righteous indignation. There was more going on than littering.

Partway down the path, just before the next clearing, he found Scott Thomas. Or what was left of him. Flies were already buzzing around the remains. The early morning sun shone down, revealing the ruin of what had once been a human being.

Parker froze in place, taking the scene in. The body was on its back. Blood not only covered the body, but saturated the ground around it. Only the buzzing of flies disturbed the stillness. Taking care where he put his feet, the sheriff moved closer. Stopping at the fringe of the blood spatters, Parker looked down at the remains. And then looked away, breathing quickly.

Robert Parker was no stranger to bloodshed or violence. He had been first on the scene of traffic fatalities and boating accidents. He had even killed a man himself. He could process this scene. Taking a deep breath and holding it, he turned back to the body.

The head was barely still attached to the torso. The throat had been savaged, torn open and shredded, exposing the neck vertebra. Even with all the blood, the whiteness of the bones shone in the sunlight.

The left arm was mangled, much of the flesh torn off. The entire right arm was missing, gone from the shoulder down. The chest and abdomen were torn up, as well, while further down…

Parker turned away again and lost it. Veteran of bloody crime scenes or not, this one was too much. His stomach rebelled, and, for the first time since a junior high football practice, he threw up. All over his shoes.

Shuddering, Parker wiped his mouth with the back of his hand, and resumed looking at the ruined body. The abdomen looked as though most of the man's stomach and innards had been eaten, along with his privates and most of the legs. A bloody sandal lay a few feet away; the other was still on one of the victim's feet, which had been severed from the lower leg.

Winslow showed up. The deputy broke into a run when he saw that Parker had found something, but the Sheriff waved him back without even looking at him.

"Get Lem," was all he said. When Winslow hesitated, Parker snapped "Now."

Jimmy called the senior deputy with his walkie-talkie, and then stepped up to look at what the sheriff was studying. It looked like a dead body. It was a dead body. Very dead. In fact, it looked eaten. He looked closer.

When the young deputy noticed that the victim's groin had been savaged, and that his privates were gone, he too lost control. Winslow staggered to the side a little and threw up. Parker noted with some amusement that it was at the exact same spot that he had puked, too.

Lem arrived to see his boss standing with an arm around the smaller deputy's shoulders, speaking softly to him. Finishing, he patted the man and gestured towards the parking lot behind Lem. Winslow nodded and slipped past Ron.

"What did you find, boss? Is that the Thomas kid?"

Parker nodded. "What's left of him. Careful, Lem; it ain't pretty."

Lem glanced at the body and then back up at his boss. He nodded. Looking back down, he swallowed back the bile that threatened to come up, and tried to look at the scene with clinical detachment. It almost worked.

"No wonder you sent Jimmy away. Not the sort of thing for a rookie, huh? Shi-it," he pronounced, dragging out the middle.

"He's alright. Bad scene. He'll be fine, I think. Just threw him a little."

Lem looked back at his boss closely. Usually not the most understanding or supportive of men, Parker was being almost human now. And then the deputy saw the sheriff's shoes. Understanding flashed across Lem's face and he smiled.

"Nice to know that the boss is still human, too. 'Bout lost it myself, seeing the hole where his jewels are supposed to be," Lem stated. "What you think, Bob, animal attack? Sure don't look like no person coulda done this. Or even a group, like them bikers."

"Don't know what you mean. Fuckin' kid puked all over my shoes. Sent him away so he wouldn't contaminate the scene any more than he already has," Parker grunted. Don't look like any person coulda done this, though. You're right about that, at least.

"Still gotta run this as a crime scene, Lem. Call it in, have Winslow start taping off the area. Let's close the park, okay? And call the hospital again. We really need to talk to the girl, now. See what they can do.

"What else? We'll need an ambulance, but make sure you get the coroner out here; need him more'n the ambulance. Great, and that means old Doc Simon. Maybe you can talk to him. Man hasn't spoken civil to me since I ticketed him for driving impaired ten years back. Asshole," Parker grunted, unaware that he was talking much more than normal, letting Lem know just how much the body was bothering him, too.

"Got it, boss," Lem said, chewing his frayed toothpick. He took out his cell phone again and moved away.

"So what the hell could have done this?" Parker muttered to himself, forcing himself to look at the body again. "Fuckin' throat is completely ruined. Had to be something big. Big enough to take an arm. And a foot. Shit."

The sheriff studied the ground around the body. The grass was pretty trampled, and blood was splattered everywhere. There! A footprint. Looked like a dog. A really big dog. 'A wolf,' a voice in the back of his head said. Scowling, he found another. Only the print was too large even for a wolf. And there were no wolves left in West Texas. Hadn't been for forty years. And then a third print. Looking closely, he found a profusion of the huge footprints, some with blood in them.

He followed them away from the body, back to the clearing where the bikers had been. And there they ended. Parker put his hands on his hips and stared off in the distance, ignoring the growing chaos around him.

CHAPTER 3

Iowa Park was a peaceful little town in western Texas. Normal early mornings started out slowly, with neighbors getting the paper off of the front porch and waving or exchanging pleasantries. Downtown enjoyed a busy, but sedate, breakfast crowd. Even during festival season, mornings started out quietly.

The Fenris Firar, unaware of Iowa Park's history, and certainly uncaring, disrupted that routine, shattering the serenity of the beautiful morning with the thunder of loud motorcycles. People stopped what they were doing and looked in the direction of the oncoming storm. Conversations ceased, and a motorist or two even pulled over as the herd of outlaw bikers swept into town.

Hard men rode in on a variety of big v-twin Harleys. The riders didn't consist of only men, either- at least half a dozen of the bikers were women, and several had their own rides. One or two looked attractive in a dangerous, wild sort of way. Two or three plainly did not look attractive in any sort of way, though they still looked dangerous and wild.

The brutish man on the first Harley led the way down the main street towards Albertson's Grocery. His lip curled in derision as the pack pulled into the parking lot en masse, cutting off traffic. The fact that no one honked or yelled only fueled his justification for hating people.

The mass of bikes came to a halt, bunched up in several parking spots. As one, they dismounted their bikes, shook out their hair, and followed their massive leader into the grocery store. Not only did the automatic doors slide aside for them, so did the early morning crowd of shoppers.

Conversations died out throughout the store as people became aware of them. The bikers seemed amused at the reaction. Sarcastic smiles came to many of their faces as they stalked through the store towards the deli, where an elderly couple stood at the counter ordering breakfast. They turned, eyes lighting up with fear as they became aware of the large motley group assembled behind them.

"Please, sir, ma'am, by all means, continue. We'll just wait our turn," the leader said, hands clasped behind his back, smiling with feigned innocence and politeness. Hearty laughs followed this statement, from his mob.

"We j-just want coffees, to go, please," the old man stammered, ashamed that he was afraid, but too smart to say or do anything about being intimidated.

The cashier, who looked to be no older than 18, rang them up, gave them their coffees, and then looked up, face flushed.

"And what can we get you all?"

"Sir, we would like to try your all-you-can-eat breakfast; the one that says it's $4.99. Is that for all of us, or are you gonna charge us five bucks each to eat here?" the leader said, still feigning politeness.

"Uh, sir, that's supposed to be $4.99 for each person. I think I could do like a senior citizen discount for y'all if you'd like," the cashier replied nervously. "It does include your drink, too."

"Well… Jerry, is it?" the leader asked, reaching forwards to flick the young man's nametag. "That's mighty nice of you. Do I look like a senior citizen to you? Do you perhaps feel that we lack the means to pay for our food?" More laughter from his followers.

A new voice came, from behind the clearly spooked young cashier. "It's okay Jerry, I'll get this one." The deli manger stepped in front of Jerry, and smiled at the big biker.

"Hi. I'm the manager, Bill Jameson. I'd be happy to take your order. If'n y'all are plannin' on eatin' here though, it may take a bit to get enough food out for ya."

The biker seemed even more amused by the middle-aged dumpy man who stood before him, trying to look as though nothing out of the norm was going on.

"Bill, this looks like the nicest establishment that we've been invited to eat at in quite some time. As it so happens, we are VERY hungry, and would all really like to eat here. I've got a hunger that nothing ever seems to completely satisfy." This last was said with a leer at one of the girls in the kitchen, pouring pancake batter onto the grill. She twitched, pouring batter onto the floor. More laughter.

"Well, Bill, never let it be said that the Fenris Firar doesn't pay their way. Here," he said, digging into his jeans and pulling out a wad of crumpled up bills. Counting off twenties, he handed the manager seven of them, waved off his change, and grandly gestured for his troop to precede him to the tables.

"I ain't sure that there's enough room for all of us to sit together, Lobo. You want I should move some of these nice people?" one of the larger, scruffier men asked, grinning at a family of four sitting at a nearby table. They hurriedly rose and left the deli.

"Naw, Ulric, we'll just spread out and maybe sit with some of our new friends," the leader said, sitting at a booth and slipping his arm around a middle-aged woman, who sat cringing under his touch.

"Please, sir, we don't want no trouble. Y'all just be patient a minute and we'll get the tables rearranged for you to all sit together," pleaded Jameson, coming out from behind the counter.

Lobo rose to meet the smaller man, still with a malicious smile on his face. "We don't want no trouble, neither, Mr. Bill. We just want breakfast. Have I mentioned that we're powerful hungry? We may not even need no plates or spoons, right guys?"

Immediately several members of the pack reached over the counter and grabbed handfuls of food. Eggs, bacon, and pancakes were shoved into mouths amidst coarse laughter. One or two bikers took food off of other patrons' plates. Again, no one complained.

Jameson looked uncomfortable. Clearly, he didn't want to push the issue with the hostile, and probably volatile, group. Suddenly he looked past Lobo, towards the entrance of the store, and visibly relaxed. "Sir, you folks will need to just be patient for another moment and we'll have you served. Coffees all around?"

Lobo sneered at him. "Wow. Pretty confident now, huh? Like that one pig that came in is gonna make a big difference with us? It doesn't. But like I said, all we want to do is eat."

"How did you know…I mean, sir, we want to…umm," Jameson trailed off, trying to figure out how the man knew that one of Iowa Park's deputies had come in the main entrance. He hadn't turned his head at all.

"Bill, Bill, Bill. I don't need to see everywhere. I can SMELL pig from a looong way off," Lobo said, grinning. "It's okay. Don't panic. Just bring me some coffee. Now!" the last was growled into Bill's face. Along with everything else, the biker had breath that smelled as though something had died in his mouth and rotted there.

Bill put a sickly smile on his face and backed up. With any luck at all, nothing would happen beyond a lot of scary looking people eating breakfast here this morning. He'd have a great story to tell his wife, and avoid any actual violence. Whoever called the police would get free breakfast here for a week, he vowed.

The entire gang was now sitting at a variety of booths and tables, some with other occupants, some without. All looked smugly at the approaching officer.

Ray Becker had been a sheriff's deputy for five years. In that time he'd broken up bar fights, arrested drunks, been in a couple of high speed chases, and even talked down a suicidal man with a gun. Despite all that, he preferred the day shift, and the more tranquil pace that went with it. Writing speeding tickets and commiserating with the locals about the tourists over a morning donut was more fun than fighting drunks, or chasing kids around in the dark.

Becker didn't like the looks of the biker gang in the deli one bit. What few other customers were still in there with them looked stressed and nervous, their stares beseeching him to do something. The twenty or so bikers all looked at him as well. They looked less than impressed.

Suddenly self-conscious, Becker hitched up his belt, loosened his baton slightly, and stared back. Fixing what he hoped was a confident smile on his face, he strode up to the group.

"Mornin', y'all," he said, nodding at the bikers. He casually stepped up to the counter, looked at Bill Jameson, and ordered breakfast.

The manager's eyes widened in disbelief. Here the law finally showed up to rescue him, and all the guy was doing was ordering breakfast? What the hell? He paid taxes for this? Muffled laughter came from the seated bikers.

Becker paid for his food, accepted his cup of coffee from Jameson, then went and sat down across from the leader of the gang. Taking a small sip of his hot brew, he looked up at Lobo.

"Nice mornin', huh? Might get some rain later on, though. Don't suppose that'd be the first time y'all get rained on, eh?"

Lobo looked at him with mild puzzlement. He could smell the sweat on this man, knew he was scared, but there was no outward sign of it. No shaking hands, no averted eyes, no catch in his voice. Perhaps bluster and threats weren't the right way to proceed this time.

"Hell, sheriff, that's the only time some of these bums bathe!" he boomed, deliberately giving the deputy a promotion. "A lil' water never hurt no one."

"Deputy. Not sheriff. I ain't that important. I'm just kinda addicted to the coffee here. Pancakes ain't bad, either," Becker said, quietly. "Hope y'all don't mind if I join you this morning." There was no challenge in his words, nor was there in his expression. He looked and acted exactly as though he was sitting in the middle of a group of ranchers, or retirees.

Nonplussed, Lobo glanced around at his pack. A couple shrugged, looking away. There were some muttered comments about not eating with pigs, but no one moved. Now wasn't the time to start trouble.

With studied indifference, Lobo slumped his massive shoulders slightly. He stretched, and then sprawled back, leaning into the bench. Then he smiled hugely at the deputy.

"Why, no deputy, we wouldn't mind at all. In fact, we'd be honored. Been a long time since we broke bread with a lawman." This last was delivered with a sarcastic edge to it, eliciting chuckles from the assembly.

"Thanks. Ray Becker," the deputy said, nodding at the leader of the motorcycle gang. "So, Fenris Firar…what does that mean?"

"Lobo. This is my motley crew…Fenris Firar. Just sounded cool, ya know? Giant wolf and all that. Nobody messed with the wolf."

Becker looked at the muscular man in front of him. He appeared to be around 40 years old, with a gold hoop in his left ear, and a leather cord, with a high school ring hanging from it, around his neck. Noting the Longview High inscription, Ray asked, "So, Lobo, y'all from east of here?"

"No. I been all over, but home used to be south of Albuquerque. Why, you gonna write a book about me?"

"Too much work. I just like to talk with folks," he stated, taking another small sip of coffee. "Don't get to meet many bikers. Been ridin' long? I had a Honda Goldwing long time ago, but gave it up. Wife didn't like riding on the back, and was afraid to ride her own."

"Well, mister pig…, I mean, mister lawman, it's been a whole heap of fun, but we gots to go. Wouldn't want to wear out our welcome, ya know what I mean?" Lobo stood, towering over the seated deputy. He glared down at the man, knowing that the cop had diffused their scene, and lowered their intimidation level for these townsfolk. And worse, there was little that the hulking biker could do about it without provoking a full-scale war. That, he could ill afford.

Leaning down, Lobo rested his hands on the table. He put his face inches from Becker's. "You'll be seein' more of us, pig. Lots more. Have a nice day."

As if rehearsed, all twenty-five bikers stood up, dropping their plates on the various surfaces in a symphony of crashes. Smiling with malevolence, they strutted out of the deli, leaving in their wake one shaken deli manager, one worried sheriff's deputy, and one mess.

Once outside, Lobo whirled towards one of his minions. He snarled, "Aardwolf, get me the address for Bill Jameson. We know he's at work, let's pay a little visit to his house. We need more cash. Caleb," he said, turning to another, "take Winnie with you and clean them out. Quietly. We'll meet up at the truck stop on 287 further west of town. Ramona, you and Wrench take the side houses, like always."

The man known as Aardwolf returned with a crumpled page of the phone book in his hand, his scarred face creased in a broad smile. Somehow the smile contorted his already grotesque face into something even worse. He held out the paper for Lobo, who grinned, plucked the paper with one hand, then gave Aardwolf a high five with the other hand.

"Good boy, Aardie. Now git that ugly mug of yours behind me before I hurl. Now, let's see…Bill and Kathryn Jameson, 217 Rogers Avenue. All right, y'all, mount up. Let's ride," he said, throwing a leg over his hog. Soon, all the massive bikes were revving, splitting the morning calm with thunderous fury.

Twenty-two motorcycles pulled out of the grocery store parking lot. Eighteen bikes continued down the main street of Iowa Park. Four Harleys turned left after only a block, and headed for a small residential area of town.

The Fenris Firar had been operating this game for a long time. The main body of bikers, including the loudest of the machines, would cruise around town, being very visible. A small group would split off to "visit" homes that the gang knew would be empty.

The home would be burgled; valuable objects taken, belongings trashed, and the house on each side would be visited as well. The bikes would of course be parked several blocks away. After cleaning out the houses, the bikers would slip back to their bikes, and rejoin the pack. Police would wonder about them, question them, and note the coincidence, but the gang had an alibi—most of the town had seen the bikers cruising around town when the robbery went down.

The outlaw bikers were much more than mere burglars. They routinely held up convenience stores, waylaid unwary travelers, stole from people at bars, and had even helped an occasional hitchhiker "disappear." These were all things that local cops would become aware of, or at least suspect, but could never prove.

Back at Albertson's, Bill Jameson watched the last of the bikers leave, and then, after taking a deep breath, turned to the sheriff's deputy. Ray Becker was still sitting at his booth, drinking coffee, looking for all the world as though nothing out of the ordinary had happened.

"Deputy Becker, not that I don't appreciate the sheriff's department showing up and all, but what the hell was that? You just sat down with 'em and acted like they was regular folks! They durn near trashed the place; they done treated all our customers bad; and they insulted you."

Delayed stress made Jameson talk faster and louder than he probably intended. "We coulda been killed, and you acted like they was the best most law-abidin' citizens in this here county! What, you was waitin' fer me to kick 'em out?" Exasperated, the slightly pudgy middle-aged deli manager waved his arms in a big circle. "Oh yeah, I coulda taken all of 'em. I got me a gun, and a badge, and a baaad attitude!"

Ray waited for the man to wind down before saying, mildly, "Bill, sit down. Have a cup of coffee, and just relax. It's over. Nothin' really got broken, and nobody got hurt. You're a little scared, and a little upset, and that's okay. You did real good with those guys. Just calm down a bit, and go real easy on insulting the law, you hear?"

Jameson looked at the deputy, who stared him right in the eyes, calmly, with no anger. He ran his hand over his face, up over his balding head, and then nodded.

"Fair enough, Ray. Can you tell me what the heck just happened? I'll feel better knowing that you acted on some plan and not just let them bikers walk all over us."

Ray noticed that all of the deli staff was standing around close enough to overhear. He smiled, knowing that regardless of what he said now, these people would embellish and exaggerate his words until they bore no resemblance to the original. So he might as well stick with the truth.

"The truth is, I kinda made this up as I went," he began. He looked around at the faces, noting their expressions. "Look, those bikers are bad news. Anyone can see that. There was about twenty-five of them, and one of me. I have one gun. At least ten of those dudes were armed. You all noticed that, right?" Seeing nods, he continued. "My coming in being all big and bad, pulling my gun, being 'The Man' would have escalated things, and people would have gotten hurt. Most times, when the shit hits the fan, pardon me ladies," he nodded towards the three women in the group, who smiled nervously and nodded back, "people panic."

"So, when it gets rough, you want to be the calmest. Don't give a bad person anything to push against. Keep things low key, and be rational. That's what I did with those bikers. They won't be hard to find. You can bet we'll be checking up on them, too—find out where they're from, where they've been, who they really are, and so on. There will be a strong police presence wherever they are from now on, you can bet on that." Ray smiled reassuringly as he added the last.

What Ray Becker couldn't tell the Albertson's employees was something that he couldn't admit to anyone, even himself. The truth was, he was famous for being cool under pressure, of never panicking under fire, and he was a total fraud. He always went cool and deliberate because secretly he was convinced that if forced to fight for his life he would come up lacking. No one knew of the nightmares, the secret drinking binges that for a while became the only way to fall asleep, and for the briefest of times, the sleeping tablet abuse.

He had managed to keep his fears secret from his fellow officers, his friends, and even his family. Ray believed that he handled the bikers effectively, but he also thought that they were not looking for trouble then, either. Just breakfast. The same breakfast that he had eaten, and would throw up once no one was around to see him.

"Deputy Becker, do you think that they'll come back here?" The young woman's question broke Ray's unpleasant reverie, and brought him back to the deli.

"Dorrie, I don't think they meant any harm today. I think that they are probably criminals, but I don't think that they are stupid. They won't be causing you all any problems," he said, reaching out and touching her plump shoulder. 'The personal touch always seems more reassuring,' he thought.

"Alright, y'all, if you have no more questions, I gotta go. Got reports to fill out about these guys. Bad guys to chase, donuts to track down, you know."

Becker rose from his seat, picked up his hat, placed it on his head, nodded to Bill Jameson, and walked out of the deli after slipping a fork into his pocket. He called dispatch and filled them in on what had happened, then called Sheriff Parker to talk to him. After that he walked around the corner and threw up.

●● ◖◉◗ ●●

While Ray Becker was being sick in the alley behind Albertson's, the biker gang known as the Fenris Firar was driving around the Wal-Mart parking lot. Iowa Park wasn't really big enough to cruise around in for long, so they made do with playing parking lot games.

The three women who rode "bitch" on the hogs got dropped off at the front entrance. They each grabbed a shopping cart, and shoved them into the traffic lanes. Several of the bikers zoomed up behind the carts and bumped into them, shoving them forwards. The race was on.

As the biker chicks rolled in more carts, more bikes entered the race. The object was simple: be the first person to get your cart all the way to end of the parking lot and out into the road itself. No rules. Just good simple fun. "Shopping Center Crazy" is what Lobo had coined this game, taking the title from an old J. Geils Band song called Rage In A Cage.

After several minutes of near miss traffic accidents, and screaming Wal-Mart shoppers, the bikers took off. Fun was fun, but if they outstayed their welcome the cops would catch them. The goal right now was to be seen but not stopped.

"C'mon, get yer asses back on board!" Lobo called as three bikes roared up to the standing biker women.

"Fuckin' A, Lobo," one responded, as she hopped on the back of Aardwolf's chopper. She kicked a wobbly cart with her left leg as Aardwolf dumped the clutch and cracked the throttle. Rear tire shrieking, the old shovelhead tore out of the lot after the rest of the gang.

Leaving Wal-Mart, Lobo directed his gang back onto the main drag to be seen. Obvious, in-your-face type seen. Not 'I think they were around somewhere, officer, but I'm not sure,' but rather, 'hell yes they were here, I remember the whole thing.' So they ran up on the sidewalk, scattering pedestrians as they went. Garbage cans, tastefully mounted on posts at several street corners, were broken off and sent rolling down the street. Paper and other refuse spilled out everywhere. Visual proof that the Firar had been there. Penny ante stuff, that may eventually get them run out of town, but not arrested or locked up.

Lobo's antics were very effective for short-term gains. Every resident of Iowa Park would angrily remember the rude behavior of these dirty outcasts, which would create enough doubt and confusion to cover their short crime wave.

Caleb, Winnie, Ramona, and Wrench were busy while their comrades were being loud and stupid. They were the smallest of the biker gang, and the best suited to stealth.

They were also the most gifted in the art of breaking and entering. Minutes after leaving the rest of the pack, they were on a side street, breaking into not only Bill Jameson's house, but the houses next to him as well.

Fifteen minutes later, the foursome were gone, leaving behind a total of three burgled and trashed homes, and one unconscious deli manager, who'd been sent home by his concerned employees to rest. Unfortunately for him, he'd gotten home just in time to walk in on Caleb and Winnie putting the finishing touches on his living room.

CHAPTER 4

Sheriff Parker's day just seemed to keep getting worse. No sooner had he managed to leave the park where Scott Thomas' body was discovered, than he was told of the biker gang's Albertson's escapade.

After calling, Ray Becker stopped in at the station to fill him in on all the details. While Becker was going over the encounter again, the desk officer poked his head in to Parker's office.

"Sheriff, those bikers are at it again. They're terrorizin' customers over at Wal-Mart now. Something about crashing carts into cars and people in the parkin' lot…"

Parker groaned. Between the hysterical girl, still unresponsive despite the shrink's first visit, the dead body eaten by animals, and now these damn bikers, he was ready to give up. Or shoot someone. Although, given the grief he'd been put through the last time that had happened, maybe he shouldn't even think about doing that.

"Yeah, alright. Did Bev send anybody over there?" he asked, knowing that of course, one of the patrol units would have been sent.

"Oh, yeah, sheriff, Bev sent Rob and Mike over. I just wanted to let you know that we've been getting' calls from people here at the station all morning, complainin' 'bout these bikers, wantin' to know what y'all are goin' to do."

"Deputy Randall, do I look busy to you?"

"Uh, yeah, sheriff, but you normally look busy. I just assumed you'd want to know 'bout this," the older man whined. Parker liked almost everyone he worked with; young, old, new, experienced, they all had good qualities. Jeremiah Randall was the exception. Close to retirement age, the skinny old guy with the incongruous potbelly drove him nuts. There were days when Parker stayed out in the field just to avoid putting up with him.

"If I look busy, then I probably am, Randall. It's been a hell of a day already, and I don't want to be interrupted by something as stupid as guys crashing shopping carts in a damn parking lot!" Parker rose from his desk as he spoke, punctuating his speech by slamming his hand down on top of his desk. Papers jumped, coffee spilled, and even Becker, who was expecting the tirade, started slightly.

"Get back to your desk, shuffle papers, answer the phone, do anything, just don't bother me with piddly shit," Parker fumed, ignoring the spreading spill on his desk.

"Awright, you don't have to shout, sheriff, I'm goin'. Just tryin' to do my job. Ya know, when Clem was sheriff here, he never yelled at nobody. He knew how to treat people," Randall trailed off, shuffling off to the front desk.

Becker finished up his account of the biker breakfast, concluding with Jameson getting sent home by his concerned staff. "If it's okay by you, sheriff, I'd like to swing by his house after while, make sure he's doin' okay. His wife's away visitin' her mother over in Dallas for the weekend." Becker always seemed to know these sorts of things about everyone.

"Fine, Ray. You do that. Maybe swing through Wally World first and check up on Bowen and Martin, too. See that they have everythin' under control."

"Sure thing, boss. See ya." Becker mock saluted, and left the office, stopping at the desk to say a few words with Randall. Suddenly Becker stuck his head back in Parker's door.

"Oh, yeah, sheriff, I picked this up at the deli for you," he said, laying a fork carefully on the desk.

"What the hell is that?" Parker asked.

"A fork. People use them to eat with."

"No kidding, smart ass. What's the deal with this one, here on my desk?" Parker barked.

"Mr. Lobo used it. It should have his fingerprints on it. Thought we could send it off, see if we get a hit." Ray said, unperturbed by Parker's attitude.

"Yeah, okay, good call. Bag it up and send it off," Parker said. Ray left with a half-smile on his face.

Parker leaned back and put his feet on the desk. Crossing his hands behind his head, he closed his eyes and tried to imagine living in North Carolina, going to Panther football games, maybe seeing the Tar Heels play basketball, and walking his black lab along the coast. Maybe in a year, when his nephew graduated, and headed off to college, he could realize that dream. He'd be free of his responsibilities then, mostly. Find some kind of dead-end, flunky job with no demands or pressure, and just enjoy a new start.

His desk phone buzzed, and Parker jumped. Damn. He'd actually drifted off.

"Parker."

"Sheriff, it's Ray. The bikers were gone by the time Bowen and Martin showed up at Wal-Mart—they just missed them. I'm at Bill Jameson's house now, and he's been hurt. The house has been burglarized. Looks like someone broke in, and while they were looting he walked in on them. Got hit in the head with a pipe or something. We're waitin' on the ambulance. Bob, he don't look good. He's not conscious, barely breathing."

Becker had called him by his first name. Normally his deputies didn't do that. Becker only called him by his first name when he was worried.

"Alright, Ray. Anything taken from the house?"

"Sheriff, it's a mess. The whole place looks trashed. I can't tell what, if anything, has been taken; it just looks wrecked to me. Happened awhile before I showed up, too. I'd think maybe those bikers came after him, but I don't think the times match up very well. They were in sight right up 'til I showed up at Wal-Mart. Guess they headed down 287 towards New Mexico, last anyone saw of them."

"Fine. Try and get a hold of his wife in Dallas, okay? If you can't, or don't have time, give the number to Randall and have him do it. We'll send Bowen and Martin over to work the house."

"Sheriff, they're already here. They were only a couple blocks away when I called in. They say that the back door was pried open with a crowbar. I'd say that's what Bill got whacked with, too. You want me to stay here or go with the ambulance?"

Parker considered. A simple break-in, even compounded by the assault, could be handled by his younger deputies working the scene. Having Becker's calm experience at the hospital was better than leaving him at the house.

"Ray, go with the ambulance—stay with Jameson. Let me know if there's any change. I'll head over to the house and take a look around."

The day felt like it would never end. Maybe it was the full moon. It always seemed to make people crazy. Two more days, he told himself. Then the moon would be noticeably waxing, and then things would calm down. Right.

Parker heaved himself to his feet with a sigh. Putting his belt back on, he slipped out past deputy Randall without a word and slammed his car door. Angry at life, he slapped the car into gear and shot out of the parking lot, tires squealing. On the way out to Jameson's he called his wife on his cell phone, and told her he would be late again. Mary, ever the patient and understanding wife, wasn't even surprised at that. She was, however, surprised that he had called her at all.

CHAPTER 5

The practice field at Iowa Park High School was a loud, busy place. Some thirty or forty youths, dressed in their football gear, were stretching out and joking with each other. Around the edges of the field, closer to the bleachers than the players, attractive young ladies in shorts and t-shirts were jumping and clapping, practicing their cheers for the first game. Latecomers were straggling out to the field, being chided by assistant coaches with clipboards and whistles.

A sharp staccato split the air, overwhelming all other sounds. As everyone turned to face the south end of the field, a teen-ager on a motorcycle popped into view, emerging from behind the bus barn. The helmeted young man pulled his dirt bike up into a wheelie and shot onto the football field.

Players cheered as he roared past them, holding the wheelie for the entire length of the field. Coaches scowled and waved at him, angrily shouting to clear the field. Cheerleaders clapped and jumped, laughing.

The rider dropped the front wheel of the Honda and slammed on the rear brake, sliding to a stop in front of the team and its coaches. He pulled off his helmet, revealing a strong, handsome face, with closely cropped brown hair. A huge smile was plastered foolishly across his face, especially considering the forbidding looks on the faces of the grown men around him.

"Awesome, dude," one of the players shouted.

"Drew, you rock. You are the man," laughed another, a large hefty teen with the number 79 on his practice jersey. One of the coaches spun on him and pointed with a rolled up notebook.

"Jones, stay out of this—you're in enough hot water as it is," the coach said, causing the lineman to drop his head and turn away.

"Mr. Collins, may we ask what in the world you are doing? You are late for practice, which is a five lap penalty, and this idiocy is worth at least five more," said a tall, formidable looking man with a whistle around his neck. "You may be our star quarterback, but that does not entitle you to be stupid. Actually, you should be setting a better example for the team. Do you feel that there is any good explanation for your behavior?"

"Well, Drew, we're waiting…what do have to say for yourself?"

"Coach, I got a date! For Friday after the game," the young man exclaimed enthusiastically.

Laughter erupted among the players grouped around the field. Scattered cheering was heard, as well as wolf whistles. Even two of the coaches grinned and looked away.

Coach Stanton caught himself starting to smile, and quickly wiped his face blank. Assuming a stern look, he raised his voice to include all of his players. "Well, since this is so very important to you, Drew, and apparently to the rest of your team, they may share in your punishment. That's ten laps for all of you. After scrimmage. Drew, get your butt into the locker room and get changed. The rest of y'all form up by squads."

The group of players and coaches broke up. Drew was left by himself. Still smiling, he pushed his XR350 under the bleachers, hung his helmet on the right side handlebar, and then sprinted into the locker room to get ready for practice. He knew that he was in trouble for being late, and that he probably deserved it. Despite appearing nonchalant, Drew was nervous about Coach Stanton being upset with him. He had benched players before for being late, or for being stupid, and Drew had just been both.

This season was Drew's last, and he had a shot at a scholarship. Last season, two or three scouts had come to see him, and this year the team was even better. He definitely didn't want to screw things up by getting benched.

The young quarterback pulled his jersey over the bulky shoulder pads, grabbed his helmet, and ran back out onto the field. Hoots and more laughter greeted him.

"Hey Romo, I mean Romeo, who's the new chick?"

"Shut up, Jones, at least I got a girl. Your last date was a guy," Drew shot back, grinning.

"Maybe so, but he had great tits, man." Doug said, slapping his best friend's shoulder. "So," the bulky lineman continued, more quietly, "do you think Coach is really mad at you?"

"I don't know. I hope not. If I get benched Uncle Bob will kill me. And it'll kill my dad." he said, looking sorrowful. "Sometimes I think I'm too stupid to play quarterback."

"But then I look at you," he went on, grinning slyly, "and I realize that I couldn't be as stupid as y'all are, so I have to be the QB. And Coach knows, that, too."

"Bitch," Doug stated.

"Jerk," Drew quoted back.

The two friends separated to work with their units for practice. Coach Stanton didn't seem too upset with Drew, and as practice went on, he began to relax and enjoy the drills. In addition to being a gifted athlete, he enjoyed working hard and training. Practice was never dull for him; he reveled in constantly perfecting his skills. For football, anyway. Bookwork was another story.

After a fast-paced two-minute drill, in which Drew performed exceptionally well, he earned praise from Coach Stanton. Drew was actually hoping that the ten lap punishment would be forgiven, or at least forgotten.

"All right guys, that's it for today. Good work, for a bunch a lazy bums who took the summer off. Practice tomorrow morning at 8 am sharp. Please be on time—you hear me Collins? Don't make me send the cops out for you." Coach Stanton watched as the players started for the locker room, then blew his whistle again, freezing them in their tracks.

"Boys, are we forgetting something? Mr. Collins has a date, remember? You all done volunteered to assist in his getting in shape for this girl. Ten laps, right? Hit it, gentlemen."

Drew fell into step with Doug as he started lumbering around the field. He jogged easily next to his friend, looking embarrassed as he caught several dirty looks from other players.

"Man, I'm sorry, Jones. I didn't mean to get everyone in trouble. I was just jazzed about…well, you know."

"So level with me, man. Who is she? Why were you late?" Jones had to ask his questions in bursts, as he kept running out of breath. "C'mon, fess up. Who?"

"Okay. You know that hot chick from biology last year, Megan Stuart? She moved here halfway through the year? Her."

"Dude, the one with the great ass? Always wore those short pants? Blonde with big blue eyes? Cool," Jones huffed, impressed. "At least I know that I'll have died for a good cause. Do her once for me, buddy. These laps are gonna kill me."

"Shut up, dork," Drew retorted. "This isn't so bad, and you know it. You're just outta shape. The only exercise you got all summer was jerking off."

"Yeah, maybe so, but I was thinkin' 'bout you when I done it."

"Sorry, dude, but I've got better taste than to put out for a jerk like you, find another guy," Drew quipped.

Jones, a legend at Iowa Park High for being an over-the-top outrageous ladies man, couldn't dignify his buddy with a response, because, truth be told, he was out of shape, and couldn't get enough breath to talk.

He settled for shooting Drew the bird, with both hands. Collins grinned and kept running, moving past Jones to catch up with two of his receivers.

After practice, the tall young man hopped back on his bike and set off for home. Jones shouted something about the Boy Scout camping trip that he'd volunteered to help with, but he merely waved to him and smiled.

Drew Collins' riding style was somewhat unique. He rode a Honda XR350, which was an older four-stroke "enduro" bike. Enduro meant "dual-purpose", as in street and off-road riding, so that's exactly what Drew did. He cut across ditches, through yards, vacant lots, down streets and alleys, and sometimes even sidewalks. Not particularly legal, or even smart, but definitely fun.

He loved his bike. The big red machine, with its long suspension and tall seat height, was seemingly made for his tall frame, and its relatively light weight made for great tricks. It had enough power to run down the highway, or pull him out of trouble with mud or sand, and was technically street legal, since it had lights and turn signals. Not that he ever bothered with those, they were just useful to have.

By using this unorthodox method of travel, Drew was able to get home in considerably less time than the normal, boring (legal) route that took twenty-five minutes. And so, sixteen minutes after exiting school property, Drew pulled into his driveway. Pushing the button on his key fob, he opened the garage door.

The Collins family residence was a single floor ranch that had the benefit of a two-car garage. The left side, nearest the living area of the house, contained the car, a nondescript Ford Taurus.

The right side housed the important stuff. That was the door that opened when Drew hit the remote.

He pulled his Honda into the spotless garage. He cut the engine and walked the bike around so that it faced out, parking it right next to his father's bike.

The older Collins worked as a mechanic at the Iowa Park Harley Davidson dealership. After his wife was killed, the man, already visibly reserved, had withdrawn completely, speaking only when spoken to, and even then mostly in single word answers. He'd devoted himself to the big twin-cylinder bikes.

Without a partner, he traded in his classic Electra Glide touring bike for a new 883R Sportster. The smaller v-twin was patterned after the flat-track racers that had helped make Harleys famous in decades past. Time had caught up with the company, but they still retained the style, image, and sound that made the Milwaukee-based motorcycles famous.

James Collins had purchased his new bike, then proceeded to "fix' all of the performance issues that its detractors claimed existed. He bumped the engine's output to 1200 cubic centimeters, put in performance cams, a Screamin' Eagle air breather system, and re-jetted the carbs. The bike was given a new exhaust as well, and even more changes that weren't visible to the casual observer.

Drew finished putting away his helmet and gear, looked again at his father's monster, and went into the house.

His father was sitting in his chair, watching the news. Despite being only forty-five, he looked at least sixty. The last three years had aged him three decades. He'd lost twenty or thirty pounds from an already lean frame, and his formerly dark hair was now streaked with gray.

James Collins didn't look up as his son came in. When Drew asked what he wanted for dinner, he simply pointed at the screen. His son glanced at the old twenty-five inch television, and stopped.

Drew's uncle was on the news, talking about a body that had been found that morning. "Once again, this is Connie Wyskoff with Action 4 News, out at Pine Cone Park in Iowa Park, talking with Sheriff Robert Parker. Right now there is no indication of foul play, but we have been warned that the public should be aware of the possibility of a large pack of feral dogs in the area." After that last long sentence, she took a deep breath and continued.

"So, Brad and Jenny, we expect further developments in this case tomorrow, when the autopsy is completed. Until then, this is Connie Wyskoff, Action 4 News."

The scene then cut back to the newsroom, with two appropriately somber looking, well-groomed thirty-somethings staring earnestly out at their viewers.

Drew used the break to speak.

"Dad, Doug wants me to help him tomorrow night with a Cub Scout camping trip. He's short on chaperons, and asked if I could go. It'd be an overnight, but I'd be back home by noon on Sunday. I've got practice in the morning, then I'll be home for lunch, and then I think we have to leave around 2 or 3 in the afternoon."

His father looked at him without expression. "That's okay. I work in the morning. Kinda backed up in the shop. Probably not get home 'til after you leave." He rose again from his chair, taking a dish into the kitchen. He hesitated, turned back to his son, and added, "The Taurus still needs the oil changed."

"I know, dad. I'll do it Sunday. I was gonna take the bike tomorrow, anyway."

"I'll help. Wanted to look at the cruise control. Didn't work last week."

"Cool," Drew said. "Hey, you comin' to the game next week? It's just in Wichita Falls; you know, Tom Landry High School? Uncle Bob's goin', you could probably catch a ride with him."

"We'll see. I want to see all your games this year, Andrew. Next year I'll be watching you on TV," James said, with the ghost of smile on his face. The expression vanished quickly, replaced with the same tired look that his face normally had engraved on it. He walked back into the living room.

Drew watched his father settle into the recliner like it was a casket. He knew his father would remain there until it was time to turn in to bed. He shook his head. There had to be something he could do to shake his father out of this. He thought about calling his aunt and uncle. In times past, they had helped get the elder Collins out of the house. Recently, though, it seemed as though his uncle Bob was getting to be *too* much like his father. God, it wasn't *his* fault. The creep that killed his mom had been wasted on drugs, and tried to kill the sheriff, too. Luckily, uncle Bob was faster on the draw and shot him. No reason to feel bad about that.

The loss of his mom was still with Drew. Initially, he'd wanted to hurt someone, anyone. The need to strike back at the world for depriving him of his mother was almost overwhelming. That rage had largely dissipated, leaving for a time numbness; a feeling that nothing mattered. His studies suffered, his activities suffered, and his friendships suffered as well.

Being young and outgoing, though, he was unable to maintain that numbness. Gradually, the feeling went away, much as anesthetic wears away by degrees until the body is once again whole and aware. The pain was still there, lingering just behind everything else in his life, but the need to live again triumphed over the depression.

But he still felt guilty that he couldn't get his father to feel that same way. Except for working on a motorcycle or watching the television, he seemed to have no interest in the world around him. He attended most of Drew's games, but while he watched, he seemed unmoved by either triumph or tragedy on the field. Even the prospect of his son getting a college scholarship based on his athletic prowess was worthy of a mere, "congratulations, son; if that's what you want."

Drew shook his head and walked down the hall to his room, closing the door on his father and problems that he wasn't able to fix. He focused on packing for his camp out. That, at least, he could handle.

Chapter 6

The Fenris Firar reconnected at the truck stop on Highway 287, west of town. Lobo was pissed when he heard about Jameson coming home. He didn't care that Winnie had clubbed him, but he was furious that the man had walked in on Caleb, and he hadn't been aware of it.

"You fuckin' idiot!" he screamed, punching the much smaller man. Caleb saw the punch coming, and even tried to avoid it, but Lobo was much faster than he looked. His straight right caught Caleb on the left cheek, and dropped the man onto the asphalt parking lot, where he lay, clutching his head.

Lobo stepped forwards, as if to kick his minion. Winnie moved, and Lobo turned to her and growled. She froze. The gang leader shook his head in disgust and stepped back.

"C'mon, you lot, let's eat. Did you at least score enough that we can eat the shit that they serve here?"

"Yeah, boss. Jameson didn't have shit, but the neighbors had some good stuff. Ramona scored almost a thousand bucks and some nice jewelry," Winnie said, kneeling by Caleb and helping him to sit up.

Lobo turned on the raven-haired beauty. While Winnie was short and stocky, Ramona was slender, tall, and had jet-black hair. Her most arresting feature though, was her eyes. The pupils were black, but the iris was silver. Not gray, or bluish, but shining silver. She exuded sex appeal. She was also violent, even by Fenris Firar standards.

"Well, bitch, where is it? Or would you prefer that I find it myself," he leered.

The leather clad female flinched. The attentions of the pack leader were something she never wished to experience again. Better by far to give up whatever she found at the house. She handed over a bank bag full of cash and jewels.

Lobo looked at her in disbelief. "Like they had this stuff lying around the house in a bank bag. What gives?"

Ramona looked him square in the eye this time. "The money was in the bag in the top dresser drawer. I scooped the rings and stuff out of the jewelry box. It was easier to carry this way."

"Back off, bitch. Just thought it was weird, that's all. Like they gift-wrapped it for us, you know," Lobo grumbled. He was the acknowledged leader of the Fenris Firar, but he was not necessarily popular with his gang members. His grip on leadership was tenuous at best. He led through sheer force, being the biggest and most violent of the gang, but he couldn't overstep his bounds, lest it cause a total rebellion. Singly, the members were at his mercy, but collectively the pack could overwhelm him.

For now, he backed down. In a more normal tone, he laid out the plan for the rest of the day.

"Okay, we need to find a place to hole up for the night. A nice out of the way field, maybe near a cattle ranch, since we'll need to feed afterwards. No roads, no fuck-ups this time."

"Wrench, Ramona, you two are on that. You can eat later. Aardwolf, take Piggy and pick up food and booze for the rest of us." He tossed a couple hundred dollars over to the scar-faced man, who nodded eagerly and put the money in his vest pocket. The rough looking, middle-aged biker chick, who bore the nickname of Piggy for obvious reasons, walked into the diner with him.

Wrench and Ramona re-mounted their bikes and roared off down the road, while the rest of the Firar sprawled in the grass at the end of the parking lot. Until the two scouts came back, they had nothing to do but eat and kill time.

After two hours of cruising around the surrounding countryside, the scouts finally found an abandoned farm that would suit their needs. It even had a large, ramshackle barn, and an old pole building that was suitable for stowing the bikes. The duo turned around in the dirt driveway, and started heading back to the main road. Wrench shifted up into second gear and felt something give.

"Fuck," he growled. Pulling in the clutch and coasting to a stop, he looked down at his left foot. The gearshift lever was at an odd angle. "Damn, I think the lever broke."

Ramona rode up beside him and looked it over as well. "The lever looks fine. Maybe the shaft cracked or stripped. Can you still ride?"

"Yeah, I'm just stuck in second. We'll have to go slow, and run it to that dealership we saw by Wal-Mart. Lobo's gonna be pissed," he said.

"Screw Lobo. What's he gonna do, leave you behind? We're the ones that make most of our money. He can spend some of it keepin' our rides healthy," Ramona spat off to the side. "Asshole," she added, not sure if she was referring to their leader, or the neurotic guy that she rode with.

"Come on already. We got to stop and get money from our fearless leader, get to the shop and get the bike fixed, and still get back before dark. I would have liked lunch, too…"

They limped the big hog back onto 287, then rode slowly at the side of the road. Most people left them alone, although a couple young toughs, noticing that they were having trouble, honked and flipped them off.

Once back at the truck stop, they explained what happened to Lobo, and after assuring him that they had indeed found a safe haven for the night, secured cash to go and get the bike fixed.

Ramona gave Caleb and Winnie detailed directions to the farmland, then led Wrench back out onto Highway 287 heading back towards Iowa Park. The ten-mile trip took half an hour. After what seemed an eternity, they finally saw the trademark Harley Davidson logo on the big street sign they had passed earlier: Bernie's Harley Davidson.

Bernard Tompkins had owned a Harley-Davidson dealership since the late 70's. He suffered through the AMF years, stubbornly keeping with the American motorcycle company. When they'd turned it around at the end of the 1980's and regained their former glory, Bernie's became the largest motorcycle dealership in four counties.

Despite his success, Bernie worked the floor himself most days, and still spent time in the shop as well. He prided himself on staying in touch with his roots, and "keeping it real," as his grandkids called it.

This Friday afternoon, he had only one associate working on the floor with him. Business was slow, and the two of them were closing down, when they both looked up at a very familiar sound. Big v-twins were pulling into the lot.

A twenty-something female in a leather coat and pants climbed off of her Sportster and stepped just inside the front door. Her companion stayed on his bike, idling in the lot in front of the service door.

"Hey, you guys still open? We got a problem," the black-haired beauty called. "His gear shaft is stripped or maybe cracked; he's stuck in second gear. We need it fixed."

Bernie came out from behind the register and smiled at his attractive customer. "Now, miss, we're closin' up now, our mechanics have done gone home for the day. I'll have one here right at eight o'clock sharp, though. We can get ya taken care of then."

The woman looked uncertainly out at her companion, who sat revving his bike and staring off into space. She looked back at Bernie in his colorful Harley bowling shirt, and smirked.

"Yeah, okay. If you'll open the door, I'll have Wrench pull his bike in. He can ride with me tonight, and then we can come back in tomorrow to pick it up."

Bernie sent his employee to open the gate while Ramona stepped back outside to tell Wrench what was going on. He scowled, clearly looking unhappy, but in the end nodded and rode his dirty panhead into the service bay.

"Okay, y'all, what name do you want me to put on this?" Bernie asked, grabbing a ticket and a pen.

"Don't worry about a name, old man. Do you think that you'll forget us overnight?" Wrench grumped. "Just fix the damn bike!"

Tompkins recoiled slightly. 'There's no need for rude behavior,' he thought indignantly. He dealt with rich new Harley owners, and hard-core Harley riders both, and regardless of their station, they were all respectful of him. Came from years of living with the bikes. Serious riders could tell, and treated him accordingly.

"Sir, we just need to know who the bike belongs to so no one else tries to take it while y'all aren't here. It's for you; we ain't trying to pry or anything."

"Wrench knows that, he's just being a hard-ass. Probably comes from not having rear shocks," the woman replied, elbowing the other biker in the ribs to keep him from saying anything more. "We appreciate your help. What time will we be ready to roll?"

Bernie appeared mollified. He smiled again at the young woman, "well, now, young lady, we open at eight, and we're open 'til noon. I 'spect your bike should be done by then. Might want to give us a call first, just to be sure."

"Fine. We'll see you tomorrow," she said, herding the grumbling male biker out of the service area and towards the door. Bernie made note of the logo on both their jackets: a snarling black wolf's head. 'Nasty looking,' he thought. 'Every gang needs to feel so tough. Even that young lady had a hard edge to her. Probably wild in the sack,' he mused.

Bernie smiled again, amused at the direction his thoughts had taken. 'What would Millie think?' Knowing her, she'd probably think the same thing, if she saw the biker chick. His smile remained as he closed up the store.

Ramona slung her leg over her 883 Hugger and fired it up. Wrench got on behind her, grumbling about riding "bitch" behind a woman. She goosed the throttle, almost throwing the jerk off. Served him right.

She cruised through town, taking her time heading back to the farm. 'It's a nice enough town,' she thought. 'Looks a little boring… Probably was a lot boring. Probably have square dances and shit like that,' she decided. Even living with her curse was preferable to country bars and line dancing.

From the rear, she heard renewed complaining. Wrench had gotten his harness boot tangled up in one of the saddlebags. Sighing, she slowed so he could extricate himself without falling off.

Ramona again cursed the day that bound her fate to these thugs on bikes. Life on the wild side wasn't always everything that it was cracked up to be. Running away from home at sixteen had seemed like the only option way back then. Escaping from an oppressive home life had led her to a worse fate—her role in this outlaw biker gang.

It was her life now, though, so she'd have to make the best of it. It wasn't like she could just pack up and move back home. Laughing grimly at the image of that scene, she accelerated through the early evening traffic, heading out to the sticks.

The Fenris Firar had taken over the old Pearson place. The house had long since been torn down, but the barn and outbuildings were still in decent repair. Lobo assumed that they remained in use after the owner had moved on. Maybe some asshole neighbor rented or bought the land.

Whatever the reason, it was perfect for the roving biker gang, and with any luck, they could camp out here for a long while. After stashing the bikes in the garage, out of sight from anyone traveling on the gravel road, they started unpacking their few belongings. The gang traveled light by necessity. It made for easy camp set up.

Ulric and a couple others were sent to search for fresh water. Piggy and Winnie volunteered to search for bathroom facilities. Lobo himself checked the barn for electricity. Not that they'd risk using lights at night. Too visible. Somebody might ask questions, or come see who was there, or worse yet, call the cops.

Finding a hanging light bulb in an abandoned horse stall, he pulled the string. He grinned as the light came on. Totally unnecessary tonight and tomorrow night, but maybe with proper shielding, they could use some lights inside later. There were always things to do for distraction and "entertainment" purposes. Some of them required light.

Just as he was starting to fret over the continued absence of Wrench and Ramona, his ears picked up the sound of a bike coming down the gravel road. Just one. He grimaced, and walked out into the yard to wait for them.

Ramona pulled in the drive, stopped long enough for Wrench to get off close to Lobo, then continued on to the shed to hide her bike with the others. When she came out from the old building she could hear Wrench arguing with Lobo.

"Honest, Lobo, it wasn't my idea. The shop didn't have no mechanics there that late anyhow. Ramona set it up, talk to her," he whined. 'Nice. Make it all my fault,' she thought. 'Like there had been a choice.' She took a deep breath and walked up to the two men.

"The place looks good, Lobo. We should be safe here for a while, huh?"

"So, Ramona, another trip to town in the morning, eh? Look, we got to be visible but not around every fucking day. Try not to schedule more stuff without my approval in the future, got it?"

Ramona looked at Lobo. He seemed calm, and was trying to be nice and rational. She'd keep things that way, then. Calm, rational.

"You got it, boss. But we really had no choice. We couldn't limp it all the way back here without attracting more attention. I thought it was better to leave it there out of sight."

Lobo seemed to consider this. "You know, you got a pretty little head on those shoulders. Has its uses, doesn't it? Just don't try to get too cute, okay, Moanin' 'Mona," he sneered. "C'mon and get some food. We still got a couple hours before nightfall."

Lobo sauntered off towards the barn, where the rest of the pack was gathered. After exchanging glances, Wrench and Ramona followed him into the old musty building and up the ladder to the hayloft.

All twenty-five members of Fenris Firar were now present, sitting in a large circle in the hay. In the middle of the floor were two or three blankets with various cold cuts and bread scattered on them. Cheese and bottles of beer completed the repast. Lobo looked around through the gathering gloom at his pack.

"Dig in," he said simply. The motley assortment of bikers obliged. In short order there was no food left on the blankets.

Large contented belches issued from several of the men, and one or two of the women.

"Okay," Lobo said, "it's time again. Stay close tonight. I knew we'd need to feed again right after, so I had Ulric bring one of the cows from the next field over. It's tethered just over the hill. You'll be able to scent it right away.

"Don't be stupid," he added.

He and the rest of the gang rose. They began removing their personal items, then clothing. They carefully folded the clothes and stacked them in piles, laying their personal effects on top. Then they lined up to climb down the ladder, following Lobo's lead.

Once outside, they drifted slowly apart. The night was almost upon them. The sun had vanished below the horizon, and the full moon was visible, low in the sky. Over the next several hours it would climb higher, and shine brighter.

Lobo stared at the moon. It called to him, pulling at his very soul. It was his mistress, and not only could he not resist its pull, he had no desire to.

Eagerly he welcomed the first sensations of tingling along his arms and legs. Deeper within, he felt his bones twist and grow. The accompanying pain, by this time, was an almost masochistic pleasure. He howled in ecstasy, dropping to all fours.

Around him, other members of the Fenris Firar were growling and starting to twitch, the full moon triggering rapid hormone releases of their own.

Bathed by the moon's pale light, the bikers convulsed and dropped to the ground, kicking and snapping spasmodically. Chemical changes in the body created by the hormones led to riotous changes in the forms writhing on the ground.

Long dark hairs erupted all along the crawling forms, thickening into a dense pelt. Individual bikers screamed, their faces losing their humanity as jaws elongated and changed shape. Teeth mutated, canines growing to alarming lengths next to the incisors. The formerly small ears, set close to the sides of the head, rotated forwards and moved higher up on the now decidedly lupine head.

Several of the gang members, Lobo included, regained their feet. They now went upon all fours; their arms having transformed into forelimbs that ended in large black-tipped nails, long tails trailing behind them.

As the transformations came to a conclusion the remainder of the pack rose. All twenty-five members of the motorcycle gang now stalked around the pasture as wolves, the moon looking down on them; the only witness to the horrible secret of the Fenris Firar.

A ravenous hunger consumed the pack. This was the time that the beasts were at their most dangerous: right after the change. No matter how much the lycanthropes ate prior to turning, their transformation left them starving, due to the immense amounts of energy consumed by the process. Almost as one, they scented the cow just over the hill. Their amazingly enhanced sense of smell was 250 times as acute as the best humans. They could almost "see" with their delicate noses.

And what they could "see" was food. The pack was so consumed with hunger that they could not even stalk their prey. They howled and bayed, and bolted off to find the cow.

The cow was hobbled so that it could move around, but not escape. It sensed the pack coming and lowed, and then attempted to flee. The bovine had no chance.

Lobo arrived first and leapt onto the cow, savagely tearing into its throat. Blood spurted as he ripped his head from side to side. Others fastened themselves to the cow's flanks and legs and dragged the larger animal off of its feet. For a few moments, it struggled, then was still, as the snarling wolf pack tore it to shreds and began to feed.

Overhead the full moon rose high into the night sky.

CHAPTER 7

Saturday dawned, bright and clear. Drew, who'd turned in early in anticipation of a big day, stretched luxuriously and rolled over again, pulling the blanket over his head to shut out the alarm. Then, grinning to himself, he reached over and slapped at his alarm clock. The persistent ringing came to an abrupt halt.

The young athlete rolled to his feet and padded down the hall to the bathroom. After a quick shower and a shave (once a week whether necessary or not), he dressed and went out to the kitchen. There was no sign of his father, who had risen and left the house before Drew's alarm even thought of going off.

As Drew prepared to start his bike, he glanced over once more at the orange racing bike. Idly, he wondered what it'd be like to ride his dad's pride and joy. 'Probably kill myself on a machine like that,' he thought. He'd asked his father once about riding it, and the elder Collins had stared at him for a moment or two, and then quietly told him to wait until he "grew up."

Shaking his head at the memory, and the feelings of frustration and insult, he kicked his bike over. The finely tuned XR fired up immediately. He pulled out of the garage and thumbed the button to close the door behind him.

Tearing off down the road, Drew reveled again in the feeling of freedom that riding always brought him. From the day he got his first bicycle, he was drawn to two-wheeled conveyance. Getting his driver's license for a car was only useful for going out on dates, as most of the girls he knew weren't into bikes.

His thoughts remained on girls, as they frequently did. For all his success on the football field, Drew was shy around girls. He considered his new "girlfriend" Megan. Although he had admired her since her family moved to Iowa Park two years ago, he hadn't spoken with her until this week. Finding out that they shared similar tastes in music served as an icebreaker for Drew, and he finally got her alone to talk with her. For her part, Megan seemed very interested in him, and flattered that the school's best athlete was expressing an interest in her.

Drew grinned behind his helmet. He was *very* interested in her. Maybe she even liked motorbikes, or at least riding on them. He'd take her anywhere she wanted to go.

Enjoying the ride to the football field, the high school senior looked around at the scenery. Even at this early hour on a weekend, there were attractive women out and about. His gaze lingered on one woman's rear end as she walked a Schnauzer on a leash. A car horn sounded directly in front of him, followed by shrieking tires.

Drew jerked his head back around to look ahead. Right in front of him was a Jeep, which had slammed to a stop as the distracted biker rode through a stop sign.

"Pay attention, asshole!" a young woman shouted at him from behind the wheel of the Cherokee. She punctuated her curse with an inappropriate finger gesture, and took off.

"Whoops. Sorry, babe," he said, mostly to himself since the Jeep had already gone. Chastising himself for being so easily distracted, Drew paid closer attention to the road, and finished the trip to practice without further mishap.

Practice itself was uneventful, especially compared to the previous evening. Drew managed to get through the entire thing without getting into trouble, and after two hours, the team hit the showers. As they were getting dressed, Drew and Doug discussed their plans for later that day.

"Now, we're gonna meet at Grace Methodist Church around 2:30, okay? We'll pack all our stuff into the vans, I think, then head out to the park. If you wanna ride your bike, that's okay, but come to the church first anyway," Doug said. "That way we can load your shit and you don't have to cart it all the way yourself."

"Cool. Sunday, then, we break camp early?" Drew asked. "I promised my Dad I'd be home by early afternoon to change the oil in the Ford."

"No problem. Want help with the car?" Doug asked. Despite his bluster, he could be a pretty stand-up guy.

"Nah, Dad and I are gonna do it. Spend a little time together. Maybe we'll even talk. He said last night that he wants to go to our first game next Friday."

"That'll be cool. He can go with my folks if he wants. They won't mind. Dad likes him, even if he never speaks," Doug teased. "Actually, I think dad likes him *because* he never speaks. He's told me that I should be more like him."

"Thanks anyway, but I know Dad. If he goes, he'll go by himself, probably on the Sportster. He'll sit alone, watch the game, then go home right after," Drew said, sadly.

Doug watched his friend's expression change, and quickly moved on. "So, when's the last time you slept in a tent, boy? Remember to bring an air mattress. And your own toilet paper. You'll thank me later. Wiping your ass with poison ivy does not make for a good time."

"The voice of experience?"

"Naw, but I seen somebody else do it. Clever."

"How many kids are coming?"

Doug started counting on his fingers, mumbling names to himself. "Twelve, I think. All between seven and twelve years old. Toilet trained, but stupid, ya know. It'll be fun," he said. "We'll do brats and hot dogs on the fire for supper, maybe grill some fish if anybody manages to catch anything."

"Sounds good. I'm gonna head home, then, and get my stuff ready. I'll see you at Grace at 2 or so." Drew fist-bumped his buddy, then walked out to his bike. Slinging his leg over the side, he looked up again at the sky. Crystal clear and blue. Yep, a beautiful day.

The morning started differently for Drew Collins' uncle. After a breakfast that consisted of too hot coffees, and too cold egg-amuffins, Sheriff Parker went in to the office to follow up on the Thomas case.

Once seated at his desk, Parker looked through his messages. Both of them. One was a note from Becker about the bikers' leader wearing a class ring on a cord around his neck. The other was from Jeremiah Randall informing him that Kathryn Jameson wanted him to call her at the hospital. That was it. He snorted in disgust. Parker expected lab and autopsy results by now. He had neither.

The sheriff of Iowa Park poured himself a cup of coffee (his third), and reached for the phone. He called Becker first.

"Becker? Parker. What's this about a ring?"

The off-duty deputy explained that he'd seen a ring on a leather cord around Lobo's neck at the deli, a class ring with Longview High engraved on it. He further explained that by Lobo's own admission he was from south of Albuquerque, not Longview.

"So what exactly does that mean, Ray? Not that it isn't fascinating, of course," Parker asked, somewhat sarcastically.

"Sheriff, it don't have to mean anything right now. I just thought you should know. The body from the park was ID'd as from Longview, right? And I heard that the bikers were there before they showed up at Albertson's. I just thought that it might be relevant," Becker told him, reasonably enough, which just pissed off Parker that much more.

"Well, thank you very much, Deputy Becker. Obliged," he growled into the receiver before setting it none too gently back into its cradle.

Now, with his two messages dealt with, he could get to work. Or at least find out where his stuff was, so he could get started on his work. He looked up the number for the morgue.

"Morgue here," came an unreasonably cheerful and chipper voice.

"This is Sheriff Parker. Where's my autopsy report on Scott Thomas—the body that was discovered Friday morning?"

"Sheriff, Doctor Simon don't work weekends. He said that he'd get to it on Monday first thing. I looked at the body, too, sir, and I'd bet on a large animal attack, probably more than one," the young voice added helpfully.

"Great." Parker once again hung up on the person that he was talking to. The fuckin' old man was really being a pain. Odds were that it was an animal attack, but he needed to know as soon as possible. So far as he knew, there were no wolves or packs of wild dogs running loose around Iowa Park.

As he sat pondering his next move, his phone rang. Parker reached out and picked it up before it could ring a second time.

"Parker."

"Sheriff, this is Dan Simon out at Mercy Hospital. The girl that was brought in Friday morning, Rita Ibarra, is talking. I thought that you should know. My colleague from Wichita Falls, Dr. Novak, is with her. She's pretty shaky, but I think you can come out and talk with her. Her folks are here, too. Also," he added with a slight nervous chuckle, "Nurse Bishop is off duty now."

"Thanks, doc. I'm terrified of five foot four brunettes. I'll be along shortly. She say anything of importance yet?"

"Sheriff, she's awful upset still. They're tryin' to just talk with her 'bout easy stuff, calm her down."

"Got ya. I'll be there soon. I don't suppose..." Parker's voice trailed off.

"What, sheriff?"

"Nothin'. I was gonna ask if you could get your dad to do an autopsy for me yet today, but that ain't fair. He knows it's important to me, he wouldn't listen to you any more than he would me, I guess."

"Sheriff, my father is the most stubborn man I've ever met. He makes you look positively wishy-washy. If I ask, it'll probably take twice as long to get done. Sorry," he added.

"Yeah, about what I thought. Look, it's just after nine now. I'll be over there in about twenty minutes. See if I can talk with the girl first, then I'll talk to her parents." Parker broke the connection, hanging up in the middle of the doctor's response, once again getting the last word. He got up from his desk, put on his hat, and went out to his car. The drive to the hospital was automatic by this time. His body made the trip without conscious thought while his mind wandered, thinking over possibilities.

●●◖◖◯◗●●

James Collins clocked in and looked at the appointment book to see what needed to be done. As was his habit, he spoke to no one, beyond a simple "good morning" in response to the sales counter girl's greeting as he walked in.

Just inside the garage door was an old panhead. It was filthy, in obvious need of care, but James found it beautiful nonetheless. Looking it over, he quickly noticed the gearshift lever hanging at an odd angle.

Leaving the chopper for a moment, he went back to the desk and looked closer at the work log. Sure enough, there was a note to fix the old bike; 'suspected broken or cracked gear shaft.' The owner was expected to stop in before closing to pick it up. Seeing nothing else pressing on the list, he returned to the dirty chopper.

Running his hand slowly over the tank, he walked around the bike in a circle. He checked the handgrips and handlebar. Satisfied, he straightened the bike up, put up the kickstand, and walked the bike back deeper into the service area where his tools awaited.

Taking his time, James inspected the bike more closely. In addition to accumulated dirt and grit, he saw what appeared to be dried blood on the seat and rear shocks. James shrugged it off. It could have been anything. What was mildly disturbing was the large open-ended wrench covered in the same dried substance that was tucked inside the frame, under the battery. Bizarre, but also not his concern.

Directing his attention to the suspected problem, he reached out and took the lever in his right hand. Twisting and pulling, the middle-aged mechanic pried the gearshift completely away from the bike. James looked at the lever in his hand. It was predictably old and crusty.

He took a hand towel to the lever. Wiping away most of the grime (with considerable effort), he stared at what was left. The lever had cracked, the screw that tightened it to the shaft was the only thing holding it together. If James removed the screw the lever would fall in two pieces.

James smiled, ever so slightly. The owner expected the repair to be more costly. Replacing the shaft coming out of the transmission was expensive. Replacing the gearshift lever was less than twenty bucks, assuming that there was no damage to the shaft. Spraying the shaft down with WD-40 and wiping it off confirmed that it was fine. A new lever and the chopper would be functional again. However…

The mechanic loved these old bikes. It was a shame that people abused them this way; didn't seem to care about them. They deserved better.

He checked the oil. Just as he suspected, it was dirty, thick, and dark, likely unchanged in many thousands of miles. The bike needed an oil change desperately. Obviously the filter would be bad as well. Considering how much money the owner had saved with the gearshift lever fix, he or she could easily afford the oil change.

James changed the oil, replaced the oil filter, and cleaned the air filter, which was plugged almost solid with debris. He included the oil and filter in the bill but not his labor. He didn't dare clean the whole bike, knowing that some bikers intentionally let them get grungy, the term being "rat bikes." He himself didn't understand the attraction, but he respected other's rights too much to do anything about it. He could however, make sure that it was more mechanically, if not cosmetically, sound.

After finishing the panhead, James Collins went back to working on a long-term project, reassembling a custom chopper that another wealthy rider had dropped off months ago. There was no rush on this bike; it was destined to be a display piece in a garage. It was, however, a tremendous project for James, for it allowed him to immerse himself in the total restoration of a beautiful machine.

Time tended to flow by him unaccounted for anyway, and this morning he was more lost in his own world than normal. It came as surprise to him then, when Lucy, the sales girl, came back to tell him that in addition to it being noon, the owner of the panhead was here to get his bike.

For a moment, James was confused as to why Lucy would come get him. He didn't work with the customers; he just fixed the bikes. There was a completed bill with a full description of everything right on the service counter. Then he realized that there was no one at the service counter. He and Lucy were the only people in the shop, so the responsibility fell to him.

Sighing, he wiped his hands and left his chopper project. Walking out to the service desk with Lucy, he looked up to see who was responsible for the old panhead's neglected condition.

Standing in front of the desk were two people, both wearing leather jackets. Not at all unusual at a Harley shop. But it was the intensity of the two that made them different than the normal biker that needed repairs. Violence almost radiated off of them.

The female, a striking-looking young woman with leather pants and boots and jet-black hair, looked up at him suddenly. Her eyes were purest silver.

"So, Mr. Mechanic, is our bike fixed yet? The '49 panhead with the green tank." Her voice, when she spoke, was soft but raspy. "We dropped it off last night, and the boss man promised that it'd be done by now."

"It's done," Collins said, nodding at the bill on the desk in front of him.

"So, what was wrong with it? Was the shaft ruined or not?" the woman snapped, glaring at the older man.

"No, the shaft was fine. Just the lever. I put a new one on." More quiet responses from James, who stared at the bill rather than look at the two obviously confrontational bikers. Lucy shifted from one foot to the other nervously.

"Hey," the other biker, a short-bearded and small, but vicious-looking, man suddenly said, "what's this other shit? I didn't need no oil change." He stepped close to the desk and leaned forwards. "We didn't tell you to do that. We said to fix what was wrong and that's it."

Wrench poked the quiet mechanic in the chest with his right hand. "You tryin' to rip us off, man? We ain't paying for this shit. I got half a mind to rip you a new asshole, bro', ya understand? The Fenris Firar don't take being screwed with. We ain't paying for this," he said again, loudly.

James looked at the floor. Softly, he said, "Your bike needed it. The filter was clogged and the oil was bad. I didn't want the bike to get damaged."

Wrench and Ramona looked at the guy. He was obviously scared of them. Wrench sneered. What a wimp. He was prey, like cattle. He didn't deserve to be treated any better than a cow or a sheep, because that's what he was.

"Well, shithead, we ain't payin' for any extra work. What you gonna do about it?"

Collins still didn't look up. Without turning his head, he said to Lucy, "just charge them for the lever. It was $37.95 plus tax." Then he walked off, into the back, where his work was. And no people.

Lucy smiled apprehensively at the bikers. She stepped behind the service desk and rang up the bill. Ramona threw two twenty-dollar bills down and then walked away. Wrench leered at the girl, then suggestively licked his lips. Lucy paled and looked away.

Wrench laughed. 'Humans are such chicken-shits.' No one stood up to the true hunters, the Fenris Firar. Lobo was right, they deserved no better than what the gang gave them. If this girl wasn't interested in giving, then perhaps she should have it taken from her.

Ramona was waiting outside, already on her Sportster. The 883 was idling, shaking slightly despite the engine being rubber-mounted. She was impatient to be gone. She had no more sympathy for chicken-shit people than the rest of the Firar, but something about the old guy fixing the bike for the sake of the bike touched her. She was angry at Wrench, too, for being such a jerk.

When he reappeared outside the service door with his chopper, she brusquely gestured for him to join her and take off. He smirked and shook his head. He rubbed his fingers together on his left hand, and then licked them and looked inside Bernie's, where Lucy was arranging clothes on a sales rack. Ramona shook her head angrily. Wrench again grinned and indicated that he was waiting here for the girl.

Ramona knew that she couldn't win this fight. Lobo would side with Wrench, he would probably even reward the little shit for bringing the girl back to the farm.

"Fuckin' man-whore mother-fucker," she screamed at Wrench, who of course couldn't hear her over the sound of the bikes. He merely waived at her, and turned away to find a place to lurk until the girl came out.

Ramona tore out of the parking lot, furious at Wrench, Lobo, herself, and the entire world. She needed space to clear her head. 'Just ride until the rage subsides,' she thought. Forcing herself to slow down to the speed limit, she cruised across town, barely noticing the landscape as she passed.

Riding through a residential area, she looked to her right in surprise as another motorcycle zipped across a yard and pulled up next to her on the street. The tall young man was riding a red dirt bike, carrying an overstuffed backpack on his shoulders, and wearing a black full-face helmet.

As he glanced over at her, his blue eyes widened behind the plastic shield. Then they crinkled as he smiled widely and waved. Revving the bike, he pulled up in a wheelie, and accelerated past her, showing off.

Despite herself, Ramona smiled. 'What a dork. With any luck, he'll crash, right here. That would wipe that silly smile right off his face.'

She twisted the throttle and shot past the startled biker, who dropped his front wheel down and stared after her.

Shrugging his shoulders, Drew continued over to the Methodist Church to meet the Boy Scout troop for their campout.

CHAPTER 8

By two-thirty in the afternoon, all eleven boys were assembled in the church parking lot, surrounded by piles of camping gear. Nervous parents buzzed around them, going over last-second checks to ensure that their child had everything that they needed for the overnight trip. Two gray passenger vans, with 'Grace Methodist Church' painted on the sides, sat nearby with their doors open.

Doug Jones stood next to his father, going over a checklist on his clipboard. He stood almost a foot taller than his dad, and outweighed him by close to a hundred pounds. The elder Jones frequently teased his wife that she must have been cheating on him with the milkman to produce such a moose.

Drew waved at his friend as he walked up. Doug, glancing over and seeing his best friend behind the group of children, beamed and waved back. Several of the kids recognized the young quarterback from the football team and shouted out welcomes to him. The senior stopped to talk with the youngsters, exchanging fist bumps with many of them.

"Hey, c'mon, break it up. You guys can talk football all night once we get to the campsite. We got to get all our gear loaded in the back of the vans, and then get loaded up ourselves. Drew's goin' too, so you can bother him all weekend." Turning to his friend, he asked, "You're still planning on riding that two-wheeled contraption, right? You can ride with us if you want. There's still room, I think."

"I'm still riding. Too much fun. Why would I want to sit in a crowded van full of brats." He was punched by one of the kids. "And get beaten up—rug rat!" he said, shoving the kid back.

"Anyway, I'll go first, if you'll show me the way. I don't want to eat all that dust following the whole convoy."

"Have it your way. I think the kids want you to ride with them, though," Doug replied. "You should spend more time doin' stuff like this, you know. The little guys relate to you. Maybe it's because you're just an overgrown kid yourself."

"Look who's talking, you overstuffed ape. I spend enough time watchin' over you to qualify for any number of merit badges. Remember the time you got caught in the biology lab with Suzy Edmonds in the seventh grade? I told the teacher that you two were playing hide-and-go-seek with me, and that I couldn't find you. I got detention for that. What did you get?" Drew grinned, knowing full well that his buddy had kissed Suzy in that lab, marking the first time he ever kissed a girl.

"Yeah, well, okay. I do owe you for that. I cover for you, too, ya know," Doug groused.

"Oh, yeah, you cover for me. Is that what you call telling Miss Phillips that I was late for class because I was getting a handjob? I wasn't even doing anything—I was in the library. We both got detention for that, you jerk."

"Hey Doug, what's a handjob?" one of the youngsters asked, pulling on Doug's arm for attention.

"Oops. Shi...I mean, shoot. Sorry," Drew said, red-faced from embarrassment, as the older, more worldly kids laughed. Doug grinned at his friend, and then looked down at the second-grader hanging from his elbow.

"Now Steve, don't you worry none about that. That's for when you get older. Right now we're gonna put all our stuff in that van right there. And maybe, just maybe, we're gonna load you in the back with the luggage. Whadda ya think about that?"

Steve giggled and swung on the big tackle's arm. Then he looked at Drew, and said, "Hey, can I ride with you on your motorcycle? It looks cool."

"Not today, big guy. I've only got the one helmet, and it's way too big for you. Maybe I can give you a ride later, though. After we get to camp. Fair enough?"

"Awesome!" Steve ran off, zooming his imaginary motorcycle past his laughing friends. Doug and Drew watched him go, then looked at each other. Both burst out laughing. "Sorry, man. Told you I wasn't cut out for this," Collins said.

"Could have been worse. He could have asked what a blowjob was. Then what would we have done?"

"Guess we'd have to send him to your sister," Drew responded quickly, ducking the clipboard that came sailing at his head. "C'mon, Doug, stop messing around and let's get these fine young lads loaded up for their trip."

"Bitch."

"Jerk."

The two walked after the boys, and with the help of the other two guides, quickly got the camping supplies and children safely loaded into the vehicles.

By two in the afternoon, James Collins was able to forget all about the rude bikers from earlier in the day. Spending a few hours assembling the gears in the rebuilt transmission for the chopper had narrowed his focus, squeezing out everything but his work.

Lucy intruded on his tranquil world shortly after two. Being twenty-six, she had other things to do on Saturday afternoons than hang out at the Harley shop, especially after hours. The day had dragged on long enough, it was time to go.

"Uh, James? I closed out the register and shut the door. Can you finish up so we can set the alarm and get out of here? I kinda have a date today," she added.

Truth be told, James Collins creeped Lucy out. While he was polite and soft-spoken, the older man with the sad eyes unnerved her. His stillness, and the fact that he never initiated a conversation, made it uncomfortable to be around him.

Even earlier, when that biker guy was being hostile, he had been no help. If things had gotten uglier, she would have had to deal with it on her own, which was definitely not in her job description.

James carefully put away his tools, and crated up the chopper parts. With the service area closed down, he shut off the lights and stood next to the side door. Lucy came hurrying up with her purse in one hand and the keys in the other.

"Okay, let's see," she mumbled, sorting through her keys. "This one for the door, this one for the deadbolt, and the alarm code is 4-2-7-5-3-9. I should remember that; right James? It's Harley on the keypad. Kinda simple. Here we go," she said, opening the door and ushering the silent mechanic through first.

Following James out, she turned and double-locked the door to the service shop. The alarm she had armed would go active in another ten seconds. She waited for the faint beep that would tell her that everything was as it should be, and she could mercifully get away. James Collins had already walked off towards his car.

Her waiting ears were rewarded with a faint but distinct beep from the other side of the door. Smiling, Lucy straightened up and turned around, heading towards the back of the lot where she had parked her car.

Partway there she paused. James had driven? He always rode his bike. He had an amazingly tricked-out Sportster that everyone at Bernie's raved about. She looked back over her shoulder, and sure enough the man was getting into a gray Ford Taurus. Funny that a guy could have such an eye-catching bike, yet drive such a boring car. Of course, she thought, a little uncharitably, the car matched the mechanic much more than the bike did.

Lucy smirked slightly at the thought and turned back towards her car. She just caught a dark blur descending towards her head, and registered the leather-clad biker from earlier behind the blurring shape rushing at her. Then an explosion of pain erupted from her temple as the heavy wrench struck her. Lucy's legs buckled and she hit the ground immediately.

Wrench checked the parking lot for witnesses. There was no one around, except for the wimpy mechanic guy in his beater car, just starting to leave the lot. Quickly, he hoisted the unconscious girl onto his shoulder and scurried off to his bike, hidden around the corner.

Sitting on his seat, he set the lightweight girl in front of him and quick-coupled a strap around both her chest and his. She slumped, but was held upright against him. In the span of ten seconds, Wrench was out of Bernie's parking lot.

Wrench rode quickly, feeling excited, aroused, and nervous all at once. He knew that he needed to get to the farm before the girl woke up, but he also knew that he shouldn't drive straight there, in case someone saw him. With that thought in mind, he looked behind him.

The Taurus was following behind him. 'Shit! That fucking mechanic,' he thought. That was not in his plan; he'd thought that the chicken-shit wrench-monkey had pulled out and not noticed anything. Since he was trying to close the gap between them, that obviously wasn't the case.

Wrench goosed the throttle and shot forwards. The chopper was built for show, rather than speed, but could out-pace a four-cylinder Taurus, and could maneuver places that the car couldn't go.

The biker immediately cut down an alley. Zooming around garbage cans and dumpsters, he looked back. The Taurus wasn't in sight.

Wrench grinned. He roared across the street into another alley that led away from the questing gray car. After a few minutes of high-speed maneuvering, the scout for the Fenris Firar was convinced that no one was following.

●● ◖◉◗ ●●

Robert Parker had arrived at Mercy Hospital. This time, no one greeted him at the door. Lem was off duty, as was Nurse Bishop, thank God. He took the stairs up to the third floor, and entered the waiting area of the intensive care unit.

A frantic-looking Hispanic couple were pacing in the quiet room. They immediately stopped and looked at him when he entered. The sheriff held up his hand in an attempt to forestall their questions. It didn't work.

"Sheriff, what's going on? What's wrong with my little girl?" the woman cried. "Where has she been? Please, tell me." The man, for his part, unleashed a torrent of Spanish that Parker couldn't begin to understand. It had been way too fast and heavily inflected for his meager command of the language.

"Mrs. Ibarra, I can't answer any of those questions yet. You need to talk to her doctors when you can. I need to have some questions answered, too," he said, addressing the pleading woman, "Please excuse me."

He gently pushed past the worried couple without another word. They started to follow him, then drifted to an uncertain stop. The man put his arms around the distraught woman as she once again burst into tears.

Parker stepped into the ICU and was met by a sturdy-looking nurse of late middle age. She reached out and took his arm, pulling him closer as she spoke.

"Sheriff, Miss Ibarra is awake and talking with Dr. Novak. She's traumatized, but says that she's willing to talk to you. I understand you have a job to do, but please be gentle. Try to let Dr. Novak help question her or help Rita with her answers, okay? She seems to be really good at this sort of thing."

"Fine, no problem." Why did everyone insist on telling him how to do his job? 'Do I just radiate incompetence?'

The nurse must have read some of what he was thinking in his expression, because she squeezed his arm again and said, "look, Sheriff. I know that you know this stuff, okay, and I know that you must be pretty good at your job. It's just that this kid's been through something horrible, and we're all feeling responsible for her, you know?" She smiled reassuringly and released his arm.

He stepped beyond the curtain. Huddled on the hospital bed was the tiny looking teen-ager, similar to the last time he had seen her. But the look on her face was different. Where previously there had been no recognition, nor animation, there at all, this time her face looked gaunt. Dark circles had formed her eyes, which were darting around constantly. She had also developed a twitch, as if she expected to have to run for her life at any second.

Standing next to her was a middle-aged, pleasant looking woman in a white blouse and blue skirt. Gray streaks lined her black hair. She was holding Rita's hand gently in her own, and speaking quietly to her. She looked up at Parker's approach and smiled.

"Hello, Sheriff, I'm Paula Novak. Doctor Simon thought that I could be some help with Rita, so I came over last night from Wichita Falls," she said, before looking down at the girl. "Rita here is a real trooper. She didn't want to talk last night, but this morning she asked for a drink, and has been talking since. She's kind of a chatterbox in fact," she added, giving Rita's hand a gentle squeeze.

Rita started to flinch, then took a deep breath and slumped back down. She still looked so tiny. Even Parker, who was definitely not a "touchy-feely" kind of guy, wanted to pick her up and hold her safe.

He fought down the urge to hold her other hand, instead sitting in a chair by the bed. After receiving an encouraging nod from the psychiatrist, he looked again at Rita.

"Rita," he began in a soft rumble, "my name is Robert Parker. I'm the sheriff here. You may know my nephew, Andrew Collins. He's a senior at your school, plays quarterback on the football team." Recognition of the name showed briefly in the girl's face before the haunted look resumed. Parker continued.

"Rita, your folks are right outside this here curtain. In a couple of minutes, we're gonna bring them in to see you? Before we do, though, there are a couple questions that we need to ask about Thursday night, okay?" The girl twitched again, starting to struggle.

Dr. Novak held her hand, and she seemed to calm down. "Very good, Rita. That's my girl. I'm here with you, remember, and you are completely safe now. What's done is done, and can't hurt you anymore. The sheriff is here to protect you," the doctor said, soothingly. Parker paused, letting the doc finish. She was good at her job. The girl finally looked up at the bulky lawman sitting beside her and nodded.

"Rita, you were with a young man, a college boy, Thursday night, weren't you? It's okay, you're not in any trouble. Your folks don't even have to know. Just nod if I'm right, okay? It will make this easier if I do most of the talking, I suppose," he glanced again at the shrink, seeing her nod slightly at his last comment.

"So, Rita, you were out with Scott, right? You took a ride in his car. Remember the nice Mustang?"

Slowly the girl nodded, looking at the sheets covering her feet. Beyond that nod she was still.

"Okay, so you stopped at the park to go for a walk, right?" Again, a slow nod. Parker was encouraged. Maybe this wouldn't be so bad. Still, he knew that he had to tread very lightly.

"Very good, Rita. Now here it gets a little fuzzy for me. You got out of the car and went down the left trail, going for a nice walk. Then something bad happened. Did you get attacked? Did something try to hurt you?"

Rita began to shiver. Tears squeezed out of her tightly shut eyes, and ran down her cheeks. She shook her head vigorously from side to side, as if trying to drive out the images in her head. Dr. Novak continued to hold her hand, and slowly slipped onto the bed beside her, wrapping her free arm around the trembling girl, pulling gently so that the teen's body leaned against her own.

The girl's shakes subsided. She nodded again, almost imperceptibly. Parker knew the next part would be the worst. Trying his best to be gentle, following Dr. Novak's example, he started to lean forwards to ask his next question.

Rita shrank back from him, turning her face away and burying it in the doctor's shoulder. The doctor shook her head and motioned to Parker to back off. He froze, then realized his mistake. He knew that he couldn't move at her, it would panic the girl, make him appear aggressive.

He leaned back in his chair and waited. Once she eased back to sitting up, mostly on her own, he tried again.

"Rita, when you were attacked, what happened? Did you get hurt by a person?" He paused, waiting for an answer. She didn't move.

"Okay, Rita, you're doing great. Were you and Scott attacked by a dog, or maybe more than one? Was it an animal?"

Rita twitched again. She turned her body slightly, pivoting towards the woman holding her. She looked up into her face and locked onto her eyes. Her mouth worked, as if trying to speak. Then she broke eye contact and looked again at the sheets. Her hands moved, twisting the sheets into her fists.

The sheriff waited. He was going to get his answer. The psychiatrist whispered in the girl's ear. Rita took a deep breath, and let it out in a burst of speech.

"It was wolves. Huge wolves. Like on TV. Los lobos! Los lobos del Diablo! Wolves. Just like on the jackets! They jumped on Scott and-and *ate* him! They ran at me, and I ran and ran and ran until I couldn't see anymore. Then I ran 'cause I knew they were after me and I could hear them coming" her small body shook with fear. "Then I don't remember any more. I was here," she said, and trailed off into sobs. She buried her face in her hands and pulled away from Dr. Novak's comforting embrace.

Dr. Novak looked at Parker. She raised an eyebrow inquiringly. He shook his head. Most of what she said made sense. The jacket reference was lost on him. He wanted to ask the distraught girl more, but Novak shook her head and motioned for him to go. He nodded and rose slowly to his feet.

"Thank you Rita. You did great. We'll talk more later, okay? I'm gonna give you a couple minutes with Dr. Novak, and then if it's okay with the doctor we'll let your parents come in and visit with you."

He walked back to the waiting room where the Ibarras were still pacing. They came up to him. He wished that a doctor were here to talk with them. He supposed one would, later. Right now, he was stuck with this duty.

"Mr. and Mrs. Ibarra, your daughter is awake. She's talking, but very shaken. It seems that she was witness to an animal attack. A friend that she was with was killed. She's pretty upset, as you may imagine. Dr. Novak is with her now, and she's a good doc. When she comes out you can talk with her more, and hopefully you can go see your little girl."

While the Ibarras had questions, Parker had no answers. He shook his head and told them they'd have to wait for the doctor. Excusing himself, he went to the nurse's station to have them page Dr. Simon.

Dr. Novak came out looking concerned, but not upset. She stopped at the desk to speak with Parker.

"Sheriff, you handled that well. Rita's gonna get better, I think, but she'll need help. I'm gonna let her folks see her. Tell Dr. Simon for me that I'll see him later and go over treatment."

"Sure. And doc…thanks. You do good work."

"Thank you sheriff. So do you. You were surprisingly gentle. Frequently people with your size lack touch and finesse when dealing with people. You did just fine in there," she said, and then left the station to get the Ibarras.

Parker turned back to the ICU nurse with a smug look. She'd heard everything that the shrink had said about him. 'So there,' he thought. 'Not quite the moron that you thought I was, huh?' She returned his look, not seeming to be overwhelmingly impressed, despite the good doctor's words of praise.

He sighed. Just can't win with some people.

CHAPTER 9

Drew arrived at the park shortly after three-thirty in the afternoon. The vans spilled into the parking lot right behind him. Dust boiled past him, doors opened, and excited chatter reached his ears almost immediately.

The young man grinned and took off his helmet. This actually looked like it was going to be fun. He hadn't been camping in three or four years. As long as his lunatic friend Jones didn't throw him in the lake or anything stupid, he reminded himself. Doug *had* threatened to get him tonight.

'We'll see who gets who,' Drew told the hulking young man silently, as the lineman piled sleeping bags and other gear on the ground.

Doug looked over at his friend, who was watching him, still sitting on his bike. "Hey, slacker, get with it. Help my dad get the rest of the gear divided up," he called, cheerfully.

"Yeah, yeah, yeah," Drew grumbled, getting off of his Honda and joining the throng of kids. Mr. Jones smiled at Drew as he came up to the group.

"Mr. Collins, good to see you. You did a good job of leading us here. Nice to see a young man that obeys traffic rules and drives sensibly. Your dad must be proud of you. I wish that *my* son showed such wisdom and maturity when he drives." The older Jones rolled his eyes towards his son, who grinned at his father and stuck his tongue out at Drew.

Mr. Jones smiled mischievously at the quarterback. "Of course, perhaps you're not always being so mature. I seem to recall my yard being damaged by a certain young man cutting across it full-throttle one afternoon. And then there was the now infamous wheelie onto the practice field." He smiled widely now, enjoying Drew's embarrassment.

"Please try to refrain from any such antics this weekend, Mr. Collins. We are attempting to mold these young boys into good citizens. We don't need them exposed to such bad examples, right?"

Doug, who had come up to them during his father's lecture, was grinning from ear to ear. He sternly pointed his finger at his best friend, and in his best mock-disappointed-father voice, intoned, "Boys, you see this young man? He is a fallen man, a tragic figure. He stands before you today, a pathetic failure of our modern school system. Pity him, but do not attempt to emulate him."

Drew slumped and held out his hands, palms up, in a sign of surrender. In a broken voice, he said, "Mr. Jones, Doug, you're absolutely right. I give up my wicked ways. Take me into Cub Scout custody. I vow to mend my ways and become a model scout, so that I too can be a good citizen, like the two of you. Do you have those cute little yellow scarves in my size?"

Kids guffawed. Mr. Jones laughed and turned back to the van, to get the last of the gear out. Doug pretended to slap handcuffs on Drew's extended hands, vowing to the giggling kids that he would indeed put a yellow scarf on Drew.

Doug's father pulled out his clipboard, and raised his hand for quiet. When he had the group's attention, he went over assignments.

"Okay, guys, here's the deal. There are eleven of you, and four of us. Each counselor will be responsible for three of you, except for those unlucky two who will be under my watchful eye." Giggles here, along with a couple of groans.

"Doug will take Jonas, Jake, and...let's see, do we have another J? Yes, Jimmy!" More giggles, as 'Jimmy' was actually Timmy.

"Now, Mr. Roberts will take Terence, Rick, and Peter with him. And now, the winners of the Drew Collins look-alike contest: Steve, Paul, and Ben." Scattered cheers followed that announcement.

"And that leaves the following unfortunates with me: Michael and Eric Vaughn," the troop leader finished up.

"All right kiddies, this is how it works: you little rug rats will carry everything, and we'll just follow along behind you with the whips, to keep you in line. Come over here and we'll divide up the stuff," Doug stated, swinging Jake off his feet and dropping him on a gear bag.

"Jake, my man, you need to help carry stuff, we ain't carryin' your fat butt all the way to the camp. Get up!" he growled. Jake scrambled up off of the gear, and then tripped and fell over Jonas' foot. More giggling.

Drew smiled. This was going to be fun. The kids seemed well behaved, and the Jones duo really knew how to relate to the campers. He should have a pretty easy time of this. He and Sam Roberts, another long-time helper, would set up the tents while Doug and his father took the kids on a hike.

They worked in silence, setting up four large tents in a semi-circle around the cooking area. Then they filled air mattresses, utilizing the pumps and adapter kits for the van's power outlet. Much better than the old way, Drew decided. Camping had come a long way in the last ten years. It was much more comfortable now.

By the time they had the mattresses filled and divided up among the tents, the rest of the troop had returned. Sam and Drew could hear them long before they came into sight. Doug had them enthusiastically singing, loudly and mostly off-key.

"There she was, just a-walkin' down the street; singin' do-wah-ditty-ditty-dum-ditty-do!" Drew grinned. He assumed that Doug's father would never allow his son to teach them the schoolyard version that he and Doug used to sing. He was right.

"Before I knew it, she was walkin' next me; singin' do-wah-ditty-ditty-dum-ditty-do; holdin' my hand just as natural as could be!" The loud and musically challenged group marched into sight.

"She looked good—she looked good—she looked fine—she looked fine—and I nearly lost mind," the kids collapsed into laughter, ending the sing-along, as Doug comically flopped into a camp chair, throwing his gear onto the ground and moaning in fake anguish.

"Drew, you gotta save me! These kids are gonna be the death of me. They work me too hard, they sing too loud, and they complain all the time! What am I to do?"

Doug was piled on by at least seven of the campers, resulting in the chair breaking, sending Doug and the kids sprawling onto the hard ground.

"Boys, that's enough!" Doug's father barked. "Look, we just started and we've already got broken equipment. Have fun, but cut back on the clowning around. Doug, that'll be your chair for the rest of this camping trip, you hear?"

"Sorry daddy," Doug muttered from under three children, in his best 'Billy Madison' voice. More giggles from the pile.

The boys moved to the tents, fighting and arguing with each other over which group got which tent. Before the good-natured pushing got too animated, Mr. Roberts stepped in.

"Boys, this red one is my group's. My stuff is already in it. The green one is Drew's, the blue one is Mr. Jones and the twins', and the last one over there is for Doug and his group. We done put it further away 'cause Doug tends to have bad gas at night on these here trips."

Doug punctuated Sam's pronouncement by putting his hands to his mouth and making a loud farting sound. Everyone laughed and joined in, Drew and Mr. Roberts included.

"Ewww! Somebody cut a REAL one!" Steve said, holding his nose.

"That was you," somebody called. "He who smelled it dealt it."

"Nuh-uh, you dope. I was clear over here," he yelled back. "Couldn't have been me."

"Then how could you smell it?" he was challenged, by one of the older kids.

"I got a good nose. My sister is a nurse, and she can smell things clear across the room. I guess I can, too."

"Your sister is hot!" the older boy said, causing more laughter and a couple of the other kids to wolf whistle.

"Mr. Jones, Doug, make 'em quit," Steve pleaded.

"Steve, your sister Amy is hot; what can I say?" Doug laughed. "Too bad she doesn't like younger football players like me."

"Gentlemen, and the rest of this rotten Scout pack, let's get changed to go to the lake. Swimming trunks for the lot of you. Fishin' poles for those of you that are hungry for fish. Please remember to not snag the swimmers—we ain't cleanin' and eatin' any Scouts!" Doug intoned, getting up off of the ground.

"C'mon, let's go," the elder Jones said, grabbing his pole and tackle box. It was his favorite part of the trip, the fishing. He enjoyed catching a big fish almost as much as he liked working with the young people.

Soon all eleven kids were clambering down the short path to the lake, with three of the counselors. Mr. Roberts opted to remain at the camp and get preparations under way for supper.

Drew and his friend took charge of the children who wanted to swim. The bulk of the youngsters went with them.

Dusk was approaching as the Scouts returned to their camp. Mr. Roberts had tiki torches arranged in a large circle around the fire pit. He lit them immediately, telling the boys that it would help keep away the mosquitoes.

Drew helped light the fire. Tonight they would have fish, brats, hot dogs, and potatoes cooked in the fire, and cottage cheese and chips. Later there would be toasted marshmallows and maybe s'mores. Hopefully there would be no campfire sing-alongs.

●●◖◉◗●●

Pain. Dull, rhythmic, throbbing pain. Lucy's return to consciousness was dominated by a headache that encompassed her entire world. She attempted to raise her hands to her head and discovered that she couldn't.

She opened her eyes. Sunlight assaulted her pounding head, and she closed them again, tightly. Gingerly, she tried again. Through slitted eyelids she took in her surroundings.

She appeared to be in a hayloft. The late afternoon sun was streaming in through the open loft door. Turning her head, Lucy was able to see more. There were clothes scattered around her, and she was lying on a blanket in the center of the loft. Her hands were bound above her head with what felt like twine.

The young woman's initial confusion quickly gave way to fear, as she remembered the attack in the parking lot at Bernie's. The biker prick from that morning had hit her with something. He must have brought her here. Dread filled her as her mind went over the possibilities.

She looked down. Her clothes were still on her. That at least was encouraging. Vaguely, she wondered what her date was thinking right now. Did he think that she stood him up? Was he going to be pissed? Lucy shook her head at the ridiculousness of that random thought. An internet date being stood up was the least of her problems right now.

A dry cough from above and behind her made her flinch. She wasn't alone. She struggled with her bonds, only now realizing that her legs were also tied. Twine around each ankle kept her feet apart, and prevented her from being able to turn around.

A dark shape moved in front of her, framed by the sun. Leaning down, the shape took on detail. It was the biker from earlier, the one that chick had called Wrench. He leered at her.

"Hiya, baby. Remember me? We wasn't properly introduced before. They call me Wrench. I thought we should get better acquainted before the fun really starts. You didn't seem so interested in me before, at the store, but you'll be interested in me soon. I'll be the focus of your whole life, little girlie." He reached out, taking her chin in his hand. She shrank back from him, trying to pull away.

The biker slapped her across the face, hard. He gripped her chin again, digging his fingers into her skin painfully. His other hand grabbed her breast, twisting it. He kissed her hard on the mouth and then let go.

Rising back up, he grinned down at her. "Bitch, you have no idea of the fun we're gonna have with you. I'm gonna bring some friends to introduce to you. We're gonna have a party tonight. And then, dinner," he ended ominously, walking out of sight.

Lucy twisted and pulled at her bonds, panicking at the thought of the biker's return with "friends." She had no doubt that he meant to rape her. The twine cut cruelly into her wrists and ankles, but despite her frenzied attempts, didn't give. She began to scream, hoping that someone could hear her and come to the rescue.

She heard creaking sounds, like someone climbing a ladder. Several someones, in fact. Then footsteps, coming closer. A dozen people appeared, now standing over her.

"Please, let me go. I didn't do anything. I won't say anything to anybody. Just leave me alone, please. Untie me," she whimpered, pleading with them.

One of the shapes loomed closer. It was another man, and he was huge. His evil, bearded face thrust close to hers. He inhaled deeply, as if drinking in her fear. Reaching out, his dirty hand traced gently down her tear-streaked face, touching her throat, and continued down her chest and torso.

"Mmm, nice. Young. Smells good. Wrench, you done good," he said, his deep voice soft but filled with menace.

"Please," she sobbed, "don't hurt me. I won't tell anyone. Just let me go."

"Little one, you're right. You won't tell anyone. Just you relax. We're gonna have some fun before supper, okay?"

The big man reached out again, placing his hand around her throat. She started to cry out, but he shook his head, putting his finger to his lips with his other hand. The girl stopped, staring at him, trembling.

His hand gripped the top of her shirt and ripped downwards. Lucy cried out in terror as the biker tore away her bra, exposing her breasts.

Around her, voices raised in triumph. Harsh guttural cheers accompanied the man's stripping of their prey. Lucy's pants and underwear were ripped off her feebly struggling form. Her screams were cut off as Lobo pressed his mouth against hers, biting into her lips.

Lobo rose up off of the girl. He looked around at his pack. They trembled with anticipation. He began to remove his clothes. Lucy whimpered again, as the assembled bikers cheered and began tearing off their own clothes as well.

Her cries were drowned out as the pack converged on her, yelling and howling with primeval lust.

CHAPTER 10

Ramona had spent the entire afternoon riding up and down various side roads, trying to calm down. Her life was not going the way she wanted it to. Granted, no one's life went according to plan, but her very existence was a curse. Since the gang had found her on the side of the road four years earlier, she had fallen deeper and deeper into a nightmare that she could never have imagined when she ran away from her groping stepfather.

The first night had been okay. The bikers had pulled over when they spotted her. The men were rude and made offensive comments, but no one had touched her. They'd camped out at a nearby rest stop, fed her, and let her crash with them. The next day they put her on the back of Wrench's bike, and took her with them.

A week later she was initiated into the Fenris Firar. Lobo "made love" to her in the late afternoon, an act of violence that was nothing more than rape. Afterwards, she'd been set free to run away into the deserted countryside.

She ran for hours, exhausted and weeping, until after dark, when she heard the first howls. Terrified, she ran faster, losing her purse and what was left of her belongings. The howling grew more frequent, and closer.

Soon she could hear growls on either side of her. She fell, too tired to run any further. She regained her feet, determined to at least fight whatever was chasing her. Staring out into the night, she became aware of large shapes circling her. She couldn't make out what they were at first, but they were huge.

One came closer, and she could see it clearly. It was a wolf; monstrous, massive, and clearly larger than it was supposed to be.

Long fangs glistened in the moonlight as it snarled at her. She tried to back away from it, but others encircled her from behind.

The wolf leapt on her, and bit her shoulder. Trapped under it, there was nothing she could do to protect herself. Ramona remembered feeling totally helpless. She was going to die. But she didn't. The wolf jumped off and ran away. The others followed.

The next morning the pack found her again. Roughly, they cleaned and bandaged her wound, and explained to her that she was now a part of the Fenris Firar. Like it or not, her curse bound her to them, tighter than the bonds of marriage or family.

Ramona snorted, riding down the highway towards the farm. Some family. The only way she survived was by being more violent than any of the others. No one messed with her, because she would die before she gave up. Even Lobo, after one more attempted "date," backed off. His penis had healed from the knife cut she'd inflicted on it, even if his pride hadn't.

The young woman had no illusions about what she would find when she returned to the farm. Wrench had remained behind at the shop to grab that girl. Odds were, the pack would be "playing with their food," as Lobo was fond of calling it.

She'd even participated in such games a time or two. The bloodlust was strong during the full moon, even during the day as a human. Ramona, early on in her time as a lycanthrope, had given in to her more primal urges, mating more than once with Wrench, and taking part in hunts that involved humans.

Now, she had grown to be revolted by such behavior. If her curse decreed that she had to be both beast and human, so be it. She would spend her allotted time as a wolf in true wolf fashion—avoiding mankind. Being a beast didn't require one to be evil; that was simply Lobo's take on it, since he himself was evil.

Ramona's philosophical debate continued until she reached the abandoned farm. She parked her bike in the shed with the others, noting Wrench's panhead in the corner, with what looked, and smelled, like fresh blood on it. She shook her head and growled.

There was no one about. No sentries, or anyone just lazing around to watch the sun go down. That meant only one thing.

She stalked into the barn. She could hear movement up in the hayloft. Her heightened senses picked out grunts, heavy bodies shifting, thumping, and faint groans. Ramona went up the ladder.

The scene that greeted her was exactly what she expected. In the middle of the floor was a pile of bodies. Under a squirming mass of naked bikers, both male and female, was the brunette from the Harley shop, being gang-raped. Several bikers held her arms and legs as three others thrust violently into her from various positions.

Piggy looked over at her, her thick features twisted in the dim light. "Ramona, you want some? She ain't done yet." The fat biker smiled.

Ramona looked away.

"Aww, come on, bitch. How long has it been since you had any fun with us? Come on, she's good stuff, or was half an hour or so ago," Wrench added, laughing as he wiped himself off.

Lobo, still thrusting with enthusiasm into the girl's mouth, stopped long enough to look over. As the violated girl gagged and choked, he grinned and resumed.

"Hey, Ramona, remind you of our time together? We can do it again, anytime you want," he rasped.

Rage flashed across the Ramona's face. She spit at Lobo and whirled away. There was nothing that she could do to help the unfortunate woman in the hayloft, but she didn't have to take part in it.

She heard raucous laughter behind her as she fled the barn. Ramona ran off across the yard, with no purpose other than to get as far away from the scene in the hayloft as possible. Reaching the top of the hill, she continued over the top and out into the field beyond, out of sight of the barn, and into the gathering gloom.

Lucy floated in and out of consciousness, her mind unable to deal with everything that she had been subjected to. Dimly, part of her brain recognized that the torture had stopped. Her eyelids fluttered, trying to open. Blearily, through the spit and other bodily fluids covering her face, she looked around the hayloft, which was now mostly dark.

She could still hear bodies moving, but it was too dark to see anything well. It occurred to her that she was still alive. Trembling, she raised herself up onto her elbows. The effort was almost too much for her.

A sudden bright light made her shut her eyes and avert her face. Guttural laughter sounded all around her.

"Hey, bitch, look…look at us," a voice taunted her from close by.

"C'mon baby, the party isn't over yet," another called.

A third voice added, "Yeah, the appetizer was good, but the main course is about to be served."

"Little girl, look. You don't want to miss this part. This is where the fun really starts," the leader growled, holding her head up by grabbing her hair in his fist. "I said look," he repeated, slapping her.

Lucy opened her eyes. There were torches lit around the hayloft, bathing the hay in soft yellow light. Crouched around her were her tormentors, all leering.

"Do you see the moon outside, little sheep? Isn't it pretty? It is to us. It fills us with strength, gives us courage, it makes us…hungry," came Lobo's hoarse voice. He released the girl's head and stepped around to stand in front of her.

He crouched down, looking somehow more primal than he did standing upright. The pack all crowded in on the distraught woman, making horrible growling noises.

Lucy blinked. Her sense of reality was slipping away faster and faster. She actually thought that she saw fangs in the mouths of the bikers as they snapped and growled at her. As dense hairs sprouted from their naked forms, she lost what little sanity had been left to her.

"No-o-o-o-o-o!" she screamed as the monstrous figures leaped upon her, shredding her flesh with teeth and claws. Mercifully, the end finally came for the young woman.

Ramona made her way as far as she could from the farm before the moon rose. She had to stay as far away from populated areas as possible. She knew that she retained some semblance of who she was while in wolf form, but not enough for rational thought or detailed decision making.

In her present state of anger, she would be unsafe for anyone unfortunate enough to run into her in the dark. She wanted no more blood on her hands. There was more than enough already.

She raised her head. She could smell water, a lot of it. She ran harder, trying to get to the water before the change took her. If she could throw herself into the water perhaps it would cool the fiery rage burning in her. Or maybe she would just drown, and all this would be over. 'That wouldn't be such a bad thing, either,' she thought.

Ramona felt the first itching sensations of the change starting in her arms, along the surface of her skin. It was time. Quickly, she stripped out of her clothes and left them under a bush. As the moon worked its curse on her body her mind concentrated on one last thought: reach the water.

The black wolf burst from the bushes, its silver eyes blazing. It leapt down the path toward the lake that its incredible sense of smell had told it lay just ahead.

CHAPTER 11

Drew sighed. The campfire sing-along was now in full swing. His best friend was dancing around the fire, waving his arms in the air, leading the young scouts in singing, and acting like a complete fool. The singing was terrible at best, but it was at least loud enough to be unintelligible.

"Okay, guys, we're going to quiet down some," Doug's father said, stepping in front of his son. Scattered boos greeted his announcement. "I thought instead that we would tell ghost stories," he said quietly, deliberating lowering his voice to add some measure of menace to his words.

The camp fell silent, each child looking around at his friends. Shining young faces reflected the firelight.

Every Scout was watching Mr. Jones, as he sat down on a stump close to the fire. He was still, staring into the fire to heighten the tension. Finally, he began his tale.

"About twenty years ago, not so very far from here, a young man went out on a date with his girlfriend. He took her to dinner, then to a movie, and then he thought that he'd bring her to the lake. They drove back to this very spot, and he shut off the car. They sat for a while, talking about life, and what they wanted to do when they got older. It got late. So the young man went to start the car and drive them home.

"But the car wouldn't start. His girlfriend was wearing high heels, so she couldn't walk all the way back. He decided to walk out to the road and try to get help. So his girlfriend rolled up the windows, locked the doors, and waited in the dark car for him to come back.

"After a while she got kinda scared, sitting there all alone out at the lake. It gets creepy here after all," he now had all the kids looking around, staring out into the dark.

Mr. Jones continued his story, his voice low and hypnotic. "So while she waited for her boyfriend, she turned on the radio. After a song or two, the DJ came on with a news bulletin. Apparently a vicious killer had just escaped from the penitentiary, and was loose in the area. People were being advised to stay indoors and lock all the doors and windows. The girl shivered, and double-checked the door locks on the car.

"The wind began to blow, gently. She could hear branches on the tree by the car, scraping back and forth across the roof...swoosh, swoosh. It started to sprinkle lightly; she could hear the patter of raindrops on the roof as well.

"Time went on. The radio trailed off as the car battery died, and the rain stopped. She was left alone in the dark with the wind and the tree branches... swoosh, swoosh.

"Just before daylight, she was awakened by headlights coming her way. A squad car pulled up to the front of her boyfriend's car, lights flashing. Two cops got out, guns in hand and flashlights shining all around.

"One came up to her, motioning at her to unlock the door. She did, and got out of the car. The big cop put his arm around her and ushered her towards the squad car. She tried to turn around and get her purse, but the two policemen told her not to turn around.

" 'Just get in the car, miss.' They said. When she got into the car, though, she looked back at her car. Her boyfriend was hanging upside down from the tree branch, his throat cut, blood pooled on the roof of the car, his fingertips just touching the roof, sliding back and forth...swoosh, swoosh. The girl screamed...Aaaaaah!" Mr. Jones finished with a loud shriek, causing many of the kids to jump and scream as well.

Some of the older kids groaned. They'd heard this story before.

"Aw, come on, Mr. Jones, that story is lame. We heard that when we was like five. It ain't even a ghost story, anyway," one of the twelve year-olds complained.

"Maybe so, but it isn't just some story, guys. This really happened up here, back in 1984. That girl was my sister. They never caught the killer, but they say that he still roams this very park, looking for people who stray away from their camp in the middle of the night," Jones, said, looking very serious.

"Yeah, sure," another kid sneered, with others joining in.

"Grrraaaah!" A huge form hurtled out of the darkness, landing in the midst of the boys, bowling them over with his outstretched arms. Campers screamed and ran in all directions.

In spite of himself, Drew yelled out loud and jumped back. The huge figure turned to face him. It was Doug, who had slipped away during his father's story and put on a dark cloak.

Sam Roberts, who alone in the group hadn't moved, chuckled.

"Got 'em again, boys. That stunt works every year. Even made Mr. Quarterback here jump a foot or two. Doug, y'all may have to check your buddy here fer clean shorts."

Doug laughed uproariously at Drew's jumpiness. "Dad does tell a good tale, don't he? Bet you never noticed the big mouth disappearing, did you?"

Drew shook his head. He and the boys had been played masterfully. The little guys would have nightmares for sure tonight, if any of them slept at all after that.

"Um, guys, shouldn't they be coming back now?" Drew said, noticing that only two or three of the boys who had run off shrieking were back.

"Yeah, we'll probably have to go find a couple of them. Happens almost every year. I'll stay here with Sam and call them back, you two boys go round 'em up," the older Jones said, his eyes still twinkling in the firelight.

Drew and Doug headed out into the darkness, armed with flashlights. They split up, Doug chasing down the kids that had run away from the lake, and Drew going after the ones that had bolted in the direction of the water.

The quarterback glanced up at the night sky. The moon was out, and the sky was clear. Stars sparkled. There was plenty of light to find your way around. He debated shutting off the flashlight, but decided against it. The kids could see the light and come to him.

He worked his way closer to the lake, calling out to the Scouts. A couple of boys came to him, looking sheepish.

"Guys, it's okay. That was just Doug scaring you. Go back to the camp; I'll be up in a minute. Anybody else out here?" he called.

Bushes moved further down the path, closer to the water. Drew kept moving, swinging his light in big circles, partly to make it easy for them to see where he was, and partly just to amuse himself.

Suddenly, over the excited chatter of the kids behind him at camp, he could hear other noises. Somewhere ahead on his right, he heard a small voice crying, and a low rumbling growl. He raced forwards. Hurtling a long rock, he broke clear of the brush. Just at the water's edge huddled a small child. Drew recognized Steve, the little seven-year old that had been put in his care.

In front of the crying boy was a huge black animal. It spun as the teen-ager ran towards the boy. The ferocious looking wolf growled horribly at Drew and snapped its teeth in the air.

Drew threw his flashlight at the wolf's face. His aim was true, and the heavy Mag-light struck the snarling creature square between the eyes. The teen flung himself between the wolf and the child, reaching towards Steve to pull him close, as the wolf roared in pain and anger.

The wolf reacted violently. As Drew put out his left arm to grab Steve, the beast leapt up and clamped down on Drew's forearm with its jaws. Growling with rage, it shook its head from side to side, tearing at his arm horribly.

The young man screamed in pain and anger, yanking his arm free and punching at the animal with his right hand. The wolf sprang back, crouching, snarling with hate.

Drew was terrified. There weren't supposed to be any wolves left in western Texas, and even if there were, they weren't nearly this big, and they were supposed to be afraid of humans. This big wolf didn't seem the least bit afraid of them.

Collins stared at the wolf. He crouched down, trying to figure out what to do next. They were both pinned against the lake, with an angry wolf staring them down. His left arm was held against his side, the blood running freely down his hand and dripping onto the ground. He felt the little kid pressed against the back of his hip, whimpering. The wolf stared back, head and tail held low.

The wolf's eyes blazed at him, their silver color reflecting the moonlight. Drew looked into the animal's eyes, feeling a strange sense of déjà vu. He had never seen a wolf up close before, but there was something familiar about this...

The wolf broke the contact, snarled once more at the two humans, turned, and bolted off down the trail. In the blink of an eye the coal-black canine was gone.

Drew slumped, feeling weak. His arm was bleeding profusely. It didn't hurt much, but he had the feeling that would change soon.

As if from far away, he heard raised voices. Doug's father appeared, along with Sam Roberts. Steve cried out and flung himself into the elder Jones' arms, sobbing hysterically.

Sam ran up to Drew, staring in shock at his ravaged arm.

"Son, what the hell happened? What did this?" he blurted out, reaching out to support the tall young man, who had begun to slip to the ground.

Doug showed up on Drew's right, and slipped under his shoulder, holding him up. The other Scouts crowded around them, asking questions in a constant barrage.

Drew looked at his friend. He was starting to feel very shaky. Doug's face was blurry at the edges, and beyond his face there was blackness. He felt blood running between his fingers and glanced down at his left arm.

"Oh God," he said in a shocked voice. His left forearm was mangled. In a couple of places, the white bones of his radius and ulna were visible. Blood poured from the torn flesh, Drew saw it was literally pumping out in rhythmic little spurts in one spot. His legs gave out, and he slumped into the two men's grip.

"Easy Drew, it's okay, buddy. I gotcha. Don't look at it. We'll get you fixed up," Doug said, trying to reassure and distract his friend at the same time. "C'mon, let's go back to the camp and we'll get your arm wrapped up."

David Jones watched his son maneuver the injured teen towards their camp. Deciding that he and Sam had Drew handled, he directed his attention to the excited and scared Cub Scouts clustered about.

"Okay boys, let's stay out of their way. Rick, run ahead of them and get the first aid kit out of my tent. It's in the black bag on my air mattress." He paused while one of the older boys raced off. "The rest of you form up into two rows behind me, Steve, you stay right here where you are," he smiled down at the seven-year old, who clung wide-eyed to his left hand. They formed up and followed the other counselors back towards the campsite.

Roberts and Doug were half-dragging, half-carrying Drew towards the camp. The big football player was fading. In an effort to keep him from passing out completely, or going into shock, Doug kept trying to get Drew to talk to him.

"So, Drew, next time you want to get back to nature, can you find a better playmate? Maybe a big squirrel, or an armadillo or something? Huh, whaddya say, buddy?"

Collins tried to smile, failed, and mumbled something unintelligible.

"What? Drew, my boy, you gotta speak up. We couldn't hear you. Say it again, big fella." Doug said, speaking in his friend's ear.

"Pretty wolf. Big pretty wolf. Nice eyes," he said, more clearly this time. He tried to look again at his arm, cradled against his side. "Bit the shit out of me," he added.

"Yeah, well, pretty or not, stay away from the aminals with big teeth. They's vicious," Jones said, trying to keep his tone light.

"Aminals?" Drew said, head lolling. "Did you get bit, too? They're animals, you big dumb lineman."

"I'm dumb? I didn't just get my ass all bit up trying to make friends with some monster-ass wolf. It didn't want to play fetch, you moron," Doug shot back, glad that his friend was sounding clearer. They were almost back to camp. He could see one of the kids coming back down the path towards them with a first aid kit.

Doug waved the kid back. They'd wrap the arm up at the camp, where they could sit down, and have better light. The kid, Jones thought that it was Rick or Peter, skidded to a stop and then raced back to the fire.

CHAPTER 12

The hospital emergency room was busy. Parker, Lem, and James Collins were waiting outside the entrance with Doctor Simon and a nurse when the two vans from the camping Scout troop pulled in.

Drew, drifting in and out of consciousness, was gently lifted out of his seat by Doug and the male nurse, and laid on a gurney. Dr. Simon checked his vitals as he was wheeled into the hospital. James Collins followed along after them, wringing his hands in despair.

No stranger to emergency room scenes, Parker stayed back and let the professionals do their jobs. He had already done what he could, pulling Dr. Simon out, and browbeating the hospital staff into making his incoming nephew their new top priority.

Sam Roberts and David Jones left to take the children home, leaving Doug behind to watch over his friend.

Dr. Simon directed the young man's gurney to the elevator, taking him straight to the surgical floor. As they waited for the elevator to arrive, he snapped at the nurse, "Go and get Amy. Tell her to hustle over here and prep this kid for surgery. He's already lost a lot of blood. I need him typed, and order at least four units from the blood bank. Meet us at the OR with them. Go!"

The young man didn't waste time answering the doctor; he just took off. In the ER, polite was a luxury they didn't always have time for. Efficiency was the valuable commodity. The new nurse might be inexperienced, but was clearly savvy.

By the time the elevator doors dinged softly, Amy Bishop was beside the bed, gently unwrapping the blood-soaked gauze from Drew's arm. The ER nurse was quick and thorough- she asked no questions, though they were burning within her. She knew the wounds had been acquired at the Cub Scouts' camp out, and her little brother had been there. But she didn't know what had happened beyond the basics: a counselor had been attacked by a large animal while defending one of the children.

With the wrappings gone, one look at Drew's arm was sufficient to keep her questions at bay. Bone was showing in his forearm. Despite the tight tourniquet, blood was still dripping from the savage tears. Whatever had attacked the teen-ager had been serious. This was no simple dog bite, like she had thought.

The doors of the elevator opened, and she and Doctor Simon pushed the gurney inside, taking the semi-conscious teen up to surgery.

●●☾◉☽●●

Three hours later, the door to the waiting room opened to admit the large shape of Doug Jones. He was smiling. Behind him, looking very small in the wake of the big lineman, was the surgeon. Doug gestured towards the apprehensive trio of Parker, Lem and the elder Collins. The doctor stepped towards them, and they quickly surrounded him, looking from Doug to the doctor, questions on their lips.

Dr. Bramble raised his hand. He looked tired; he had been called in late at night to perform emergency surgery on the weekend. He spoke quietly in the mostly empty room.

"Folks, Drew is out of surgery. He's in recovery right now. You can't see him yet, but he's fine. We stopped the bleeding and repaired most of the damage to his arm. He'll be okay, barring complications. We won't know for a while yet whether he has any nerve damage or not. He may not regain full use of his hand; it's too soon to tell.

"We'll keep him the rest of the night, and then put him in a private room in the morning. You'll be able to see him then. Do you have any questions?"

James' eyes had filled up, and his throat was tight. His son would be okay. He shook his head, staring at the floor, while Mary Parker held his arm and whispered reassuringly in his ear.

Sheriff Parker gruffly thanked the tired man. He still had some questions before the doctor left.

"So, doc, does he have many stitches? Will there be much scarring? He plays football, is he still gonna be able to throw the ball and everything?"

Bramble considered. "Drew needed quite a few stitches. He will have some scarring on his arm. Maybe skin grafts will help later on, but they're probably not necessary. As for playing football, I just don't know. Of course, I know who Drew Collins is, and I would hope that someday he can continue his football career, but I wouldn't count on it if I were you. I'm sorry, we'll know more in a few days."

He paused, and seeing there were no more questions forthcoming, left the room, presumably going back home to bed.

Doug looked at his best friend's family. He had no idea what to say. This wasn't the time for jokes. He'd stayed just outside the operating room for over three hours to see if Drew was going to be okay, and now that he was out of danger, Doug had no idea what came next.

"Jones, don't just stand there like an idiot, boy, tell me what happened out there," Parker barked. The young man jumped at the sharpness of the sheriff's voice.

"Uh, well, we was out at the camp, you know, and my dad and me, we told this ghost story. I mean, it ain't precisely a ghost story, there's this serial killer and all, but no ghosts. So, uh, anyway," the boy stammered, seeing the impatient look on the sheriff's face, "uh, yeah, so we told this story, and the kids kinda freaked and ran away."

Doug went on, telling them how they split up to go and get the children rounded up; about Drew going to the lake and finding Steve Bishop pinned against the water by a black wolf; and how when Drew intervened, the wolf bit him, then ran off.

"What do you mean, a black wolf? There are no wolves in west Texas anymore, hasn't been for thirty years. And them was red wolves. Did you see this happen yourself?" Parker asked, clearly skeptical.

"I didn't see Drew get bit, but I saw the wolf run off. It was a wolf, sheriff, no dog or coyote. It was big, too, real big."

"Okay Jones, you saw a black wolf that ran off. Then what?"

"Sheriff, we wrapped up Drew's arm, and put a tourniquet on it to try and stop the bleeding. We got the kids all in the vans and came here to the hospital. That's all I know," Doug ended awkwardly.

Parker looked hard at the teenager. He was clearly rattled, but firmly believed what he thought he had seen.

"I'll run you home, Mr. Jones. Mary, can you take Jim home? We can all come back in the morning to see how Drew's doin', right?"

James Collins protested mildly. He didn't want to leave Drew at the hospital alone. He didn't want to go back to an empty house by himself, either. Mary seemed to understand this. She took his hand, patted it, and told him that he could come back to their house and sleep on the couch until morning. Then she'd bring him back to see his son.

●●❨❪❾❫●●

Drew awoke to sunlight. The room he had been moved to had the blinds open, letting in the late morning sun. He looked around. There was no one else there; he had been given a private room.

He thought back to the previous night. He remembered the story that Doug and his father had told, he remembered the kids running away, running after them, and finding Steve by the water, menaced by the black wolf.

The recollection of being bitten made his arm twitch. He looked down at his left arm, lying on the clean white sheets, completely wrapped from elbow to fingertips in white gauze. His other arm had an IV in it. He sat up, shifting upwards in the bed, careful not to disturb his arm any more than necessary.

There was a knock at the door. Drew cleared his throat, noticing that he was very thirsty, and called out, "Come in."

A nurse entered, smiling. She fussed around Drew for a moment, straightening his blanket and pillows and adjusting his arm before saying, "You have visitors, young man. They came in to see you as soon as we brought you in, but they really want to see you now that you're awake. Are you ready for some company?"

"Um, yeah, okay. Who's out there?"

"Your father, aunt and uncle. Also, there is a large, somewhat heavy-looking guy who has almost needed restrained several times. Your best friend, I take it?" she said cheerfully.

Drew nodded. The idea of Doug being restrained by the nursing staff was funny. The image of two or three middle-aged nurses in crocs and scrubs holding back his determined best friend was silly.

The nurse took her patient's broad smile to indicate enthusiasm and readiness for company. She swept over to the door, pulling it open and announcing to the people in the hallway, "Come on in, folks, he's ready for y'all."

His father came in first, looking positively haggard. Sheriff Parker followed, looking grim. His wife, Drew's aunt Mary, trailed behind him, smiling brightly. Finally, behind her loomed Doug Jones, grinning like an imbecile.

"Drew Collins, you look good. You gave us all quite a scare with this, you know," his aunt started. "Your poor father didn't sleep a wink last night, huddled on our couch. He must have drunk an entire pot of coffee, too. Maybe now he'll be able to sleep. How are you?"

Drew looked guiltily at his father. He really didn't want to make his father's life any worse than it was. Not that he'd planned this. He had merely reacted to a situation.

His uncle Bob went next. "Young man, you made me proud. Hero, huh? Still not sure about what you claim attacked you, but pretty brave nonetheless. You get better, huh? Got a game next week. Looking forwards to seeing you this season." He gripped his nephew's right shoulder tightly, and then stepped back.

"Hero my ass! One little nip from a dog and you fold up like a sissy! Some big-time quarterback you are. Didn't occur to you to duck when the doggie jumped at you?" Doug boomed out, causing Drew to laugh. His family, who had tensed up at the teen's seemingly insensitive comments, relaxed as they saw their effect on Drew.

"Now, now," the nurse scolded, herding the big young man away from the bed. "You can all come back in a few minutes. Right now I need some time alone with our patient."

Doug leered over the nurse's shoulder at the last comment. He made obscene gestures with his hands, making Drew blush and smile at the same time. He flipped off his buddy, and mouthed, 'Bitch.'

Doug smiled serenely back at him and mouthed, 'Jerk.' He left the room, closing the door behind him.

The nurse looked at Drew and smiled as well. She motioned towards the bathroom. He nodded and sat at the edge of the bed. Rising carefully, he walked the few feet to the bathroom, with the nurse walking beside him with his IV pole.

He turned to the nurse with a reddening face. "You don't need to actually go in with me, do you? I can handle this part, right?"

"Well, since you seem to be pretty stable on your feet, we'll let you try this solo. If you have problems, there is a red call button right next to the toilet, okay? I'll be right out here."

"Thanks, ma'am. I'll just be a minute," the relieved young man said. 'Thank God,' he thought. The idea of the woman in the bathroom with him while using the toilet was scarier than facing an all-out blitz on third and long.

After he finished, he opened the bathroom door, and was met immediately by the attentive nurse.

"Everything go okay?"

"Yeah, just fine," he mumbled, awkward at being questioned about how his piss went. He moved back to the bed and sat down. The efficient Miss Stubblefield whisked his IV pole into place and pulled back the sheets for him.

"Uh, can I get some clothes? I mean, at least like, underwear?" Drew asked.

"Soon. We'll let the doctor look at you, now that you're awake, and we'll check your arm. Are you in any pain? Does your arm hurt?" she said, mothering him back onto the bed, and getting his arm arranged correctly. "You're due for some pain meds. Since you're awake, maybe you can just take a tablet. Lay back, now, I'll let your family back in, and then go get the doctor for you."

This time Doug was the first one back in. He looked at his friend in amusement.

"So, how was she? Didn't take very long, dude, she too good for ya?" he cracked. "Gotta watch them older ones, they got experience."

Collins shook his head in mock exasperation. "You know, Jones, they have shots for problems like yours. As long as you're here, maybe you could get fixed or something."

"Ain't no problem with me. Nothing that a hottie in a nurse's outfit couldn't fix, huh?" Doug enthused, rubbing his hands together. " You shoulda seen the one last night that worked on you. Steve Bishop's older sister. Wow! Major babe. Too bad she always dates losers. Maybe I'll convince her to make an exception in my case."

"Doug, the only 'hottie' in a nurse's outfit you could get, would be the Joker visiting Harvey Two-Face in the hospital," Drew laughed. "As for Amy Bishop, she doesn't date losers as bad as you, no matter how much her little brother likes you."

Parker cleared his throat. "Well, I gotta go. I'll talk to you all later. Bye, Drew, you take care of yourself," the sheriff said, patting his nephew's shoulder again and walking out.

He was replaced by the doctor; who walked in just as the bulky sheriff was stepping out. Parker, remembering crashing into Simon just two days earlier the same way, sidestepped adroitly and avoided the collision.

Doug watched the averted near crash, and turned triumphantly to his friend in the bed.

"See, doofus, that's how it's done. How hard is it to move out of the way? Even an old, slow guy like your uncle can do it!" Jones jibed, adding hastily to the retreating broad back of the sheriff, "No offense, Sheriff Parker; just trying to make a point."

Doug's attempt at humor fell flat. No one smiled, except for the doctor who had just entered the room. He smiled at the people gathered around the bed of his patient

"Hi Drew, how are you feeling? Good to see you awake today. We met earlier in the morning, but you were mostly out of it."

"That's how he is normally, doc. Hard to tell, though, if you don't know him like we do," Doug threw in. Mary looked embarrassed, and shushed him.

The doctor seemed mildly amused, treating Doug as if he were a mentally handicapped child.

"Young man, why don't you go out to the nurse's desk and get yourself a soda? They keep 7-Up back there, and I'll bet they'd give you some. That way the grown-ups can talk," he said, speaking slowly and clearly.

Drew burst out laughing as Doug stood nonplussed, obviously trying to figure out if the doctor was teasing him, or if he really thought that he was slow.

"Doug, I think he's kidding. You can stay, just shut up. Linemen are supposed to be seen and not heard." The young man turned his attention from his friend to the doctor.

"So, doctor, can I lose this IV? And get some real clothes;?" He looked down at his hospital gown. "Not that this robe isn't quite the fashion statement, it just isn't me."

"You need to finish out this bag on the IV. We put this in to help replenish fluids, since you had lost so much, and now you're getting antibiotics to help fight off infection. Once this bag runs out, we'll take out the IV and just give you pills and lots and lots of fluids. Fair enough?"

Drew nodded.

"I will be back later this afternoon to change the dressing on your arm and check things out more thoroughly. Go easy on the nurses here, just to warn you. They can be mean to big, tough football players who misbehave, got it?" he asked, as he turned away to talk with Drew's father.

"Yeah, doc...what about the clothes? Can I put on some sweatpants, maybe, and a t-shirt or something?"

"Oh," the doctor said, turning back to his patient. "Well, the t-shirt is out for now. We have to put you in things that won't involve your arm. I don't see why you can't have some sweats or something, though."

Drew sighed with relief. No way he could be comfortable lying around in this geeky robe, with his ass hanging out. He could live without the tee, for now. He looked around.

The doctor was talking with his father and aunt. Doug was half listening to them and half trying to catch the eye of the other nurse at the desk with Stubblefield.

'Unbelievable,' Drew thought. 'It's like all he ever thinks about. He's even worse than I am.' He leaned back, relaxing. 'I'm tired,' he thought with mild surprise. He closed his eyes briefly, to rest them. And promptly fell asleep.

CHAPTER 13

Dawn came for the Fenris Firar. The farm was quiet. The majority of the pack had been up in the hayloft when the moon had risen, and were still up there when the sun intruded, changing them back to the human, or mostly human, forms they wore when the moon wasn't full.

Lobo looked around at the blood-drenched loft. He sniffed, inhaling deeply. The scent of blood and sex still filled the air. The remains of last night's entertainment were scattered around in the hay. He smiled. Life was good.

Mentally, he took inventory of his pack.

Fourteen of them were in the hayloft with him. That left ten downstairs or outside. He dressed quickly, and climbed down the ladder. Five more bikers were getting dressed on the ground floor of the barn.

Lobo stepped outside. Using both eyes and nose, he found four more members of the Fenris Firar. Only Ramona remained unaccounted for. He remembered her showing up just before dark, and walking in on their fun.

The bitch had blown a gasket and run off. Going into the garage, he found her Sportster, still there, which meant she must have run off on foot. Lobo grinned- that made for some interesting possibilities.

Others joined him outside. Ulric, his massive lieutenant, touched his arm. Lobo turned to regard the only member of the Firar that was actually larger than he was. Ulric followed him because he wasn't smart enough to lead the pack, and both of them knew it. It kept the lieutenant loyal, which in turn made him useful.

"Yeah, Ulric, what is it?"

"We're gonna need more food. We ate everything last night. What should we do?"

"Starve, if yer in charge. So what, I gotta do all the thinking here? Just go back into town and get food. They love us at Albertson's," he said, which was greeted with laughter and scattered cheers.

"Uh, Lobo, we probably shouldn't actually go into town for a while," Wrench said, nervously.

"Why the hell not?" Lobo demanded.

"Um, well, you remember that I grabbed that girl yesterday from the Harley shop?" He hesitated, clearly nervous. "That chicken-shit mechanic might have seen me grab the girl."

"You were SEEN? You idiot! Someone saw you snatch that girl, and you never told me? I oughta kill you right now, and leave your dead body next to hers. Jesus, Wrench, are you stupid," he growled, cuffing the cowering man behind the ear with an enormous fist.

"I'm sorry, Lobo, I knew that you'd like the girl, so I brought her to you. Not like that bitch Ramona. She told me not to stay after and get her. She split on me. If she'd been there watchin' out like she's supposed to, nothin' woulda happened."

"So this is Ramona's fault, then? Is that right? Maybe when she gets back I'll let you two fight it out. Winner goes with us, loser stays behind with the girl."

Wrench actually looked relieved, which only angered Lobo more.

"Wrench, you idiot. You know we can't do that. You were the one seen," Lobo turned away in disgust. "Leave me alone, I gotta think."

He knew that they'd have to leave the area, long before he wanted to. Lobo was smart enough to know that the farm had way too much evidence of their presence. There was no way to clean up the hayloft and get rid of the body, and they'd already had bad luck with the guy at the park. The cops had shown up too soon, and they barely got away without being questioned. This time they couldn't just leave the scene as it was.

"Okay, here's what we're gonna do. We're gonna head north to Oklahoma, maybe drift over to Arkansas. Gather all our stuff; get the bikes loaded up. The barn needs to burn, all the way to the ground. Same with the garage."

Lobo pointed. "Aardwolf, Caleb, find me some gas or oil or kerosene, anything that burns. Lots of it. Okay, assholes, move it!"

The big biker stomped over to his bike and pulled it out of the garage. The old soft tail rolled easily under his touch; he'd had this bike for a long time, and it felt as much a part of him as the wolf. He packed up his few meager belongings and strapped them to the back of his sissy bar.

Having taken care of his things, Lobo returned to damage control. They had to eliminate as much of their presence at the abandoned farm as possible. He knew that a big fire would attract attention, but if they could make it hot and fast enough, it would destroy most of the evidence before anyone could put it out.

He looked around for his men. Caleb and Aardwolf both were returning, with cans of fuel in their hands. Aardwolf was grinning.

"Lobo, I found something good. There's a diesel gas barrel on the other side of the garage that's still pretty full. We can go back and get more."

Lobo smiled. Aardwolf was dumb, but at least he was competent and dedicated. Not nearly as prone to make bad decisions as Wrench or some of the others.

"Aardwolf, you are my favorite pack member. Go find some more containers. I want at least twenty-five gallons up in the loft. Give me another fifteen or so in the garage where the bikes were, and then spread more all around on the grounds. Douse the cow carcass, too, okay?"

Maybe this wouldn't be so bad after all, so long as there was no solid evidence against them. The locals could complain and investigate, but wouldn't follow them.

He smiled again. Then he looked at the white Hugger that sat alone, waiting for its rider. Ramona's bike. Damn it, she wasn't back yet. Where in the hell was she? She wouldn't take off without her ride, even if she left the pack.

Lobo's sinister smile faded. 'Now what,' he thought. Leave without her and take the bike; or leave without her and leave the bike, hoping for her to show up before the cops? 'Damn. Stupid-ass woman. More trouble than she's worth.' Once more, he regretted taking her in, and making her one of his pack.

Piggy came over to him. She looked from him to Ramona's bike and back again. The question was obvious. Piggy was one of the chicks that still rode bitch, and wanted the bike for her own.

"Yeah, Piggy, it's time to roll. The bike's all yours. We're riding outta here in five minutes. Get ready." He looked out at the assembling pack.

"Let's get some fire going! Light the loft first, then the barn, and the garage, and then fire the lot after we pull out. Did you hear me, Caleb— *after* we pull out, numb nuts!"

Caleb nodded enthusiastically.

"Okay, let's get on with...well, well, look who showed up," Lobo said, scenting the approaching female before the others. They all spun to see Ramona striding up to them, her face expressionless.

"Hey, bitch, guess what? Lobo gave me your bike, so find another ride!" Piggy gloated, thrusting her bloated-looking face forwards at the advancing woman.

Ramona never hesitated, never even changed expression. Without warning she spun, kicking out and catching Piggy on the side of the head with her right heel. Landing from the sudden spinning kick, Ramona continued on to her bike, stepping past the prone woman she had dropped. The raven-haired beauty put her key in the ignition, turned it, then thumbed the starter button on her 883. It fired right up, idling with the famous Harley shudder. She looked at Lobo, who shrugged, got on his own bike and shouted "Set this place ablaze!"

Hurriedly, Winnie and Caleb dropped torches in the hayloft and climbed down. One of them set the lower barn on fire while the other set a match to the garage.

As Piggy got quietly to her feet, Aardwolf pulled up next to her on his hog. She got on back, wiping blood from her chin, and casting a murderous look at Ramona, who merely smiled back at her.

The Fenris Firar pulled out of the farmyard. As the last of them took off down the gravel, Caleb tossed a diesel-soaked rag onto the driveway, after lighting it on fire. Then he turned his back on the roaring blaze, following his pack mates slowly down the road.

Behind the outlaw gang, the farm burned. The diesel fire burned darkly, huge billowing clouds of black smoke spreading across the sky. Far off, alarms began to sound.

The fire alarms got everyone's attention. Owing to Lucy Parson's abduction the previous day, the citizens of Iowa Park were already on alert. Less than five minutes after the rising column of smoke had been sighted, fire trucks were rolling out.

Deputy Ray Becker was the first person on the scene. Pulling his car off to the side of the road, he looked around at the old farm. The fire was amazing. A roaring pyre was already consuming the barn. The garage was blazing; even the driveway itself was burning. He couldn't even get in the lane.

Becker got out of his car and looked around, but saw nothing in the surrounding area; no movement, no people anywhere. As the fire in the driveway subsided, more vehicles showed up. Two or three neighbors pulled up in trucks, and the first of Iowa Park's three fire trucks made its way down the lane.

Sheriff Robert Parker came flying up, sliding to a halt next to Becker's car. The man got out of his Charger, nodded at his deputy, and stared at the blaze. He sighed.

It was obviously arson, but Parker had a sinking feeling that it had been set to cover up something unpleasant. The shit that was happening this week; he had just left the hospital, and his nephew, and walked out to see the smoke and hear the sirens.

"Becker, do you want my job?"

"Sheriff?"

"I said, do you want my job? It may be available soon at this rate," Parker said. He wasn't sure if he was joking or not.

Neither did Ray. He stared at his boss for a time, then chose to ignore the question.

"Sheriff, I got here first. Didn't see anything, or anybody, around. Whoever set this used a lot of diesel, I'm betting."

"Yeah, I figured that. Tell the fire crews to be careful; there must be a barrel around here, somewhere. Wouldn't want it to blow up on us," the grim-faced man responded.

Becker went off to talk with the leader of the volunteer fire department. They huddled at the edge of the blaze, pointing and talking strategy. Eventually, Becker nodded, slapped the man on the shoulder, and came back to where Parker stood.

The truck sprayed down the driveway with water, putting out the dwindling fires there, before the crews cautiously moved in. They found the gas barrel at the far end of the garage, and hosed it down thoroughly.

The other two fire engines pulled down the drive, one stopping at the garage behind the first, and the other coming to a halt in front of the barn. Both immediately began spraying water on the fires.

Parker looked at his deputy. Becker shrugged. "I told them to put them all out as fast as possible. Tom said that they usually don't bother when it's just farm buildings and they're this far gone, but I figured there might be important evidence."

"What do you think?"

"I think that we're gonna find something bad here. What about you?"

"Guess we'll find out. A fire like this, couldn't have been set but ten or fifteen minutes before you got here, tops. Whoever it was can't be too far away yet. Go call it in. See if we can cut 'em off. Bet they headed north to avoid town."

"Sure thing, boss. Maybe they'll come out around Clara, tryin' to cross the line and head up towards Lawton. I'll be right back." Ray walked off, calling dispatch as he went. He didn't need to leave Parker's side to make the call, but knew that the sheriff wanted to be left alone to think about things. He often did.

Becker called Bev, explaining the situation and what the sheriff wanted done. She sent both cars north of where they were to try and intercept the gang, and then called in help. Both the state police and county. Bev knew her business.

Two hours later, the police had found no one. The biker gang had simply vanished. The fires at the farm were largely put out, and the remains of a cow had been discovered at the edge of the property, partially burned.

Firefighters had also discovered what appeared to be human remains in the wreckage of the barn, but they were too burned to tell what gender the person had been.

CHAPTER 14

Drew flexed his arm, happy to be free of the annoying IV. The small band-aid that had taken its place was much less of a nuisance. The only problem with it was that some "sadistic" nurse had used a little kid's version, adorned with Sponge Bob. Doug was impressed with it, promising to bring him some Sponge Bob diapers and footy pajamas to go with it on his next visit.

Chuckling, Drew looked at his left arm, now re-wrapped, and clean. The old dressing had become discolored with blood and whatever goo that they had covered his wound in. He attempted to make a fist and found that while he could close his hand, he couldn't clench it tightly. Opening his hand was a problem as well; he could relax his fist, letting the fingers uncurl slightly, but he couldn't open his hand wide.

Frowning, Drew tried again with no luck. Putting his right hand over his left, he forced the hand wide open. The effort hurt the outside of his left forearm. He made a fist; this time the inside of his left forearm hurt. Damn.

When the doctor had tested his fingers for sensitivity earlier, he had felt the light pricks on the pads of each finger. Relieved, the doc had told his father and aunt that there didn't appear to be any nerve damage, which likely meant a full recovery. The only question was how long it would take- there was still a serious amount of tendon and ligament damage to deal with.

Now alone, he was starting to feel the pain from his injuries. It started as a dull ache, easy to ignore. Then his forearm felt heavy, and sensitive to the touch. In fact, it was feeling sensitive to anything that touched it. Drew swore that he could feel the pressure of the gauze wrappings, and the pillow under his arm. The bones in his forearm began to ache more, becoming harder to block out.

As the pain grew, Drew became more restless. He was no stranger to pain; he'd received more than his share of injuries playing sports. This was simply something that he would have to tough out, he told himself.

But an hour later, he was in agony. The bones in his arm felt like they were on fire. The burning spread up his arm; his entire left side was inflamed. He took another pain pill, but it did no good.

Drew was bathed in sweat. He felt shaky and weak. He couldn't rest, and watching the television was not helping. He needed out. Despite his shakiness, he opened his door and looked out into the hallway.

There was no one around. The young man stepped out into the hall and set off down the corridor, a little wobbly, but stable. The walking seemed to help, and the pain subsided as he went.

As he passed another nurse's station, he heard them talking in excited voices about a fire outside of town. There were rumors already of a human body found, badly burned and unrecognizable. The trio of nurses was of the opinion that the body would turn out to be Lucy Parsons, the girl who'd disappeared after her shift at Bernie's Harley shop the previous day.

Drew kept going, looking for a private phone. He wanted to call his dad, make sure that he was okay. He also wanted to call his uncle, and find out what was going on. But as he lifted the receiver, he hesitated.

The young Collins had never called his uncle about business, and the thought of interrupting him on the job, especially during something as serious as this, made him nervous. Maybe he'd wait for a while. His father was due to come back to the hospital later that night, and uncle Bob as well. They could talk then.

Drew walked back to his room, feeling unsettled. The pain had receded, but the news of the fire and discovery of a body had made him feel queasy.

Doug was standing outside his door. The young man had gone home at lunchtime, supposedly to sleep the afternoon away, and possibly come back late in the evening. Obviously he hadn't done that.

"So, playing hooky already? Do the nurses know that you went on a cruise?"

"No, and I won't tell if you don't. Get in my room, you big ox, and try not to knock anything over," Drew responded, pushing at his friend with his good arm.

Once inside, Doug overwhelmed a chair while Drew sat on his bed. Jones motioned at his friend's bandaged arm.

"You saw the doctor after I left. What's up? Can you play again?"

"Don't know. They say that there isn't any nerve damage, but the muscle tissue needs time to heal. Doc said I'll be out for at least a month, probably longer. The season'll be half over by then."

"Shit, that sucks. What're we gonna do for a quarterback? Simpson can't play the spot. Coach stuck him there because he knew that we wouldn't use him," Jones said, sadly.

"Tell me about it," Drew replied, exasperated. "I tried to make a fist, and couldn't. I can't even straighten my hand out all the way without it killing my arm. Fuckin' sucks."

"When do you get to go home?" Doug asked.

"If things go okay, I get to check out Tuesday morning. That's *if* there's no infection, and *if* I don't develop 'complications' or some shit like that. A lot of 'ifs,'" Drew replied. "And I still need to come back like every day to get the arm looked at."

"Cool. We can ditch school and hang out at your house all day until practice. You can still come to practice, right?" Doug asked. "Simpson's gonna need all the help you can give him."

Drew laughed. "What the hell do you mean, 'we' can hang out at my house? I thought that I was the one who was hurt." He jabbed a finger at his friend. "*You* need to be in school; your grades won't take the abuse."

"Screw my grades, this is about helping my buddy the hero get back on his feet," Doug insisted. "Of course, I will have to drive you back in here for your appointments with the nurses. There's no way you can ride that two-wheeled disaster that you call a motorcycle now."

"Hey, what about my bike? Is it still out at the camp? I don't want anything to happen to it," Drew said anxiously.

"Relax, doofus, your dad brought it home already. Your aunt Mary drove him out to get it."

Drew breathed a sigh of relief. "Hey, did you hear anything about the fire? I heard some nurses talking down the hall about it. They said they found a human body there, all burned up."

"Nope. I heard the sirens, but that's it. Does your uncle know anything?"

"I don't know. I was just gonna call him when you showed up. Do you think I should call him now, or wait a while? He's gotta be really busy with this stuff right now... What do you think?" Drew asked, unsure of himself.

"What do I think? Is the great, all-knowing quarterback now asking for help from a dumb lineman? Wow, your injury must have affected your head, too," Jones replied. "Seriously, though, I don't think that there's anything you could do anyway, so just wait. The sheriff doesn't seem like a man that likes being bothered."

Drew thought about what his buddy had said. Despite his impatience, he had to agree. He'd leave the sheriff to his work, and try to deal with the inactivity of just sitting in his hospital room.

At least Doug was there. He brought a sense of comedy to everything that he did, even the serious stuff. He was the biggest clown in western Texas. Literally.

"Okay, if we're just gonna sit around, can we at least watch TV? I'm bored. If we don't do something fun, I'm just gonna go home," Doug whined, only mostly kidding.

"Oh, you big baby. Let's go see if there's a ball game on the idiot box for you."

The two young men were in luck: the Rangers were playing a late game, and it was on ABC. They settled in to watch.

Once the game ended, Doug lobbied for staying the night, putting up a cot in his buddy's room, or just sleeping in a chair. Drew vetoed the idea, not because he didn't enjoy Doug's company, but because he was tired. He also wanted to look at his arm some, without anyone around.

He was getting worried about his injury, a lot more than he let on. Drew had heard the doctor telling his father that the ligament damage would require further surgeries to fully repair. The recovery time from these operations could take up to a year, and the fact that he couldn't make a fist or straighten out his hand completely meant bad things.

Once Doug left, Drew sat down on the edge of his bed and pulled the ever-present hospital tray over to his left side. He put his arm on it, first spreading out a clean towel over the flat surface.

Carefully, he unwrapped the yards of gauze wrapped around his forearm. Then, after piling the gauze on the corner of the tray, he gingerly picked at the bandages against his skin. They pulled free with only minimal pain.

Drew Collins stared at his arm. It looked like something out of a horror movie. Angry red skin with jagged edges was stitched together in seemingly random patterns, beginning just below his elbow, and ending right at his left wrist. Due to swelling (at least, he hoped it was just swelling) his forearm was lumpy and uneven.

The flesh twitched and pulsed, almost with a life of its own. Drew wasn't consciously flexing, or doing anything to cause this bizarre shifting of skin and muscle. He swallowed nervously, resisting the urge to gag. His arm didn't look like it belonged to him anymore, and that thought terrified him. He was glad he made Jones go home. Drew didn't want anyone to see his arm like this.

Morbidly drawn to his wounds, he stared in perverse fascination. That fucking wolf had really done a number on him. He was lucky to be alive, he told himself. He needed the convincing; looking at his arm, he didn't feel lucky at all.

Drew placed the old bandages back over his forearm and rewrapped the gauze covering with a shaking hand. He sat back against the bed and closed his eyes. The room seemed to spin, his stomach lurching dangerously.

The young man opened his eyes and rose to his feet. Moving to the window, he opened the blinds and stared out at the mostly full moon. It seemed to stare back at him. His arm itched. He could feel it twitching and pulsing under the wrappings.

As Drew stood at the window his arm began to ache again. The pain centered in the bones of his forearm, as if they were trying to expand and shift. His hand also hurt now, his fingers throbbing and curling into claws. He moaned and tucked his arm against his side. Turning away from the window, he stalked out of his room, heading down the hallway, trying to escape the pain by keeping moving. It didn't work very well, but at least he had other things to keep his mind occupied. His room suddenly felt very small and very confining.

●●◖◯◗●●

Drew returned after eleven pm. He'd been out roaming the halls, hiding in various stairwells, and even once slipped outside, to walk in the night air. Nothing had seemed to help; he was out of sorts, and in pain. The meds served to blunt his senses, and make him feel groggy, but his arm still felt like it was on fire. Between the aching in his bones, and the itching along his skin, it was driving him insane.

He looked around his room in frustration. There was a piece of paper on his tray- a short note from his father. Apparently his dad had come in to see him while he was out pacing around. Great. Maybe he should call home.

'Never mind,' he told himself; it was after ten. His folks told him to never call anyone after ten pm unless it was an emergency. This didn't really qualify, and his father normally went to sleep early.

He sat down on his bed. The remote for the TV was right at hand, but nothing caught his interest. He lay back and pulled the blanket up to his chin. He closed his eyes and tried to sleep.

Drew shivered with pain. He snuggled deeper into the bed, drawing the sheets and the blanket around him. Gradually the pain seemed to diminish. His eyes closed as his body relaxed. His mind drifted as he fell asleep.

He was riding his Honda, cutting across yards and zipping onto side streets. The ground flew by under him as he rode, the wind blowing in his face. He pulled up beside another rider. The Harley rider turned to look at him.

It was a young woman, beautiful, with long jet-black hair streaming out behind her head as she rode. She was dressed in a black leather jacket and leather pants, with high boots snug on her calves. Drew was captured by her eyes as she looked his way: they were pure silver.

Those eyes seemed to dominate Drew's semi-conscious mind. They floated in front of him as the rest of the image blurred. Those blazing silver orbs seemed to burn into his brain. The background shifted and came back into focus.

Framing the luminescent eyes was a black face with pointed canines and flattened ears, the snarling visage of an angry wolf staring at him. In his dream, the focus pulled back, and he could now see the wolf's body as well. It was the naked body of a shapely, erotic woman. Then it too blurred, shifted, and reappeared, becoming the black-furred body of an immense wolf.

The wolf with shining silver eyes roared with anger and leaped at Drew, its teeth growing larger until they filled his vision. He backpedaled frantically, trying to keep out of reach of the ravening mouth, but his dream feet seemed to be engulfed in mud. The teeth reached him, and with a huge snap, closed over him. Pain engulfed him as he felt his blood spurt.

His mind recoiled in shock; contact was broken, and the image disappeared as Drew cried out and thrashed. He awoke to the after-image of the silver eyes and snapping teeth chasing him. Shaking, he pulled the blanket about him again, and fell back into troubled sleep.

Later, he moaned again in his sleep. He tossed and turned, twisting the sheets into knots around his body. He shook his head from side to side, fighting the frightening images that now filled his dreams. As the night wore on, his face cleared and his body relaxed. Normal sleep claimed him.

The double image of the woman and the wolf, both with the same eyes remained in the back of his subconscious, however, and it was a tired, haggard, and confused man that finally awoke to face Monday morning.

CHAPTER 15

Sunday evening for the Fenris Firar found them in a different state. After fleeing the farm just outside Iowa Park, they made their way on county roads to the north and east of Wichita Falls, eventually leading to the town of Lawton, Oklahoma. Certain that law enforcement officials would have warned any decent-sized city about the gang, Lobo kept them out of sight and undercover. They stopped behind an all-night truck stop after dark.

The moon was no longer full, but it still exerted a strong pull on the lycanthropes. It did not trigger the enormous physical changes that the full moon did; however, it still created an increased state of arousal and propensity for violence. The leader of the Firar, while being violent, also was not stupid. He knew that in this excited state, coupled with their recent attention-getting activities, the gang needed to stay secluded.

Therefore, he sent Winnie and Aardwolf, his least violent members, into the truck stop for food and drink. While they were gone, he directed the remainder of the Firar to set up camp over the hill from the road.

"Make sure no one can see us. Before we bed down, I want to know that there aren't any side roads running back there to surprise us. No fire either. Tomorrow we'll find a better place to hold up."

"Yeah. You got it, Lobo," Ulric said, the hulking lieutenant dividing up bikers to carry tents and bed rolls over the hill. He sent Wrench and Ramona around the perimeter to check for paths, roads, or nearby homes.

By the time that Winnie and Aardwolf came back with several bags bulging with food, the Firar had a rough campsite set up.

Lobo set two watches for the night, consisting of two members, one north and one south of the campsite. The first pair ate quickly and departed. The second pair ate quickly as well, then went to sleep off to the side. The remaining bikers sat around in a rough circle, sprawled out on the ground in various stages of undress. Most had their boots and shirts off, including a couple of the women.

They were a hard bodied lot; there were the usual different body types, but there was no excess body fat on any member of this gang. The demands of the change burned away any and all extra calories they consumed. The challenge was in getting enough to eat regularly.

Lobo looked around at his group, his glance falling on Ramona, who sat staring at the ground, not speaking, or looking around at anyone. She had been silent the entire day, not uttering a single word since rejoining her pack members late Sunday morning.

"So, Moanin' Mona, got anything to say about last night?" Lobo asked.

"No," she replied, still not looking up. "Just think that you are disgusting, and wrong in what you do. That girl wasn't worth the price we're gonna pay for your evening of 'fun'."

"That ain't what I meant, girlie, and you know it. I want to know where you were all night? You know you're not allowed to just run off and leave your pack during the moon."

She looked up at him, then slowly around at the pack. Many of them were staring at her. Most of the others were ambivalent towards her. They weren't hostile, but they weren't friendly, either. 'That may soon change,' she told herself. A couple of the faces in the circle were actually glaring at her. Wrench and Piggy, along with one or two of their cronies.

She looked back at Lobo, who sat staring at her curiously. He could tell that she had something uncomfortable or bad to tell. Ramona took a deep breath, and then let it out slowly. "I ran away last night. I knew that I was coming back—I just needed to get away from what was going on. I was mad. I just took off running, with no idea where I was going

"When it was almost dark I could smell water, lots of it. I thought that maybe if I threw myself in the water it would calm me down. I hate getting wet when I'm changed, ya know?" She looked around, some of the assembled pack nodded in agreement. Lobo's face was neutral; he was waiting for the punch line.

Ramona continued, "I ran for the water. When I reached the lake I was going to jump in, at least I think I would have. There was a little boy in the way. He was right in the path, trapped between me and the water. Then someone jumped between us and threw a flashlight at me."

Ramona stopped, unwilling to go on. She didn't want to admit to the next part. Lobo was not going to give her a choice.

"So, then what happened? What did you do?" he demanded.

Ramona hung her head. Softly she said, "I bit him."

"You what? Did you kill him?"

"I bit him. This guy jumped between me and the little boy, and I tore the shit out of his arm. But he's alive, I'm sure," she almost whispered.

"You WHAT? You bit a human, and left him alive? And then you go all fucking day without saying anything?" Lobo roared, coming to his feet with a bound. "Jesus Christ, girl, do you have any idea what kind of shit that puts us in?"

He towered over the girl, who didn't raise a hand to defend herself. She didn't even look up as he kicked at her viciously. His foot, mercifully without its heavy harness boot, landed on her left cheek. Ramona went down in a heap, and lay unmoving as Lobo stomped around her, raving. The others stood also, and spoke loudly to each other. None got between Lobo and Ramona.

The pack leader grabbed her hair and hauled her to her feet. Holding her head at a painful angle, he brought his face to within an inch of hers. "You stupid bitch. You *know* we can't leave someone behind that will turn at the next full moon. Damn it all, we're two hundred miles away from this guy, with cops everywhere looking for us, and now we've got to deal with this?" he growled, shaking her.

"I should just kill you now and send Ulric back to take care of your mess. But I don't want to risk losing a valuable pack member because you fucked up. You're gonna have to fix this one. You have any bright ideas, bitch?" he yelled, throwing her back to the ground.

"I don't know," she yelled back. "I didn't plan this, it just happened. And anyway, it isn't my fucking fault the cops are after us. Asshole there," she motioned at Wrench, "is the one that grabbed that girl."

Wrench stepped forwards, snarling. He went to kick at Ramona, who was still on the ground, but Lobo backhanded him, almost dismissively, and knocked him back.

"Knock it off, Wrench. She's right about that. You fucked up too, asshole. Did you think that I wanted that bitch brought to our camp if you left a witness to you pinching her? Fuck, I'm surrounded by morons.

He looked down at the prone woman. "But that doesn't change your fuckup, Moanin' Mona. Do you know who it was that you bit?"

She shook her head.

Lobo swore under his breath. "So go back, stay low, and find out who it was, and how they're doing. Find out who the old mechanic is, too, and where he lives. We may have to deal with him, too."

"Lobo, do you really trust her to go back by herself? Remember, it's her fault that we're in this fix," Wrench said, glaring at the woman. "She could fuck it up more."

Lobo snarled at the smaller man. "Of course not. But who the fuck am I gonna send her back with? You?" He jabbed a finger into Wrench's chest, and he flinched. "I send you back, and the cops'll pinch you before you dismount." He narrowed his eyes, thinking. "Still, we need somebody." He looked around at the assembly.

"Caleb."

"Uh, Lobo, the thing is…we're kinda a slow burn there. I'm not sure that it's such a good idea to go back right now."

Lobo glared at the scout, who stood his ground but looked down at his feet. He looked around at the rest of his pack.

"Is there anyone with the balls to go and protect the safety of this pack? I'll go myself if I have to. "Mona can't go by herself. Ain't none of us know what she'd do on her own."

No one moved, except for Wrench, who obviously wanted to speak but didn't dare. He scowled again at Ramona and then looked at Lobo. He took a deep breath and stepped forwards.

"Lobo, let me go. I know that guy saw me. So what? If we go in low profile and stay outta sight, what difference does it make?" He shot a venomous look at Ramona. "At least you know I'll be watchin' out for the interests of the Firar."

Lobo looked at Wrench speculatively. He wasn't the brightest member of the pack, but he *was* loyal. And he detested Ramona. Plus, if shit went down in Iowa Parks (or whatever the hell that place was called), they would get Wrench and Ramona. And by a strange coincidence, those were the two that they had good descriptions of. He smiled.

"Fine, Wrench. You and Ramona go back and clean up the fuckin' messes you made. Don't leave just yet, though. Wait a bit; say, maybe a week. We got plenty of time before the next moon. Let things calm down a bit before you go back." He shook his head. "I wouldn't even take the bikes. Find an old car or something, stay out of sight. Got it?"

Wrench nodded, satisfied. Ramona looked distinctly unhappy, not that Lobo cared. She'd better do what she was supposed to. Her time in the pack could be coming to an end.

The pack resettled, in preparation for resting for the night. The first couple of nights after the full moon cycle were always early ones for the Firar. The extra energy expended, in addition to the lack of sleep for the better part of three days, took its toll on the lycanthropes, and they paid the price afterwards.

Chapter 16

Robert Parker woke up early on Monday morning, fifteen minutes before his alarm was set to go off. His wife was lying next to him, gently snoring. He smiled momentarily, as he listened to Mary 'performing.' He had mentioned to her before that she snored, and she had indignantly replied that, "no, ladies did *not* snore."

The fleeting smile was gone quickly, as the events of the past few days intruded upon his consciousness. Today was Monday. Mondays were always bad.

He groaned, causing Mary to interrupt her symphony. She caught her breath, snorted, and then rolled over and put her arm around her husband.

Parker gently disengaged her arm and slipped out of the bed. He reached over and shut off his alarm, so his wife could continue to sleep. She was a substitute teacher at the elementary school, and didn't have to work today.

He went out to the kitchen and started the coffee maker, then headed to the bathroom for his morning routine. He and Mary had established a pattern that worked for their mornings years ago. He got up first, started the coffee (that they both were mildly addicted to), used the toilet, brushed his teeth, shaved, and took a shower.

Once he was done, Mary would rouse herself, sometimes with his help, and then take over the bathroom. What entered the bathroom was a weary, zombie-like woman, with badly messed hair, an old robe and frayed slippers. What came out was a bright, vivacious forty-five year old woman who could easily pass for thirty-five, with perfect hair and clear, sparkling eyes. Parker wished that whatever miracles occurred in the bathroom when she was in there would happen when he was in there, too. All that ever seemed to happen for him was the toilet would clog.

He walked out to the kitchen and sat down, pouring himself a cup of coffee. The sun was just coming up, its tentative rays coming in through the window over the sink.

After drinking his first cup of the day, he contemplated breakfast. Knowing the amount of shit that he'd be dealing with on this day, he opted to merely have a second cup of coffee. He wasn't up for solid food.

By seven-fifteen he was out the door, quietly kissing his sleeping wife on the cheek and putting on his hat as he left. Shortly after seven-thirty five he was at his desk, with his third cup of coffee and the paper. He scanned the headlines, looking to see how the semi-local reporters weighed in on the events at Iowa Park. Thus far, it appeared that they were not blaming the Sheriff's department for the ongoing mess, but that could change very quickly.

Becker knocked at his door and ducked inside, joined by Lem. They pulled up chairs and sat around his desk expectantly. 'Damn them,' he thought. So poised and relaxed. And why shouldn't they be? It was his responsibility to solve everything, and give everyone else direction. All they had to do was whatever he told them to.

"What? You guys are looking at me like somehow I know what to do, or what's going on." He ran his hand over his balding head. "I've been over my head since I took this damn job."

Lem smiled around his first toothpick of the day. He shifted slightly in his seat to get more comfortable. Tipping his hat back, he cleared his throat.

"Well, boss, things're a right mess; we all know that. We also know that things'll sort out, they always seem to. Today we'll get that autopsy result on Thomas, mebbe an ID on the body from yesterday, and who knows, mebbe even get a hit on that biker's prints that Ray got."

Becker nodded. "We should get something. I'll call the state police in an hour or so; they don't seem to get rolling until after nine. Bill Jameson's awake, too. Hospital told Lem we could see him. Maybe pay a visit to the Ibarra girl, then stop in on your nephew while we're there."

"Yeah, works. Let's call Simon first, see if we can light a fire under him. Maybe get us more info on the bodies in the morgue before we head over there." Parker looked over at Lem, who was just coming off of his shift, as opposed to Becker, who was just starting his.

"Lem, you want to tag along?"

The deputy smiled even more broadly. The toothpick tilted dangerously, almost falling out of his mouth. Parker scowled at the man. It was totally wrong to be this happy on a Monday this early, with this much shit going wrong.

"You authorizin' the OT, sheriff? I'd be happy to come along, if'n I'd be gettin' paid." The toothpick recovered and bobbed from one side of his mouth to the other.

"What the hell, come with us. I'll find a way to justify it to the bean counters. I gotta bad feeling about this whole thing, and I'll bet that before it's done, this little bit of overtime'll be a drop in the bucket."

Lem stood, stretching. He yawned widely and then looked at the others. "Let me make a couple of calls before we take off." He stepped out of the office and walked to his desk.

He was replaced in the office by the unwelcome presence of Jeremiah Randall, who slunk in with a printout in his hand. The desk sergeant always seemed to have a paper in his hand. Probably felt that it justified his intrusions, Parker thought. It didn't.

Randall waved his hand vaguely at Parker. His face was animated, especially for a Monday morning. Becker glanced from sheriff to desk sergeant, and nodded toward the door, planning on leaving the sheriff alone with the annoying man.

The desk sergeant saw the look and put out his arm, barring the deputy from leaving. His eyes swept from one man to the other. He held up the paper.

"Sheriff, we just got this teletype from the Staties. Bad things, sheriff, bad things." He sidled up to the desk, extending the page towards the sheriff.

"For God's sake, Randall, give me the teletype," Parker growled and snatched the paper from the older man's hand. The sheriff held it up so that he could read it. "Great. Just fuckin' great." He handed it to Becker.

Ray smoothed the crumpled paper out on the desk and read aloud… "Be on the lookout for an escaped convict. Larry Lee Tate, of Shreveport, Louisiana, escaped from custody Sunday night at approximately ten-thirty pm, while being transferred to a new maximum-security psychiatric ward at a Texas State Penitentiary. Tate was convicted for the brutal murder of fourteen female college students in Houston during a six-year span, from 1995 to 2001. He has admitted to killing over thirty people in his lifetime, and is considered at-large and extremely dangerous."

Parker snorted at the last. "At-large and extremely dangerous. No shit. Crazy mass murderer serial killer, loose and running around here. Last fucking thing we need," Parker swore. "Maybe he and the bikers can all get eaten by the monster wolves running around that no one has seen."

"Sheriff, nobody says that Tate is actually runnin' around here yet, just that he could be headin' this way," Randall replied. "I thought that maybe we'd want to work up a warnin' for the town and such, ya know."

Parker rounded on the sergeant. "And say what, exactly? Don't go out at night, there's wild wolves running amok; don't go to stores, there's bikers running amuck; don't stay home, there's people breaking into houses; and don't go out on the roads, there's a serial killer on the loose?" He shot the man a withering look. "Jesus, Randall, get a grip. We got work to do."

Becker shot his boss a look of mild reproach. Randall was right, and they both knew it. Parker was just taking out his frustrations on the older man. Ray cleared his throat. Parker glanced over at him, read the look, and sighed.

"Yeah, okay, Jerry, write something up for me to sign later, and we'll get it to the press. Word it careful so we don't cause a panic. Things are bad enough already."

Randall straightened. He puffed his thin chest out with pride and said, "Yes sir, I'll get on this right away. I should have it done in an hour or so." He walked out, mumbling to himself.

"Jesus," Parker said, once Randall had gone. "You sure that you don't want this job?" he asked Becker again.

"Boss, you know I don't want your job. I just bring the headaches to you now; what would I do if you weren't here?" The other man grinned at Parker. "I got a gravy job, sheriff. You get the crap end of it."

Becker made it seem like a casual dismissal, but inwardly his guts twisted whenever Parker made this joke. The idea of being responsible for life-or-death decisions, and possibly sending men out to die made him feel sick.

The deputy stepped out into the hallway to check on Lem's progress. He saw Randall walking towards the sheriff's office again. Looking past the desk sergeant, he could see an older couple standing at the front desk.

He stopped Randall. "What's up, Jeremiah?"

"I gotta get the sheriff. We got Scott Thomas' parents at the desk, wantin' to talk."

"Tell you what, Jeremiah, why don't we take this one? I'll talk with them, and we'll let Sheriff Parker keep working on the other stuff. I'll go on up."

Randall looked undecided for a moment, but shrugged and nodded. Becker was probably better suited to talking with the two distraught parents than the gruff and volatile sheriff, anyway. He nodded his head and reversed his steps, leading Ray to the front desk.

"Mr. and Mrs. Thomas, this here is Deputy Ray Becker. He'll talk with you about your son. Deputy Becker, these're the Thomas's, Dean and Pamela."

Becker shook hands with each of them, smiling gently. He asked them if they would like to sit down.

"Let's go sit at my desk, shall we? This way...my desk is the messy one in the corner," Becker said. "I wish that we could be meeting under better circumstances," he added, sitting behind his desk, which was spotless.

After a brief pause, Dean Thomas spoke.

"Officer, I mean Deputy, we'd like to know more about what happened to Scott. We know that he's dead, but how did it happen?"

"Mr. and Mrs. Thomas, not to be too blunt, but the autopsy results aren't done yet," Becker began. "We'll know more later this morning."

"What we do know is that it looks as though Scott and a young lady stopped at a park just outside of town late Thursday night, and were attacked by animals of some sort. The young lady is really shook up, and hasn't been able to talk much, but she did say that they were attacked by wolves."

"Excuse me, did you say 'wolves'?" Mr. Thomas interjected.

"Yes, sir, I did," Becker said quietly. "Now we haven't heard of any wolves in these here parts for thirty years or so, but just Saturday night the sheriff's own nephew was attacked at a Cub Scout campout by what appeared to be a large wolf as well. As unlikely as it sounds, we have been looking for a pack of wolves these past few days, but nothing has come up."

"Uh, sheriff, er, deputy, we got Scott's things from the hospital, and we're missing something. Scott always wore his class ring, and we'd like…well, we'd like him to be wearing it when he's buried. Do you have his ring?"

Becker paused. He had to tell them the truth, but he couldn't tell them everything. They would have heartache enough without knowing that their son had been eaten, and would be buried without his entire arm, along with other body parts.

"Mr. and Mrs. Thomas, I'm very sorry, but there was no ring recovered with his effects. If you could describe the ring, we'll certainly keep an eye out for it, but we've searched the park thoroughly. I'm sorry."

"It was a white gold class ring. Longview High School, class of 2007. It had his name inscribed on it. He loved that ring. He even wore it during baseball season, when all his friends took theirs off. When he went to prom, he wouldn't let his girlfriend wear it, he insisted that we get her a nice ring to wear instead," she sniffled, dabbing at her eyes with a hankie.

In Becker's mind, he saw a ring, suspended from a leather thong around a biker's neck. The leader of the Fenris Firar, Lobo, had been wearing it on Friday morning at Albertson's Deli, not half an hour after the mangled body of Scott Thomas was discovered in Pine Cone Park. Mrs. Thomas' description matched the picture in his head.

Becker made notes on a card, not because he needed to, but because it looked good for the Thomas's. It would seem to them that the deputy, and the department, cared about their son, and were doing everything that they could.

He looked up from his notes at the couple. They were studying him, as if trying to gauge his seriousness, or ability, from his note taking.

"Folks, we're doing all we can. We are very sorry for your loss," Becker told them. "If there is anything that we can do for you, please don't hesitate to contact us.

"Deputy Randall there, the guy at the desk," Becker motioned, "will be around every day, and will take care of you, whether you stop in or call. And if we find the ring, we'll get it to you immediately."

"We will also call you this afternoon if there is anything from the doctor's report different than what we've already told you. Is there anything else that we can help you with?" he asked, looking from one to the other?

The weeping couple shook their heads, rising from their chairs. They shook Becker's hand, and made their way out of the office.

Becker watched them go, sensing his comrades as they came up beside him. Parker stopped at his right, while Lem stood behind his left shoulder and put his hand on it.

"That was nice, Ray. If anythin' bad ever happens to anyone Ah know, Ah want you to be the one to come see me," the lanky deputy said.

Parker was more practical. "Okay, that's done, and Lem made his calls. The hospital's waiting for us. Let's go." He put on his hat and walked out, going right past Randall without a word.

Lem and Ray looked at each other and shrugged slightly. They followed after the sheriff, but paused at the desk to say good-bye to the irascible desk sergeant.

Lem drove to the hospital, filling them in on his calls. The coroner's office was ready for them. Dr. Simon, Sr., would be in his office, with some preliminary findings on the Thomas autopsy, and would talk with them regarding the new body.

Rita Ibarra was mostly unchanged, although Dr. Novak wanted to talk with Parker if he could spare a moment or two. And Bill Jameson was awake and talking.

"Awright, guys, let's do Jameson first and get it out of the way, then we'll see Simon. After that, we'll see the Ibarra kid, and then we'll stop in on Drew," Parker said. Lem and Ray nodded, seeing the logic behind the order.

Upon seeing the lawmen, Bill's wife, Kathryn, launched into a semi-hysterical rant about the injury to her husband, and the sheriff department's inability, or unwillingness, to deal with the crime wave that had hit their town.

Bill himself could add nothing of value to the conversation. He had seen an average-sized man in his living room, wearing all black. Then he had felt a sharp pain at the back of his head, and had woken up in the hospital.

Parker assured the couple that they were doing all that they could to bring the robber or robbers to justice, and that this case was their top priority. Then the cops beat a hasty retreat, heading to the morgue and one Dan Simon, Senior, coroner.

"Well, it's about time that you guys showed up." The crusty old doctor greeted them, with his usual charm. "All that grumblin' and complainin' about bein' in a hurry, and then you show up late?"

"We're glad to see you too, doc," Parker said, sitting down in the only other chair in the small room. Becker and Lem lounged against the wall. "So what's the deal with the Thomas case?"

Simon looked at them with distaste. He cleared his throat, ready to give his report, so that the annoying cops would leave him in peace.

"Scott Thomas, nineteen years old. Had alcohol in his blood, but not enough to qualify as drunk." Simon continued, glancing down at his report. "The boy died of an animal attack, just as I told you he did. Apparently, he was attacked by a pack of large canines. Hairs found on the body indicate wolves. We sent them in, and were told this morning that they matched almost one hundred percent to gray wolves.

"Cause of death was one massive bite to the throat, severing the carotid artery, and also ripping out the windpipe. Victim was dead before he hit the ground. The rest of the wounds seemed to be inflicted post mortem, and are consistent with feeding behavior.

"Anything else?" Simon asked, looking at the men.

Lem leaned slightly forward from his position on the door jamb. "Yeah, any chance that the bikers that were seen leaving the park at day break had anything to do with this?"

"Not unless they keep a powerful lot of wolves as pets. Did you boys see them bikers with big ol' wolves runnin' with 'em?" The doc asked, smirking at them.

"Okay doctor, do you have anything yet on the body that was brought in yesterday afternoon?" Becker asked.

"Yeah, a couple things. It was a female; early to mid twenties, most likely. Burned really badly, but you knew that. Let's see," he mumbled, pulling a stack of reports closer and sorting through them.

"Ah, yes," he said, taking one out and glancing through it. "Female, around 5'4", badly burned. Evidence of rape—probably multiple rapes, since traces of more than one type of semen was recovered. Human semen, I might add," he said, looking out at them again, obviously waiting for them to ask why.

"Doc, of course it would be human semen. Since when does a woman get abducted and raped by anything else?" Parker grumped.

"Since when does a woman get abducted, raped, burned, and eaten by wolves all in the same evening?" Simon retorted, enjoying the sudden looks of shock on the faces of the deputies and their boss.

"Are you telling us that she was eaten, too? By wolves?" Becker asked, disbelief evident in his voice.

Simon nodded. "This young woman's body had bite marks identical to the ones found on Scott Thomas. The body was severely burned, but there is no mistake. She was at least chewed on by the same beasties that got the Thomas kid. I understand that Drew Collins is here in the hospital, suffering from a bite from a wolf as well? Perhaps you gentlemen should start looking for this pack of wolves, since they seem to be everywhere."

The three lawmen exchanged looks. Their day had just gotten much worse. Parker looked back at the coroner and tried for a way out.

"Dr. Simon, have you identified the woman yet?" Maybe it was someone else. Some hitchhiker that had been sleeping in the barn and been attacked, accidentally knocking over a lantern or something.

"No. It'll be a couple days probably. Not much to go on for positive ID. Probably do dental records. Send me over the missing girl's files and we'll cross check them. Now, if that's all, I've got work to do." He stood, indicating their time was up.

Wordlessly the sheriff and his two deputies moved out of the coroner's office and out into the hallway. Once out of Simon's earshot, Lem turned to his comrades in arms.

"W-e-l-l, shit, boys. Now what?"

"Now we go and see how the Ibarra girl is doing. Dr. Novak promised to meet with us. We'll try and figure this thing out later. Right now we proceed with our business," the sheriff said.

Parker led them up the stairs to meet with the shrink, and then check on Rita's progress. He stoically refused to think about the coroner's disturbing findings. He would sort it all out later.

●●❪◉❫●●

Dr. Novak met them outside Rita's room with a small, professional smile. She politely shook hands with Lem and Ray, then looked closely at Parker. "Sheriff, how are you holding up? You look tired. We could make some time to just sit and talk through all of this, if you would like."

Parker looked uncomfortable. He shrugged and mumbled, "I'm fine, doc. Tell us about the Ibarra kid."

"Rita, sheriff. Her name is Rita," She looked sternly but patiently at the surly cop. "She'll do better if you refer to her by her first name. Calling her the 'Ibarra kid' is not conducive to her recovery."

She grinned abruptly. "Of course, that may be just what she expects from a grumpy old guy like you. Perhaps being friendly and compassionate would only confuse her. You did fine the last time you were here; let's just see how this time works out.

"As for how she's doing," Novak continued, "we believe she is still in shock. She eats, drinks, uses the toilet on her own, and answers direct questions; but she volunteers no information on her own. She shows no initiative at all. We are hopeful that with continued therapy she will recover, since she has no physical injuries to deal with."

Novak shook her head and shrugged. "Frankly, sheriff, I don't see what you hope to gain from talking with her further. She has offered no new information," she concluded, staring at the sheriff, as if trying to gauge his intentions.

"Dr. Novak, I'm not here to upset her, or you for that matter. We're just at a loss here. The coroner's findings back up the Iba…uh, Rita's story completely, but there's a problem that I was hoping she could help me with."

"Fine, let's go in and see her together, shall we? You gentlemen can wait out here for us." She took the sheriff's elbow and led him away from his deputies. Lem glanced briefly at Becker and then looked away quickly, trying not to grin.

Rita Ibarra looked unchanged. The tiny teen lay in her bed, staring almost blankly at the TV. She looked over when Novak greeted her, but showed no signs of recognition or emotion.

Parker wanted to get this done quickly, so that he could go and visit his nephew. He cleared his throat and stepped up to the bed. Novak let him lead.

"Rita, hi. It's Sheriff Parker, again. I'd like to ask you a couple more questions, if you're okay with that. Is it okay with you if we talk a little bit more?"

Rita nodded absently. Parker took that to be agreement, and, after getting a supportive nod from Novak, he continued.

"Rita, when we talked last, you told me that wolves attacked you and your boyfriend. Do you remember that?"

Another nod, just a little troubled.

"Good, Rita. Very good," he said, earning another approving nod from the psychiatrist. "Okay, Rita, now here's what I don't understand. When you told us about the wolves last time, you said, 'just like the jackets.' Rita, what did you mean by that?"

Rita's brow furrowed. She flinched, as though seeing the attack again in her mind. She began to twitch nervously, reaching out to Dr. Novak for support. The psychiatrist held her upset patient. She spoke softly to the girl, encouraging her to take her time, and answer the question from the sheriff. Gradually, Rita's shakes subsided, and she began to speak quietly.

"We took his car and left the party, going to the park to make out. When we got there, we went down the trail to find a nice place and we saw all these bikes parked there. There was no one around, just the bikes. Further down the trail we found clothes scattered all over. There were jackets, with this mean-looking patch on it; it was a wolf.

"Then we saw these wolves, they were huge. They was eatin' this deer, and then this wolf hit Scott and there was all this blood, and-and..." she trailed off, burying her face against Novak's shoulder.

Parker didn't like what he had heard, but he had been expecting it. He had personally witnessed the gang leaving the site that morning. He just couldn't see the connection between the bikers and the wolves. At least not consciously.

He quietly thanked Rita for talking with him, telling her that she had done well, and that he hoped that he hadn't upset her too much. Then he bid the teen and the doctor goodbye.

Once in the hallway he collected Becker and Lem. It was time to check in on his nephew, Drew, and see what kind of night he'd had.

CHAPTER 17

Drew Collins awoke sometime after daybreak. His sleep had been filled with nightmares, waking him time and again, covered in sweat and shaking with fear. Those silver eyes chased him in his dreams, showing him images that he couldn't banish, and left him feeling both drained, and exhausted. Finally he gave up on sleep entirely, staring at the ceiling until his mind zoned out completely.

In addition to his nightmares, the pain in his body had spread. His forearm no longer ached and itched like it had before: now his entire left side felt...wrong. As he lay in his bed, Drew tried to figure out why he felt like this. The doctors hadn't told him anything about these pains, or the feeling of *wrongness* that had invaded his body.

His bones ached, and his blood seemed too hot for his body. Despite the fact that he didn't have a fever, he was flushed. He mentioned it to a nurse, but she dismissed his feelings, telling him that everything was fine.

Drew heard footsteps in the hallway, approaching his door. He lay still, pretending to be asleep, but unsure why he was doing so. Sheriff Parker's gruff voice could be made out, telling the nurses at the station that they were going in to see him.

The distinct sound of a cell phone being closed could be heard as well. Drew listened as one of his uncle's deputies spoke about the call.

"Sheriff, we got a hit on the prints that I lifted from the deli. Wasn't local, though. The Royal Canadian Mounted Police's system had him in their files, if you can believe it. He told me he was from New Mexico. If you can't trust an outlaw biker, who can you trust?"

131

"Ray, cut the shit and tell me what you got," Parker growled, just outside Drew's door. The young man strained to hear.

"Okay, the guy we know as 'Lobo' is one Fletcher Burroughs, from Saskatchewan. Born in 1964, son of a whore and some john; in and out of trouble as a youth, moved up to assault as a teen; vanished in his twenties after a warrant was issued in relation to a murder rap."

"And this Canadian is now running a biker gang in the southwest United States?" Lem asked.

"Appears so. The murder is still open, too. Pretty gruesome. Body was all hacked up and dismembered, and they say animals may have gotten to the body after the murder took place. Sound familiar to anyone else?" Becker asked, looking at his boss and friend.

"Yeah, it does. Maybe we can do the Mounties a favor if we ever catch this guy. Right now we don't seem to be doing well at finding them, though. All right, clam up, let's not say anything around Drew about this shit," Parker said, knocking on the hospital door.

Quietly, the sheriff pushed open the door and peered around the corner. His nephew appeared to be asleep. The three lawmen slipped into the room, closing the door behind them.

"Drew? Hey, Drew, you awake?" the sheriff asked softly.

Drew shifted and opened his eyes, trying to look like someone who had just woken up.

"Hi, Uncle Bob. I was just sleeping." He sat up, yawning and stretching. "What's up?"

"Good morning, sleepyhead. How do you feel?" Parker asked, looking critically at his nephew. Despite Drew's nonchalance, he looked rough. His eyes were bloodshot, and there were dark circles under them. His face looked haggard. 'Just like Jim…', Parker thought.

"I'm fine, just a little tired, that's all. The arm feels great," Drew said, holding up his arm and rotating it around. Actually, Drew wasn't lying about that part. His arm did feel better than it had last night. His hand was closed in a tight fist. How did he do that? Yesterday it hurt to even try, and now he made a fist so naturally, he hadn't even noticed.

"Good, good. I understand that they're going to send you home after lunch today. Do you need a ride?"

"I don't know. I think that dad went to work this morning. Doesn't he have to sign me out?"

The door swept open and a nurse bustled in. "Yes, young man, as a matter of fact he does. He'll be here around eleven to talk with the doctor about your care, and then you can go afterwards," she said, interrupting their talk.

"You, Mr. Collins, could use some cleaning up. Do you feel up to taking a shower? I can assist you, if you need," she added.

Drew blushed; embarrassed to no end in front of his uncle and the two other policemen. The tall redhead, Lem, laughed out loud.

"Sheriff, maybe we should leave so that young Drew here can have his bath. We can come back later, or just stop by the house this afternoon."

"Shut it, Lem. We've got some questions for Drew before we leave. Nurse, give us a couple of minutes," Parker said, not really asking, as he shooed the mildly protesting nurse back out into the hall.

Turning back to his nephew, the sheriff smiled. Drew was red-faced. Despite his size and skills on the football field, and all the hardships that he'd been through, he *was* still a teen-ager after all.

"Drew, you said that you were bitten by a large dog or something, right? We're trying to get our info straight, there's a couple of weird parts that don't make sense."

"Wolf," Drew corrected. "I was bitten by a wolf. Black, with silver eyes. It might have been dark out, but I know what I saw. It was *definitely* not a dog." he added. He was getting annoyed with everyone doubting what he had seen.

"Drew, we don't doubt that you were bit by a wolf. Two others have been attacked over the weekend, too. We just don't see how the wolves and the bikers connect," Lem said, drawing an irritated look from the sheriff.

Drew had wondered about the connection between the bikers and the wolves himself, or at least the one that had bitten him. His wolf had the exact same eyes that the woman on the Sportster had. But that would mean…no, that couldn't be.

"Well, Drew, you take care of yourself. I'll come 'round tonight at the house and check on you. Your dad should be here in a couple of hours. We gotta go," Parker said, leaving the room with Becker and Lem in tow.

Drew sat back, thinking about his nightmares. About the wolf and the beautiful young woman with the same eyes. His reverie was brought to a halt by the reappearance of the bulky nurse with a towel and soap. 'Swell,' he thought.

●● ◖ ◗ ●●

Two hours later, Drew sat on the edge of the bed in his own clothes. His father stood next to him, looking very haggard, but clear-eyed. A doctor with two nurses stood in front of them, going over the conditions of his release.

"So, you understand that if you feel up to it, you may attend school tomorrow, but no activities whatsoever. Also, just so we're clear, *no* motorcycle." The doctor said the last two words loud and clear. He knew what Drew was thinking. "We'll see you back here on Friday at nine am to have another look at the arm, and review your medications. Also, we need to see about getting you the rabies vaccine. It's really much less painful than it used to be. If it's necessary, we can give you the treatments right here. Any questions?"

Drew shook his head. He just wanted out of the hospital. The doctor smiled automatically, wished them well, and left. The two nurses busied themselves with what was left. One gave the senior Collins Drew's discharge papers to sign, while the other pulled a wheelchair into the room.

Drew's eyes widened at the sight of the chair. He looked at the nurse in dismay.

"No way. I don't need that thing. I can walk just fine," he insisted.

"Mr. Collins, it is hospital policy that all discharged patients are conveyed to the door in a wheelchair by an employee of the hospital. Sorry," she added, far too cheerfully to actually be contrite for anything.

"Drew, hush. Just get in the chair and let's go," his father said quietly. He picked up his son's bag of possessions and walked out.

Having no choice, Drew huffed and sat in the chair with poor grace. He crossed his arms and looked straight ahead, his cheeks red.

The first nurse grinned at him and took the handlebars. She pretended to rev up the chair like it was a motorcycle, and actually made 'vvvroom' noises at Drew, who smiled despite himself.

Once at the entrance to the hospital, Drew sat waiting in the chair while his father brought the car around. He clenched and unclenched his fists. His left hand now closed without pain, but both arms ached, as did his shoulders. He twisted his head from side to side; it, too, was sore and stiff. 'Probably just from trying to sleep in the rotten hospital bed,' he told himself.

As soon as the car pulled up, Drew bounded out of the chair, before either nurse could take an arm to help. He turned and smiled at them, bowed slightly, and then got into the passenger seat. The nurses waved as the car drove off.

●● ❨◐❩●●

The remainder of Drew Collins' afternoon was filled with Sports Center. Once they'd gotten home, he'd been placed on the couch with the remote control, a summer sausage, Ritz crackers, and a Mountain Dew Big Slam. His father then left, going back to Bernie's, even though they'd given him the day off.

Drew idly clicked through the channels, finding nothing of interest despite having one hundred plus stations. He ended up staring at the same Sports Center show all afternoon, eating the entire summer sausage, and gulping down the soda.

By the time he finished the crackers, it was past the end of football practice. He expected Doug and a couple of the other guys to show up before supper, and likely before his father returned home.

He got up from the couch and went into the kitchen in search of more food. Potato chips…pop tarts…soup. Soup? It was early September in Texas, who had soup in their cupboard around here? Annoyed, Drew moved the cans out of the way.

Canned ham. Now, that was more like it. He peeled the tin open, grabbed a fork, and went back into the living room. He was half-finished with the five-pound ham when the doorbell rang.

Drew went to the door, expecting to see his football buddies. Instead, there was an attractive blonde girl standing on the front step.

"Megan?" he said, somewhat at a loss. "Hi. Um, come in." The girl smiled at him and slipped under his outstretched right arm, which was holding the door open.

She stopped in the middle of the living room and turned back to face him. Drew closed the door and looked self-consciously at his mess on the couch. Megan followed his eyes to the scattered cracker crumbs and half empty ham tin. She giggled.

"Sorry Drew, did I interrupt your feast? I can come back later. I just wanted to see you. I heard at school that you were attacked," she said, eyes wide.

"Uh, yeah. It was no big deal. Some kid was being stalked by a wolf and I chased it off."

"And that's all, huh? Then how come you spent two nights in the hospital? And why is your arm all wrapped up? Drew, tell me the truth," she demanded, drawing close to him.

"Megan, honest, it was nothing. I threw a flashlight at the wolf and it bit me. Can't blame it, can you? I'll be fine."

"So do we still have a date Friday night after the game?" Megan asked expectantly. She smiled at him, and the young man swallowed.

He forced a smile onto his face and answered, "Sure. No problem. We might have to ride with Doug and his date, though."

"That's okay. I like Doug. He's sorta cute, in a big gorilla with octopus hands kinda way," she said, giggling again.

The visual of Doug in a gorilla costume with eight hands, all trying to grope his girlfriend, was pretty spot on. And funny. Drew laughed with Megan and allowed himself to relax.

"So, who is Doug taking out to eat after the game, then?" she asked, still smiling at her joke.

"I have no idea. His girlfriends change every day, or at least after every therapy session. They get wise to him quick and run screaming for the hills," he responded, trying to be funny. Supposedly girls liked men that could make them laugh.

It worked. Megan giggled and grabbed his arm. His left arm. Drew cringed, expecting it to hurt immensely. There was a slight feeling of pressure, but nothing else. The girl recoiled after feeling the bandage beneath her fingers, eye wide with horror.

"Oh God, Drew, I'm so sorry. I forgot. Are you okay?"

Drew smiled at her. "Yeah, it's okay. I'm fine. I told you that it was no big deal. Didn't hurt a bit. Relax," he told her, putting his arm around her shoulders.

She leaned against him. She was soft. The young man put his other arm around her as well. She looked up at him, eyes shining. Obeying an impulse as old as the human race, Drew dipped his head, slowly bringing his lips down to hers. Their lips brushed.

"Hey shithead, what's goin' on in here?" Doug's loud voice blasted through the screen door. "Here we come, all the way out here to visit our fallen comrade, bringing gifts and sustenance and all that, and here you are…"

Megan pulled away, red-faced with embarrassment. Drew glared over her head at his friend. Doug pretended not to notice, and opened the screen. Six members of the team came barging in, laden with a variety of snacks and soft drinks.

Drew looked over at Megan and sighed. The girl was leaving. And just when things were getting interesting. With obvious reluctance he looked back at his teammates, who were rummaging through his cupboards for bowls, glasses, and plates.

"Hey Megan! I'll walk you out, okay?" he called, pushing one teammate aside and intercepting the girl at the door. She looked up at him, nodded, and gave him a small smile.

Together, they walked outside and to her car in silence, not touching, but moving very close to each other. Drew opened the door for her and stepped back.

"Megan," he began, as the blonde slid into the driver's seat. She looked up at him.

"Yes, Drew?"

Drew ducked his head and kissed her full on the mouth. He pulled away quickly, and mumbled, "Thanks for coming to see me. See you at school tomorrow."

Megan stared at his retreating back. She smiled widely. Hunk city. She started her car and drove away, still smiling.

Drew was also grinning as he went back into his house. He was greeted with a chorus of cheers and wolf whistles. Doug tossed a can of Mountain Dew to him, which he caught with his left hand without thinking. Jones frowned at him.

"Should you be doing that? Dude, remember I saw your arm. Take it easy."

"It's okay, mom. I'm fine. Geez, you're as bad as that nurse from ER that kept coming in and talking to me. Give it a rest," he said.

"Umm, which ER nurse? You don't mean Amy Bishop, do you?" Doug asked. "She is so hot."

"God, you're impossible. By the way, which one of your bevy of hot chicks have you trapped into going out to supper with us Friday after the game?"

"Sam. She's fun, and she gets along with Megan, too. Nothing serious, you know," Doug grinned.

The rest of the evening passed uneventfully. The team managed to eat prodigious amounts of food without breaking anything, and dispersed when Drew's father got home just after eight.

●●❨◐◑❩●●

Sometime deep in the night, Drew surged up from his bed. In agony, he yelled out at the top of his lungs. His entire body felt like it was on fire; his bones burning away and his skin being consumed by the flames.

He awoke, chest heaving, sitting bolt upright in the middle of the bed. He was covered in sweat, and shaking badly. Drew looked around in panic. What was happening to him?

The door to his room opened. His father, still dressed in his clothes from the previous day, looked in.

"Drew," he asked hesitantly, "Are you okay, son? I heard a yell."

"Yeah, I think so," he replied, rubbing his arms and hugging himself. He ached everywhere. "Yeah, dad, I'm fine. Just a bad dream, I think."

James Collins stared at him blankly. "Okay. Well, if you need anything, just let me know," the gaunt man mumbled, pulling the door closed and shuffling off to his own room.

Drew looked at the clock: it was three thirty in the morning. 'God,' he thought. 'What the hell is going on?' He shouldn't hurt like this. His arm barely gave him a twinge, but the rest of his body felt as though he was having a bad reaction to a drug, or like there was fire in his blood. Maybe the medicine they had given him was bad or something. He vowed to stop taking the pills.

He wished that he could remember the dream that he'd been having. He had the vague sense that he'd been running, chasing something. Or someone. Megan? The biker chick? Who or whatever, he had the impression that his chase had been somehow sexual in nature.

Drew got out of bed and went in to the bathroom. He ran the water in the sink and then cupped his hands in it. He noticed that they had stopped shaking. Leaning down, he poured water on the back of his head.

He straightened back up and shook his head. Water droplets flew out in every direction. Drew stared at himself in the mirror. A handsome young man stared back at him, water running down his face. His blue eyes bored into his reflection's, trying to see what was going on inside.

Nothing. Drew sighed and went back to bed. As he fell asleep, he saw his blue-colored eyes staring at him, and they were slowly replaced by a pair of startling silver ones. They watched him dream, seeming to hover over his bed.

•• ❨ ◉ ❩ ••

Ronald Lemly and Jimmy Winslow were sitting in their cars, facing opposite directions in the Albertson's parking lot. It was a slow night in Iowa Park. Finally. There had been enough excitement in the last four nights to last the rest of the year, Lem thought.

The veteran officer looked at his young coworker. Winslow was looking around, head bobbing in time to music only he could hear. Lem was grateful for that. He'd heard some of Jimmy's tunes after work a couple of times, and he had no desire to ever hear more.

Rap was a strange thing to him. It wasn't singing; nor was it playing instruments, exactly. It made no sense to him, at all. Give him the Grand Old Opry any day. Ricky Scaggs; now that was music. Old Hank Williams. Cole Porter. Johnny Cash.

Lem glanced again at Jimmy. He grinned. The young deputy was now "singing" under his breath. The words to the rap song in his head could just be made out.

"Jimmy," Lem said, intruding on his song. "Did you run down the name of that biker gang like I asked you to?"

"Um, not yet Lem. I been kinda busy with stuff. I'll work on it after I get off tomorrow though."

"Sure. No rush. Just thought that a name as weird as Fenris Firar ought to be worth lookin' into. Figgered that a young guy like you would be handy with a computer, could maybe find somethin' that I couldn't."

"Yeah, I'll dig something up."

"Cool. Well, I'm gonna roll. Wanted to make extra passes through Pine Cone Park for a spell, see if we can spot them wolves. Funny that we ain't seen nothing out of them except for when they attacked people."

"Ya know, Lem, I'm kinda confused by that. I didn't think that we had wolves here no more. Haven't never seen any sign of wolves before. It's like they showed up same time as them bikers did, and left same time, too."

Lem was silent. His thoughts had been running along the same path as the rookie's. For all his shortcomings, Winslow wasn't stupid. Parker may be right about him, Lem thought. With some time and direction, the kid could be a good cop.

"Yeah, confuses me too. Make sure you track down that name for us, huh? I'll talk with you later," he said, starting his car and pulling out of Albertson's.

Jimmy sat in the parking lot for a time. He remembered growing up in Dallas, watching TV with his brother and sisters. His older brother had liked monster movies. Halloween had been Erik's favorite holiday, and he'd tormented his younger brother regularly, trying to scare him. Werewolves had been one of Erik's favorite monsters; the idea of becoming something else had attracted the young boy in the projects.

Six short years later, he'd become something else: a statistic. The teen-ager had joined a gang and become just another senseless victim of a drive-by shooting.

Jimmy had vowed to be different. He'd promised God and his mother (was there a difference in the 'hood?) that he would make his life count for something. And so, despite losing all of his friends, and suffering the scorn and ridicule of all the people that knew him, he'd applied to be a cop.

No one, including his mother, had expected him to succeed. That he made it through the Academy and became a sheriff's deputy was a shock, even to Jimmy himself. Now, he was determined to make a name for himself; to prove that he was a real cop.

'Okay,' he thought, back in Albertson's parking lot; the Fenris Firar. Goofy name. Why not just the Lobos, or something else? The Wolfpack, maybe? Make it something catchy, easy to remember. Gangs usually did that. Black or white, human nature was constant. It was all about appearance. He was looking forward to Googling the biker gang later.

Right now he had this boring shift to finish. He pulled out of the parking lot, squealing the tires just a bit. Good to be a cop, he thought, glancing around to see if anyone had seen him. The 24-hour grocery store was deserted, except for employees. No one was watching his exit from the lot.

CHAPTER 18

Tuesday dawned bright and clear in Iowa Park. Drew Collins woke up sore and confused. The remainder of his night had been filled with shadowy dreams that teased him, and left him with a feeling of yearning.

At least he didn't hurt as bad as when he'd woken up at three thirty. Then, he had felt like he was about to die. Now he just felt as if he'd been beaten up by the Baltimore Ravens' entire defense.

He got up and shuffled to the bathroom. The shower was still steamy, and a wet towel was spread out across the bar. His father had already been there, and gone.

Drew made himself breakfast. While normally just cereal or toast was all he bothered with, today he whipped up an omelet, stuffing it full of ham and cheese. He ate quickly, collecting his things for school.

He hurried out to the garage, and stopped. His bike sat in its normal spot, waiting for him. He started to take the key down from the rack, then shook his head. 'No motorcycle,' he reminded himself. 'Too much stress on the arm.' With a sigh, the teen-ager snatched up the keys to the Ford Taurus

Twenty minutes later Drew pulled in the parking lot of Iowa Park High School. The lot was already over half full, and he had to park a ways out from the front door. As he started walking between the cars towards the front entrance, he was spotted by some underclassmen.

In seconds he was surrounded by well wishing, and curious, other students. All seemed to be talking at once to him, and expecting him to answer back. He caught himself tensing up angrily, and then grinned. 'Enjoy your celebrity,' he heard Doug's voice say in his head.

"Guys, look, it's no big deal. I was attacked by a wolf that was trying to get to a little kid at a Cub Scout campout. While we were fighting I got bit on the arm. The doctors say that there isn't any nerve damage and that I should be okay before too long."

Amidst the choruses of "whoa, dude," and "shit, man," he heard one guy whisper to his buddy, "Can't be that bad. Check it out: he's got his backpack on that arm. Gotta weigh twenty pounds."

The senior glanced at his left shoulder. Sure enough, he had slung the heavy backpack over his injured arm. He normally carried his stuff on his left side, and apparently he just put it there out of habit. Funny; it didn't seem to hurt at all.

"Oops. Probably shouldn't do that," he said, grinning at the girls. "So doped on pain meds that I didn't feel a thing."

Nonchalantly, Drew switched the bag over to his right side, where it hung awkwardly. He was about to stretch out his arm, and draw some attention to the bandages that covered it when a booming voice called out to him from across the parking lot.

"Drew Collins! You gimpy-butt, sissified, glory-boy quarterback! What are you doing?"

"Hi Jones. How's the master masturbator this morning? You seem grumpy; didn't your hand want to put out last night?" he shot back, drawing loud laughs from the group.

"It's your hand that's off the dating scene, pretty boy. I do just fine," the massive lineman retorted, pushing his way through the smaller students to get to Drew.

"Okay boys and girls, we have to get to class now. Later, you can all sign Collins' face or something. Scat!" He shooed the other kids away.

Once the underclassmen were gone, his cheerful face assumed a more serious expression. He looked at Drew's arm, then stared hard at his best friend. "Collins, what the hell is going on?"

"What do you mean? Nothing's going on. I feel better, and don't want to sit home and twiddle my thumbs all day."

"That ain't what I mean, Drew. I seen your arm Saturday night. It was tore to shit. You 'bout lost it, and now you act like it don't even hurt. I know you aren't taking too many pain meds; I bet you ain't even takin' the ones you're supposed to be on."

Drew shrugged. Walking in to the building, he threw out over his shoulder at Doug, "I don't know. I feel fine. Just go with it. You don't make a big deal about it and I won't tell anybody that you snuck a slug of your dad's whiskey at breakfast."

Jones looked after his best friend in shock. "How the hell did you know that? I brushed my teeth afterwards and everything?"

Drew smiled and shook his head.

Tuesday promised to be much more fun than Monday. The circus was in town now, with Drew back. Rumor had it that the local paper was sending someone to interview him at lunch.

By the end of third period, Drew was ready to leave. Or kill someone. Or lots of someones. Every class was the same: everyone whispered about him, from beginning to end, shooting glances his way, without even trying to be discreet. Even the teachers seemed distracted. Drew felt more like a zoo specimen than a student. He was so fed up with everyone at school, he even considered going home. A mental image of himself sitting in the living room, staring at the TV like his father did at night, convinced him to stay. Besides, he reminded himself, gym class was fourth period, and that was his favorite.

Doug and Drew had set up their schedules to have Phys Ed right before lunch. It gave them a goof off class together, then lunch afterwards. Gym was the most fun class that they had, too, and there were cute girls in fourth period.

Drew entered the guys' locker room to the expected shouts of people calling out and yelling to get his attention. He endured it with what he considered admirable grace and patience, although the gym teacher disagreed with his choice of vocabulary when telling everyone to please leave him alone for a short time. 'Can't please everyone,' Collins told himself, glaring at Mr. Rew's back.

He sat in front of his locker and started pulling out his gym clothes. A heavy hand slammed down on his right shoulder, and

Jones's deep voice said, "Collins, what the hell are you doing? You don't get to dress out for class. You gotta sit your ass out, remember? Wolf bite, arm injury, doctor's note, any of that ring a bell?"

"Oh yeah. I can't dress out, can I? Kinda pointless to get dressed in gym clothes to sit and watch. Duh!"

Jones laughed. "Yeah, and you say us linemen are dumb. You been all kinds of stupid this week. Maybe when you do get better, you can join us in the trenches where you don't need to be smart. Now move your broken ass over and let me get changed. Some of us actually get to play today."

Drew shrugged and slid over. Bored, he stood up, walked out of the locker room and into the gym, to see what he'd be missing in class. He saw bases and a yellow plastic bat on the floor. Whiffle ball. He actually enjoyed that game, no matter how elementary school it seemed.

Once everyone came out from the changing rooms, Mr. Rew divided up the class into two teams, and sent Jones' team up to bat. Drew was assigned a spot sitting on the stage behind home plate. He sat down with poor grace. They could have at least let him pitch. It's not like his right arm had been injured. He could toss the ball underhand without hurting himself.

It's so easy that even Beth Cahill could do it, and about all she was good for was sex, if the stories were true. She looked hot enough, Drew thought, watching the big-chested blond toss the whiffle ball towards the plate.

'I wonder how much of those stories are true,' he wondered, staring at her. He focused on her chest, seeing it sway and bounce as she threw the ball again. He could just see the faintest hint of her nipples pressing against the fabric of her t-shirt, even through the bra she was wearing.

Drew licked his lips. He shifted his position on the stage, leaning forward. Beth laughed at something that Doug said as he stepped up to the plate, and threw the ball harder. This produced more spectacular results than Drew was prepared for. As he watched her breasts jump, he was struck in the forehead by the ball.

Jones had fouled the pitch straight back, having been caught off guard by the girl's change of pace, and swinging late. The glancing blow shot the ball right into Drew's face, rebounding with a loud, hollow sound.

The entire class roared with laughter. Drew turned bright red. Doug looked at him sadly. He shook his head.

"Folks, that's what happens when quarterbacks get too big for their britches. They forget that sometimes they have to move. If he keeps getting hit like this, he won't even be able to be a dumb lineman. He may have to be team manager, or even towel boy," he said, to more laughter and jeers.

He smiled ruefully. 'When do I outgrow this shit?' He was pretty sure that Tony Romo didn't have these kinds of problems. Then again, remembering his bad games and stupid mistakes when Jessica Simpson had shown up to watch, maybe he did.

Beth managed to throw the ball to Doug without causing further injury to Drew, though he was still distracted by her movements. God, she even smelled hot. Even from over on the stage, he thought he could smell her perfume. Or something else, like musk, or body wash.

Drew abruptly got up and walked off. The game went on without him to watch, teen-agers laughing and engaging in horseplay. Drew stopped at the drinking fountain and splashed water on his face, trying to calm down. He took several deep breaths. Gradually, his pulse slowed back down to normal, and he could think about other things than just Beth Cahill's body.

He looked back at the whiffle ball contest. Doug's team was now in the field, and the other team was up to bat. Of course, Beth was at the plate. Her back was to Drew. She crouched over slightly, seeming to aim her butt right at him.

'Damn,' he thought. 'Give me a break. I can't take this.' He looked away as the curvaceous girl hit the ball and ran to first base. She stared at him speculatively from first as he glanced up, hands locked in front of him, tensing and un-tensing his arms.

Beth smiled at him. Drew caught his breath as she seemed to take a deep breath, stretching her t-shirt tight across her chest, and waved at him. From across the gymnasium he could see her lick her lips slightly, moistening them.

Pulse once again pounding, Drew pushed open the doors to the hallway, and escaped the gym. He went into a bathroom, this time dunking his head in the sink, running cold water over his entire head. He was shaking.

He sat down in a bathroom stall and put his head in his hands. What the hell was happening to him? He knew that all teen-aged boys were horny, and he was no exception. He thought about girls constantly, and fantasized about the "Girls Gone Wild" chicks, and Hooters Girls, just like every other male he knew.

He also knew that this was beyond normal. He had known Beth Cahill since elementary school. They had always gotten along okay, but neither showed much interest in the other. Drew was too serious and sports-oriented, and Beth was way too much a party-girl. Why he suddenly couldn't control himself in the same room with her was a mystery.

The bathroom door opened and three guys came in, talking loudly. Drew recognized their voices; they were sophomores, players on the junior varsity football team.

"Man, did you hear about Rita Ibarra? She hooked up with some college guy over the weekend, and then while they were doin' it, the guy was killed by a wolf. Ripped his throat out, covered her in blood, left her trapped underneath the corpse for like, hours. Supposedly she's totally freaked out, in a coma or like a vegetable or something."

"I heard something like that. I heard she was goin' down on him, and this wolf jumped right over her and tore his head off," another said.

"Guys, you are full of shit. My mom works with her mom, and she told me that they were just walking in the park when they got attacked by a bunch of wolves. The guy tried to protect her and got killed, and she ran away. She's in the hospital now, but she's getting better."

"Yeah, right, Juan, they was just walkin' in the park. They was in Pine Cum Park after midnight, and they wasn't doin' nuthin';

right. That's just her mom talkin', tryin' to protect her little girl's rep," the first said.

"So did you hear about Drew Collins?" Juan said, changing the subject. "He got attacked by a wolf, too. Bit the shit outta his arm, damn near killed him."

"What, was he out in Pine Cum Park, too, git'n his rocks off?" the third boy asked, trying to sound as tough as his friends.

"No," Juan said, "he was out on a Scout trip and got between a wolf and some little kid; saved the kid's life. I guess he almost died."

"Wow. That took balls. He's helping me with my game, too, you know," said the third boy, who Drew knew to be Terry, the JV quarterback.

"Yeah, yeah, Drew Collins, big stud quarterback. I bet that's not what went down there, either. Weird family, ya know," the first threw in.

"What do you mean?" Terry asked.

"You know his mom died, right? Some crackhead shot her, and then her brother the sheriff hunted him down and blasted him outta existence. Was an official inquiry and everything, but it got swept under the rug and all. He's a spoiled big-shot crybaby, if you ask me."

The stall door slammed open as Drew launched himself out of the stall at the first kid, an acne-mottled sophomore named Stevens. Stevens turned to see him emerge from behind the door and raised his arms to protect himself.

The older boy crashed into him hard, driving him against the sink, then bashing his head against the mirror. It broke under the impact. The other two boys grabbed Drew's arms, trying to pull him off of their friend.

"Drew, man, he didn't mean anything by it. He's just talkin' stupid, it's okay."

"C'mon, Collins, back off. You're hurting him," Juan grunted, trying unsuccessfully to pry his left arm off of Stevens' throat. Drew growled and shoved again, bouncing the smaller boy's head against the broken glass a second time.

Stevens slumped, the second impact knocking him unconscious. Drew let go, watching him slide off of the sink and fall to the ground. He shuddered, staring down at the boy on the floor.

"Never talk about my family, asshole. My mother is dead, and my uncle did nothing wrong. The motherfucker that shot my mom tried to shoot him too, and my uncle shot first. That druggie ruined my family," he snarled.

He turned on the other boys in the bathroom. "Do I need to repeat myself, or do you two assholes understand?"

"We get it, Collins. Jesus," Juan said, holding his hands out in front of him. "Just back off. I gotta get the nurse," he slipped out past Drew.

Terry looked at Drew, white as a sheet. He looked down at his friend, who was slowly moving his hands up to his head, curled into a ball amidst the broken pieces of mirror.

"Man, Drew, I know he can be an asshole sometimes, but did you have to do that to him? He didn't mean any harm," Terry asked, kneeling beside his buddy.

Drew sneered. The stupid punk had gotten what he deserved. People should learn to keep their mouths shut about things that didn't concern them. They'd live longer.

'Yeah,' he told himself. They'd...what the fuck had just happened? Did he really just beat up a little kid for running his mouth? Maybe the guy deserved something for trash talking, but he might have really hurt him.

He was coming unglued. He knelt down beside Terry and helped Stevens to his feet. Miraculously, the sophomore hadn't been cut by the mirror. He was shaky, but balanced himself by holding on to the sink.

Drew began to apologize for losing his temper and slamming him into the wall. Stevens waved him off, turning away. Terry bent over and began picking up pieces of the mirror, throwing them into the trash.

The bathroom door burst open and Juan came in, followed by the principal and the nurse. Juan rushed over to Stevens to see how he was. The principal took in the broken mirror, the shaky teen, and Drew, standing in front of him with a stricken look on his face.

"Mr. Collins, what exactly is going on in here?" he asked.

Before Drew could answer, Stevens said, "Nothing, Mr. Phelps. I slipped and hit my head on the sink. I'm okay."

Juan looked as though he had swallowed a huge goldfish. He opened his mouth to argue, but Terry glared at him and shook his head.

"Is that true? Mr. Collins?"

"Umm, yeah, I guess so. I was in the stall."

The nurse checked on Stevens. "I want to see you in the office, Mr. Stevens. You seem to be okay, but let's check, all right?"

Jeremy Stevens nodded, then looked briefly in Drew's direction before walking out of the bathroom. The nurse followed him out.

Principal Phelps stood his ground. He was silent. The boys shifted uncomfortably. Drew was motionless, waiting to see what was going to happen. No one spoke. Finally the principle sighed. He looked from one student to the next, his gaze coming to rest on Drew.

"Okay boys, I think we all know that there is more going on here than what I was told. Anyone care to make a statement?"

Juan mumbled under his breath, "No hablo ingles," and walked past the administrator. The man didn't seem to hear him, although the words carried to Drew clearly.

Terry looked Mr. Phelps straight in the eye. He took a deep breath and said, "Mr. Phelps, I was standing right there. I was talking with Jeremy when he slipped. He was goofin' around, you know how he is; and he lost his balance and hit his head."

Phelps stared into the sophomore's eyes and saw only sincerity. He also knew that he was being bull-shitted. There just wasn't anything that he could do about it.

"Okay, Mr. Hooks, go back to class. Drew, let's go to the office, shall we? I understand that there's a reporter from Wichita Falls here to interview you about your escapades from the weekend. Did you know that the paper was sending someone here to the school?

Drew looked at Terry and mouthed a thanks. Hooks nodded and walked out, leaving Collins to follow Mr. Phelps to the office to meet with the reporter.

●● (●) ●●

There was a middle-aged man in a cheap suit sitting in Phelps' office, holding a notebook. He stood up as the two entered, smiling brightly. He introduced himself as Matthew Roth, before asking Drew to sketch out the events on Saturday as best he could, in his own words.

Drew was no stranger to being interviewed; he had been in the paper repeatedly, and even on TV because of his prowess on the football field. But right now he was not in the mood for the media. His emotions were churning, and he felt desperately out of touch with reality.

He focused on the man in front of him. The guy was blathering on about the camping trip, going into boring details that had already been supplied by Mr. Jones. Drew waited impatiently for him to finish.

Finally, just as Drew was almost convinced that he was going to miss his twenty-year class reunion, the old guy wound down. He looked encouragingly at Drew, raising his pen to the notebook.

"What?" Drew asked, not having caught what he was supposed to say.

"Mr. Collins, Mr. Roth asked you how you felt when the wolf attacked you," Phelps said.

Drew raised an eyebrow. "How do you think I felt? I was scared shitless. I thought I was going to die. I didn't think at all at first, you know, when it was goin' after Stevie, but when it looked at me, it fuckin' scared me," he snapped, earning a look of massive displeasure from his principal.

Phelps hurriedly spoke into the awkward silence.

"I think what Mr. Collins meant was he was frightened, but didn't think about it when he saw little Stevie Bishop at risk. He just reacted, and saved the boy. I'm sure that you can print something to that effect and not use our student's unfortunate choice of phrasing," he said, glaring at Drew, who shrugged in a 'what-did-I-do' fashion.

Mr. Roth seemed unfazed. He merely scribbled in his notebook, nodding sagely. He looked up at length, cleared his throat, and asked Drew if he "considered himself a hero" or not.

Drew snorted. "Of course not. What a stupid question. I just reacted to a situation. If I'd have known that wolf was gonna go after me and rip the hell outa my arm, I probably would have run away. Jesus, Mr. Phelps," he grumbled, looking at the principal, "do I have to keep doing this? They could have at least sent somebody decent to talk to me. This guy hasn't taken a shower in at least two days. Betcha he had his breakfast out of a bottle, too."

"Mr. Collins, that will be quite enough. Get to your class. I'll finish up with Mr. Roth here, and then we'll discuss your attitude in more detail, perhaps after school."

He turned to the reporter, who looked stunned, and was self-consciously patting his hair and straightening his clothes. As furious as he was, Phelps couldn't help noticing that Collins was probably right. Not that it mattered; no student at Iowa Park High School had the right to treat a member of the press in such a fashion. But still, Phelps could discern a slight, ripe body odor, buried under cologne, and the veins in Roth's nose told a tale of alcohol abuse. On closer inspection Roth was probably younger than he appeared, maybe still in his thirties.

Phelps walked Drew to the door of the office. He reached out and placed a hand on the young man's shoulder. Drew startled him by reacting violently to the touch, pivoting away and bringing his hands up quickly, as if to strike at him. Then the boy dropped his hands sheepishly, and looked down at the floor.

"Mr. Collins, I want you in the office at three-thirty for detention, do you understand me? We will talk about your attitude, offensive language, and this sudden predisposition towards violence that you seem to have developed. I understand that you've been through a lot recently, and in the past, but that doesn't excuse your behavior."

"Yes, sir. Sorry," Drew said, head down. He had no idea what was making him act this way, but he was well aware he was out of control. Detention seemed the least of his troubles. As he walked away he could hear Mr. Phelps apologizing again to the reporter.

●● ◖ ◗ ◖ ◗ ◗●●

Walking into the commons for lunch meant being around other people. Lots and lots of other people. Drew wasn't sure he was up for that, and started to to bypass the doors. He could smell burned lasagna coming from inside, and paused. He wanted to go in. Food was food, and he was starving; he had been all day.

A new, familiar smell in the air froze him in place. Drew relaxed. It was Doug, trying to sneak up behind him. Drew could hear his mammoth sneakers on the tile. Just as his big friend was about to mess up hair, (or just rub his head, since Drew's hair was too short to muss), the quarterback spun and grabbed Jones's outstretched hand.

"Ha! Gotcha, you big dork. Are you predictable or what?" He laughed, feeling as good as he had all day.

"I'm a dork? You're the only guy I know that can save a kid over the weekend, becoming a hero to all, then beat up another little kid, abuse a reporter, and get detention all in the same half day. Been busy, haven't you?"

"How did you know about all that? I didn't tell anyone about the detention, or the reporter," Drew said, pushing his friend in the chest lightly. "Who cares, anyway, the guy was lame. And for your information, that 'little kid' was Jeremy Stevens—he's almost my size, and a total jerk. Should learn to keep his mouth shut. Kinda like you."

"Who do you think arranged for that reporter to be here in the first place, idiot? He talked to me and my dad last night, and I told him that you'd be here today, and all hot and bothered to tell your story. And then you pull this. You'll never be rich and famous now, dude," Doug admonished, laughing. "Want lunch? I'm famished. Even the cafeteria lasagna sounds good to me."

"Yeah, I suppose. They burnt it, though," Drew responded absently, looking down the hall at three girls walking away.

"And you know this how? Have you already been in there?"

"No, doofus. You can smell the stuff clear down the hall. And the green beans that we have every time we have lasagna. And the wheat bread roll, *and* that god-awful dessert stuff they must make in hell and ship through the sewers to our school."

"You can smell all that from here? Right. And I'm taking over as QB for the team until you get back. C'mon, Cyrano, let's go eat," Doug said, pushing open the doors to the cafeteria and wading in. Drew followed in his wake, and in no time had a plate full of passable government issue school lunch food.

The food was everything Drew had predicted, much to Doug's chagrin. The subpar meal only added to the stress of Drew's first day back. He was ready to bolt, but knew that he couldn't. He had to make it through the rest of the day. The young man resigned himself to suffering through his classes, vowing to stay calm and under control—no one was going to make him act crazy.

No sooner had he made that vow, than Megan Stuart appeared. Drew flinched when he saw her. God, she was cute. No, beyond cute; she was hot. Maybe they could skip their next class and go somewhere…

"Hi Drew. How's your first day back? Are you doing okay?" She smiled brightly at him. 'Little miss innocence,' Drew thought. They could fix that.

"Hey sweet thing. I'm doin' fine, how's your day going?"

She seemed confused. "Drew? Are you sure you're okay?"

Drew took a deep breath and tried to clear his head. Obviously, being calm and collected was going to be more difficult than he thought. He forced a normal expression onto his face.

"Hi Megan. I'm sorry. It's been a tough day and I'm really out of it. I was going to go home, but I should try to finish out the day. I need to go, but I'll call you tonight, if that's okay?"

Megan's face cleared. She smiled even more brightly at him, and tossed her head, sweeping her blond hair around and off of her shoulders.

"Yes, I'd like that. I'll be home after seven. Take care of yourself, Drew. Bye," she said over her shoulder as she walked away.

He watched her go with appreciation. Doug was right; she did have a great ass. He caught the direction his thoughts were taking and forced them back onto more 'wholesome' lines. She was really nice, and cared about him.

The last two classes were a pain, but Drew made it through them without mishap. When the final bell rang, he headed back to the office to serve out his detention.

CHAPTER 19

When Sheriff Parker walked into his office on Wednesday morning, there was a pile of news waiting for him, none of it good. He had dispatches from the State Patrol, informing him that Larry Lee Tate had been sighted two counties over, and negative reports from various other law enforcement agencies regarding the motorcycle gang.

There was also a folder sitting on his desk from Jimmy Winslow. He sat down in his chair holding his second cup of coffee of the day, and opened the manila folder.

Inside were a couple of sheets of computer paper. The first was a print out of two words with definitions.

__Fenris__, or Fenrir, was a monstrous wolf of Norse mythology, the offspring of the mad god Loki. The wolf, according to the legend, will trigger the Apocalypse, and kills the leader of the Gods, Odin.

__Firar__ was another Norse word, that refers to people, whether a group or community, or a general term denoting humanity.

The second page was a typed explanation from Jimmy of what he had found. Apparently the young man thought the sheriff couldn't put two and two together himself. Of course the biker's name, Fenris Firar, would mean Fenris' people, or people of the wolf. Bikers weren't known for being subtle or deep thinkers.

The sheriff put aside the folder and sorted through the rest of his messages, futilely hoping they would read differently than they had the first time. They didn't; there was still a psycho-killer on the loose nearby, and no new leads on where that biker gang was.

He glanced out front and saw Randall heading his way, with his usual concerned expression on his face. Parker sighed. Would it be too much to ask that Jeremiah took a day off once in a while, if for no reason other than to just give him some peace in the office?

Randall knocked on his doorframe, even though he could see that Parker was staring right at him.

"What is it, Jerry?"

"Well, Sheriff, I got a call this morning from Bernie, at the Harley dealership. He had a question concerning Lucy Parsons that he needed to talk with you about. I have the number right here," he said, laying a paper with Bernie's phone number down on his desk.

"Okay. I'll probably head over to Bernie's and talk with him in person. I'll be out of the office for a while."

Parker got to his feet and walked the sergeant back to the front desk, stopping to refill his mug before leaving the office.

It was a short drive to the Harley shop. When he arrived, Bernie was there to greet him.

"Good morning, Sheriff. How can I help you? You didn't have to come out here for me, I just had a simple question."

"Morning, Bernie. I wanted to talk with you some more concerning Lucy Parsons, and the two bikers that were here last week. Can we go to your office?"

"Sure thing, sheriff. It's this way," the older man said, leading him to a spotless, well-decorated office off to the side of the clothing section. He sat in his leather chair, and motioned the lawman towards the comfortable looking seat opposite him.

"Well, what can I help you with? I thought that I had given you everything that you needed from our end. Lucy had no relatives in this area, and we didn't know any of her friends or boyfriends."

"Bernie, you actually called me this morning. What did you want? Can I help you in some way? I don't have anything new to report. The gang still hasn't shown up anywhere, and we still can't tell conclusively how Lucy died. I'm sorry."

"Sheriff, I just wanted to know what we should do with Lucy's personal effects. She had a locker with some stuff in it; wasn't much, but it shouldn't just sit here or get thrown out, you know?"

"Just box it up and drop it off at the station. I'll have Randall find out where to send it. Anything else?"

"Not really. I think we're gonna have a rally next month, kind of a memorial service of our own for her. You all might want to be here, just in case one of them shows up for it. I'll let you know the date as soon as we have it figured out."

"Sounds like a good idea, Bernie. Thanks, I'll keep you posted on things, okay?"

●● ◖◖◍◗◗ ◖◖

The Fenris Firar were lying low. For the past several days, they had been hiding out, avoiding the public eye. Other than a supply run or two, the gang kept from venturing anywhere near people.

But they were also getting restless. There had been two fights, both coming to bloodshed before being broken up. Lying around and staying quiet was not in the nature of the lycanthropes. Lobo knew he wouldn't be able to keep his unruly gang under wraps for much longer. He also didn't want to- he was as restless as any of them. He decided that what they needed was a diversion, some fun that wouldn't expose them to unnecessary risk.

"Firar, I think it's time for the Olympics. They start tomorrow. Let's get it set up. I want the obstacle course; the eating contest; the hunt; and the rest. You know the drill," he growled, before turning away to drag Ramona and Wrench off to the side. "Not you, Ramona. Or Wrench. You two are leaving. Time to go back to Texas and clean up that fuckin' mess you made.

"Don't fuck this up. Get well away from here, then steal a car and head back to that hick town. Lay low. No trouble making— you hear me, Wrench?"

The smaller man nodded.

Lobo continued. "Find out who that kid is. Recruit him or kill him. Or just bring him to me to decide, if you can. Check on that mechanic, too. Get rid of him if it works out. We don't want anyone that can testify against us. Any questions?"

Wrench glared at Ramona before asking, "Yeah, Lobo. Who's in charge, me or her?"

"Jesus, does someone have to be in charge? There's only two of you going. Just get it done." The hulking leader pushed both bikers towards their rides. "Now go, before I get pissed and end your miserable time with the Firar."

Ramona got on her Sportster without a word. She knew that she had no decision in the matter, and that she if she didn't go back to check on the person that she'd bitten, Lobo would only send someone else.

The leather-clad woman glanced over at her male counterpart, her lip curled in disgust. Wrench was not just dirty, he was stupid. Having to take him with her almost guaranteed that they'd be spotted, or get caught.

'Maybe getting caught wouldn't be that bad,' she reflected bitterly. That'd end this messed-up existence of hers, and provide some entertaining moments, as well. She could see the scene at some jail or prison when the first full moon rose on the Fenris Firar.

Oh, yeah, that'd be fun, all right. For all of fifteen minutes, until they all got shot. So much for that idea. Still, there had to be something better than this.

Wrench and Ramona fired up their bikes and took off, riding away from the Firar's temporary hideout, heading in roundabout fashion back to Iowa Park and the unsuspecting Collins family.

CHAPTER 20

Drew got up on Wednesday feeling better than he had in weeks. No pain in his arm, no aching bones, and best of all, no nightmares. He was filled with energy, and a feeling that the world was his.

Like the day before, he was particularly famished before school, and made himself an omelet stuffed with cheese and an overabundance of ham. The young man wolfed it down on his way out to the garage.

Dripping cheese and egg crumbs on the otherwise spotless floor, Drew grabbed the key and walked over to his prized Honda. Without a second thought he put on his helmet and swung his leg over the seat. He was grounded from the motorcycle until his arm was better, but as far as he was concerned, his arm was fine. It was a beautiful day outside, and he was going to enjoy it. He fired up his machine and tore off to school.

Once in the parking lot, he was met by Doug, who got out of his parent's Thunderbird. He looked at his best friend sitting on the motorcycle with obvious concern.

"Morning, Collins. The doc clear you to ride that beast again already?"

"Shut up, mom, I'm fine. Who needs doctors, anyway?" he teased his friend. "My arm doesn't hurt at all, and I wanted to enjoy the weather. Almost left the damn helmet off, too. Gonna tell on me?"

"No you dope. I'm just worried," Doug replied. "Yesterday you about got kicked out of school, and now you show up on your bike, using your arm again in ways that you're not supposed to. What am I supposed to think?"

"You're supposed to be my best friend and support me. So stop being a worrywart and relax. Come on, let's go inside."

Doug and Drew walked past the office, checking out the girls in the hallway. Beth Cahill sashayed past them, smiling broadly at Drew. Both boys whistled low, and high-fived each other after she passed.

Jeremy Stevens and Juan Hernandez went by, pointedly looking the other way. Jones scowled at them both.

"Pricks," he grumbled under his breath. Drew grinned.

"Easy, big guy. Don't get me in trouble today, too. I did enough of that yesterday to last the rest of the year," the senior said. "Mr. Phelps cut me serious slack yesterday, but he probably won't if I screw up again."

"What are you doing, Collins?" Doug asked, pointing at Drew's left arm.

Drew looked down. He was scratching his forearm, and hadn't even noticed. Now that he was aware of it, his arm did itch something fierce.

"It feels like there's ants under the dressing. This sucks. I'm stopping in the john to look at it," he said, heading for the nearest bathroom. Doug ducked in with him, curious to see Drew's wounds now that they'd been cleaned and wrapped for a few days. The way Drew was acting, you'd think that there wasn't anything wrong with it, but Doug knew better. He'd been there when it happened.

Drew stopped at the sink, checking to make sure they were alone. The stalls were empty. He glanced at Doug, and then quickly unwrapped the gauze dressing from around his forearm. He piled it on the counter, and then carefully peeled back the bandages covering his injuries.

His left forearm was whole. The wounds had closed. There were a series of purplish scars all down the length of his arm, from elbow to wrist, but even those were faint.

Drew scratched at his arm more, flaking off some dead skin from the line of scars. Doug's eyes widened to the point they seemed about to fall out of his head.

"I don't fuckin' believe it!" he gasped, looking like he wanted to grab Drew's arm and prod at the scars. "No way that can be real. How the hell is your arm *healed*?"

Drew looked at his best friend, Doug's shock mirrored in his own eyes. He couldn't believe it, either. He looked back at his arm and flexed it. Muscles bunched and relaxed. He made a fist and held it up.

Doug was white. Hesitantly, he reached out and touched Drew's forearm. Drew's skin was slightly warm, but otherwise fine. The skin over the scars felt smooth, not even dimpled where the teeth had punctured him.

"What the hell?" Doug exclaimed. "It feels normal! How is that possible?"

Drew hurriedly started replacing the bandages and dressing, hiding the injury. "We got to get to class."

"And what do we do about this?" Doug demanded, pointing at Drew's arm.

"Nothing. Not a word. I don't know what's going on, Doug, but promise me—not a word to anybody."

"I don't know, man, this isn't like any of the other shit that we've been through, Drew, and you know it! We gotta tell somebody; the school nurse, your doctor, somebody. You may not be okay."

"Jones, I'm fine," Drew said, trying to convince himself as much as his worried friend. "I'm better than okay. You saw my arm; it's better. What's to be upset about?"

"If I keep mum about this for now, you've got to promise me that you'll go see your doctor later. I'll even drive you, but you gotta see somebody."

"Yeah, yeah, yeah… I gotta see somebody. God, give it a rest. I'll go after practice. Now, let's go," Drew spat out, getting annoyed by his friend's insistence. You'd think that he had some horrid disease, or was wasting away in all manner of grotesque ways, rather than merely healing ahead of schedule.

Collins and Jones walked out of the bathroom and headed for their respective first period classes, both lost in thought. While

Drew was fuming about Doug's paranoid reaction, Doug was ill at ease at the unnaturalness of Drew's recovery.

Drew's first three class periods passed without incident. He made it through each boring session, keeping himself entertained by separating out the boys and girls in the room by scent alone.

'It's amazing,' he thought to himself, 'how many people just don't bathe enough.' Covering their stink with heavy perfumes and deodorants is not the same as being clean, he told his classmates silently. 'And for God's sake, brush your teeth.'

Closing his eyes, which was easy to do in Miss Shimeck's English Lit class anyway, he concentrated on hearing small movements in the room. Drew began to pick up on scuffling foot noises, throats being cleared, papers being rattled, and even the faint scratching sound of pens writing.

He could hear various students breathing; some easy and deep, some rapid and shallow, and a couple wheezing with allergies. Blocking out the droning sound of the teacher's voice, he focused even more.

Vaguely, multiple drum sounds came to him. Heartbeats, he realized with surprise. He was actually hearing hearts beating in the chests of the people around him. He leaned back, lost in the wonder of it all.

"Eh-hem! Mr. Collins, are you with us today?" Miss Shimeck's aged nasal twang intruded on his world of sound. "Hello, earth to Drew Collins…"

He sat forwards and opened his eyes. The entire class was looking at him, most with broad smiles on their faces. The teacher however, was not amused. She was staring hard at him, displeasure radiating from her fragile old form.

"Mr. Collins, did you not hear my question? Is it, or is it not, rude to have students sleep through a teacher's lecture? You may not find Shakespeare to be as exciting as your football games, young man, but you will do me the courtesy of staying awake for my class. Do I make myself clear, Mister Collins?"

Drew fumed. How dare the old bag embarrass him like that in front of his pack! Didn't she know how old and easy to take out she was? She survived by his indulgence, he was the dominant...

Drew reigned in his temper, suddenly realizing that once again, his new emotional problems were threatening to get the best of him. He lowered his head.

"I'm sorry, Miss Shimeck, it won't happen again."

"See that it doesn't. Now, back to our lesson," she told the class, who all quietly and regretfully returned their attention to the teacher.

●● ◖◖◗◗ ●●

By gym class, he was ready to burst. His energy level was shooting through the roof, and his tolerance for school, and all the morons around him, was all but used up.

He found Doug in the dressing room. Sneaking up on the big man, he pounced on his back as he was opening his locker. Quickly putting the lineman in a half nelson, he leveraged his friend to the floor.

Doug swore and twisted around, coming face-to-face with his grinning buddy. The murderous look disappeared off his face.

"Damn it, Collins, you jack ass! What are you doing, trying to get yourself killed? I coulda tore your head off!" he ranted.

"Not a chance, you gorilla. You're way too slow. I had you, and you know it. Now get changed, we got whiffle ball to play," Drew said happily. Taking his two hundred and forty pound friend off of his feet, even from behind, was something he'd never done before.

"Drew, you twit, you can't play. You're supposed to be hurt, remember?"

"Yeah, I know, but consider this: if my arm is better, I can play Friday night, right? Do you think we can win with Simpson at quarterback? Think about that," Drew said, walking out of the locker room.

Out in the gym, he was immediately assaulted by the sweet smell of Beth Cahill. The senior girl was standing just outside the door to the boys' changing area, almost as if she'd been specifically waiting for Drew to appear.

He turned to look at her, dressed in short shorts and a tank top. She was also completely made up, like she was going out on a date, rather than just dressing out for PE. If he hadn't been so wildly attracted to her, it would have been laughable.

Despite how obvious she was, it was working. Drew's mouth went dry, and his palms were uncomfortably sweaty. He cleared his throat nervously, and she smiled. Beth pushed away from the wall, which involved torso shifts that almost caused cardiac arrest on her unfortunate victim.

"Drew, how's the arm? Are you feeling better today?" she crooned, taking his right arm in both of hers, pressing it to her body. "I feel so bad for you,"

She stared into his eyes and Drew stared back, pulse pounding. He could feel her soft curves, all along his arm. Just as the moment was getting too out of control for him, Doug flung open the locker room door and tramped out into the gym.

Drew pulled back from the girl shakily. He tried to smile at her, but it didn't work. He just looked somewhat ill.

"Uh, I'm doing fine, Beth, but I gotta go," he mumbled, staggering away from the coyly smiling teen.

Doug threw a massive arm around Drew's shoulders, dragging him further away from the curvaceous peril. His own shoulders shook with merriment. After a quick look at Drew's face, though, his demeanor changed.

"Hey, what's wrong, Collins?"

Drew was shaking. His face was red; not from embarrassment, but from stress. Both hands were clenched into tight fists. His entire frame was rigid beneath Jones' arm.

"Fu-uck," Collins finally said, twitching out from under his buddy's arm. He took several deep breaths, trying to clear his head.

"Collins, what?"

"Just give me a minute," Drew snapped, almost hostile.

"To do what? You look ready to explode, dude," Jones said, looking closely at his best friend.

Drew shook his head several times, staring at the floor. 'How come I never noticed how good she smells? Man, it's...intoxicating. I wanted to throw her on the floor and..." He made an odd gesture that involved more shaking than anything else, "...right there in the middle of the damned gym..."

Finally he looked up at Doug and smiled. "Guess she just got to me," he replied, trying to put the matter to bed. "Just do me a favor? Keep me away from her for a while? I can't think rationally around Beth Cahill right now."

"Like any guy can? C'mon, lighten up. You been through a lot, and now you're reacting like you have a new lease on life, or some shit like that."

"Just promise me, you big goon," Drew said, glaring at Jones.

"Okay, okay, I'll babysit you in gym class; and after that if I need to. God, you're a pain in the ass."

When the final bell rang, Drew was more amped up for football practice than he had ever been in his life. He beat everyone out onto the field, and was busy setting up drills when the rest of the team made it out.

Doug looked at him questioningly, but said nothing as he joined his teammates. The rest of the team grumbled and settled into warm-ups, led by the enthusiastic Coach Burns.

Once those were out of the way, practice began. Coach Stanton was again at his best, blasting the offense and the defense equally. No one could do anything right, especially the offense. Under the "guidance" of Jerry Simpson, they struggled mightily.

Drew itched to step in, but wasn't even allowed to dress out, let alone scrimmage. He bit his tongue, standing on the sidelines and pacing back and forth.

Stanton glanced over at him and smiled. "Mr. Collins, do you have something that you'd like to say? Perhaps you can fix what ails our offense?"

"Coach, can I show Simpson the fake to the fullback and toss? He's hesitating, and it destroys the flow to the play. Then maybe just a little work on the play action passes? I won't over do it, I promise."

Stanton seemed undecided. Collins pushed the issue, desperate to play.

"Coach, my arm's doing great. Just ask Jones. He was there when I got bit, and he's seen the injury today. It's like new—no pain, bleeding, even the stitches are gone now. I'm fine, really." He flexed his arms wide, making fists and smiling.

The head coach looked over at Burns, who shrugged. He obviously didn't think that Simpson could do the job, and had been pushing for Collins to play as soon as he could.

"Okay, Drew, step in. Remember, go easy. You're not dressed out; no running the ball yourself, and get rid of it quickly." He then turned to his defense. "Guys, no hitting the QB. Step sharp, though. Mr. Collins is going to show us all how to play quarterback."

For the next half hour, Drew got to run the offense. The change was remarkable. Almost every play worked, and the defense was back on their heels the entire time. Collins seemed faster and smoother than ever.

When Stanton blew his whistle, Jones looked across the line at his friend, flipped him the bird, and smiled. Maybe everything would be okay.

Collins wiped sweat from his face and smiled hugely. He high-fived a couple of his linemen, and then turned to his coach.

"So, Coach, how was that? Can I play on Friday?"

"Mr. Collins, you bring me a doctor's release, and you can play. Fair enough?"

"Sure thing, coach. I'll bring it Friday to the game," the young man said happily. He turned and walked away, catching up with Doug, who was on his way to the water table.

"So genius, how are you going to get a doctor's note by Friday? Are you really going to go to the doc's office?"

"Shut up, dork. I'm playing on Friday, and no one's going to stop me. We'll figure something out."

"Yeah, uh-huh. Good luck with that one. C'mon, let's get a drink while we still can. You may be done playing for the day, but I've got work in the trenches yet," Doug grumbled, casting a dirty look at Coach Stanton's back.

CHAPTER 21

Daybreak found Ramona and Wrench twenty miles outside of Iowa Park. A day and a half of riding, just the two of them, had not improved Ramona's mood. In fact, she was more taciturn and short-tempered than normal. Wrench, while nowhere near a candidate for Mensa, nevertheless knew enough to leave her alone as much as possible.

Still, after riding all night, he was grumpy and irritable himself. As they came to a stop at a gas station, he yelled at the raven-haired woman, "Where the hell are we?"

Ramona tried to pretend she hadn't heard him, hoping he'd shut up and leave her alone. Fat chance, he was too stupid to take a hint. Wrench understood subtlety only slightly better than he did astrophysics.

She sighed as he yelled again. Motioning with her right hand at the small town beyond the Shell station, she snapped back, "This is Elliot. Little shit-hole of a town. We should find a car or truck here and stash the bikes."

"Whatever," Wrench replied, trying to act as if he could have come up with the idea himself. No matter how much he wanted to be in charge, he just wasn't smart enough. That didn't make him any easier to deal with, though. "So, smarty-bitch, where do you think we're gonna find wheels that we can afford? Lobo didn't send us back with a lot of dough."

"Wrench, we're gonna get gas here, then cruise around for a farm house or something that looks like it ain't busy. We'll hold up there and use whatever vehicle we can find—just hotwire the damn thing. We don't need anything fancy, just something other than the bikes."

Wrench thought for a moment. It made sense, except for one thing. "Uh, Ramona, didn't we just do the whole farmhouse thing? Maybe we should just like, rent a room or something."

"Brilliant, Wrench. We're supposed to be hiding, remember? The fewer people that know where we're staying, the better." She rolled her eyes, obviously implying that she considered her companion an idiot.

The eye rolling wasn't lost on Wrench. The vicious little man snarled, swinging his fist at her, despite being too far away. Since the punch didn't reach, he spit at her. It struck her jacket.

Ramona growled back, kicking out at Wrench's bike as she gunned her own. Her booted foot caught his shin as she rode past.

"Shit!" he roared in pain, taking off after her. It wasn't much of a race: Ramona stopped after twenty or thirty yards at the nearest gas pump.

"Wrench, we can fight later. Fill up the bikes and wait here," Ramona told him when he caught up to her. "I'll go in and pay for the gas and get some food, maybe see about a place close by to crash at," as she walked off, leaving him no choice in the matter.

"Whatever, bitch," he grumbled, slopping gas into his tank.

Ramona came out with a couple bags of groceries and the closest thing to a smile that Wrench had seen on her face in a long time. She tossed her hair and walked quickly to her bike.

"Well, what's up? You look like the cat that just swallowed the canary."

"I think we got lucky. There's a shitty trailer park just around the bend, full of migrant workers. Odds are there'll be an empty one there that we can use. C'mon, let's go," she said, firing up her bike and taking off.

Wrench swore as he kicked his bike over and took off after her. The least she could have done was warn him, maybe even wait for him, instead of making him catch up to her. Bitch.

A mile down the road, there was indeed a small trailer park, with fifteen to twenty old, beat up mobile homes scattered haphazardly around a central office. Ramona pulled up to the battered permanent building with the weather-beaten sign that said simply, "Office."

She knocked loudly on the cheap door. Getting no response, she twisted the knob and shoved. It pushed open with some difficulty, and she stared inside. A large, fat Hispanic man sat at an old desk, reading a skin magazine. He looked up as she entered the room.

"Que? What do you want?"

"You got an open place to stay? Need a trailer for a month. I have cash," Ramona said, waving a wad of bills in front of his sweaty face. He looked from the money to the attractive woman holding the bills. His face twisted into a disturbing grin as he took in her lithe form and obvious curves.

"Yeah, I got what you need. We can discuss payment later," he said, leering at her.

The silver-eyed woman stared hard at the disgusting fat man. He continued smirking at her, either oblivious to her anger, or just indifferent to it. He smacked his thick lips and sat forward in his chair, which creaked alarmingly but held.

"Here," he tossed a key onto the desk in front of her. A grungy piece of tape on the side had the number 12 written on it in blue magic marker.

"I'll be by later to collect your… rent. If you need anything, anything at all, come see me," the vile smelling man asked, absently rubbing at his crotch. "Comprende chica?

Ramona swept up the key and spun out of the ramshackle office, giving the fat man a great view of her ass as she left. Just let him come by later and try to collect his rent. She looked forward to his visit.

Lot twelve was just about what she expected: an old 12 by 50, piece of shit mobile home from the 60's. It was indistinguishable from the other trailers that surrounded it, and without the piece of cardboard with the big blue '12' on it, they wouldn't have been able to guess which one was theirs.

Wrench glanced at their new dingy white home, taking in the piles of trash, the broken down steps, and the poorly patched roof. His face twisted in disgust. Even outlaw bikers had standards.

"Why are we staying here? This is the worst shit hole I've ever seen."

"Don't be dense," Ramona replied. "Or at least, no denser than you have to be. We have to be inconspicuous—that means stay where no one notices, or cares, who we are. This place is perfect. Now shut up and stick the bikes behind the trailer, so that they can't be seen from the road. I'll go in and open the windows. My bet is that this place could use airing out."

That turned out to be an understatement. The trailer smelled like several cats had died in the living room. The refrigerator seemed to keep the air inside it only slightly cooler than the air in the room, and half the lights were burned out or missing. There was only one bedroom, with a nasty bare mattress. Ramona gave a mental shrug; she'd sleep on the ratty couch in the living room. At least the bathroom seemed functional.

She quickly stacked the supplies from the convenience store on a grime-covered counter top, then sat down to look through the local paper that she'd picked up. The young woman scanned the headlines as she flipped through the pages.

There! An article on the mysterious animal attacks plaguing the area around Iowa Park. It was only a short follow-up to a previous story, but contained vital information for the Firar female.

"There is still nothing new to report on the rash of animal attacks in and around Iowa Park. Police reports indicate that they have made no progress thus far in locating the elusive pack of wolves believed to be responsible for the death of at least one college student, and the injuries of two high school students. A second fatality, the victim of abduction, is also believed to be related, although authorities are not certain of the connection.

Police have issued a warning for residents of Iowa Park to stay indoors after dark, and to be on the lookout for the wolves. Drew Collins, the senior from Iowa Park High School who was attacked and injured late Saturday evening, is recovering and has been released from Mercy Hospital. The other victim, who has asked to remain anonymous, has yet to be released, but is reported to have no physical injuries."

Drew Collins. She had a name now. In a town the size of Iowa Park, it couldn't be hard to find him. Tomorrow she'd get a hold of a computer and look him up. She still had to find more info on the mechanic, too. That would be harder, since he'd seen her as well as Wrench. She couldn't just walk into the Harley shop and ask around.

Those were problems for the next day, however. For tonight, she still had to deal with Wrench, the sleeping arrangements, and probably that fat pig from the office. She sighed.

●● ◖◉◗◑ ◕●

Lobo looked around him, and smiled in satisfaction. The games were progressing. The pack seemed happy enough with the distraction, and threw themselves enthusiastically into the raucousness. Mankind had always used sport to determine pecking order, the original Olympics being just an excuse for warriors to compete in non-lethal fashion for position, and the Firar were no different.

Currently, the sumo challenge was taking place. Amidst a circle of beer cans, Ulric was reigning supreme, hurling his competition outside the ring with enthusiasm, accompanied by coarse epithets.

The ring itself was surrounded by members of the Firar, all drinking beer and mocking those getting tossed. Aardwolf was the latest victim, getting thrown headfirst into the dirt. Ulric raised his arms in triumph and roared.

"Who's next? C'mon, ya pussies! Bring it," the massive biker called, turning a full circle, trying to goad someone to enter the ring. No one moved.

"Ah, ya chickens," he finally said, lowering his arms. He looked up the hill to where Lobo was standing. The lieutenant smiled slowly, looking directly at his equally massive boss.

The challenge was unmistakable. Winnie and Caleb whistled. The rest of the pack began to cheer and clap, adding their support to the match. Lobo looked at his pack and saw only enthusiasm for a big match, not hope for a change in leadership.

The cheers turned to full-throated yells and howls as Lobo stepped into the circle of beer cans. The gigantic leader of the Fenris Firar pulled off his faded, stained leather vest and threw it aside. Mockingly, he bowed to Ulric and motioned to him. Both men crouched in mock sumo fashion, facing off three feet away from each other.

Piggy stepped in between the two, her right hand raised high. She looked at Ulric, then at Lobo. He nodded, eyes locked on his lieutenant. The stocky woman dropped her hand, yelling, "Bonzai!" and jumped back.

The two muscular men surged up out of their stances, slamming into each other with a tremendous crash. Both drove their forearms up into the other man's chest, trying to drive the other backwards, or at least off balance.

Initially, it was a stalemate. Muscles flexed and swelled, sweat poured, and teeth were bared as each man strove to overpower the other. Ulric shoved upwards, knocking Lobo's hands off of his chest. Unleashing a primal scream, the second-in-command extended outwards, stepping forward to tip over his leader.

Lobo pivoted, slapping Ulric resoundingly across the side of his head. Ulric staggered, losing his balance for an instant. Lobo drove his shoulder into the burly man's side, shoving hard at his exposed back.

The lieutenant was knocked forward, somersaulting to his feet immediately, scattering the cans that formed the boundary for the match. He spun around, facing his leader. The scowl on his face was priceless. For a moment, Lobo thought his most dedicated follower might actually attack him. He sneered.

Ulric postured for a moment longer, then grinned. He held his hand up and stepped back into the ring for Lobo to high-five him.

"Cool. Good move, boss," the largest of the lycans said, smiling broadly. It was no disgrace to be beaten by the alpha male of the pack. It was to be expected. The rest of the pack cheered as well, with only a couple of catcalls aimed at Ulric.

"Next event!" Lobo called out, accepting a beer from Graybeard. He chugged it down quickly, and crumpled the can up in his massive fist. He belched loudly with satisfaction. What was the next event? He couldn't remember.

Oh, yeah. The hot dog eating contest. One of everyone's favorites, mostly because everyone was entered in this one. They'd learned from previous Olympics that size didn't necessarily matter in this particular event. Wrench had won last time. Only he wasn't here now, Lobo reminded himself. He briefly wondered what his missing pair was up to, then dismissed them from his mind.

"Okay, c'mon, let's get this going. Where's the stuff? Get this thing set up—what, do I have to do everything?" he growled. Pack members scrambled to set up tables, and brought out plates laden with pre-counted stacks of hot dogs piled on them.

Twenty-three plates of thirty hot dogs each were placed on three tables. The Firar all took up stations in front of the plates. They all looked at Lobo, waiting for the signal to begin. The hairy leader held one hand high, the other just above his plate of hot dogs.

As he dropped one hand, Lobo grabbed three wieners with the other and shoved them in his mouth, signaling the beginning of the race. Not completely fair, but no one was going to argue with him, especially since everyone knew it didn't matter.

With Wrench gone, Aardwolf was the odds-on favorite to win. The dim-witted man had just barely lost to Wrench last time, and now it wasn't even competitive. He swallowed his last hot dog whole before anyone else was down to eight.

"Fuck," Lobo grumbled through a mouthful of Oscar Mayer's finest. "Aardwolf wins. Shoulda known- I don't think the mangy fucker even chews."

Aardwolf smiled at Lobo happily, slobber dripping off of his chin. There were members of the Firar who swore that Aardwolf was actually cleaner eating as a wolf than as a man. Probably smarter, too.

"Okay, gang, that just leaves one more event for our Olympics," Lobo intoned, rubbing his hands together. "We'll take a short break to get set up, and then we're on for the 'Bitch Toss.'"

Hoots of delight came from mouths still full of hot dogs. While not everyone competed in this event, it was also a gang favorite. The entire pack worked together to assemble two runways with beer cans. Distances were stepped off, with cloth markers dropped every foot.

Ulric and two others appeared, carrying two large burlap sacks. They dumped them out on the ground, disgorging two small, very dirty vagrants. The bums blinked, looking around at the bikers that surrounded them. One whimpered.

"Relax, boys, you're just here to help us play a game. Help us out for a half hour and we'll send you on your way with a new bottle. Okay?" Lobo asked, all smiles.

"Don't hurt us, mister, we didn't do nuthin'," the stronger looking homeless man pleaded. He looked at the ground, expecting to be kicked or hit. The life of a vagrant was a hard one, and being abused by those who felt superior was part of everyday existence.

"What'd I say?" Lobo roared. "I told you that if you behave and help us out we'll let you go. Mess with us and you'll never bum cigarettes or booze from anyone ever again; got it?"

"Yeah, okay, mister," the other man whined. "Whatever, just don't hurt us."

Winnie stepped between them and grabbed a handful of dirty shirt in each hand. She hauled both men to their feet. They stood uneasily, cringing under the amused gaze of the bikers. She smirked at them, reveling in their fear.

"Okay boys, here's the deal. See these two lanes made up of beer cans? We gonna have a contest. We're gonna take turns throwin', and see who can throw the farthest. Your job is pretty simple, boys," she continued, grinning at her fellow bikers. "Your job is to just relax, and stay where you land. We gotta measure and see who gets the farthest, okay? So don't move or you'll make them mad."

The bums looked startled, as it dawned on them that they were going to get thrown around repeatedly for the amusement of the outlaws. They looked at the gang, trying to see a way out; then, with resignation, they looked at each other and slumped in defeat.

The Firar, experts in reading body language, followed the entire process with glee. Seeing the shoulders of the two bums slump, they broke out in laughter.

"So, who are our first contestants? Step right up, gentlemen, and pick up your bitch," Lobo called, as Ulric and another man each grabbed a bum by the back of the pants and hair, hoisting them unceremoniously off of their feet.

The two homeless men hung limply from their captors' grasps. They knew that this was going to hurt; they also knew that if they resisted, they would probably be killed. Best to suffer the coming indignities stoically, and hope they would be released mostly unbroken.

"One, two, three!" Winnie shouted. The two members of the Firar grunted as they let fly, throwing the small men as far as they could. The vagrants sailed out into the night, arms flailing wildly. They crashed to the ground and lay still. Winnie placed empty beer cans at the head of each bum, to mark the spot where they landed.

"Next," she called dragging the men back to the starting position. Two more bikers pushed up front to throw the vagrants. They also tossed the men with great enthusiasm.

Over the course of the next half hour, the bikers threw the homeless men over a dozen times, catapulting them through the air to land awkwardly on the hard ground. When the dust finally settled, Ulric was declared champion, and the revelry wound down for the night.

The hobos were marched several hundred yards away, and Graybeard handed each a bottle of cheap whiskey, warning them to keep quiet.

"If you guys tell anyone that we're here, or that we harassed you in any way, we will find you. And when we do, no one will find you. Ever. You got it? Good," he said, pushing the men in the chest, making them stumble backwards.

"Now get walking. Remember, not a word, or tonight will seem like a pleasant diversion." The oldest of the bikers stared hard at their retreating forms, watching them until they passed from sight, limping and swigging from their bottles. Another day in the life of a faceless vagrant.

●●◖◖◗◗●●

Ramona tossed and turned on the couch. It was a broken-down piece of shit, but since she was used to sleeping on the ground, it wasn't too bad. Her bigger problem was Wrench, who, against all wisdom, tried to talk her into sleeping with him in the bedroom. He'd needed forcibly reminding that no meant NO, and was currently sulking in his room, nursing a dislocated wrist.

Around midnight, she heard a scraping sound on the lock to the front door. A key was inserted and turned, quietly. She lay still, pretending to be asleep. This had been expected. She was a little surprised that he was here this early, but knew that he'd come.

The door eased open, surprisingly quiet for being old and crappy. A vague shape slipped in to the room before the door was closed again. Ramona could hear heavy breathing from a fat man, trying to keep quiet. She could also smell him from across the room: stale sweat, dirty clothes, beer, and grilled onions with beans. 'Altogether a lovely date,' she thought.

The biker kept her eyes closed until the man was standing over her. He reached out and stroked her hair with a grubby hand. Despite the dimness of the trailer, he seemed to know his way around. Probably not the first time that he'd shown up here to collect his… rent.

He leaned over her. She could hear him inhaling, trying to smell her, and she could sense his excitement at the lecherous act he was about to begin. He reached down lower.

The fat man's hand had just started to fasten on firm flesh when Ramona erupted into motion. She surged up off of the couch, knocking his hand away from her chest and reaching out to cup his head in both her hands. With a savage wrench, she snapped his neck.

Fredrico Valdez died in shock, not even realizing what had happened to him. His last impression was a visual image of silver eyes blazing into his with total fury. His body dropped to the floor with a loud crash.

Wrench was out of the bedroom quickly, peering into the living room with an expectant smile. He had been told by his partner that she'd have a visitor to deal with at some point during the night, and that he wasn't to interfere.

"Well, what's up?"

"What's up is that there's one less piece of shit in the world," she spat, rising from the couch. "Help me go through his pockets, see if he has anything useful. He certainly wasn't worth anything alive," she said contemptuously, kicking his side.

The fat manager had less than five dollars in cash, and a matchbook from a strip club. High roller. Even Wrench seemed put off by the stench wafting off of the dead man. He reached into the back pocket, grinned, and pulled out a ring of keys. "Lookee here; we got us some keys. Could be we scored us a ride."

He straightened, spinning the ring around his finger. "So what the fuck do we do with this? He already stinks, and a couple of days in this heat, he's gonna draw flies from three counties away."

"Let's go see what these keys fit, then we'll figure it out," Ramona said, swiping the keys from Wrench's hand in a deft motion. He never was the most observant member of the pack.

They discovered an old Dodge van sitting behind the office building that looked serviceable. Two of the keys that the unfortunate Fredrico had carried fit it. Ramona almost smiled; at least some of this was working out. She looked at Wrench, who was making motions at her to give him the keys, so that he could drive. Once again, she sighed. So predictable. Odds were that once they drove the van back to the trailer, he'd need her help loading up the body, too.

CHAPTER 22

School on Thursday was a study in frustration for Drew. The kids were moronic and childish, the teachers boring and overbearing, and even his best friend was acting differently; he seemed subdued and thoughtful. Drew kept catching Doug watching him out of the corner of his eye.

"Jones, what's going on?" he asked at one point. Doug looked uncomfortable, mumbling something about Drew seeming less tolerant of people than he used to be, and some blathering about not being patient. Shit.

The only bright spot was Beth Cahill. The blond vamp was rapidly passing the 'obvious' stage, and proceeding to blatantly throwing herself at him. Megan Stuart saw them flirting in the hall at lunch time, threw a hissy fit, and ran off crying. But that was her problem. Drew was a free man; he could talk to whoever he wanted.

Football practice had gone just fine, as far as Drew was concerned. He got all the repetitions with the first team, and Simpson watched. Even Coach Stanton seemed happy with him, but he kept bringing up the doctor's note to be able to play in the game the next night. He'd have to do something about that damn note. It'd be just like them to keep him out of the game even though he felt fine.

Friday finally arrived. Drew Collins had waited almost ten months for this day, the first football game of senior year. He felt as though he could explode. He awoke before his alarm went off, and almost leaped out of bed.

Before he left for school, he carefully crafted a fake note from a piece of hospital stationery he had brought home with him. Signing it so sloppily that it couldn't possibly be identified, he folded it up and stuck it in his pocket.

He skipped breakfast, being far too wound up to eat. He barely even noticed that his father was still in his room. Drew collected all of his things and loaded up the car. Since tonight's opening game was away, he had to take all of his things now, to put on the bus. Which sucked, since he couldn't take his beloved motorcycle to school.

Once at school, he found Doug. Their friendship had been strained of late, with Drew being more short-tempered and secretive. He had blown off his best friend several times over the past couple of days, but he needed his help on this. Doug was to provide corroboration that Drew had indeed visited the doctor.

"I've got the note here," he said, pulling his buddy off to the side. "All you've got to do is back me up. Tell them that you were there and heard the doctor say that I could play. And then it's good-bye Tom Landry High! They won't have a chance," he gushed, his enthusiasm causing him to raise his voice.

"Yeah, yeah," Doug said, hushing his friend with his hands, "fine. Are you *sure* that you're okay?"

"For the last time, I'm fine, Mom. You saw my arm the other day. It's better now than it was then. Now quit worrying and let's get through this damn boring day."

The two pushed their way through the milling students to their first period classes, parting with a fist bump and an exchanged smile. Doug, though, stared after his friend for a moment or two, a concerned look on his face. Drew didn't seem to notice.

The young Collins was in high spirits, taking active roles in all of his classes, asking questions and offering his opinion on various subjects. His teachers seemed pleased, especially Miss Shimek, who seemed to think he was finally starting to take his studies seriously.

By the time gym class rolled around, he was feeling on top of the world. He dressed out for class for the first time since his injury, showing his note to Mr.Rew, who accepted it at face value and simply waved him towards the locker room.

He clowned with Doug during the whiffle ball game, flexing absurdly whenever Beth Cahill was near. She seemed entertained, giggling and posing back at him. At one point, after he hit a home run, she slapped his butt as he ran around the bases. He shook his finger at her and grinned.

After class Beth was waiting for him outside the locker room. She smiled hugely at him as he walked out. Drew flexed once more, just for kicks, and laughed with her as she took his arm. They started off down the hallway.

Drew looked down at her and smirked. "I think that I owe you this," he said, swatting her butt lightly. She jumped and slapped him playfully. "So, are you coming to the game tonight?" he asked, pulling her closer to him.

"Why, of course. I wouldn't miss a chance to see the stud in action," she replied, slyly shifting his hand back down to her butt. She winked and swirled away from him, heading off to lunch.

Drew stared after her, mouth dry. His hands clenched, and he trembled. He had a different kind of action in mind than just the football game. God, she was hot.

Doug joined him. He stared off in the same direction that Drew was. He just caught a glimpse of Beth disappearing into the cafeteria. He turned and looked at his best friend. Collins was trembling, muscles clenched, face flushed, and he was whimpering quietly.

"What the fuck? Jesus, Collins, get a grip on yourself. You're acting like a dog in heat or something." Drew didn't move. Jones reached out and pushed at his friend. "Dude, chill."

Drew spun, snarling. He knocked Doug's hand aside and struck him solidly in the face. Jones staggered back in shock, his nose bleeding.

Drew's vision cleared, and he saw his buddy standing in front of him with a bloody nose, dimly realizing what he had done. All he had seen had been Beth Cahill.

"Aw, man. Doug, I'm sorry. Really. I don't know what came over me. I didn't even know it was you. You okay?"

Doug wiped his nose. He looked at the blood on his hand, and then scowled at his friend.

"You asshole. What the fuck were you thinking? Shit. You could have broken my nose. I oughta bust you one back, you little shit-head." Jones pulled a handkerchief out of his pocket and wiped off his face and hand.

"Jones, it was an accident. I'm sorry," Drew said, moving closer to check on his friend. "Come on, let's go get lunch. Are you that big a pansy, I thought you were tougher than that," he teased, slapping Doug on the shoulder.

He stepped past his friend, intent on getting some food in him. Skipping breakfast had been a big mistake. Maybe he could eat twice, or take some freshman's lunch in addition to his own.

Jones shrugged and followed his best friend into the cafeteria. He'd live, and he needed food as much as Collins did. Didn't he outweigh Drew by fifty pounds? He was a growing boy.

●● ◖◯◗ ●●

By Friday afternoon, Ramona had discovered, care of the computer at the public library in Iowa Park, that Andrew Collins' father was one James Collins, a mechanic at Bernie's Harley-Davidson shop. The odds of the mechanic that they knew as 'Jim' being anyone other than James Collins were pretty slim. She dug further.

There was a story about one Helen Collins from three years earlier, gunned down in a convenience store robbery gone wrong. The killer had run off on foot, and been cornered by the Iowa Park sheriff, one Robert Parker. There had been an exchange of gunfire, and the young man had died. The sheriff had been cleared of any wrongdoing by a review board.

Apparently that had been only the second murder to happen in this quiet town of 6500 people since the year 2000. 'And then the Firar had come to town,' she thought. 'Add two more, and we're not done yet,' she told the monitor, bitterly.

She paused to catalog what she'd learned. First, the young man she'd bitten was Drew Collins, senior at Iowa Park, starting quarterback for the Hawks, and by all accounts, a good person who happened to get attacked by a wolf simply because he tried to save a little boy from getting mauled.

Secondly, this young man had already suffered a terrible loss when his mother had been brutally shot by a crack head, who in turn was shot by the local sheriff, who also turns out to be the boy's uncle.

Thirdly, the young man's father, already devastated by the loss of his wife, might also be the only witness to identify Wrench and Ramona as the bikers who had been in the shop just prior to the girl being snatched.

And now she had to find this guy's only son, explain to him that he was cursed, and see if he would be a good addition to the motorcycle gang that had helped destroy his life. Oh, yeah, this would go well.

'Don't forget, Ramona,' she told herself, 'there's a good chance that the same gang he needs to join-or-die may have to kill his father.'

She debated how much to tell Wrench. Probably as little as possible; that psycho would go off, do something stupid, and just make matters worse. Not that things could get a whole hell of a lot worse for the Collins family than they already were.

She left the Tom Burnett Memorial Library and headed back to Elliot, where she had left Wrench. Hopefully the stupid little shit hadn't gotten himself in any trouble while she was gone. They had a football game to go to tonight, to see the one and only Drew Collins in action.

●● ◖◉◗ ●●

Coach Stanton studied the note in his hand critically. He had thought that Drew had been bluffing about getting a release to play. The story went that he'd been hurt pretty badly during the attack, and for a doctor to clear him this early was definitely unusual. They were generally pretty cautious about such things.

After squinting at the completely illegible signature on the note, and considering the hospital stationery on which it was written, he looked at Drew. He really needed his star quarterback for the first game of the season.

"Looks like you're starting tonight then."

"Yes!" Drew pumped his fist in the air, and then high-fived Doug Jones. Life was good.

●●◐◖◯◗◑●●

The rivalry between Iowa Park and Landry High was strong, owing to the close proximity between schools. Landry High had been on top recently, but last year Iowa Park had squeaked by on a late touchdown run by Drew. This year promised to be another good game, despite what Drew and his teammates were saying about their rivals.

After a short trip, the bus stopped and emptied out its cargo of players, coaches, cheerleaders, and gear. Fans were already milling about the bleachers. The concession stands were opening up, and the marching band was assembling on the field to run their half-time show.

Collins was almost shaking with energy. Normally calm and cool before, during, and after games, now he was a bundle of nerves. He paced up and down the locker room, slapping shoulders and psyching up the other players. His manic display didn't go unnoticed.

"Drew, dude, chill out. Come on, just get dressed," Jones said, pulling him over to a seat in front of his locker. "What's the matter with you? You're making everybody nervous. You're supposed to be the calm one, remember? I'm the jump and shout and scream guy."

Doug lowered his voice, "Are you sure you're okay? I mean, seriously, can you do this?"

"Yeah, I'm fine. Just a little antsy, I guess. Feel ready to hit somebody. Wish I still got to play defense, you know? Other guys get to play both ways, why can't I?"

Doug looked again at his best friend. "Since when do you want to get dirty playin' defense? Prima donna quarterbacks don't have to sweat and work and stuff like us guys in the trenches. Besides, Coach don't want to lose you to some injury playin' D. Just concentrate on your job, okay?"

"Yeah, yeah... sucks, though," Drew said, pulling on his shoulder pads. He quickly finished dressing out and pulled his mouthpiece out of its plastic case, sticking it on his facemask. He spun around on his bench to face the other players, waiting for the coaches to send them out to warm up.

The stands were mostly full by the time the players finished their warm-ups and went back inside for last minute instructions. The Texas crowd was enthusiastic and loud. Security was on hand to ensure that the exuberance didn't overextend into violence.

Ramona and Wrench stood at the end of the visitor's bleachers, trying their best to blend in. Both decided to forego their normal leathery look for nondescript sweatshirts and jeans, in an effort to not stand out. The young woman had tucked her hair up under a cap, and wore sunglasses to hide her distinctive eyes.

Wrench, true to form, wore a grubby trench coat over his stolen Hawks sweatshirt. He was also of the opinion that such subterfuge was beneath him. His loud disagreement with Ramona's choices only vanished once she reminded him that Lobo had told them to go undercover.

The girl looked around at the people attending the game. They seemed happy, and excited about the upcoming sporting event. 'Like the outcome had anything to do with real life,' she thought. Pathetic. 'Get a life,' she silently told the people around her.

Not that she had a real life. Hers was an unreal existence; one that the people around her couldn't begin to comprehend. Hell, she didn't even understand her life. Survival itself was a day-to-day, moment-by-moment occurrence; any attempt at having an actual 'life' of any sort was beyond her at the present. And so here she was, spying on the innocent young man that she had afflicted with a terrible curse.

The rival teams ran out on to the field, accompanied by loud cheers from both sets of bleachers. The coaches for each team ran out as well, albeit with more reserve and dignity than the teenagers displayed.

After losing the coin toss to start the game, the Hawks kicked off. Landry High was unable to move the ball, thanks largely to the efforts of Iowa Park's massive tackle in the middle, Doug Jones.

He stuffed the Cowboy's tailback for a loss on third down, then narrowly missed blocking the following punt.

Drew ran onto the field, and stepped into the huddle. Doug, already with sweat pouring down his face, grinned at him and said, "Okay hotshot, let's do it."

Collins clapped his hands sharply to get everyone's attention. He called his first play: a play-action pass to Wilkins. "On two, guys. Ready—break!"

The Hawks bolted out of the huddle, lining up quickly. Drew looked over the defense and decided they were lined up correctly for the play they had called. He barked out the signals at the line of scrimmage.

The ball was snapped up into his hands, and he spun, faking a handoff to his running back, then turning to look downfield. Wilkins was cutting across the middle, but he was covered. As he started to throw short to his tight end, he saw Toby Johnson far downfield, sprinting into the clear. He was at least five yards behind everyone.

Drew double clutched, pulling the ball back in, and then fired deep, putting everything he had into the throw. At the ten yard line Toby turned and gathered the ball in, trapping it against his chest. He trotted the rest of the way into the endzone, and flipped the ball to the referee, sprinting back up the field to chest bump with his quarterback.

Collins set up the extra point attempt, holding the ball for the kicker. It was good, and just like that the Hawks were up 7-0. One play, 68 yards. He ran off the field happily, high-fiving his coach as he reached the sideline.

Iowa Park held on the next series, too, getting the ball back on downs right at midfield. This time Drew worked the ball downfield slowly, mixing runs with passes, until they were on the two-yard line.

Coach Stanton hesitated, then sent in the play. He didn't want to call a quarterback sneak, knowing that Drew was injured, but the play would work, he was sure of it. Plus Collins seemed to be fine.

Drew received the play from the sideline and grinned. He got to keep the ball and run it himself. Cool. He relished the chance to get hit, and to hit someone back. Confidently, he announced the play in the huddle, ignoring the look of surprise and worry on Doug Jones' face as he listened to his friend.

Collins took the snap and faked a handoff into the line. His fullback ran into a solid wall and stopped short of the endzone. Drew still had the ball, however, and was sprinting around the right end, heading for the goal line, one of the Landry linebackers in pursuit, angling to cut him off before he could cross the line. As Drew cut towards the endzone, the linebacker leapt at him, arms extended. Collins reached out with his left, and stiff-armed the bigger player, shoving him forcefully to the ground.

Drew danced into the endzone, holding the ball aloft. As his teammates surrounded him, he spiked the ball and leapt into Jones' arms. The big tackle held him up in the air for a moment, then dropped him back to the ground and slapped him on the side on the helmet.

"Dumb ass. Take care of that arm, you nit. What were you thinking?" Doug scolded.

"I was thinking that I needed to get into the endzone. The arm's fine," Drew responded, still smiling. "Come on, let's set up for the extra point. We still have work to do."

On the sideline after the extra point was made, Collins restlessly paced. He felt too full of energy to simply stand and watch the defense. They should let him play D, too.

He glanced around. In the stands, he could see classmates, their parents, and others, cheering on his team, and talking amongst themselves. He recognized most of them. Iowa Park was a small, close-knit community. It seemed like the entire town made the short drive to Wichita Falls.

His eyes were drawn to Beth Cahill, sitting in the middle of the stands with a group of her friends. She made eye contact and smiled. Drew smiled back, flashing her a thumbs up. The blonde blew him a kiss, and laughed. Her friends nudged her and giggled. Drew was brought back to the game by a loud roar from the other sideline.

Tom Landry High scored a touchdown of their own. Doug Jones came raging over to the sideline, screaming to anyone who'd listen that he had been held by two guys on the other team. Coach Stanton yelled at him to calm down, that they'd get it back.

After a short kickoff, and shorter return by Toby Johnson, Drew took to the field, intent on scoring another touchdown. He changed the first play that Stanton sent in, so that he could run the ball again.

Collins called his own number on the third play from scrimmage as well. He ran the option, a play that the Hawks never used with him in the game. Coach Stanton looked on from the sidelines as Drew called his own plays the rest of the drive, getting more and more livid as the drive progressed.

When Drew finally threw a short touchdown pass to his tight end, and then ran off the field, Stanton was waiting for him. He grabbed his quarterback's arm, and tried to yank the young man closer. The big man was used to being able to muscle his players when necessary, and his QB's disobedience warranted at least a rant.

Stanton pulled on Drew's arm, drawing him in. As the coach started yelling in his ear, the quarterback threw his arm up and back, knocking the coach's hand free. He growled in the coach's face and whirled away. Taking off his helmet, the young man hurled it at the water cooler and sat down at the end of the bench, holding his face in his hands.

No one approached him. Stanton glared at him for a moment, then directed his attention back to the field of play. The game continued. Landry High was not able to score this time, Jones breaking through his double team to sack the quarterback for a big loss on third down.

After the Cowboys punted, Coach Stanton sent Collins back in, with the admonition that if he changed even one play, he'd be benched. Drew looked his coach dead in the face, expressionless, and ran onto the field.

Stanton sent in the first play: a running play for the tailback. Drew called it in the huddle, and then stepped up to the line. The Cowboys crowded the line, guessing a running play was coming.

Drew saw it, glanced over at the sideline at his coach, and ran the play anyway. It didn't go anywhere.

On second down the head coach sent in another running play. Drew shook his head. The man was punishing him. He called the pitch, then broke the huddle. Once again, the Cowboys crowded the line. Drew glared again at Stanton, who was scowling at him.

'Screw him,' Drew decided. He called an audible at the line, changing the play to a play-action pass. As the middle linebacker for Landry crashed into the line to stop the run, Drew turned and fired the football to his tight end, who had run into the spot vacated by the defender. The play was good for twenty yards.

Coach Stanton called timeout. As Drew came over to the sideline, the big man was fuming. "I told you not to change a single play, Collins; what the hell was that?"

"Coach, they were ready for the run. You saw them. I know you did. I called the last play and it didn't work. I would have run this one, but they were set up for it. What do you want me to do; lose the game or win?" Drew shouted.

"I expect you to do as you're told. Changing the last play at the line was okay. Just don't go 'cowboy' on me and ignore the plays like you did the last drive," Stanton growled back, in his quarterback's face. "This is a team sport, Collins, not a personal showcase for you. Got it?"

"Yeah, I got it. Can we go play now? What do you want me to run?"

For the rest of the game, Drew ran the plays that Stanton sent in. The game itself ceased to be interesting by halftime, as Iowa Park had run up a 35-7 score. Stanton took his quarterback out of the game early in the third quarter, after Collins threw his third touchdown.

Drew stood on the sidelines and helped send in plays to Simpson. The junior still looked lost on the field, despite the four-touchdown lead. Collins gritted his teeth, refraining from asking Stanton to send him back in. In an effort to calm himself down, he took a mental step back from the game.

He closed his eyes and took a deep breath. The sounds of the game surrounded him. He could hear activities both on the field, and closer to him. He could pick out individual sounds from his team on the sidelines. There was a lineman behind him spitting out a mouthful of water. Over to his left, he could hear Coach Stanton talking rapidly to an assistant.

He could hear various people in the stands talking. A random word or two made their way to his ears. He grinned, hearing one of Beth's friends referring to him as a stud. He heard a hoarse voice, grating on his ears, complaining that it was enough, they could leave.

Drew turned to find the last voice. At the corner of the bleachers, there was a couple standing, talking to each other. They didn't seem to be agreeing, either. The man, the same person Drew had heard, was gesturing towards the parking lot. The woman was standing her ground, shaking her head.

The guy grabbed her arm, and the woman reacted with surprising violence. She grabbed the man by the throat with her free hand and twisted her arm out his his grip, moving very close to her partner. The young woman sneered in his face and thrust him away from her. He swore and stumbled away, heading towards the parking lot.

'Violent chick,' Drew thought, grinning. Little prick probably deserved it, though.' He should have stuck around for the rest of the game. After all, he had to, even though he didn't get to play anymore. He sighed, smile fading. Despite the big win, he felt unsatisfied. He also knew that there would be consequences to his earlier disobedience on the field.

By game's end, Drew was feeling stressed. He knew that not only was he in trouble for changing the coach's plays, his fake note ruse was bound to be discovered at some point. His uncle had been in the crowd during the game, and there was no way the sheriff would be fooled by the note. He'd seen Drew's arm at the hospital.

He was in a foul mood in the locker room. Oblivious to the good humor and horseplay around him, he sat at his locker with his head down. Jones came thumping over to sit beside him, wearing a towel, and dripping wet from the shower.

"Hey, hotshot. Why so glum? You got to play, we kicked their asses, and nobody got hurt. You look like you're ready to go in front of a firing squad. Or to a fight. Cheer up, dude."

Drew looked up. He forced a smile onto his face as he answered his big friend. "Yeah, we won, but I'm gonna be in deep shit," he said. "My uncle was at the game. He'll know I forged a note" he said glumly. "Then, just in case I wasn't stupid enough, I go and call my own plays and get in trouble with Coach." Drew stood up. "And to top it all off, I'm not even tired. I feel like the game didn't happen. I have all this fuckin' energy to blow, and the game's already over."

"Not tired? You should play defense, too. You know, like us grunts. You'd be tired, then. You didn't even have to play the whole game; Coach pulled you out like right after the third quarter started."

Drew sat back down and glared at his locker. "I know I should play defense. They won't let me." He slammed his helmet down on the bench. "It's not my fault they pulled me out early—I asked to go back in and they said no."

Doug laughed at his friend. He took everything so literally.

"I'm just kidding you, dude. You're our quarterback; you don't get to indulge in things like defense and blowouts. We need you healthy." He thumped Drew's back, rising to get dressed. "We won 48-14—enjoy it."

Drew dressed, and went outside to wait. The bus wouldn't leave for another half hour, most likely. He took a deep breath of the night air, feeling better. Looking around, he saw random groups of people milling, going over the game. He saw his aunt and uncle, talking with parents of other players, and ducked his head.

"Hey, big guy, nice game," came a sweet voice. The sound of Beth's words arrived at the same time as her scent reached his nostrils. He turned to see her approaching and smiled.

"Beth," Drew said, feeling awkward. "I saw you in the stands," he added lamely.

"I know. You were great today," she said, moving in close to him. "Do you feel okay? You looked a little sick or something on the sidelines."

"Uh, yeah. I just didn't want to come out of the game, you know. I want to play defense, too, and they won't let me," Drew said, sounding petulant, even to himself. "Sorry," he muttered, looking away. "I'm a jerk. The game was great, and we won. I should be satisfied with that, and be happy."

Beth reached up and trapped his face between her hands, turning him back to face her. She gazed into his eyes, concerned.

"Hey, it's a big deal to me if you're unhappy. You should be happy after a game like that, and if you're not, maybe I can help." She drew his face down to hers, kissing him on the mouth with ardor.

Drew stiffened in surprise, then kissed her back hungrily. His arms went around her, and pulled her tightly against him. The girl pressed against him, burying her tongue in his mouth. Her hands strayed down, grabbing onto his butt.

The young man responded instantly, growing hard, and pushing even harder against the voluptuous blond. One hand worked free to slide up her side, fastening on to a large breast. His other hand slid down to settle on her butt. She gasped and slid a hand to the front of his jeans.

Beth fumbled with his belt, pulling it open and unbuttoning his pants. She slipped down his chest, kneeling in front of him. She started to pull his underwear down.

Drew was suddenly aware of the fact they were outside; behind the bleachers, but still out in public. He looked around. If they got caught...

At the other end of the bleachers another woman stood, watching them. She removed her sunglasses and stared at Drew, who froze, staring at her flashing silver eyes. His erection failed immediately, as old nightmares erupted into his conscious brain.

He pushed Beth away from him, pulling up his pants and struggling to get past the surprised, and now upset, girl. "Hey," he cried out, buttoning his jeans and stumbling out from behind the bleachers. "Who are you?"

There was no one there. He looked frantically left and right, but the enigmatic woman was gone. He could just get a whiff of her scent, lingering on the air where she had been. He spun around to see where Beth had gotten to, and caught a glimpse of her retreating around the other end of the stands. Shit.

Drew heard other players coming out of the locker room, laughing and joking with each other. Shaking his head, he joined them in filing onto the bus for the return trip to Iowa Park. Taking a seat for himself, he turned to look out the window; still searching for the woman. She was nowhere to be seen.

Ramona watched Drew looking around, trying to spot her. She watched him board the bus and sit down, still vainly trying to locate her. She smirked. She'd caught him with his pants down, literally. Good thing Wrench hadn't seen them; he'd be all over her, trying to get her to do the same. Fat chance.

After the bus pulled away, she stepped out from her hiding place and walked back to the van. She thought about what she'd learned about her 'victim.' Obviously, he had recovered from his wounds already, a sure sign that he had contracted the disease. Sometimes they didn't. Collins had.

Watching him move during the game, he was well on his way to changing, too. Judging from the way people had talked about him during the game, he was previously a jock, and enjoyed success on the athletic field. To her discerning eyes, though, his movement was more feral than athletic. His movements had an edge to them, a hint of violence barely contained. That was part of every lycans' fundamental nature. It would be much more pronounced after his first transformation, but was already visible to someone looking for it.

She also noticed that he was handsome, in a rough and tumble way. She wasn't much of a football fan, but she knew that quarterback was usually considered the 'glamour' position, and the most likely to look like a big 'boy toy.' Collins looked more like a linebacker—someone who liked hitting people. At least he did to her, and her 'vast' knowledge of football.

Wrench was fidgeting behind the wheel of the van when she got there. "'Bout time," he grumbled as she got in the passenger side.

"Bite me," she shot back, settling in and putting on her seat belt.

The wiry little man put the van in gear and burned out of the parking lot. In the decrepit old Dodge, it wasn't very awe-inspiring. The battered old vehicle spun gravel and slewed sideways, power steering whining, and then lurched out into traffic, leaving teen-agers behind in the lot, laughing.

Wrench didn't seem to notice. He was pissed. He'd spent the whole night at this stupid high school football game, checking out the chicks, knowing full well that Ramona wouldn't let him bring home a 'guest.' And after the debacle with Lucy, Lobo would probably back her. He swore to himself.

Maybe this new guy, Drew or whatever, would provide some fun. Maybe he'd even get to kill him. Or at least that asshole mechanic. Wrench had staked out the Harley shop earlier, but there had been no sign of the guy. Tomorrow, perhaps.

Entertaining dark thoughts of primal pleasure, the biker drove back to the trailer. From time to time, he glanced over at his partner, but the woman was silent and uncommunicative, lost in her own thoughts. Wrench doubted that they were the same as his, unfortunately. Another boring night at their stupid trashy temporary home.

CHAPTER 23

When Drew arrived home after the game, his uncle's car was in the driveway. Waiting for him in the living room were his aunt and uncle, along with his father. All wore worried expressions. His uncle was also scowling.

The moment Drew was in the room, Parker laid into him. "What the hell was all that? How did you play in that football game? I talked with Stanton, and he said that you had a doctor's note."

Drew took a step back. His uncle was right in his face, furious. His nostrils were flared, his cheeks red, his eyes blazing. The older man put out his right hand and reached towards Drew's bandaged left arm. "Let me see your arm," he said.

Drew put his arm behind his back. The sheriff grabbed his nephew's shirt and pulled him closer, reaching again for the left arm. Drew twisted away and swore.

"Andrew Collins, you stop that right this instant!" Aunt Mary said, stepping between her husband and her nephew. "Let us see your arm right now." She stood with her arms crossed, tapping her foot expectantly.

Drew's lip curled. Who did she think she was, his mother? He started to fire back at her, and caught himself. These people cared about him, and were angry because they were concerned. His posture changed, and he became a normal seventeen-year old boy again.

He held out his arm for inspection. Parker gingerly prodded the bandages, then swiftly unwrapped the gauze. As the last of the dressing fell to the floor, the three adults leaned in closer to stare in awe at Drew's arm.

"Good Lord A' mighty! Would you look at that," Mary breathed. "How is that possible?"

Her husband looked shocked. The sheriff glanced suspiciously at his nephew's face, and saw embarrassment in his eyes. "Okay, Drew, what's up? Don't tell me that the hospital did some new treatment or some shit like that—I called them and you never showed up for your appointment today. So explain that," he said, pointing at the healed forearm.

Drew shrugged. His left arm looked almost the same as his right. The only evidence of his injuries was a small line of faint scars on the outside of his forearm, running from his wrist to his elbow.

"I don't know, uncle Bob. I didn't do anything. It hurt like…really bad for a couple of days, then it just went away. When I took the bandages off to change them, the skin was healed up, and the stitches were gone. I wanted to play in the game, so I lied about going to the doctor."

Parker's eyes narrowed. "How do you feel?"

"I feel fine, Uncle Bob. Really," Drew proclaimed. "I can't explain it, but what's the problem? My arm got better and I feel fine."

"Drew, this is a problem, regardless of how you feel. This kind of healing is unnatural. Has anything else happened?"

"Like what? I didn't grow wings or anything," Drew said, throwing his arms in the air. "God, you'd think that getting better and having energy and wanting to play football were all crimes or something." He turned to leave. "I'm going to my room, okay? It's been kind of a big day. By the way, we won. Not that anybody cares," he said, stomping away down the hall.

As soon as Drew's door slammed, Parker looked at his wife and brother-in-law. Mary still looked bewildered, James confused. As for himself, he was scared almost out of his mind. There was no rational explanation for Drew's healing, and he refused to consider any other options.

"Jim, this doesn't make sense. People don't heal like that. The doctors told us that he may never regain full use of his arm, and now less than a week later, he's better than ever," Parker stated, his voice rising despite himself. "And he got into a fight in school, is arguing with everyone around him, and generally acts like a bully. What the hell is going on?"

James looked up, shaking his head at Parker. "What are you trying to say, Bob? That my son is turning into something straight out of one of them old monster movies?" he said. "Lon Chaney, the Wolfman, right? Come on."

"I didn't say that," Parker grumbled. 'Out loud,' he added in his head.

"What are you saying, then?" Mary asked, still confused, and more than a little scared.

"I don't know. There's so much going on right now that doesn't make sense. First that body in the park, then the burned out farm, and now Drew. All three have wolves involved, but we can't find any sign of them," Parker said. "And those damn bikers figure into the first two, but not the last one. It can't be what I'm thinking, but I can't shake the feeling that it's all connected." His eyes narrowed. "If that gang was involved with Drew, too, I'd say that it has to be what I think, no matter how impossible."

"What? That the bikers that took Lucy were werewolves? Is that what you're trying to tell me, Bob? Jesus, and you think that I need help? You're nuts!" James exclaimed.

Mary quietly spoke. "Robert, there must be a different explanation. There are no such things as werewolves. Men can't turn into animals. At least, not like that. I don't know what's up with Drew, but it can't be related to him getting bitten by a wolf."

"Don't you think that I know that? Its just...there's no other explanation."

"Come on, Bob, if the bikers were what you think they are, wouldn't there be a connection to Drew as well? He got bit out in the middle of nowhere, with no one around but a bunch of Cub Scouts. No bikers. The only motorcycle within miles of that place was his," James argued.

Drew burst out of his room. He'd been listening behind his door to the entire conversation, his anger turning first into astonishment, then to fear. He came back into the living room, his eyes wide.

"There is a connection. The wolf that bit me, the big black one, had these silver eyes. I still have nightmares about those eyes. One of the bikers, this hot chick, um," he stammered, looking momentarily embarrassed, " I mean, a woman with long black hair, has the same crazy silver eyes. I saw her on the street once while I was riding around. She was smiling at me, and I…um," he paused again, nonplussed.

"Anyway, I saw her at the game tonight, too. She was dressed different, though, like in disguise. She took off her shades, and I could see her eyes. It was her."

James looked at his son skeptically. He raised his eyebrows. "So what are you saying, son? This woman is also the wolf that bit you? Does that make any sense at all?" He began to shake his head. "No, I refuse to believe anything that stupid."

Parker sighed. His guts had twisted during his nephew's story. It was one more piece to an already impossible puzzle that was his responsibility to solve. He just didn't think that he wanted to.

"I didn't say I believed anything like that, either, dad. It's just really weird, that's all. Like those bikers are everywhere, you know?" Drew said.

The elder Collins threw his hands up. "Well, I'm not going to have this stupid conversation in my home anymore tonight. Bob, Mary, thanks for coming over. Have a good night," James said, moving his company towards the door.

Parker stared back over his shoulder at his nephew, who looked back at him, his expression bleak. The older man sighed and followed his wife out into the night.

As the Parkers got into their car and prepared to leave, another car pulled into the driveway, blocking them in. Doug Jones jumped out of the front seat of his car and started for the front door of the house. Halfway there, he noticed the sheriff and his wife in their car, and stopped in mid stride.

"Hi, Sheriff Parker. Sorry, I'll move the car right away. I just needed to see Drew for a minute."

"Hi, Doug. No problem," the sheriff said, as Mary waved at her nephew's best friend. "Nice game tonight."

After moving the car, Jones headed back to the house. Drew met him at the door, stepping outside. "Hey Doug, what's up?"

Doug glared at his best friend. Drew, already stressed, stared back in confusion. Then he glanced at Doug's car, saw his girlfriend Sam in the passenger seat, and another shadow in the back. His heart sank. Shit, he'd completely forgotten about his 'date' after the game.

"Hey, asshole, forget something?" Doug whispered. " You were supposed to ride back with us, in my car, the one that my sister drove over to the game for us." He motioned towards his vehicle. "We were supposed to go out to eat, remember? It would have been bad enough with you along. Sam likes Megan, and hates Beth. After you switched dates for tonight, she almost refused to go, but I talked her into it." He shifted closer. "Then you go and stand us up, leave me sitting at Denny's with two chicks that just sat and glared at each other for an hour!"

"Man, I'm sorry. It just got to be too much and I forgot." 'Which is true,' Drew added, to himself. He took a deep breath and looked at Doug. "Look, right now isn't a good time. My dad is freaked out. My uncle, the SHERIFF, is freaked out. I got a lot on my mind." Drew shook his head. "I'll call you tomorrow, okay? Tell Beth... I don't know. I messed up big, and she's not even my type. What was I thinking?"

Doug stared at his friend in disgust. "So you're just going to go back into the house and leave me to clean up after your mess. This fuckin' sucks. Thanks for nothing, shithead."

Doug got back into his car, held up his hand to forestall questions from the back seat, and drove off.

Drew watched them leave, then turned back into his house. He dreaded going back into the living room and facing his father. Apparently his dad felt the same way, because as he stood outside, Drew saw the bedroom light go on. Even from out in the driveway, he could hear the door close.

With a growing sense of anger and frustration, he decided to go for a walk. The house seemed too confining. Maybe the cool night would provide some answers, or at least a distraction from his problems.

Deputy Jimmy Winslow sat at his desk at the mostly deserted station. He knew that he should be out patrolling: it was Friday night, after all. The first football game of the season had just ended, and the teenagers would be out in force, celebrating.

Instead, he continued his research. Over the course of the past several days, Winslow had spent many hours assembling a file on the outlaw biker gang known as the Fenris Firar. By cross-referencing information from the Internet with police files, he was able to piece together a large history of the gang's movements and possible activities.

Jimmy was aware that Sheriff Parker hadn't been impressed with his initial report. This time around, there would be enough information and conclusions to get a passing grade from even the toughest of critics: his boss.

Thinking about his boss made the young deputy realize that perhaps it was time to get back on the streets. If something went down, and he wasn't out patrolling like he was supposed to be, he'd be in serious trouble. Hastily sliding all of his papers into a folder, he went back out to his squad car. He had a long night in front of him, driving in circles and chasing teenagers who thought that everything was a joke.

In his haste to get back to his assigned duty, Deputy Winslow missed one of his files; a printout of a missing persons report from San Antonio, three years earlier. The black and white photo of a striking-looking eighteen-year old named Ramona Warner sat forgotten on the desk. The report was one of a suspected runaway that had possibly run afoul of a known outlaw motorcycle gang. Distinguishing characteristic of this girl was her striking silver eyes. Those eyes stared out at the empty room with no expression.

CHAPTER 24

Robert Parker was silent on the drive home from the Collins' house. His wife kept looking over at him from the passenger seat, but he wouldn't meet her eyes. He was afraid of what he might see. He really didn't want to talk about things right now.

Either his wife would think he'd lost his mind, or worse, she might agree with him. Normal people didn't consider the possibilities he was thinking of. And he refused to consider what the consequences were for his nephew. Perhaps he should just cling to the idea that there had to be a rational explanation for everything. Damn his overactive imagination.

Once safely in their own living room, with the lights on and curtains drawn, Mary Parker felt that it was time to break the silence. "Bob, talk to me. I'm at a loss. What's going on?"

Parker shifted on his side of the couch. He looked straight at the television, which didn't offer any solace. The stupid thing wasn't even on. He sighed and finally looked at his wife of twenty-five years.

"Mary, I don't talk to you about stuff. Usually Lem fills you in on stuff at work, but even he doesn't know what I'm thinking on this. He'd probably think I'm nuts, too. Hell, right now, even I think that I'm nuts."

"So start from the beginning," she said quietly, reaching over and clasping his hand. "I'm a good listener, you know."

Parker took a deep breath and tried to organize his jumbled thoughts. Maybe she *could* help. She sure as hell deserved to know what he was thinking at least. That way, if he *was* crazy, she'd have advance warning, and be better prepared when they took him away in the little white coat.

"We get this call last week. Girl wandering on 287, covered in blood. We find what was left of a guy in Pine Cone Park, all ripped up and partially eaten. Doc says it was wolves. Only there aren't any wolves in our area, haven't been for over twenty years.

"There was this motorcycle gang parked out there—twenty bikes with no people, according to the witness. Then when we get there in the morning, they're there and take off on us.

"Then Lucy Parsons disappears right after work. The next day, we find her body, badly burned but still obviously mauled and eaten by large animals, probably wolves." Parker paused and looked his wife in the eyes, a haunted look on his face.

"That same night, Drew gets bitten by a wolf that he says has silver eyes, just like one of the bikers that was seen at Bernie's. He gets taken to the hospital, almost dies from blood loss, but then makes a miraculous recovery, and now shows almost no sign of having been bitten at all," he growled, throwing his hands up. Calming himself, he took one of Mary's hands in his own and continued.

"Oh, yeah, and the kicker: all of this happens during the full moon. Full moon ends, so do the attacks. Gang vanishes along with the wolves." He stopped, gripping her hand tightly. He brought his eyes back up to hers.

"So, do you think that I'm crazy?"

Mary pondered his words for a time before smiling at him. "I think that you work very hard, and that you're good at your job. I'm not here to tell you that you're right or wrong. If this were an old monster movie, it'd make perfect sense," she told him.

"But, sweetie, seriously, there *must* be some other explanation. Maybe these bikers disguise their crimes, mimicking wolves to cause panic and confusion," she continued, patting his hand.

"Enough to fool old Doc Simon? The guy's an ass, but he's not an idiot." Parker felt frustration building, but kept his cool. "Besides, that still wouldn't explain Drew. You saw his arm. Barely any scarring, like it's had over a decade to heal."

Mary frowned. "I don't know," she said, finally. "I'd like to think that it was a miracle—you know, something good after all the bad things that he's been through." She sighed. "Except that it just seems, somehow…wrong."

Parker picked up her train of thought. "It feels that way to me, too. And the way he hid it…makes me think that he feels wrong about it, too," he said, concern evident in his voice. "I know that he has been acting a little off, too. Short-tempered and rude. He's been through a lot, but even when Helen died, he wasn't a rude child. There's something not right here."

"Come upstairs, Bob. Let's go to bed. You're too worried about this to think clearly. Let's forget about everyone else for a while and just enjoy life for ourselves for a time." Parker allowed his wife to take his hand and lead him upstairs.

•• (◖◗) ••

The Crazy Horse Bar was busy on Friday night. Nestled under the shadow of Mount Scott, about ten miles north of Lawton, it was doubtful that any of the patrons of the place appreciated the view. The Crazy Horse was a rough scene, home to serious power drinkers, outlaws, and biker gangs. Police presence was limited; nobody was innocent, or naïve, enough to stop there by mistake, so the cops figured they had better things to do than risk life and limb enforcing the peace at a place where nobody's life was worth dying for.

This left the denizens of the bar considerable latitude. Discipline, what there was of it, was enforced by a trio of gigantic bouncers that were paid to insure that the bar kept its profits high. So long as no one was killed, almost anything went.

That night, the place was packed. At least four different biker gangs were represented. As the booze flowed, the members got more and more animated. An early scuffle ended when the bouncers clubbed both fighters unconscious and dragged them outside, dumping them off to the side of the entrance.

Lobo watched the other gangs with interest. They were a hard lot, and lived the way they looked. There were no posers here; no rich guys pretending to be 'bikers' because they rode a hog and wore leathers. These were men and women who lived hard, violent lives, and thought they could handle anything thrown at them.

That made him smirk. Maybe someday he would invite another gang to 'party' with the Firar during full moon. Then he'd see just how tough those particular bikers were. That'd be a fun party for sure. He'd have to invite one of the gangs that had female members, so there could be some 'extra' fun before the moon rose.

In the meantime, they had time to kill, and needed to keep a low profile. No reason that they couldn't have some fun anyway. He snapped his fingers. Ulric immediately leaned forward.

"Let's set up some fun. Get Aardwolf to start an arm-wrestling contest, okay? We'll match up against the other gangs. Loser buys the beers."

"Gotcha, boss," the big man said, getting up from their corner table. Several of the other outlaws watched him as he walked up to the bar. He was a big man, but he moved with more grace than most guys his size. Glances were exchanged, grudging nods made.

Aardwolf quickly made the rounds, bringing each leader a shot of whiskey, and an invitation to enter the contest. After some discussion, four tables were cleared, and bikers paired off for the game. Lines formed at each table. Free riders, those bikers in the bar who lived the life but weren't members of any gang, served as referees.

Round one went to four members of the Firar. Lobo smiled as the next group took their places at the four tables. Two of this round's participants were women from the Firar. They were matched against much heavier women from other gangs.

Winnie and Piggy slammed their opponents' arms flat on the table in seconds, earning them raucous cheers from the males. They mocked their counterparts, and high-fived each other. Maybe they weren't nearly as attractive as Ramona, Lobo observed, but they were still useful. Strong as hell, too. Maybe he'd let them square off against some of the men.

Within minutes, the Fenris Firar had wiped out the other gangs. Only Caleb lost a match, to a biker that outweighed him by at least a hundred and fifty pounds. As the victorious lycans drank their tribute, the losers glared at them. Scattered muttering and complaining was heard throughout the bar.

Lobo pulled out a hundred-dollar bill. Waving it in the air, he announced that the next round was on him. The complaints changed to cheers, and the tension eased. 'Time for the next game,' the pack leader decided.

"Okay, let's have some fun," he cried out. "Bar slide!" Caleb and Aardwolf swiped the glasses and bottles off of the long hardwood bar; and then poured booze down the entire length of its pockmarked surface.

The crowd gathered as Ulric picked Caleb up, took two quick steps, then pitched him bodily onto the bar. The little man slid completely from one end to the other, shooting off the corner and into the waiting arms of some of the Firar.

Cheers went up as more booze was poured out. The leader of a local Mexican gang grabbed one of his men and rushed forwards. He too, tossed his man the entire length of the bar. The small Hispanic surfed down the wood surface and sailed out towards the assembled Firar.

The bikers crouched with outstretched arms, and just as the other biker soared into range, they all stepped aside, letting him crash onto the floor. The Firar roared with laughter, joined by the other patrons of the bar, with the exception of the Mexican gang.

The leader of 'Los Lobos,' however, looked pissed. His man had been disrespected by the other wolf gang, and it was a slap not just at him, but all the other members of his pack. He couldn't let the slight go unpunished.

A switchblade snapped open in his right hand. The burly outlaw stepped towards the leader of the Firar, only to be met by two of the monstrous bouncers. One shook his head. The other simply brought a bat up to his shoulder and glared. More laughter followed this.

Out maneuvered, the Mexican glared and folded the blade closed. He made a big show of putting it back into his pockets and raising his hands, to show that they were empty. The bouncers nodded and stepped back.

Lobo held out his hand to the leader of the other gang. After a brief hesitation, the man took it. They clasped hands, and the leader of the Firar offered his rival a drink. Again, the other man hesitated before accepting. The breach was healed. The game continued, although each gang now had their own people on hand to catch their own 'surfer.'

Several hours later, the bar closed down for the night. The parking lot became the scene of almost a hundred bikes firing up and riding off into the darkness. The Fenris Firar left right away, all in one bunched up pack, seemingly oblivious to anyone that might be watching or trying to follow them.

After about fifteen miles, the Firar pulled over into an empty field. A few minutes after, the Mexicans showed up. They pulled in and shut off their bikes. Thirty hard-looking men got off their rides, pulling out a variety of crowbars, pipes, chains, and baseball bats. They formed into loose ranks, four rows deep, and faced Lobo and his pack.

"Gringo, you disrespected us. We're here to accept your apology," their leader growled. He held his switchblade up and scowled. "Even if I have to cut it out of you."

Lobo stood in front of his men and women, relaxed and at ease. He had manipulated the scene back at the bar to produce just this situation- the upcoming brawl would provide the real fun for his pack. The Firar, despite being slightly outnumbered, were sure to come out of this fight the winners.

The shaggy biker took off his vest and tossed it on the ground behind him. "You ask for my apology? Here it is, then: I apologize that Mexico has no real men. I apologize that their women must have sex with limp-dick chickens with no balls." He smirked at his people, and then grinned mockingly at his counterpart. "I apologize that these same chickens soil the great American motorcycles that they ride. And I apologize to the dirt here, that it will soon be covered in the blood of these worthless chicken-shits."

The squat Mexican spit in the direction of Lobo and hissed, "Chinga tu madre, puta," and then roared unintelligibly, charging headlong towards his foe, the rest of his gang following close behind.

The Fenris Firar howled into the night air, and rushed to meet the charge. The two groups crashed together, quickly dissolving into small knots of swirling chaos. Individual battles raged back and forth, punctuated by loud cries and savage yells. Blood spilled on the ground as bodies fell and remained prone.

Lobo took out the opposing leader himself, blocking his initial knife thrust, then seizing his wrist with both hands. Stepping under the man's outstretched arm, Lobo wrenched his wrist inwards, feeling it snap. The knife was driven into the Mexican's own ribs by the move.

The man's eyes widened in shock. He grunted, and started to pull the knife out, but Lobo held his arm, keeping the knife in place. He smiled into his foe's face and drove a knee into his chest, knocking him over backwards. The leader of the Firar moved on to find someone else to play with.

Ulric was similarly having fun. The big man grabbed two rival bikers and slammed them together viciously. They slumped and fell to the ground. He immediately grabbed another by the arm and yanked, dislocating his shoulder. The man yelped in pain and swung his other fist at the Firar enforcer. It landed flush on his nose, which cracked and sprayed blood.

The ugly biker growled and caught the mustached man's other fist in his left hand. Twisting his arms into a pretzel shape, he hurled him bodily into yet another biker, knocking both off their feet. By the time the second man had disentangled himself, Ulric had kicked them both in the head, knocking them unconscious.

All around the lot, the Fenris Firar took care of business. The Mexican gang, no matter how determined, was simply no match for the lycanthropes. Even in human form, the bikers were stronger and faster, not to mention more violent, than their counterparts.

Within a few minutes the fight was over. None of the Mexicans were still on their feet, while all of the Firar were standing. Many had injuries, but those would heal quickly. The same could not be said for the members of Los Lobos.

The Firar checked over their fallen foes. Despite their brutality, the outlaw bikers had been careful not to kill any of their opponents. Injured and beaten, but alive, the Mexican gang wouldn't make any trouble for the Firar. Outlaws settled things for themselves. A death, however, would probably involve cops. Or worse, the Feds

Satisfied their fallen foes would survive, the bikers mounted up and took off. All things considered, Lobo thought as they roared off into the night, it had been a decent evening.

CHAPTER 25

The next three weeks were a bureaucratic nightmare for the sheriff of Iowa Park. Robert Parker spent most of his time filling out paperwork on the recent "activities" his normally quiet town had been subjected to. Despite a towering pile of physical evidence that was added to daily, no progress had been made in the cases.

At least, not any progress that could be committed to paper. Parker felt that every new clue pointed towards his impossible conclusion, which he *knew* couldn't be voiced. With his men, he was gruff and noncommittal, insisting that there had to be a logical explanation for everything.

Alone was a different matter entirely. He would hold his head in his hands, and pray that he would wake up from this nightmare. No matter how he arranged the evidence, nor what reaches he made in an effort to explain what had happened, he saw only one answer to the questions stacked on his desk.

Winslow had brought him in a thick file that he'd painstakingly assembled on the biker gang. There were dozens of photos, bios, and news articles in it, along with interviews with various law enforcement officials. Parker looked through it once, seeing only that the inferences and conclusions seemed to point towards his own theory. So he tucked the folder away in the bottom of his desk and tried to forget about it.

The deputy was disappointed, and a little bitter, that his boss showed so little gratitude for his hard work and initiative. Every time he tried to bring up the file, Parker blew him off. There were hours of his own time poured into that file, in addition to time spent on the clock. The least the sheriff could do was show some appreciation.

Lem was completely unsuccessful in getting his boss to talk. While Parker was always closed-mouthed, he at least shared most of his thoughts with Lem during a case. This time, though, the sheriff spoke less and less as time went on.

In an act of desperation, Lem had called Mary, hoping to find out more information. The normally friendly and communicative woman was surprisingly distant and quiet, deflecting all of his questions and saying only that her husband was working hard to find answers.

Finally, Lem sat down with Ray Becker, to go over the caseload. Ray admitted to being stuck too, but advised patience with Parker. 'Big surprise,' Lem thought sarcastically. Becker always advised patience. Whoever taught Ray Becker as a child that 'patience was a virtue' beat that one into his head.

Getting nowhere with his older, more experienced coworkers, Lem started spending more time with Jimmy Winslow. The young man was serious about finding answers, and increasingly frustrated at the lack of progress. The two made an unlikely pair: the tall, lanky white man with an ever-present toothpick, and the short, young black man bursting with energy. Nevertheless, they were frequently spotted at Albertson's, drinking coffee and going over notes at all hours of the day.

Unfortunately for the duo, they failed to make any real progress on the cases. They kept coming up blank, despite the fact that two of the bikers that they were searching for were staying mere minutes away from them.

Ramona and Wrench had been hiding out at the trailer for almost twenty days, and their cover was wearing thin. The fat manager had been missed, and his van was beginning to be dangerous to drive around. So far, the police hadn't been seen at the trailer park, but that could change at any moment. It was time to move on.

'Just as well,' Ramona thought. Wrench was intolerable to live with. Out in the open, surrounded by the rest of the Firar, he was kept in check. Alone, he was a constant source of stress. That she hadn't already killed him was a small wonder.

Twice already, the two had come to blows. Neither time was serious, but it had definitely heightened the tension in the trailer. Now, they didn't even speak to each other. Wrench frequently disappeared at night, likely working out his frustrations by catching and killing wild animals, and the odd pet that was wandering loose.

Ramona devoted most of her time to covertly following the younger Collins. She was certain he hadn't seen her since that Friday night after the football game. She wasn't sure how to approach him now, but the time was drawing near.

After three weeks of observing him, Ramona was even more disheartened by what she had done to him. His life was effectively over, and he didn't even know it yet. He hadn't done anything to deserve this curse, yet he had it. That much she could tell. Very soon, he would go through his first change, and his life would never be the same.

It was Monday, and the moon would be full on Wednesday. Ramona had to find a way to warn the young man about what was coming, but she had no idea how. How do you tell a complete stranger that they have an ancient curse that would turn them into a wolf at the full moon? Definitely not a casual conversation.

The only way was to approach him directly, when he was alone. She was certain he would recognize her; it was just a question of whether or not he'd take the time to listen to her before going to the cops. Or just running away.

She'd also have to take Wrench with her, to stand watch. Hopefully he'd stay out of the conversation itself. It was doubtful that he'd have anything positive to add to it. Like he added anything positive to any situation.

"Wrench, we're getting out of here," she announced, getting up off of the couch. The raven-haired beauty grabbed her few things and tossed them into a bag, which went over her shoulder.

"Where we goin'? It ain't time for supper yet." Wrench smirked. "We gonna go watch your little boy some more? Maybe kick this thing into gear, finally? Lobo must be tired of waiting for us."

"We're going to talk with the Collins kid. He needs to know what he is, and what's going to happen to him."

"Whatever, just so long as we can get out of this shit hole."

"Yeah, we're out of here. Don't leave anything behind," she warned.

"No worries, Ramona. I got all my stuff. We gonna torch this place?" he asked hopefully. "Nothing like a little fire to liven things up."

"No," she sighed. "We set the last place on fire, remember? We don't want to advertise the fact that we were here. So, why would we do something that would announce to the cops that we hid out here?"

Wrench didn't answer. The two locked up the old trailer and left in the battered old Dodge van. Their ride was smelly, clearly on its last legs, but it had served them well. A couple more days, and they could abandon it and get their bikes back.

●● ◖◉◗◉◗◖●●

Drew's life had taken a turn for the worse. He'd looked forward to his senior year with great anticipation, and it had started out as if all his dreams were going to come true. Football practice was going well; he actually mostly enjoyed his classes; and above all, a fledgling relationship with Megan Stuart.

Then the bottom fell out. First, a wolf attack sent him to the hospital. After horrible pain, and even worse nightmares, he had healed miraculously, and was able to play ball. Only nothing was the same. He felt no joy or satisfaction in their first win of the season, even though he played well. The next two games were the same: he played great, and they won both handily, yet he still felt wrong. Even meeting Mike Leach, the head coach of Texas Tech, failed to impress him. Nothing seemed to matter.

He'd also screwed up his chances with Megan by fooling around with Beth Cahill, then dumping her with no explanation. Now, both girls were angry with him, as were their respective circles of friends.

What was worse, his friendship with Doug Jones was on the rocks. While they still remained best friends, a distance had formed between the two of them that had never existed before. They were uncomfortable with each other, and neither knew how to fix things. Lunchtime in the commons was frequently an awkward silence, as both ate quickly, and made excuses to leave.

When Drew left the practice field Monday afternoon, he noticed a white van driving by slowly. He'd seen the same beat up Dodge a couple times before, but thought nothing of it, lost in his own world as he was. This time, though, he caught a flash of long black hair on the passenger side, and a face, quickly averted.

After a quick shower, and an uncomfortable wave to Doug, Drew slipped back outside. He glanced around, trying to find the van again.

It was in the parking lot, stashed behind someone's big truck, no one inside. He tried the doors, and found them locked. Looking inside, he saw trash scattered around the interior, and two leather jackets heaped on the floor between the front seats. As he strained to see more details on the coats, he failed to notice the two shadows that appeared behind him.

"Find anything, prick?" Wrench snarled from close behind.

Drew whirled, dropping down into an instinctive crouch, teeth bared and both hands clenched into fists. He glared at the two people that had him cornered against the van.

The woman laughed, a low, throaty sound. Her posture was relaxed, hands hanging easily down at her sides. "Relax, boy, we're not here to hurt you," she said.

The other one, the male, looked like he *was* there to hurt someone. He moved closer to Drew, into striking range. His threatening stance and manner was unmistakable. This was a man about to attack.

"Down, jackass. We're here to talk to Drew, not fight," Ramona snapped. "I said, *back off*!" She stepped between the two males, pushing the shorter biker back and away from Drew. "Wrench, go for a walk. Now!"

The hairy man sneered and sauntered off, flipping the woman the bird behind her back, and making a throat-cutting motion at Drew, before disappearing behind parked vehicles. Drew watched him go, then turned his attention back to the female biker.

He knew even before she removed her sunglasses that she would have silver eyes. He'd seen her at least twice before, and recognized her hair, shape, and, surprisingly, her scent. Still, he flinched when the glasses came off and those uncanny eyes stared into his own.

"Drew, we need to talk. My name is Ramona. We've met before," she said. "There are things that you need to know, and we're running out of time."

"Who the hell are you?"

"Ramona. I just told you that. Not very bright, are you?" She raised an eyebrow at him. "I guess what they say about football players is true: just big dumb jocks."

"Yeah, yeah, I heard that part. I mean, who *are* you?" He felt his temper rising at her patronizing tone.

"That's what we need to talk about, big boy. About me, and you, and what's going to happen to you in two days," she said softly.

"Maybe I should just call the cops. They're looking for you, too."

"What, call your uncle, the big bad sheriff?" Ramona was pleased by his reaction to her words. "Don't look so surprised, Collins, I know all about you. And your father. We need to talk about that, too. So, come on, let's go somewhere to talk, okay?"

"Just tell me what you need to say, then leave me alone," Drew slipped a little to the side, hoping to find an angle to escape if the other biker returned. The woman noticed and smirked.

"All right, here's the short and nasty version: you got bit by a werewolf. In two days, there's a full moon. You'll turn into a wolf. It'll hurt like hell, and you might attack people. Stay away from everyone that you know on Wednesday night. Clear out. You can go with us."

Drew cut her off before she could say anything further. He was shaking his head vigorously. "No, no, no. That's nuts. I got bit by a wolf. There are no such things as werewolves, and you're wanted by the police. Get out of here, before I call them."

Ramona grabbed his arm. "I'm not kidding, boy. Calling the cops won't help you. You're going to turn, whether you believe it or not. Come with me. We can help you."

Drew twisted free of her grasp and pushed his way around her. The chick was freaking him out. It was unnerving, hearing his uncle's fantastic theory from this woman's lips, while staring into those eyes, the same eyes that had haunted his dreams for weeks. The same eyes that belonged to the coal-black wolf that had savaged his arm.

"Lady, I'm leaving now. Go the fuck away." He stalked off, keeping an eye out for the little guy that had been with her. He was angry enough now to actually hope to run into him.

Drew got to his bike without being stopped. He put on his helmet, fired up the Honda, and left the lot. He watched behind him the entire ride home, to see if the van followed him, but he didn't see anything.

Once at the house, he put the bike away and watched out the living room window. The van never showed. If his father was curious about his strange behavior, he didn't let it show. He just sat in his chair and glared at the television.

Eventually, Drew sighed and gave up. The bikers hadn't followed him. They probably already knew where he lived anyway. Ramona seemed to know a lot about him, she could easily have found out his address.

Ramona. The biker chick was attractive, and got under his skin. Her scent was intoxicating, and her long black hair was so luxurious that he longed to run his fingers through it. And then there was her body...

Drew brought himself out of his daydream, reminding himself that the 'hot biker chick' was also dangerous as hell, and probably crazy. The last thing he wanted was to have more to do with her. He needed to get back to reality.

Drew picked up the phone and called Megan. He had been trying to apologize to her for two weeks, but she didn't want to talk to him. Maybe now she would.

The phone rang. And rang. It clicked over to an automated message, asking the caller to leave their name and number. Drew hung up. He didn't want to leave a message for Megan on the family answering machine.

He dialed Doug's number next. His friend had his own cell phone, like most of the other kids in Iowa Park. Drew was one of the few without one. Megan probably had one, too, but Drew didn't have her number. Jones picked up on the second ring.

"Hello," Jones said.

"Hey, Doug, it's me. What are you doing right now?" Drew asked.

"Nothin'. Just ate. Was gonna kill some time before Monday Night Football. Why? What's up?"

"I had an interesting run in with a couple people after practice today, and I'm a little freaked. Can you come over?" 'Please,' Drew added mentally.

There was a hesitation on the other end. Finally, Doug cleared his throat. "Sure. I'll be over in about ten minutes. See ya." The line went dead. Drew looked at the receiver in his hand and wondered if Doug was taking lessons from his uncle. Someday, he was going to hang up first on someone.

True to his word, Doug pulled into his driveway ten minutes later. He got out of his car and went into the back yard with Drew, so they could talk without Drew's dad overhearing them. As soon as they got into the backyard, however, the dog from next door began growling and barking at them. Drew growled back under his breath, and cursed at the Rottweiler. Finally, the dog went back inside, its owner scolding it in half-hearted fashion.

"Okay, bud, tell me," Doug said.

Drew took a deep breath. "I met the bikers that Uncle Bob and the rest of the police are looking for. They came to the school to talk to me."

"No shit?" Doug was surprised. "Why the hell would they do that?"

Drew looked his friend in the eyes, then looked away. This was going to sound stupid. Or worse, crazy. He took a deep breath. "The chick that I saw before, she told me that I was bitten by...well, a werewolf. And that I'm going to turn into one at the next full moon." Drew paused, waiting for his best friend to laugh.

Doug was silent. He studied his friend closely. His eyes narrowed, and he asked, "So what do you think?"

"What do you mean, what do I think? I think she's got a screw loose. I mean, think about it: I'm going to change into a wolf? That's impossible!" Drew said with heat.

"Yeah, like your arm healing? Because that was totally normal," Doug responded. "Fast healing was always a part of being a werewolf, you know."

"This isn't a damn movie, you dork. There is no way in hell that I become a hairy monster and run around howling at the moon."

"Then why am I here, listening to this? You got to be a little worried. What gives?"

Damn. Doug was big, but he wasn't dumb. Drew wanted to talk, to make himself feel better, but there were some parts of this that he didn't want to talk about. And Jones, the big jerk, was zeroing in on those parts.

"Okay. Remember the wolf that bit me?" Drew asked. Doug nodded. "It had these really weird silver eyes."

"Yeah, you told me. So?"

"Well, Ramona, the girl, has the same eyes. The exact same eyes. Who the hell has silver eyes, Doug?" Drew began pacing back and forth. "How can she have the same color eyes as the wolf did?"

Doug didn't have an answer. None of this made sense to him. At least, not rationally. The only answer that would explain everything was straight out of a horror movie, and he wouldn't even give that idea a second thought if he hadn't seen Drew's arm for himself. It still gave him the creeps just thinking about it.

"So, what do I do? Should I call the cops or not?" Drew demanded.

"Why wouldn't you call the cops? They're both wanted, aren't they? If you don't call them, you're like an accessory, or something. Unless there's a reason not to call them?" Jones asked, looking at Collins.

Drew hesitated and looked away again. He was scared, afraid that the biker chick was right. Despite everything that his brain told him, he was worried that something was horribly wrong.

Doug seemed to read his thoughts. "Hey, Drew, come on, man. Think about it. There has to be some other answer. Maybe it's all some sick joke or something. It'll be okay. We'll figure something out."

"Like what? Exorcism? Maybe a really good shrink? Keep me inside and away from any windows during the full moon? Shit!" Collins spat.

"I was thinking more along the lines of getting you a regular doctor. You never did go back to the hospital, did you? There's no way you would have gotten away with it, except your dad is..." Doug trailed off, not knowing how to finish his thought.

"Yeah, I know," Drew agreed. "I don't know if I want to go to a doctor, though, to get poked and prodded. If they find anything weird, I'll end up some lab rat or something. And if they don't find anything, I'm back to just being crazy again."

"What, then? Just wait around for the full moon, and see what happens? I don't think that would be your best bet, either."

Drew threw his hands up in the air. "Damned if I know. I feel like I'm ready to explode all the time. I don't have any answers, I just feel like hitting someone. "

"I noticed. A little horny, too? I mean, more than normal," Doug added, seeing his friend's look. "What?" he demanded.

"Like you should talk. You're the horniest guy I know," Drew retorted, somewhat lamely. Doug was right. His libido was out of control. It had cost him his budding relationship with Megan, and was probably keeping him from calling the cops on Ramona and that creepy little guy, Wrench.

"Bite me," Doug replied sarcastically. "By the way, Beth was asking about you again. Want to try again?"

"No. I don't know what I was thinking."

"You weren't, dude. At least not with your brain. I still don't know why you dumped her in the first place. What happened that night?" Doug asked.

Drew looked embarrassed. "It was right after the first game. She met me outside, behind the bleachers. We were making out, and right there, she started to go down on me. I couldn't believe it. I looked around, to make sure no one was watching, and there she was. Ramona, just was standing at the end of the bleachers, staring at us. I ran away from Beth, and couldn't face her again."

"The biker chick caught you? That's awesome," Doug chuckled.

"Screw you, Jones. It isn't funny."

"You're right," Jones said, still laughing. "It's hilarious." Drew looked indignant for as long as he could, before he, too, started laughing.

"Okay, so it's a little funny. Seriously, though, what do I do? Ramona knew all kinds of stuff about me, and I think they've been stalking me."

"I don't know, you're supposed to be the genius. I'm just the dumb lineman."

Doug grinned at Drew. It was the best they'd gotten along in weeks. The seriousness of the situation receded in the face of their renewed camaraderie.

"So, genius? What next? Shall we stay home Wednesday night and put you in a doggie collar? We could get you some Alpo and your own food dish."

"Hey, this is serious. I have a couple of wanted felons stalking me, and we both know that there's weird shit going on."

"So, let's wait out the moon, then. Prove that it's not true, and then go from there." Doug pulled out his phone. "I think we start there. Let me make a call or two, and we'll have us a werewolf party," Doug said, still smiling.

"Nothing stupid, okay? Just us. My house after practice. Got it?" Drew asked. Doug held up his hand. Drew slapped it, and they walked back to the front yard.

As Jones got back into his car, Drew called to his best friend. "Hey, Doug... thanks."

Doug looked out at his long-time comrade and smiled. "Bitch."

"Jerk," Drew snapped back, grinning as Jones peeled out of the driveway. At least now he wasn't going through all of this alone. It felt good, for the first time in a long time.

As he walked back into his house, he froze. There was a familiar scent in the air. He looked around, stepping back out onto the driveway. Drew didn't see anything, but he knew that Ramona was out there. Damn. He couldn't find her, and wasn't sure what he'd do if he did.

Eventually, he gave up and went back inside. A silver-eyed shadow detached itself from a tree across the street and walked away.

CHAPTER 26

Drew survived Tuesday. It only lasted an eternity. Wednesday wasn't any better, but at least it marked the week being more than half over. The one and only positive thing to come out of the school day was a possible reconciliation with Megan. She actually looked at him in the hallway before lunch, offering a half smile before walking away with her friends.

The way Drew's luck was going, he considered that a major victory. Maybe after things calmed down they could be friends again...or maybe even more than that. He could use some stress relief. Yeah, like Beth was going to do before... 'wait, calm down, jerk,' he told himself. Megan wasn't like that.

Neither was he; he had morals, and standards. This had to just be some stupid phase he was going through. Soon, hopefully very soon, he'd go back to his normal, horny-but-terrified-of-girls self. Right now he felt like a walking, talking hormone. Maybe this was how Doug felt all the time.

Except Doug probably didn't feel so violent. Drew was so keyed up, he barely made it through the school day without punching someone. Football practice was even worse. Playing quarterback was a pain: he wasn't allowed to get hit in scrimmage, and obviously he couldn't hit anyone else. God, he felt like a kicker.

Once practice was over, he rode his bike home and ate a fast supper, alone. His father wasn't there, only a note saying that he was eating over at Bob and Mary's. Strange, but also good. Perhaps they could patch things up, too. It also meant that the house would be empty for the evening.

As he cleaned up the kitchen, he turned on music. His father was a die-hard aficionado of classic rock, as befit a guy into bikes, he supposed. Drew himself was more into modern rock. He turned up the volume on the stereo. Doug would have to put up with his tunes. The big lineman was a country fan.

Drew heard a sound and looked around, catching a quick glimpse of a face peering in his window. He knew who it was, the silver eyes were a dead giveaway. Walking quickly to the front door, he yanked it open and shouted, "Go the fuck away! I told you if I saw you again, I'd call the cops, and I...umm, hi," he trailed off stupidly. Standing in front of him on the porch was Megan Stuart, looking scared to death.

"Drew? Doug invited me to come over, but I'll just go, if you want," she said, backing away.

"Megan? No, stay! I mean, please stay. I'm glad you're here. I wish doofus-boy would have told me, though."

"What was all the yelling about?" Megan asked.

"Uh, I thought that I saw something in the window. I was just trying to chase them off. I didn't hear you drive in," he answered, looking away.

Heavy steps on the porch announced Doug's arrival, sounding loud and clear even over the music. "Hey guys, it's me," his cheerful voice sounded. Doug came in the door, winced at the music, and shook his head sadly. "Drew, you got to learn how to properly treat a lady. This shit is unsuitable for Ms. Stuart," he said, covering his ears and winking at Megan. "You should be serenading her with something that has a little melody and style."

"For your information, Mr. Jones, Megan is a bigger fan of this music than I am. So there," Drew retorted, sticking his tongue out at Doug, which earned him a giggle from Megan.

"I suppose," Doug grumbled. "It still sucks."

"So, what are we going to do? I was just told that we were going to keep you company tonight, because things were going badly for you. What's going on?" Megan asked.

Drew looked at Doug, who simply shrugged and looked away. He returned his attention to the attractive blond, which was easy enough to do. What to say to her, on the other hand, was more difficult.

"I have some issues with getting bitten last month. It messed with me, made me do some stupid things that I really, regret now. Tonight, I just need some company."

"Well, what should we do?" Megan asked.

Doug chose this moment to join back in. "Hey, we could raid the refrigerator, and then play a killer game of Monopoly. Or just watch a movie, I guess."

"My vote is for Monopoly. I haven't played that game in years," Megan said.

Drew shrugged. Whatever they wanted to do was fine. He was feeling restless. Digging through the closet, he found the old board game and brought it to the table. Megan poured them each a soft drink, and Doug emptied the refrigerator of everything edible he could find, throwing it all on the table next to him.

What ensued was a high-spirited, loud game, full of teenage jokes and spilled snacks. For the next few hours, Drew was able to forget his worries and just be a normal seventeen year-old. As they played, the sky outside darkened.

In mid-laugh, Drew was suddenly struck by a wave of nausea. Resisting the urge to vomit, he stood up, shakily and ashen-faced. The other two stopped and looked at him in concern.

"Drew? You okay, bud? You look a little green," Doug asked.

"Yeah, I think so. Suddenly just don't feel so hot," he said weakly. Another wave hit him, this time with an accompanying sense of wrongness that radiated from his bones. Pain, too. Shit.

"I'm gonna go to my room for a minute, okay?" Drew said. Without waiting for an answer, he bolted from the table, racing down the short hallway and slamming his door shut. Drew stood on the other side, chest heaving. Something was wrong. Way wrong.

Doug and Megan looked at each other. Both stood up and started talking at the same time.

"I'll just go and check on…"

"Wait here and I'll be right…"

Megan smiled and waved Doug back to his seat. She walked down the hall and knocked on Drew's door. She received no answer, but could hear him moving inside. Quietly, she turned the knob and pushed the door open.

Drew was standing in front of her, holding his head in his hands. He was shaking. Tentatively, she reached out and touched his arm. "Drew, are you okay?"

The young man flinched, lowering his hands and turning to look at her with bloodshot eyes. "Megan, I…I don't know. It hurts. All over." And it did. His whole body felt like it was trying to turn itself inside out.

The young woman stepped into his room and put her arms around him. Drew shivered, and hugged her back. The pain subsided. His nausea passed, leaving him feeling weak but steady.

"Drew, you are burning up. Your whole body feels flushed." Megan held his face in her hands, turning it slightly and studying him closely.

Their faces were very close. Megan was warm, soft, and oh so tender. He leaned down, pulling her closer yet. Their lips touched. Megan closed her eyes and pulled his face down more strongly, kissing him harder.

Collins moaned and held her tightly. He kicked his foot out and caught the open door, sending it solidly back into place against the doorframe. Locked in their embrace, the couple fell against the closed door and continued their kiss.

Drew's pulse raced, his heartbeat thundered in his ears. He kissed Megan fiercely, thrusting his tongue into her mouth. He pushed against her, pinning her up against the door.

Megan gasped and tried to pull away. Things were starting to happen a little too fast. She broke contact with Drew's mouth and turned her head away. Trying to catch her breath, she mumbled, "Drew, let's slow down, okay?"

Drew growled and fastened his lips on her neck, kissing her hungrily. He held her close with one arm, reaching up her shirt with his other hand. She shook her head, trying to get her hands up between them.

"Drew, no! Come on, stop it," she insisted, pushing at him. She pushed his arm back down, pulling his hand out from under her shirt. "That's enough."

Out of control, Drew ignored her. Primal forces were driving him. He seized her hair, pulling her head back further, greedily kissing her throat. He pushed away her hands and grabbed at her chest.

As Megan cried out, Drew suddenly felt an immense surge of white-hot pain lance through his entire body. His bones felt like they were exploding with molten fire. He arched his back, bringing his head up from Megan's neck. He roared in agony.

His right hand ripped downwards, tearing the girl's shirt open. In spite of the pain, the sight of her black bra, just barely covering her breasts, enflamed his passion again. He brought his hand back up, and grabbed for the top of her bra strap, intent on ripping it off of her.

The sight of his hand stopped him. The hand gripping Megan's bra strap was covered in coarse gray and black hairs, with long, curved claws where fingernails should have been. The fingers themselves were thicker and shorter than they were supposed to be.

Shock flooded through him. His nightmares were becoming reality. Suddenly, he realized what he was doing. He was in the process of hurting this girl that he cared about. He was becoming a monster, a loathsome beast.

Sickened, he released Megan and pushed her away from him. She fell to the floor, sobbing. From the other side of the door, he could hear Doug pounding on the wood, demanding to be let in.

Another wave of agony hit. His spine twisted, forcing him to hunch over. His skin was crawling, like static electricity was crackling all along his body. Drew's groping hand found the doorknob.

As the door flew open, and Doug pushed his way into the room, Drew swung his arm like a club, knocking Jones to the side, and bolting down the hallway. Barely aware of his surroundings, knowing only that he had to get away, he crashed through the kitchen window and fell into the backyard.

Rolling to his feet, he felt yet another prolonged burst of pain course through him. Bones twisted and expanded, his muscles shifting under his skin. His clothes were beginning to suffocate him, so he shed them as best he could. Long gray and black hairs had begun sprouting all over his body.

Teeth clenched, he staggered away from the house. Behind him, he could hear Doug calling for him, and Megan's hysterical crying. He needed to get away. He didn't want them to see him. He didn't want them anywhere close to him.

Drew stumbled into the wooden fence separating his house from the neighbor's back yard. Another wave of contractions hit, forcing him to his knees. From the ground, he looked back at the house, and could see Doug's face looking out through the wreckage of the kitchen window, trying to find him.

With a savage growl, Drew forced himself to his feet. He sprang over the six-foot fence, landing in a heap on the other side. Fresh agony exploded in his head, and he brought his hands to his face. The front of his skull felt like it was pushing out, the bones in his face thrusting and extending his profile dramatically. His clenched teeth shifted along with it, changing shape and size.

The hands that he brought up to his head no longer looked like hands at all. Large paws, tipped with black claws, cupped the sides of his face as he lay on his side, overwhelmed by what was happening to him. He tried to talk, to say 'no, no', but he could no longer form the words. All that emerged from his tortured throat was a hoarse whimper. The whimper faded, replaced by a low growl as he pushed his way past the pain to regain his feet.

The beast that had been Drew Collins made it on to all fours and crouched low with its eyes closed. Senses that had previously been secondary now conveyed an overload of information. His sense of smell operated on a level that he couldn't begin to understand, and his hearing was so acute, he could hear Megan Stuart back in his room getting to her feet.

Somewhere deep down, Drew still knew who he was. He retained his sense of identity, but the "what" he was had changed. His thought processes were more primitive and basic, deeper logic and higher reasoning had been replaced by instinctive urges and heightened senses.

As his restructured brain struggled to adapt, he became aware of a loud, insistent growling close by. Opening his eyes, he saw the neighbor's Rottweiler standing a few feet away, lips pulled back and baring its teeth.

The ferocious dog leaped at the wolf that had invaded its domain. Drew, in his new form, was slow to react, and failed to move quickly enough to avoid the charge. The Rott's teeth closed on his neck and ripped, drawing blood.

Drew roared and snapped back, missing the black dog's flank by less than an inch. The two canines whirled and crashed together, throwing themselves at each other with increasing ferocity. It wasn't long before both animals were covered in blood, flesh hanging in tatters from their savaged forms.

The wolf was more awkward, less instinctive than its counterpart, but much heavier. The advantage became more and more pronounced as the fight went on. The wolf shoved against the smaller Rottweiler with his chest, throwing it off balance, following up with both paws pinning its adversary to the ground. With no hesitation, the two hundred pound werewolf tore out the Rottweiler's throat. The black dog kicked a few times spasmodically, then lay still.

Drew shuddered and lowered his head. A dim part of his consciousness knew what he had done, and that there would be consequences. He couldn't be caught. He must escape.

The wolf looked back at the fence. There were two humans behind it. Their scents identified them as people that he knew and trusted, but he felt the desire to run from them, too. They couldn't see him like this.

Staggering slightly, the wolf turned away from the fence and loped the other way, towards the front yard. Easily leaping the gate, he ran across the driveway and vanished into the darkness, leaving a trail of blood behind.

•• ❰◖❍◗❱ ••

Doug Jones stood at the fence, staring at the carnage in the next yard. The Rottweiler lay in pool of its own blood, torn to shreds.

He'd heard the terrible fight, and after ensuring that Megan was okay, he approached the fence hesitantly, unsure if he wanted to see what lay on the other side.

The teenager caught a flash of an immense gray shape leaping the front gate and bolting off. He couldn't be certain in the darkness, but the shape had seemed to have a tail, and sprang over the gate like a dog. A really big dog.

He knew one thing for sure: Drew couldn't have done this. No way he could have ripped the guard dog to pieces with his bare hands. Not only that, the sounds that he'd heard weren't even remotely human. And now, Drew was gone. 'Or whatever Drew turned into,' he added mentally.

Megan Stuart stood in the kitchen, sobbing. She held her torn shirt closed with her right hand, and gripped the windowsill with her left. She was confused, only knowing that something bad had happened to Drew. Doug walked slowly back in the house and put his arm around her. He found one of Drew's shirts to put on the distraught teen, and guided her out to his car.

"Come on, Megan, let's take you home," he said gently, putting her in the passenger seat and shutting the door. After taking one last look around the yard, he put his car into gear and drove away.

CHAPTER 27

The werewolf of Iowa Park dragged itself through the bushes and side streets of town, bleeding profusely. It was badly wounded from the fight, and was rapidly weakening. It knew that it couldn't go back home, but also recognized that it needed help. The wolf recalled being taken somewhere once, a hazy memory of being hurt, and then taken care of. Big white shapes with lines on them, lit up in the dark, leading to a huge structure made of concrete and brick. Help was there.

The wolf made its way through town, avoiding people and the moving things that conveyed them from place to place. Whenever possible, the animal remained on grass, being more comfortable with the natural earth than with the oddness of the hardened ground that dominated so much of the area.

Several times it was forced to hide, waiting for groups of humans to move on. It was chased out of two yards by the domesticated animals that claimed those spaces for their own. The wolf could have easily killed them, but knew it was better to avoid confrontation.

At length the beast's patience and determination was rewarded. A bright sign appeared that the wolf recognized from some buried memory from its other existence. He saw the big building further ahead, and slowly made his way towards it, keeping to the shadows.

Now that the big wolf had reached his destination, he was at a loss for what to do. Even its limited reasoning recognized it would not be welcome past the strange opening that opened and closed on its own. The canine had no idea how to secure the help it needed.

In confusion, it laid down in the bushes a short distance from the doors.

Weak from both its exertions, and the serious amount of blood lost from its wounds, the wolf closed his eyes. Seconds later, it was unconscious.

Doug drove Megan home, talking with her in quiet tones. The girl was calmer now, but still tremendously upset. She really liked Drew, and had been willing to give him another chance after the Beth Cahill fiasco. She had gone over to help when Doug asked, believing that Drew was in need, and had been 'rewarded' with him attempting to assault her, before running away. She was not only upset, but confused.

Doug tried to explain that Drew really wasn't himself, that things were really wrong with his best friend since the attack. Tonight had gone horribly wrong, and somewhere out there in the dark, Drew was really sorry for what had happened. Doug kept apologizing for what had happened, wanting to be sure that she knew that. And he begged for her to think about things before telling anyone. Drew was alone, scared, and Doug needed to find him first.

Megan, wrapped up in her own thoughts, simply nodded and stared into the night. When Doug pulled into her driveway, she got out and walked away without a second glance. She went inside, and closed the door immediately.

Doug stared after her for a few moments before he sighed and drove off, heading back to Drew's. He thought about calling the sheriff, but he decided that involving Drew's uncle would be bad. That would make what happened tonight 'official,' and Drew could easily get into more trouble than he already was.

By the time Doug got back to the Collins house, Drew's father was there. So were Sheriff Parker, and two of his deputies. They were talking with the neighbor, a disagreeable man named Eldridge, who was wildly upset that his prize guard dog had been killed.

The stocky middle-aged man was shouting at Ray Becker, demanding to know what 'they' were going to do about this.

Becker was trying to calm the man, but Eldrige would have none of it.

"Mr. Eldridge, we're going to do everything that we can, you know that. Right now we're trying to find out all the information that we can, and as soon as we get this figured out, we'll let you know."

"You don't know what's happened? Fuckin' look!" Eldrige raved. "My dog was torn apart! Had to be a pack of 'em, no way just one dog coulda killed my Brutus. You guys need to go find the pack of dogs that did this. Or maybe it was them wolves I kept hearing about last month."

Becker didn't react to the slightly ill smelling man's yells, nor did he show his surprise at the reference to the wolves. No one had seen or heard anything in almost three weeks, and now this.

The deputy left Eldridge to stare at the remains of his dog, and walked over to Parker, who was glaring at his brother-in-law's house over the fence. James Collins stood just on the other side, expressionless.

"Sheriff...hey, are you with us?" Becker asked, snapping Parker out of his trance.

Parker shifted his glance, taking in his deputy, then looking at James briefly. "Yeah," he grunted. "What you got for me?"

"Sheriff, Mr. Eldridge was gone from roughly seven pm until just before eleven. He stopped at the bar for a drink, and then hit Blockbuster just before they closed. When he got home, his dog, Brutus, didn't come up to greet him, which was his habit. He went into the backyard, and found the remains like you see them here," Becker motioned behind him. "There's a trail of blood leading away from the scene, leads across the street into the grass."

Parker popped an anti-acid into his mouth and grimaced. The knot in his stomach was getting worse by the second. He looked again at his brother-in-law, and simply said, "Fine."

"What do want me to tell Eldridge, boss?"

"Whatever you want, Ray," the sheriff said, dismissing his deputy. "Give me a minute here, and then we'll follow those tracks." Becker took the hint and moved away, intercepting Eldridge as the man was coming over to complain again.

Once Becker was out of earshot, Parker leaned over the fence and rasped, "Jones, get your ass over here. Now."

Doug, who'd been standing nervously off to the side since getting out of his car, hurried over to the fence. He stopped beside Drew's father and peered over at the sheriff.

"Yes, sir?" he asked.

"Where's Drew?"

Doug ducked his head slightly, moving so Parker couldn't see him over the fence. He didn't want to be here, and didn't want to give the sheriff any information about Drew. He looked to Mr. Collins for help, but the older man simply stood there and stared at the ground.

"I don't know, Sheriff. I was just coming over to see him," he mumbled.

"Boy, don't bullshit me. Where the hell is he?" Parker barked, in no mood for games.

"He's not here," Jones insisted. "He ran off. Honest. I came over to look for him."

"Mr. Jones, do you know anything about what happened here? I see an extra car in the driveway, and you pulled in pretty fast," the lawman said, not backing off, despite the fact that he couldn't see the youngster that he was grilling.

"Not really, sir. Have you been over here, yet?" Jones asked, staring in fear at the twisted pile of torn and discarded clothing on his side of the fence. That must have been what Mr. Collins was staring at. If the sheriff knew about it, Drew was in big trouble.

"No, Jones, I've been busy over here. Why?" The sheriff sounded tired. Not physically tired, like after a big game, but worn out, like he was tired of life.

"No reason, Sheriff...just wondering. The other car here belongs to a friend of mine from school. If I see Drew I'll tell him that you're looking for him, though. Okay?"

"Don't leave yet. I'll be over in a couple minutes to talk some more. I just gotta finish up here," Parker said, turning away from the fence and heading towards Eldridge's front yard.

When Parker was out of earshot, Jones grabbed the clothes on the ground and raced into the house. He shoved them into the closet in Drew's room and shut the door. There was nothing that he could do about the broken picture window in the kitchen, though.

He began putting pieces of broken glass in a garbage bag. James Collins walked over and helped. After a couple minutes of working in silence, the older man cleared his throat. Jones stopped and looked at him.

"Doug, what happened? I know you were here." For the first time in at least three years, the older man made, and maintained, eye contact. "I saw Drew's clothes on the ground. I know that you two didn't fight—you don't have a mark on you. Tell me."

"Mr. Collins, I don't know, and I'm not sure I want to. He did go through the window, though, and he was in a lot of pain. I got to find him."

"Did he kill Brutus?"

Doug stammered. "I think so. I just don't know how." The boy shook his head. "Mr. Collins, if he's in trouble, I don't want to get him into more with the cops. Even if Sheriff Parker is his uncle, you know?"

Collins looked at the young man for a moment. Then he looked away and said quietly, "Go. Take your friend's car and get it out of here. I don't think Bob's seen the plate yet. Just come find me when you find my son. I have your word?"

"Yes, I promise. Thanks, Mr. Collins," Jones said, hurrying out the front door and praying that Megan left the keys in her car. Doug slid behind the wheel and as quietly as he could, started the car and crept out of the driveway.

●●◐◯◑◖●

Parker sent Becker and Winslow to follow the trail of blood. He walked around the fenced area to the Collins residence, where James was waiting for him on the porch. He noticed the missing car right away.

"Where did Jones go?"

"Home, Bob. He didn't know anything. You can talk to him tomorrow if you need to. I need to find my son. I have to go."

"Maybe you should just stay here. I'll call you if I hear anything?" Parker told him. "I'll have somebody come over and help you board over that window while you wait."

Collins nodded. He had a bad feeling they weren't going to find Drew, no matter who looked for him. For all his anger and mocking of Parker's concerns, it now looked like the impossible was, in fact, the only explanation.

•• ◖◯◗ ••

Doug drove all the way to the Stuart house and dropped off Megan's car before he realized that he didn't have a ride back. He really didn't want to knock on the door and ask Megan to drive him anywhere, so he set out on foot.

He weighed his options. Instead of walking back to Drew's, he could start looking for his friend, but where to start eluded him. Doug shook his head in bewilderment. Trying to pinpoint Drew's movements depended on who, or what, Drew was, and Doug didn't have any idea.

He recalled the deputies saying earlier that whatever had attacked the Rottweiler had also been injured. Maybe his friend would head for the hospital.

Doug decided to head over towards the hospital in a roundabout way, poking around, carefully. Whatever had happened to Drew, it hadn't changed him for the better, and if he was able to tear that guard dog apart, maybe Doug himself was at risk from his friend.

He thought about what he knew of werewolves, most of it courtesy of movies he and Drew had watched. If that was really what Drew had become, he was a risk to anyone he met. He'd also change back to himself at first light, if he lived that long.

Doug knew that he needed to find his friend as soon as possible, then somehow keep them both safe until dawn. Then they could try to figure out what to do from there. Just shrugging and walking away from the situation never entered his mind. This was his best friend.

Looking all around him constantly, Jones made his way on foot towards the hospital, hoping that he'd find his friend, and that his friend wouldn't find him first.

CHAPTER 28

Amy Bishop's shift was scheduled to end at seven am. Wednesday was a slow night, though, and when the other nurse on duty volunteered to let her go an hour early, Amy took her up on the offer. Slow nights were more tiring than busy ones, and she had more than enough hours on her timecard for the last two weeks.

The young nurse waved to her colleague and walked out the automatic door, heading towards the employee parking lot. This early in the morning, everything was quiet. She could barely hear any traffic moving; it was as though she was alone with the sunrise.

She smiled at the thought, her gaze lingering on the big hospital sign pointing to the ER entrance. The sun hit the top, and it shone like a star. Her gaze dropped to the bushes below the sign, the red-tipped leaves swayed slightly in the modest morning breeze.

Red-tipped? Amy frowned. The shrubbery around the hospital was a boring uniform green. She looked again. Several of the leaves under the sign were definitely covered in red. She stepped closer, staring at the leaves. They were coated with blood. Fresh blood, since it was still red, and not the rust-brown color blood became when it dried. She'd seen enough of each to be able to tell the difference.

Hesitantly, she reached out and touched one of the leaves. The blood came off on her fingers. A small sound made her look down.

Lying at her feet was a young man, bleeding profusely. Amy jumped and cried out in shock. Her scream made the man open his eyes, and he stared at her, in obvious pain. As he struggled to get up, Amy saw that he was naked, his body covered in wounds.

The ER nurse pulled back from his grasping hands as her training took over. She uttered soothing sounds, and pushed him back down to lay flat on the ground. Amy glanced around, looking for help. The young man needed taken inside right away.

"Help... me," the man said, sounding weak but clear. She looked back at him, starting to explain that help was on the way, and that he'd be fine. Her words died in her throat. She recognized the form on the ground beneath her. It was Drew Collins, the man who had saved her little brother.

"Drew! What happened to you?"

"Help... me," he repeated. He succeeded in grabbing hold of her sleeve, and pulled her closer. "I've got to get out of here. They're looking for me."

"Drew, you're hurt. I need to get you inside so we can fix you up."

"Please, just get me out of here." His voice was becoming stronger, his tone more insistent. "If you take me inside, the cops will find me. I need to get out of here."

Amy considered his words. He was hurt, but seemed clear-headed, and she owed him for what he had done to save her brother. She looked more closely at his injuries. He had several long cuts on his arms, legs, and torso. They appeared deep but not life threatening. Some wounds were even starting to close, the blood flow slowing to trickles.

"Please, get me away from here. I'll be fine. I promise."

Amy hesitated. All of her training told her to do this by the book, and take the injured man inside the hospital. Her instincts, however, told her to help Collins. She owed him a debt that she could never repay. But she could make a start.

Mind made up, she told him to stay put for a moment, and brought her car around. Carefully, she helped the injured man into the passenger seat and closed the door. As she came around the front of the car to get in the driver's side, Doug Jones walked right into her.

His head was down, following something on the ground, and he hadn't seen her. She had been so focused on Drew, and getting him out of the parking lot, she'd just jumped right in front of the guy.

"Whoa, Amy, sorry, I wasn't watchin' where I was goin'," the big teen said. His eyes moved past her to her car, widening as he saw who was slumped in the passenger seat. "Shit, Drew!" he exclaimed. "I've been looking for him all night!"

"What happened to him, Doug? He's cut up pretty bad, and won't go into the hospital. I was going to take him home and try to clean him up."

"Is he okay? I mean, is he going to be okay?" Doug tried to push past her, craning his neck to see Drew better. The nurse attempted to push him back, but lacked the necessary mass.

Doug hurried to Drew's side of the car. "Drew, you okay? Is it you? I mean, you know, are you you again?"

The tortured face of his best friend looked out at him. He nodded, shivering and holding his arms tightly to his chest. Jones looked back at the nurse. "I'm going with you."

Amy looked around the parking lot. There was still nobody around, but that could change at any moment. The large young man would be a pain to get rid of, and could be a help with his injured friend. She nodded toward the back seat of her car.

Doug slid his bulk into the back as Amy got in the front seat. After making sure Drew was okay, she put on her seat belt and pulled out of the ER lot. The short trip to her apartment was made in silence.

After Amy brought out a bath towel for her naked patient to cover himself with, Doug helped her move Drew inside. While still in serious pain, the young man was steadier on his feet than before.

Amy spent the next half hour cleaning and dressing Drew's cuts. Upon close examination, Amy could see that his injuries all appeared to be animal bites, likely from a large dog. This brought on a wave of relief. She'd made the decision to help him because of her family's debt to him, but she couldn't shake the nagging concern that he had wounded, or even killed, a person. That he had been hurt by an animal made it less likely he'd done anything criminal.

Additionally, his wounds didn't look nearly as bad as she had first thought- almost like they were healing on their own. When she'd first seen him, he'd looked like he was dying. Now, just a half hour later, he seemed well on the way to recovery.

Drew sat in Amy's kitchen, staring at the floor while the nurse finished. The events from the previous night flashed through his mind in frozen images; the fight, the subsequent running away, the flight to the hospital, and finally, passing out in the bushes outside the emergency room. None of it seemed real. The unimaginable pain of his nightmarish transformation, coupled with the injuries sustained during his fight with the dog, convinced him otherwise.

Drew raised his head. Doug was sitting at the table, staring at him. His face showed concern and fear. Drew didn't blame him; he felt the same way himself. One way or another, his entire life had changed, and likely not for the better.

"Thanks, Amy. I owe you big time for this," he said, as she finished and sat down next to him. "I don't know what to do, just that I have to get out of here."

"What do you mean, 'get out of here'?" Doug asked. "You mean run away? And go where?"

"I don't know, but I have to leave. My uncle will be looking for me. For all I know, Megan is going to call the cops too, and after what I did to that fucking dog, they'll throw me in jail for sure." Drew stopped and stared hard at his friend. "I can't go to jail. Not like this. Tonight's another full moon."

Amy chose that moment to break in on the conversation. She was more than a little lost as to what was going on, but she was already involved. "I probably don't want to know the answer to this, but what does the full moon have to do with anything?"

The two men exchanged looks. They remained silent, both choosing to stare at the floor rather than meet the nurse's questioning gaze.

"Guys, seriously, what difference does it make?" she insisted, looking from one to the other.

Drew finally spoke, keeping his eyes glued to the tile floor. "What happened last night will happen again tonight. Every time there's a full moon. That's why I have to leave. I've got to get far away from here before it gets dark."

"Drew, what will happen during the full moon? You sound like you think you're a werewolf or something," disbelief evident in her voice. "That's ridiculous, and you both know it."

From the look that the two boys shared, she could tell her comment wasn't off the mark. "Amy, it's true. I was there last night, and God help me, I don't know how it can be, but it is," Doug said, stumbling over the words. His rational mind still refused to accept what was happening, but he *knew* inside what was going on. Part of him had known since seeing Drew's arm.

"Okay, let's calm down a bit. There's no way that a human being can turn into a wolf," she said. "It's biologically impossible, and you both are old enough and smart enough to know that. I don't know what happened to Drew last night, but I know that he is *not* a big hairy wolf."

Drew looked up, capturing Amy's eyes with his own. They were red-rimmed and haunted. Without breaking eye contact, he held up his left arm. "Amy, remember my arm? I came into the hospital three weeks ago after being practically mauled by a wolf. Remember what it looked like? Look at it now," he held it out to her. "No sign of injury. None. How is that possible? No one heals that fast, or that completely." He practically shoved the limb in her face. "Look!"

Bishop took his extended arm in her hands and studied it. She found no signs of his bite. Frowning, she glanced at his other arm, just in case she was confused. Drew caught her look and smiled slightly.

"Scary, isn't it? Not a mark." he said.

"This doesn't mean anything. Yeah, it's bizarre, I'll give you that. Injuries like yours don't heal that quickly, or completely. But guys, it doesn't mean anything more than that," she insisted. "Now, tell me how Drew got all cut up this time, and why we can't take him to the hospital like he needs."

Doug took over for Drew. "He got into a fight with the mean-ass guard dog that lived next door to him. When he started to change, he ran away from us and jumped the fence between the properties. The dog attacked him and Drew killed it, then jumped the front gate and ran off."

Amy looked at both of them skeptically.

The big teen looked at his friend briefly before continuing. "I saw the dog, Amy. It was ripped up. No way a human being could have done that kind of damage. And it was a trained attack dog, too. Could have killed me easy. Drew wouldn't have had a chance against it."

"So now what? Drew lives out his life in his dad's back yard, eating out of a dog dish and wearing a spiked collar?" Amy said, exasperated.

"That's not funny," Drew grumbled. He shifted in his chair restlessly. "Do you have anything to eat? I'm starving."

"Yeah, I can make you some eggs, and I think that I have some sausage, too. Doug, you want some, too?" Amy asked, walking to the refrigerator.

"Sure. You want some help?" he asked, getting up and following her into the kitchen. "I make a mean omelet."

••●☾◐◉◑☽●••

Once breakfast was ready, Doug and Amy rejoined Drew at the table. All three of them ate, but Drew attacked his food with something approaching desperation. Finishing well before his friends, he looked around for more to eat. His face was flushed and covered in a light sweat. Amy noticed.

"Drew? You okay? You need more to eat? I'll make you a sandwich…or two. You're sweating, by the way. I should take your temp."

"I'm fine. Just get me those sandwiches. Got roast beef or ham?" he asked, getting up from the table and prowling into the kitchen to go through the refrigerator. Behind him, Amy and Doug watched him worriedly. He was moving markedly better than he had just an hour ago. Normally, that would be a good sign. Today it was just unnatural. That fact was starting to impress itself on the nurse, just as it already had on Doug.

Drew turned to look at the pair still sitting at the table. "What? I'm still hungry. Is that a crime?" he looked at them with irritation. "Do either of you want a sandwich, too? I can make 'em," he said, stacking slices of bread on a paper towel. "No? Okay, then, just me."

Moments later he was sitting down again, eating three sandwiches with obvious gusto. Doug and Amy continued watching him with growing unease. His movements were quick, efficient, and powerful. He bore almost no resemblance to the bleeding, semi-conscious man they had all but carried in.

Drew noticed their worried expressions and looked down in puzzlement. The paper towel was empty, except for a couple of crumbs. The sandwiches were gone. Slowly, he recalled where he was and why. His face fell.

"I've got to go. You shouldn't be around me," he stated, getting to his feet. "Thanks for your help, Amy. Doug, I'll see you later."

Both of his friends rose, too. "Just hold on, Drew. You can't just run off. You got nowhere to go and no way to get there. Let's sit back down and figure this out. If you have to leave, it should be with a plan," Doug said.

Amy added her voice. "Drew, if the police are looking for you, you need to get away from here, but you need to have someplace safe to go to. Do you know anyone that you can go stay with?"

Drew shook his head. "You don't get it. Tonight I will change into something terrible, and anyone around me could get hurt. I need to get away from everyone. I can't go and stay with relatives or friends, even if the police wouldn't look there. I couldn't put them at risk."

He paused, as if considering a new thought. "I need to find Ramona. Those bikers know what happened to me. If there are answers, they'll have them."

"Sounds like a *great* idea," Doug said sarcastically. "Except those bikers are the cause of all your problems. Oh, and they're also wanted for kidnapping, rape, and probably murder, too." Doug grabbed Drew's shoulders, almost shaking him. "Think about it- you want to avoid the cops, not hang out with the people they're looking for."

Drew was adamant about his decision. He'd made up his mind to find the enigmatic female biker and get answers from her. No amount of arguing or threatening would dissuade him. Eventually, Doug and Amy gave in.

It was decided that Drew would rest at Amy's apartment for a couple of hours, while the other two left to get necessities for his escape. Despite his situation, Drew was exhausted, and fell asleep almost the second his head hit the pillow.

Hours later, Amy's gentle touch at his shoulder brought him bolt upright in the bed, both hands clamped onto her shoulders. She screamed at his sudden movement, which brought Doug crashing into the room.

The three of them looked at each other. Shaking, Drew let go of Amy, who laughed nervously and got up off of the bed. Drew got up as well, and followed the other two out of the room.

"Drew, let me see your chest," Amy asked.

"What do you mean, you want to check out my chest? Isn't that backwards? I mean, shouldn't I want to see your..." he trailed off, seeing that his attempt at humor had fallen flat. Both Amy and Doug were looking at him with worried expressions.

He sat down in a chair and pulled up the t-shirt Amy had given him to wear. The nurse took away the bandages that she'd applied just three hours earlier, and gasped. Doug swore under his breath and looked away. Drew looked down. There were three fading scratches on the right side of his chest; otherwise, his skin was intact.

"That's... impossible!" Amy cried. Hurriedly, she pulled the rest of the dressings off of her young patient. Where the deepest wounds had been, there were mostly-healed areas with scabs. The lesser injuries were completely gone.

"It just can't be," she kept repeating, checking him over for signs of serious wounds, and finding none. It was almost as if he hadn't done anything worse than slip and fall down. Amy gave up looking and fell into a chair.

Drew's best friend sat forwards in his chair. "Drew, the cops are lookin' for you, just like you thought, your uncle especially. He knows you didn't come home last night. Your dad says that the police believe that the bite marks on the Rottweiler are the same as the ones on that college guy last month.

"I hate to say this, but I think you need to go. Lay low somewhere until we can figure this out."

Drew nodded. "Yeah, and I think I know where to find some of those answers, too. I can't ask either of you two to do any more; I don't want you to get in trouble. I need to get home long enough to get some of my stuff, and some wheels."

Doug and Amy exchanged glances. Jones said, "We kinda figured that." Reaching into his pocket, he pulled out an envelope. "Here. This is all I had in my savings account, and what Amy could get out of hers. It's just over three grand. It'll go fast, dude, so be careful with it."

Doug produced a plastic bag. "Also, I got you this at Wally World: it's a prepaid cell phone. I'm the only one with the number. This way we can keep in touch." He handed the envelope and the phone to Drew.

Amy took over. "We're going to run you over to your house now. If the coast is clear, we'll drop you off and wait. Then we'll run interference for you to get out of town. You up for that?"

Drew stood up. He took a deep breath and said, "Let's go. Thanks, guys. I'll find a way to pay you back. I promise."

Doug grinned at his friend. "You can't pay me back everything that you owe me, man, the list is too long." Getting serious, he mumbled, "Just take care of yourself and don't get killed."

•• ❰❰◯◯❱❱ ••

The trip over to the Collins residence was uneventful. Amy drove, with Doug in the passenger seat, and Drew lying down as best he could in the back. There was only Doug's car in the driveway, left over from the night before. Drew slipped out first and opened the garage. The Taurus was gone, so Amy drove her vehicle into the empty spot, so it couldn't be seen from the street.

While Doug and Amy kept watch out the living room window, Drew changed clothes, and stuffed a backpack with the few necessities he could take. When he was done, the young man put on his leather coat, grabbed his helmet, and walked into the garage. He picked up the key for his Honda, then paused.

Sitting in its accustomed place was his father's souped up Sportster. The orange racing bike rested on its stand, capturing

Drew's attention. The machine seemed to whisper to him. 'If you're going on the run, why not take the bike that can run the fastest,' it seemed to ask. 'You know you always wanted to ride me.'

Drew looked around, as if to see if anyone would stop him. Slowly, he replaced the key for the Honda and grabbed the Harley-Davidson one off the rack. On a whim, he tossed his helmet onto the workbench and left it. 'What the hell,' he told himself. Live life on the edge. As long as he was stealing his dad's bike, he might as well ride risky.

Putting on his sunglasses, Drew sat down on the Sportster. He fired it up, listening to the thumping roar of its powerful v-twin. Despite everything, he smiled. From the garage door, Doug looked at him and flashed a thumbs up. The way was clear. Drew nodded, and his friend triggered the release. The door came up, and Drew carefully let out the clutch, easing the bike out of the garage.

Doug ran back to his car and led the way down the street. Amy followed him, and Drew brought up the rear on the bike. The mini caravan worked its way on side roads to the edge of town. Just outside the city limits, Doug pulled over and stopped, the others joining on the shoulder.

Amy examined Drew's wounds one last time, shaking her head yet again as she failed to find any signs of the previous night's injuries. She patted his shoulder, and then hugged him tightly. Finally, she stepped back.

Doug took her place. He stepped up to his best friend, started to speak, and then stopped. He was at a loss. Drew looked at him and nodded. Jones handed him his overstuffed backpack, which settled into place on his back.

The moment stretched on, the two friends not knowing how to say goodbye. Drew held up his right fist; Doug hesitated a second or two, and then bumped it with his own.

"Bitch," he breathed.

"Jerk," Drew responded. He started the Sportster back up, revved it ridiculously, blinked away sudden tears, and drove off.

Amy and Doug stood on the shoulder of the road, watching him fade away into the distance. The young nurse glanced over at the hulking teen-ager standing beside her, looking lost.

"C'mon, Mr. Jones, buy a girl some lunch, okay?" Doug looked at her. He took a deep breath, wiped his eyes, and smiled. Recovering himself somewhat, he stared appreciatively at the young woman next to him.

So maybe this wasn't *all* bad, he thought.

CHAPTER 29

Drew shot down a back road, reveling in the wind blowing past his face. The souped-up Sportster throbbed with power, seeming to hurtle him over the sun-bathed landscape.

It felt good to be alive. Gone was the pain and horror of the previous night, the memories now like a long-forgotten dream. He was young, healthy, and full of energy. He barely resisted the urge to shout.

His exuberance faded as he saw his first shadow. Evidence that the sun was moving, and would eventually set, brought back to mind what had happened the last time the sun had gone down. He remembered again the searing pain, the feeling of wrongness, and the transformation. Grimly, he saw flashes of what had occurred after that, and once again, he remembered why he was fleeing from the only home he'd ever known.

The road ahead rose steeply. As he crested the hill, he saw two figures ahead of him, standing in the middle of the road. Both were dressed in black leather, standing near two bikes raised on kickstands. Ramona and Wrench, waiting for him.

Drew grimaced and slowed the Sportster. The pair ahead of him didn't move. He came to a stop just short of them. Ramona stared at him intently, her unearthly eyes boring into him. Wrench merely smirked.

At length, the two moved. Without a word, they got on their bikes and fired them up. The young woman looked over her shoulder at Drew and motioned for him to follow. They took off, resuming Drew's journey north.

After a while, they stopped for gas and food. There was a Subway at the convenience store, so the three ordered food and sat down at a table. So far, they hadn't spoken to each other. Wrench grinned at the young man sitting across from him.

"So, kid... have a nice night? Any bad dreams?" The little biker laughed. Ramona rolled her eyes and looked away.

Drew glared at the dirty man and took another bite of his club sandwich. Deliberately, he chewed and tore off more. Wrench scowled.

"Does your daddy know that you have his bike? Didn't your momma pack you any lunch? Oh, wait," he continued, seeing his shot at Drew's mother hit home. "I forgot. You don't have a momma anymore, do you?"

Drew growled and lunged out of his chair, hands reaching out to grab Wrench by the throat. The smaller man leaned away and laughed. He stood up and stepped further back as the enraged younger man pushed against the table and swung at him.

"Easy kid, I didn't mean anything," he said, smirking. "You gotta control that temper, gonna get you killed one of these days," he added, his expression darkening.

Ramona had enough. She stepped between Wrench and Drew, pushing Collins back while glaring at her biker counterpart. "Wrench, knock it off," she grated. "Asshole." She turned back to Drew.

"I tried to warn you but you wouldn't listen. I don't blame you too much, but now you know. So it's time to face facts and deal with them."

"What do you mean?" Drew fired back. "I'm not sure what the hell happened last night. I know the cops are looking for me, and that I probably hurt someone I care about." Drew paused, looking less defensive, and added, "And I think I killed a Rottweiler that attacked me."

"Uh-oh, a vicious dog killer, I better be careful," Wrench sneered from behind Ramona. The comment earned him an elbow to the ribs by the disgusted female.

"Take a hike, Wrench. We'll meet you outside." she commanded.

"I haven't finished eating yet," Wrench grumbled.

Ramona swept his sandwich off of the table and tossed it at him. He caught it poorly and the sandwich separated, sliding in sections down his torso to drop onto the floor. "Damn it!" he yelled. Turning on his heel, he kicked the remains of his lunch across the floor and stomped out.

"Asshole," Ramona repeated. She turned back to face Drew. "C'mon, Collins, sit down. We got stuff to discuss." She resumed her seat and looked pointedly at where Drew had been previously sitting.

With a last glance at the door that Wrench had gone through, Drew sat back down. He still bristled with hostility, glaring at the raven-haired biker. If she was to be believed, it was her fault that he was in this mess.

"Okay, I'm here. So discuss." Drew crossed his arms and sat back.

Ramona took in his hostile posture and sighed. "To start with, what happened last night will happen again tonight," she began. "And tomorrow night. Every month, for the rest of your life, you will change during the full moon. There's nothing that you can do about it. There is no cure for this curse."

"Which you gave me," Drew accused.

"Yeah. Sorry. So, anyway, you have to leave everything and everyone that you know. There is no way to go back to the life that you had before. You already know that, or you wouldn't have left."

Drew lowered his head. "I left because the cops were looking for me. I attacked a friend of mine, then killed the neighbor's dog. I thought that you might have answers, so I left to find you."

"For what it's worth, I am really sorry for what happened," Ramona said. "What answers there are you'll have to learn on the road. Join us, and I'll teach you everything you'll need to survive. It won't be easy, but it's better than just giving up and dying," she said, hastily adding "or being killed."

The reappearance of Wrench put an end to their conversation. The diminutive psychopath stalked down the aisle to where they sat and slammed his hands down on the table. "C'mon, kiddies, time to go. Is junior here coming, or not?"

"Shut up, Wrench," Ramona snapped, earning another growl from the biker. "He's coming with us. Drew, we'll talk more later, I promise. We need to go."

Collins slowly nodded.

The three left Subway and got back on the road. After two more hours of riding in silence, they stopped again for gas. It was now late afternoon, and shadows were beginning to lengthen.

Ramona took off her sunglasses and looked around. The rural setting was ideal for hiding out for the night, given the rapidly approaching full moon. At some point they would need to hook up with the Fenris Firar. Hopefully before Lobo decided to hunt them down.

"Wrench, you ride ahead. Find Lobo and tell him that I'm bringing Collins in. We'll meet up in two days in Amarillo," she commanded. "We'll hide out here tonight and start out in the morning. You can probably get another hundred and fifty miles before nightfall."

"Sure, 'Mona, and you can be free to play with your new toy," Wrench sneered. "How stupid do you think I am?"

Ramona slapped him, hard. "Honestly, pretty stupid, but we both knew that already," she glared. "Just go, asshole. It'll give me a chance to teach Collins the ways of the pack." She shoved him towards his machine. "Get back on your piece of shit bike and get out of here."

Wrench growled back over his shoulder as he walked the rest of the way to his panhead. He kicked the old machine over and it roared to life. He tore out of the gas station, blowing smoke and leaving a skid mark behind from burning out.

Despite the seriousness of his situation, Drew's lip curled in derision at Wrench's display. "What a pathetic ass-wipe," he said.

"Don't underestimate him, he's vicious" Ramona replied. "You can't trust him, and when he fights, don't expect it to be fair. He won't hesitate to kill you if he can."

"He's the one that took Lucy, isn't he? Did he kill her?"

Ramona looked away. "He had a big part in it." A scowl crossed her face. "We can talk about that later. Right now, we should get food, a lot of it. Then we'll find a quiet place to hide out for the night. C'mon, let's shop."

Drew rolled his eyes. "Yippee, shopping." He followed the beautiful woman into the store.

An hour later, they were settled in an empty barn, blanket on the ground, and a huge pile of food surrounding them. Ramona took off her coat and tossed it to the side. She turned back to Drew and stared at him.

"Well?" she asked, when he didn't say anything. "Here's your chance. Ask me what you want to know."

There were tons of questions in Drew's head, but he wasn't sure he wanted to hear the answers. His face hardened as he came to grips with his situation. He needed to know everything. Knowledge was key.

"We'll start easy. What I am? What do I have?"

"You're a werewolf, Drew. A lycanthrope. You have a disease that turns you into a wolf every full moon. Impossible or not, it's real. You're not born with it, as far as I know; you have to be bitten."

Drew looked hard at her. She wasn't kidding. She wasn't messing with him, trying to play on his fears over what happened the previous night. "Okay, I'm Lon Chaney, Jr. What does it mean? How does being a werewolf work? In the movies, they can never remember anything, and I do."

"You keep your brain when you change, Drew. Becoming a wolf means that your senses and your brain both change, though. You see and process the world like a wolf would," Ramona explained. "While in wolf form, you know basic things from when you were a man, and then when you're human again, you retain the images and stuff from when you were a wolf." She paused here to shrug. "They're a little confusing for both wolf and human, because the brain is different, but you still know who you are."

"Okay, then why did you attack me? It was you, wasn't it? I had nightmares about your eyes all the time. It had to be you," he accused.

She lowered her head. "Yes, it was me. I was trying to throw myself into the lake. That kid just got in the way. Then you attacked me—you started it, remember. I just reacted like any wild animal would, and bit you. I'm sorry."

"Swell. So if you were the wolf, how come you were so big? I mean, sometimes, the movies make the werewolves look gigantic, and other times they just look like regular wolves."

"Again with the movies...this isn't fiction, Drew," Ramona repeated. "Lobo says that when the transformation happens, you don't gain or lose mass. So, if you weigh two hundred pounds now, you become a two hundred pound wolf. That's twice what a normal wolf weighs. The bigger you are, the bigger the wolf."

"Okay, what else?"

Ramona considered. The curse was bad enough, but there was more. This young man deserved to know it all. "We age faster. Dogs live about seven years for each one that humans live, so we outlive them. Humans live to be about seventy normally, and dogs live to be ten or so. Because of our curse—the enhanced metabolism and time spent in lupine, that is, wolf form; we age more rapidly. I have no idea how long we live; everyone I know that has died has been killed, not just passed away.

"And that's the other thing," she added. "In the movies, werewolves can only be killed by a silver bullet. That's bullshit. We can die just like anyone else. It's just that since we heal so quickly, we have to be killed outright. Serious wounds we can recover from.

Drew sat, thinking over her words. It made sense. Or what passed for sense in this screwed up version of the world. So, he was doomed to turn into a huge wolf every month, and probably die young. "So what's with all the food?"

"Healing and turning take a lot of energy, so we have to eat a huge amount of food. Since we turn tonight, we need tons of calories. Otherwise, we start off weak, hungry, and really, really hostile. Even more than normal."

"Makes sense," Drew said. He had one more question. He didn't want to ask it at first, but now it seemed almost like an afterthought. "So what about the transform...the turning thing.

Does it hurt that bad each time?" He studied Ramona's face, wondering if she was judging him. "I mean, not to be a wuss or anything, but I've never felt that kind of pain before. I don't think I can go through that every time. I thought that I was dying."

Drew looked ashamed to admit his fear, but Ramona couldn't blame him. She'd thought that she would die too, that first month. It was something that you learned to live with. Knowing that it wasn't going to kill you made it easier. For some of the Firar, they'd grown to almost like the pain, and looked forward to it, like a rite of passage.

"It gets a little better. It won't kill you, and knowing that helps make it bearable. It's never been fun, but it can be survived. Surviving is sometimes the best that we can hope for, Drew."

"Swell," he grumbled. "Spend my life running away from everyone that matters to me, go through terrible pain regularly, and die young with no future. Does that about sum it up?" he asked, bitterly.

Ramona stared hard into his eyes. "Yeah, that about sums it up, Drew. You're going to have to deal with it. Some people don't. They either just check out and kill themselves, or give themselves over to their base impulses and become little better than beasts all of the time. You didn't strike me as that big a pussy. But go ahead: prove me wrong.

"But remember, there's more to this than just you. The pack thinks your father saw Wrench grab that girl. They're planning to kill him, so that there aren't any witnesses. If you wimp out and bail on this, your father's as good as dead."

Ramona paused, and looked away. When she continued, it was in a much softer voice. "And I guess, I'm tied up in how you take this, too. My future with the pack is tenuous. Most of them are looking for an excuse to get rid of me, and leaving you alive was sort of the last straw."

She raised her eyes again. "No one leaves the Fenris Firar. The devil's motorcycle gang has only one way out, Drew: death. If you bail, they'll track you down and kill you. Then they'll kill your father, and then probably me. So there you have it; it's all up to you. Happy now?"

Drew slumped back, resting against the wall. 'As if things couldn't get worse,' he told himself. He really was cursed- first with his mom's murder, then his dad's depression, and now this. For the first time, he understood how his father felt. How the hell did someone continue living day after day with this kind of stifling weight on him? If this was how his dad felt every day, it was a wonder that he found the strength to get out of bed in the morning.

Suddenly, it dawned on Drew what gave his father the strength to get up and face each day. It was him. James Collins had a responsibility to see his son grow up. There was no joy since the passing of his wife, but there was still duty and responsibility. That, Drew could understand.

Ramona watched the battle going on inside the young man. She could read each phase simply by observing his body language. After the shock faded, his dejection was obvious. The terrible burden of the curse was bad enough, but the added strain of lives hanging in the balance could be too much for the seventeen year old.

There was little that she could do to help him through this. Either he was strong enough to make it, or he wasn't. She sat still, barely breathing, watching to see what would happen.

Slowly, Drew seemed to come to a decision. His hands clenched into fists, and he sat up, no longer leaning on the wall. The atmosphere in the barn seemed to change. Strength was radiating from him; Ramona sensed an alpha male across from her. He was going to fight.

Drew looked at her and took a deep breath. "Okay. It's getting dark. What can I do to help get through the change? Do we need to stay away from each other? Do we eat now, or afterwards?"

"We should eat now. It makes the change a little less painful. We'll need to eat again once it's over, too. We can stay together, here in the barn," she replied. "Let's bolt the door, so that we can't get out tonight. Sometimes we want to be able to run free, but tonight I think that we should stay where it's safe."

Drew dropped the bar across the barn door, while Ramona made huge sandwiches for them. As the sun began setting, both of them felt a sense of urgency, and ate quickly. After bolting down his food, Drew looked at Ramona expectantly. "So now what?"

"Take off your clothes and stack them neatly out of the way. It doesn't do to wake up naked and have your clothing be missing or torn to shreds. It tends to get embarrassing."

'Like this isn't,' Drew told himself. He had stripped countless times after gym class or after practice, but that was with a large group of other guys. Getting naked in a barn alone with a ridiculously hot chick was totally different.

Seeing his red face, and unwillingness to start, Ramona snapped at him. "Hey, shithead, get 'em off before it's too late. What's the matter? You've wanted to see me naked since the first time you saw me, showing off on that little dirt bike of yours."

"You remember that?" he muttered. His stomach gave a lurch. He knew that feeling. It would be followed by unbearable pain in his bones, and his skin stretching until it felt like it would tear apart.

His modesty overcome by the reality of the oncoming transformation, Drew took off his shirt and folded it quickly. He glanced over at his companion as he dropped his pants. Ramona was staring right at him, and was down to her underwear. He looked away and continued.

After folding his pants, he took a deep breath and stepped out of his underwear. As he laid them on top of his other clothes, he self-consciously looked back over at Ramona. She too, was naked. Drew's mouth went dry as he stared at her toned body. She looked like one of the centerfolds in those magazines that he and Doug kept hidden from their parents.

"Enjoy it while you can, Collins," Ramona said dryly, staring back at him with interest. "In just a minute, it's going to get ugly." She grimaced, and then held up a hand. "See."

Her hand was sprouting coarse black hair. Drew had an instant to be shocked, and then the first shooting pains hit him. He stiffened. "Aargh!"

"It'll be okay, Drew. Tough it out," she gasped. She held out her hand, which Drew took in one of his own. He saw that it was changing, and tried to pull it away from the girl. Ramona refused to let go. She clung tightly to his hand, and pulled him closer. Both of them trembled and twitched, bathed in sudden sweat. The change was claiming them. As they hunched forwards, Ramona placed her forehead against Drew's. They stared into each other's eyes.

Drew stared into her silver eyes, gaining a slight sense of calmness and peace, despite the incredible pain. The transformation forced them apart, but Drew held onto the strength gained from her support. Rather than fighting, he embraced the change, rushing towards the bestial form awaiting him. The pain receded, leaving him on all fours, gasping.

The monstrous wolf took in a deep breath, steadying himself. Next to him was a coal-black female with lustrous silver eyes. They sniffed each other thoroughly, getting familiar with one another on a much deeper level than was possible for them in their puny, sense-deprived human state.

Eventually, they touched noses and snorted. Apparently satisfied with what she found, the female turned her attention to the food in the middle of the floor. Strong teeth ripped open containers, and she began to eat. The gray male joined her.

Ramona growled briefly, shouldering him away, then settled down and let him in. Side by side they devoured everything left on the ground. After nosing through the wrappers for any crumbs that might have been missed, they explored their domain. Or cage, as the case turned out.

Part of the wolves remembered that they were shut in the barn to keep safe, but the wild side of their nature resented being locked up. They examined all four corners of the barn, searching for a way out, before eventually giving up.

Eating taken care of, and their immediate environment established, all that was left were each other. Both wolves resumed sniffing and studying the other. This led to the female taking a playful nip at the male.

Drew jumped back away from Ramona, and then pawed at her. His large front paw pushed her back. She responded by diving in at his legs, grabbing his back leg between her strong jaws and biting down lightly.

The gray wolf whirled around and tackled the smaller female. They rolled, twisting and jumping, frantically wrestling around on the barn floor. Empty wrappers and food containers flew, and the carefully positioned water bowl was dumped over.

Eventually worn out, the black wolf stopped and lay down, panting hugely. The male approached, head held low. Deciding that he was welcome, Drew flopped down next to Ramona and rested. The two wolves settled down, nestling back-to-back and fell asleep.

When the wolf that was Drew Collins awoke, Ramona was already up. She was facing the larger male with her ears up, head cocked slightly to the side, studying him. The gray got to his feet and stretched luxuriously. There were definitely advantages to being a wolf—a part of Drew recognized a sense of freedom and satisfaction in just *feeling* the world around him, something he couldn't get in his human form.

The black wolf approached him. He sensed a difference in her; the way she moved was subtly altered from before. There was threat here; no, not threat, but something different. Her scent was different. It pulled at him, enticing him.

The wolf responded. It was a natural instinct. The drive to mate was as basic and strong as the urge to feed. Sometimes stronger. Drew moved beside Ramona, nuzzling her and whimpering softly. She growled at him, but didn't push him away, or bite at him. Moving carefully with deliberation, the gray wolf placed his forepaws around the female's back and moved closer. She didn't resist. The two wolves mated in the barn, taking their time, and then went back to sleep, laying side by side.

●●◖◗◖◗●●

Parker was in hell, he was sure of it. Maybe it wasn't quite as hot as it was supposed to be, but it certainly felt like he was in the abode of the damned. Everywhere he turned—damnation! Ruin. Pestilence. Death.

In addition to being stuck in a nightmare where outlaw bikers were werewolves (something he still refused to verbalize), his "pride and joy" nephew gets bitten by a wolf, attacks his girlfriend, kills a guard dog, and runs away. If this didn't push his brother-in-law over the edge, he'd eat his hat. The big one, that looked like Smoky the Bear's.

And his wife, whom he loved and practically worshipped, kept looking to him to provide answers. Real ones that would explain everything, and restore order to the universe. She'd known him his whole life. If anyone should know just how over his head he was, it was she. Irritably, he shoved his sleeping wife. She groaned and shifted further away, still sleeping. Nothing kept her from her precious shut-eye.

Lately, he hadn't been able to get to sleep until he was so tired, he just passed out. Tonight was no exception. Despite the fact that he'd had only an hour or two of sleep yesterday, he was still tossing and turning fretfully, unable to keep his eyes closed. Every time he tried, he saw Drew sprouting fangs and fur, stalking through the neighborhood, howling and running from him, while he chased his nephew with hunting dogs and torches.

The sheriff shuddered and sat up, inadvertently pulling the blanket off of his wife. "Hey, jerk. Give me my blanket back. Go to sleep, okay?" she mumbled, patting the bed where he should have been laying. Parker sighed and covered her again with the blanket.

Easing off of the bed, he slipped down the hallway to the kitchen. Plugging in the coffee maker, he glanced at the clock on the wall. 'Three thirty. Crap,' he thought. Waiting for his coffee to brew, he stared out the window into the darkness. Another full moon. Parker swore that for the rest of his life, he would stay indoors and avoid even looking at the moon when it was full.

He turned away from the window and sat with his back to it, thinking about the day ahead. He needed to interview a witness that claimed to have seen a hospital nurse put a naked man into her car and drive off the previous morning. Since they'd actually managed to track Drew's blood from his neighbor's yard to some bushes at the hospital, it could be legit.

In addition, he needed to see his best friend, and try to convince him to fill out a missing persons report on his son. No, if what Parker feared was true, there could be no official paperwork on Drew's disappearance. Regardless, he wanted to be there for James.

He was so lost in thought, he didn't notice his wife until she flipped on the kitchen light. He jumped, spilling coffee onto the table.

"Can't sleep, again?" she asked. "How am I supposed to sleep with you prowling around out here?" Mary sat down at the table with her husband.

"Come on, Mare, I wasn't prowling or making any noise. I was just having some coffee," he grumped. "Anyway, you could sleep through a tornado, and you know it."

Her stern expression softened. "I know, Bob. The noise didn't get me up; it was the smell." She patted his shoulder. "And I missed you beside me. I know you're not sleeping. What can I do to help?"

Parker put his head in his hands. Running his fingers through his hair, he sighed and looked at her. "I don't know. Nothing makes sense. There is a perfect explanation for everything that's been going on; absolutely perfect. It just isn't rational, and can't be real. So what do you do when the only theory that fits the facts is fantasy, or horror, and can't ever be put on a report?"

"Didn't Sherlock Holmes say that once you eliminate everything, what can't be, is?"

"I think he said, 'Once you've eliminated the impossible, whatever is left, no matter how improbable, must be true," he corrected. "Not that it matters, Mary, because Mr. Holmes was also a fictional character, so what he said really doesn't count."

Crap. She would bring up Sir Arthur Conan Doyle's big quote. He used it frequently with his officers, and applying it here left him with his current predicament. What was left *was* the idea that he was dealing with a werewolf biker gang. And that his nephew was likely the newest member of that pack.

Parker was silent. His wife reached out and took his hand. She held it tightly and waited. When he finally spoke, he didn't look at her.

"You know, I never thought there could be anything that I couldn't deal with. No matter what happened, I could overcome it.

In high school, we won the state championship. We weren't bigger than the other teams; we just worked harder, smarter, and wouldn't accept that we wouldn't win," he said quietly, almost as if speaking to himself.

"The army was just like that. I busted my butt and never backed down, and I got through it. When that punk shot Helen, I chased him down and shot him. No hesitation—I just drew and fired when he raised his gun. I could get through the press and the inquiries because I knew I was right."

Parker wrapped both hands around his coffee cup and stared at the contents. "I get by with James' problems because I truly believed that we would find a way to fix it. Somehow, it would all get better. We could survive the tragedy. It would just take time.

"But this isn't going to end well. There are no answers to this that don't lead to hell," he paused, looking at her for the first time. There were tears in his eyes. He hadn't cried since their wedding day. "There's no way out: not for me, not for James, and not for Drew. I can feel it.

"I go into that damned office every day, and I can see that report that Jimmy keeps adding to, sitting on my desk, like a fucking Pandora's Box, just waiting for me. I see Lucy Parsons when I close my eyes, all ripped to pieces, standing in front of me, asking me why I let this happen to her."

"I don't know if I can go on like this," he said, voice breaking. "I want to get out of here. Away from Iowa Park, away from Texas, and away from law enforcement. I just want to go somewhere we can be together, sit and watch the sun set on the ocean or some shit like that," he finished, reaching for her.

Mary came over and sat on his lap. She held him tightly in her arms, cradling his head against her breast. "Robert…Robert, look at me," she gently demanded, tipping his head back. "Do you really want to leave? We can move, if that's really what you want. We will deal with this situation. I know we can get through this. If you don't want to be a cop anymore, that's more than okay with me, you know. Not that you don't look dashing with your big hat and star, you know," he smiled slightly at that.

"We will be fine, Bob. We'll take care of each other, just like always. Now, come back to bed with me. I'll hold you. We need to sleep, baby, and it will look a little brighter in the morning."

She stood, still holding his hand. She pulled him to his feet. "Come on, let's go back to bed." Reaching out, she unplugged the coffee maker and shut the light back off. For the next four and a half hours, Mary Parker held her husband close and watched over him as he finally relaxed and fell into a deep sleep.

CHAPTER 30

Morning found Drew and Ramona side by side in the barn. The first pains of the transformation woke both wolves, and they staggered to their feet, growling. Both howled in anger, snapping their teeth in the air at the agony being done to them. Grudgingly, the pair yielded to the return to human form.

Shaking in pain and exhaustion, Drew held out his hand towards Ramona. The dark-haired woman shook her head and slowly walked over to her clothes. She began getting dressed, ignoring the young man with her.

Drew watched her for a time, then silently turned to his own clothing. His emotions were turbulent. The newly turned werewolf remembered vivid scenes from the previous night: the pain of the change, the wrestling matches, eating and sleeping together, and finally, mating. He didn't understand everything, but he was confident of one thing—she liked him. They were together.

"Ramona," he started. The girl ignored him, throwing off the bar to the door and walking outside, leaving him staring after her in confusion. His face tightened in anger. 'What the fuck,' he thought.

Ramona came back in, carrying a bag. She set it down and unpacked more food. Without speaking, she started eating. Drew came over and dug in, too. Several minutes later, after consuming everything in the sack, they cleaned up the barn, trying to remove all traces of their stay. They worked in silence, still not speaking to one another.

As they were climbing onto their bikes, Drew broke the silence. "Ramona, what's going on? Why won't you talk to me? I didn't do anything wrong." Or did I? He wondered. "I'm not leaving with you if we don't talk."

She fixed him a withering stare. "So, that's how you're going to be? Don't get your way, so you're just going to leave? Spoiled little brat. Try it. Just stay here and let me go. The pack will find you. And then see what happens."

Suddenly Drew realized what was going on. With the dawn, her concerns over the pack, and her future, had returned. Their bonding during the night had added stress to her situation. She needed to deal with it, and the first thing he did was reach out to her for support, which only made her worries worse.

"Okay, fine. Let's go. Talk when you're ready," he growled, not happy but willing to back off, for now. There'd be time on the road. The disadvantage to a two- gallon peanut tank on the Sportster was that you had to stop every two hours to fill up.

She tossed her head and fired up her machine. Drew started his, and followed her onto the road. The morning was bright and clear, even if their future wasn't. Another glorious early fall day. The bikes thundered down the back roads.

●● ◖◯◗ ●●

After a half hour or so, Drew spirits lifted, the freedom of riding working its magic. As happy as his Honda made him, it was nothing compared to blasting along on the tricked-out Sportster. Behind his dark sunglasses, the young man's eyes sparkled.

With a smirk, he nudged ahead of Ramona, taking the lead. She glanced at him, her expression hidden behind her own wraparound shades. Drew hunched over his handlebars, imitating someone racing. He looked back over at her.

With a shake of her ebony mane, Ramona expressed her disdain for Drew's actions. She accelerated forwards and pulled in front of him. She goosed the throttle a couple of times, jerking the bike ahead unevenly, and settled down. Despite herself, she grinned when Drew honked at her.

'That's better,' Drew told himself. 'At least she can respond to the ride. We'll talk later. We've got all night,' he thought. Then he frowned. Tonight was another full moon, the third in the cycle. They needed to find a place to hide out before dark. And then, the next day, he would meet the pack, come face to face with Lucy's killers.

Sobering rapidly, he followed his companion to a gas station. They pulled in and shared a gas nozzle, managing to get just over four gallons into the two Harleys. They took off again, Ramona not wanting to linger and talk. That was fine with Drew, who was now wrestling with his own thoughts.

After another stop for fuel, the pair finally pulled into a rest stop and sat at a picnic table. Drew shifted uncomfortably on the concrete seat. He wasn't used to riding for hours on end, and his butt hurt. Ramona didn't seem to notice.

Irritably, he drummed on the tabletop. "Can we at least get some food? I'll buy." He turned around, looking to see if there was any food to be had at this stupid hole. All he saw was a bank of vending machines, probably filled with outdated candy bars. 'Swell,' he thought. He pivoted back around to glare at his silent companion. Ramona endured his glower without apparent hardship.

"We can get food next stop," she said, finally breaking the silence. They were the first words out of her mouth in several hours. "Right now I want to get something straight. Whatever happened last night wasn't us, okay? I mean, I wasn't myself, I was…damn it, you know what I mean!"

Drew scowled at her. "Like I was myself? C'mon, Ramona, I'm new to all this shit. You came to me, blabbering about how my life was over, and how I needed to come with you and be this biker werewolf guy in order to save my father. So here we are, and now you act like I'm the plague or something."

"Maybe you are," she retorted. "Maybe everything in this fucked up life of mine is just getting to me. Like one night together and all of my problems are gonna go away. Right," she snorted. "We're on our way to meet with Lobo and the rest of the pack, Drew. We may be riding to our execution. This isn't some Harlequin romance novel. This is serious stuff."

"No kidding. I just left my dad, my friends, and everything that meant anything to me behind so I wouldn't cause them any more trouble. What future I have sucks." He felt his fists clench tightly as his anger rose. "But *you* talked me into this, Ramona; we have to face what's coming. It'll go better if we face it together, rather than separately, and you know it."

"Like I can trust you," Ramona said, turning her back on Drew. "I don't even know you. Everyone else has let me down, why should you be any different?" she added, staring off into space.

"This isn't about trusting each other, it's about *surviving*. I need to know my father will be okay, then I'll figure out how to live my life. You don't have to trust me, just do what you need to survive."

Silence fell. Ramona remained with her back turned to Drew. The big teen-ager stared at her profile, angry at her, and at the same time entranced. He smiled. Despite everything, he couldn't get down. His entire life was defined by his outlook. No matter how bad things got, or what kind of shit happened to him, he wouldn't stay down.

"So, do you want a shitty candy bar, then, or not? Can't go to my grave hungry." He stood up, digging in his pocket for change.

Ramona snorted. She'd tried not reacting at all, but Drew was funny. His delivery was pretty good, too. It was hard to stay angry at him, since he hadn't really done anything wrong. She rose from the table as well.

"Get me a Peanut Butter Cup? I'm going to the bathroom." She swirled away as Drew looked after her in surprise. "Hey, Mr. Big Shot Quarterback; get me a Mountain Dew, too, huh?"

Wrench found the Fenris Firar by mid-afternoon. They were holed up outside yet another dive, just outside Amarillo. It was uncanny how members of the pack could find the main group. It was like a mobile homing beacon.

He rode up on his old panhead, threading his way between sprawled pack members. No one gave him more than a cursory glance. If Wrench were a more reflective or intelligent sort, he may have noted that he was less than popular with his "family." Instead, he merely grumbled at the number of people in his way.

Lobo was waiting at the center of the makeshift camp. The burly leader was standing shirtless, with hands on hips, as the diminutive rider shut down his bike and stepped off.

"Well?" Lobo demanded, his tone belying his nonchalant posture. The leader of the werewolf gang was more concerned about Ramona and Wrench's mission than he was willing to admit.

Wrench grimaced. He stretched his shoulders, and struggled to find the right words. He had been in a hurry to get back and report, but hadn't really figured out what he was going to say when he arrived.

"Wrench," Lobo hissed, "is there something wrong with your tongue? I assume that you have something to report, right?"

"Yeah, boss, of course. I, uh, came straight to find you, once we met up with the kid that Ramona bit. I knew that you'd want to know what was goin' on," he babbled. "So I came right here, to see you."

"Great, Wrench. Now, before I have Ulric tear off your empty fucking head, *tell me what's going on!*" Lobo roared, getting the attention of the entire pack.

Wrench swallowed. "It's bad, boss. 'Mona has the hots for this guy. She stayed behind to 'teach him about being a werewolf' or some shit like that. Said she wants to meet us in Amarillo tomorrow. With the Collins kid."

"And our problem with the mechanic?"

"The mechanic's the kid's dad. She wouldn't let me go after him. I think that this is gonna be a clusterfuck, boss," Wrench said. "It ain't my fault, either. She don't listen to me, and she damn near broke my arm ."

Several of the Firar laughed at his last comment.

"Shut the fuck up!" Lobo snarled. Silence ensued. "Now, Wrench, tell me again about this kid."

"Name's Drew Collins. He's some kind of stud football player at the high school there. His mom was killed by a robber; his dad is this depressed burnout mechanic that worked on my bike. Ramona tried to talk to him before the full moon, but he blew her off. Afterwards, he took his dad's Sportster and we met him on a back road outside of town."

"And then what, Wrench? Did you all make nice and friendly?"

"She told me to leave!" Wrench whined. "I tried to tell her that we had to deal with the mechanic, but she told me to go and find you. She was talking with the kid when I left, and they seemed to be gettin' along just fine."

"Anything else about the kid?" Lobo directed. He seemed a little calmer, which Wrench took to be a good sign.

"He's pretty big. Not like you or Ulric, but big. Doesn't like me, the shit. I think he knows I took the girl. He knew her, I think. I don't like it, Lobo. I think he's trouble."

Lobo growled and spun away, knocking Wrench to the ground with a dismissive slap. He stormed away, scattering pack members in his wake. Cursing to himself, the big man paced, trying to decide what to do next. The fact that Ramona was becoming more trouble than she was worth was painfully evident to him. It was probably easier to just remove her from the pack than continue dealing with her shit.

His eyes took on a more furtive look as his pace slowed. He glanced around at his pack. By and large, they took his orders well. Ramona wasn't well liked, but he still didn't know how they would take to killing one of their own. Trial by combat was fine, but not outright murder for no reason other than being a pain in the ass. No, he'd need a reason to eliminate her.

And that kid that she was bringing with her. There was no way that he could keep this guy. He'd be a liability. What if daddy came looking for him? Maybe *that* wouldn't be so bad, he thought. They could get rid of him easily, away from Iowa Park, versus going back to grab him. As long as the guy didn't bring any cops, they were fine.

He turned back to Wrench, who was sitting and snarfing down food. "Hey, asshole, any chance that Collins' dad would come looking for him out here?"

Wrench cringed. "Uh, I don't think so, boss. It don't seem likely."

"Why not? Doesn't he like his kid?" Lobo said, scowling. "Kid took his bike, too, you said. Sounds like a couple reasons to chase him down to me."

"Guy stays home all the time, Lobo. Barely leaves his house. And, uh," he stalled, causing Lobo to glare at him, "well, I think that the sheriff in Iowa Park is the kid's uncle, too. The cop would be more likely to come after him than his dad, I think."

Lobo roared and swung at the little man. Wrench dove to the ground and rolled away. The infuriated leader kicked and stomped at the smaller man, but Wrench kept out of the way. Finally Lobo swore and turned away from him.

Regaining some limited composure, Lobo began hatching plans on how to get rid of his problems without involving the cops. It wasn't going to be easy, but he could make it happen. Staring wrathfully at Wrench, who'd helped bring this shitstorm down on him, Lobo smiled to himself grimly. Maybe he could work this to his advantage and get rid of several problems at once.

CHAPTER 31

Friday afternoon was busy for Doug Jones. While the previous day was probably the toughest of his young life, Friday was even more work. He spent the school day fending off questions from everyone as to the whereabouts of his missing best friend, and then was confronted by his stern and imposing coach.

"Mr. Jones? A word with you, if I may," Stanton said, not so discreetly seizing his elbow and guiding him in to an empty classroom. The older man punctuated the seriousness of the situation by closing the door behind them, before turning to face his lineman, both arms crossed over his chest.

"So, would you care to enlighten me as to the status of our quarterback, Mr. Jones? His father hasn't returned any of my calls, and no one seems to know anything concerning his whereabouts." he growled.

"Coach, Collins won't be at the game tonight. He can't. I can't tell you more than that, because I don't know anything else—I swear," the last was a little high-pitched and nervous, since Stanton's face had darkened alarmingly.

"You know that he won't be at the game, but you don't know why, or where he is, is that it?"

"Uh, yeah, I guess," Doug stammered. "I mean, yes, coach, that's the truth. You'll have to talk to his dad for more stuff. I haven't seen Drew, not since his last practice, coach. Honest." Jones gave the man his most sincere expression.

Stanton scowled. "Mr. Jones, I happen to know that you were at his house Wednesday night, and that some questionable things went on there that night. So don't try to lie to me like that. Straight up, Jones: what's going on?"

268

Doug squirmed. His coach was pinning him down, and keeping the pressure on. What now? Memories of his past with Drew surged through his mind, and he realized that he owed his friend more than he did his coach. Even at the possible expense of his football career. Some things were more important than that.

He held his head up, and looked Stanton in the eye. "Coach, Drew's dealing with some things that are none of my business. He's my best friend, and I would help him if I could, but I don't know where he is or what is going on right now. It's not drugs or anything like that, but I don't think that he's gonna be able to play football here ever again." Doug felt a sudden confidence. "I'm sorry, but believe me, coach: I don't know anything else about it. You'll have to talk to Mr. Collins. Sorry, coach, but I gotta go," he finished, stepping around the stern-faced man and opening the door. Without glancing back, he walked out into the hall and headed for the parking lot.

Stanton stared after him for a time, then shook his head. He made a mental note to call the Collins residence again later, then set about trying to figure out a game plan for that night without his star quarterback. So much for dreams of glory and a state championship.

Doug made it to his car without further incident, and drove home to collect his gear for the home game later that evening. When he pulled into his drive, Amy Bishop was waiting for him. He felt a brief surge of pleasure at seeing her, but then remembered the secret they shared. She stepped away from her car to meet him in the driveway.

"Doug, do you have a minute?"

"Sure, Amy. What's up?" He continued towards the house. "Come on in, I have to get my stuff for the game. Don't mind the mess," he added, momentarily embarrassed as he thought of the condition that his room was in.

"No worries, Doug. We both know there are more important things than a clean room," she replied, following him through the house. Once she got a look at his bedroom, though, she caught herself.

"I may have been wrong," she grimaced, gingerly holding up a brown banana peel that was beginning to rot. "I'll just throw this out for you and wait by the door," she added, cocking an eyebrow at him and shaking her head.

By the time Doug collected his gear and rejoined the brunette, she had perused the family's extensive photo collection.

"Ready to go?" he asked, glancing back at her as he pulled open the door. She was still lingering over a picture or two by the bookcase. "Amy? You okay?"

She looked over from the pictures. "Doug, I didn't know that you were such a cute baby. I mean, you were positively adorable."

Doug blushed. That baby picture was a constant source of embarrassment, and his parents absolutely refused to take it down. Even his sister delighted in showing it to everyone who ever came into the house. Especially his dates.

Somehow in the midst of everything going on right now, it seemed ridiculous that Amy was commenting on that photograph. He couldn't know that it looked similar to a picture that she had of her little brother, and that it reminded her of what Drew had done for the both of them.

"Yeah, I guess. I grew out of it, though," he mumbled, unsure of what to say.

The nurse smiled at him. It was a small smile, but warm and genuine, and caused Doug's mouth to go dry. Once again, he wished that she was here to see him, and not just because of Drew.

'Oh well,, back to reality,' he thought. "You wanted something, Amy?"

"Yeah, Doug, I did. The police found blood in the bushes at the hospital. They're starting to interview everyone that was there that night. They'll get to me soon. What do you think I should say?"

"I don't know...you can't tell them the truth," Doug replied. "Beyond that, your guess is as good as mine. Drew was always the thinker, I'm more the direct action type." He reddened as she looked at him with raised eyebrows. "I mean, well, you know. You don't have to look at me like that...I wasn't trying to be stupid or anything, okay?"

"Relax, Doug, I'm just giving you shit. Just trying to lighten the mood a little. Are you always this serious?"

He looked at her in surprise. No one thought of him as serious, not even the guys he played football against. He was a giant-sized practical joke waiting to happen. Everybody knew that.

"No, I'm usually not serious at all. But right now, you know, doesn't seem like the time for jokes and shit. I spend all my time trying to cover for Drew and what happened, and I worry constantly about how he's doing, and where he is."

"All the more reason to at least try to lighten up while we're going through this," Amy replied. "Otherwise we'll both go nuts." She looked at him intently. "Wanna go get some food?"

Doug did a serious double take. Was she really...? "Uh, are you asking me out? Like a date? Don't get me wrong, I mean, I'd like to go out with you, I just don't know why you'd..." he trailed off, confused.

Amy laughed. "You know, for a second there, you looked just like your baby picture. Yes, I am asking you to go and get some food with me. You can even pay—I seemed to have given all my money to your buddy. What do you think?"

The young man smiled wide, then his face fell in almost comical fashion. "I can't. I got a game. I really gotta go. We won't get done until almost eleven. I'm really sorry. Maybe you'd like to go to the game...?" he trailed off, thinking about how stupid his football game must seem to a college graduate.

Amy smiled. "Maybe next time, Doug. I'm not really into sports. It's okay," she said soothingly, seeing his crestfallen expression. "There'll be other chances. I don't think that this problem is going away any time soon, do you?"

"No, probably not. I guess I'll see you later, then. Bye, Amy." Wistfully, he watched the attractive brunette get into her little car and drive away. Almost resentfully, he threw his gear into his vehicle and drove back to school.

Matt Roth watched the game with disinterest. As far as he was concerned, it was a juvenile sport, with arbitrary rules, a pointless scoring system, and only served to elevate brainless steroid addicts above everybody else, all for the sake of "competition." None of it mattered in the end, yet it looked like the entire town had made it a point to attend, screaming and thumping their chests like a bunch of gorillas watching a fight.

Bitterly, he reflected on the mistakes that had led to him being sent here. Okay, maybe he did on occasion drink a little more than he should. Maybe he *had* missed a deadline or two in the last month. He was still a damn good reporter! He should be doing real journalism, not wasting his time covering some stupid high school football game.

He was convinced his editor was out to get him. He'd taken that piece about the Collins kid getting bit by a wolf and blown it out of proportion, trying to make it look like a big deal, when it wasn't. Some dumb jock gets bit by a dog, so what? Now here he was, suffering through a game, and the hotshot he was supposed to be watching wasn't even playing.

Once the farce finally ended, he made his way to the field to try and find Collins. Several fruitless minutes of searching confirmed the kid wasn't there. Background grumblings from other Iowa Park players sank in: the guy missed the game entirely, and no one really knew why.

Roth felt a nudge. Just a small one, but he hadn't had his interest grabbed by much of anything for a long while, and any feeling at all was novel. Perhaps there really was a story here.

He grabbed a passing player, a big guy with a blood and dirt covered 79 on his jersey. "Hey, buddy. Just a minute. Where was Drew Collins tonight? I was supposed to interview him after the game, but I haven't seen him."

The player looked down at the guy holding his arm in anger. It was bad enough they'd lost to a team this crappy, but now that same asshole reporter that had shown up hung-over at school was here, trying to get a line on their star quarterback.

"I don't know, Jack. Let go," he growled, pulling his arm away from the smaller man. He tried to push past the reporter, but Roth noticed the name on the back of his jersey and cut back in front of him.

"Hey, aren't you Doug Jones? You're supposed to be Collins' best friend, right? So if anybody'd know where he was, it'd be you, right? C'mon, Jones, level with me."

Doug was suddenly nervous, and Roth knew he had touched a nerve. The lineman knew something, but was unlikely to give it up. "Look, mister, I don't know anything about Drew, okay? I think he's sick or something. It's no big deal; everybody misses a game now and then. Now, can I go shower? I need to get on the bus with the rest of the team."

Roth let him go. He stood on the field, staring up into the night sky. There was something going on here, he could feel it. For the first time in over a year, his life had a purpose. With a steady stride, the disheveled looking reporter walked back to his car and drove out of the lot.

●●◖◖◯◗●◗●●

When sundown caught up with Drew and Ramona, they were still barely speaking to each other. The previous day was spent talking almost non-stop, with Ramona trying to prepare Drew for life as a shape-shifter. This day was spent mostly in angry silence, both young people sullen and withdrawn. Drew's infrequent attempts at conversation and levity had been ignored for the most part by his taciturn companion.

Shortly before the sun set, Ramona rode her bike off of the road, into a field. Parking around a bend, she quickly stepped away from her Sportster and started shedding her clothes. Drew followed her example wordlessly. He folded his stuff up, left it on the seat of his bike, and set off after Ramona, who had walked away without so much as a glance.

Within moments, they felt the first stirrings of the change. Drew grimaced. He hated this part. Ramona kept walking, twitching at each spasm. The moon caught them fully. No longer able to walk, they fell to the ground in agony. The reality of the transformation was grossly different from the myth, where lycanthropes ran on a beautiful field, and just *flowed* into their lupine forms.

Once the two wolves regained their feet, they shook themselves, and ran deeper into the field, seeking the fresh scent of prey. While not hostile to each other, there was a guarded tension this night, a sense of caution and distance. When they took down a young fawn, they ate separately.

The remainder of the night was spent exploring, the two never far from each other, yet distinctly apart.

•• ◖◉◗ ••

Lem brought the morning paper in to Parker's office first thing on Saturday. "Seen this yet, boss?" he drawled, dropping an open page on the desk. "Thought you might want to take a look at Roth's piece."

The sheriff sighed and pulled it close. On page two, Matt Roth had written a short article on "The Disappearance of Iowa Park's Star Quarterback," going on to tie Drew Collins' absence from Friday night's game to the sinister killings of two college-aged people earlier in the fall. Despite the vagueness of the story and complete lack of any real "evidence," the story read disturbingly close to accurate.

Parker pushed the paper away and swore. He knew his phone lines would probably be lighting up any minute now, with concerned citizens demanding to know what was going on, and what he was going to do about it. So much for keeping this thing under wraps.

Jimmy Winslow blew in to the station, carrying a paper in his fist. He hurried to the sheriff's office, excitement all over his youthful features, making him look even younger. "Sheriff, sheriff, you gotta see this!" he burst out, pushing past Lem and holding out the paper towards his boss.

Parker merely motioned at the newspaper spilled across his desk. Winslow glanced down, and flushed. "Oh, you already saw it, huh? What do you think? Are they really connected like the guy says? You know, I always thought so. I mean, we tracked the blood from the yard all over town, and it ended there at the hospital, and then, nobody's seen Drew since, ya know?" he gushed, excitement once again plastered on his face.

"So, Sheriff, what are we gonna do now? Do you want me to put out an APB for Drew? Maybe that same gang that grabbed Lucy Parsons kidnapped him, too."

Lem, noticing the darkening scowl on the sheriff's face, grabbed the deputy's arm and pulled him out of the office. Parker put his head in his hands again, closing his eyes and trying to make the migraine go away. "More coffee," he mumbled. "I just need more coffee. And maybe a magic wand." Then he could make it all go away.

Outside the now closed office door, Lem was explaining to the junior officer how they couldn't put out an APB on Drew Collins, because he hadn't been reported missing. The word from his father, at least according to the sheriff, was that Drew was home sick. The reporter was just stirring things up to sell papers.

Winslow looked doubtful. He knew there was more going on than anyone was letting on. Why was his department trying to cover it up? He turned away from Lemly, making a silent vow that he would follow up on everything himself.

Lem watched the young man walk away angrily, and knew he was far from satisfied. Of course, neither was he. He also thought the biker gang had something to do with Collins' disappearance, even if Parker and James Collins were trying to pretend the boy wasn't missing.

Looking through the glass into his boss' office, he wasn't surprised to see the sheriff sitting with his head in his hands. He'd seen a lot of that pose over the last month. For the first time, Lem wondered if Parker was no longer fit to run the sheriff's department. Maybe he should retire, turn the whole mess over to someone else. The idea depressed him. No one else could run this place like Parker. He'd snap out of this. He just needed some time.

Chapter 32

The next morning, things were tense between Drew and Ramona. Once dressed, Ramona launched into a lecture about how he should act when they met up with the Fenris Firar later in the day.

"Once we find the pack, keep your mouth shut. Let me introduce you, but don't talk unless Lobo asks you a direct question. Don't respond to anyone else—Lobo is the only one that matters.

"Keep your head down, and don't make eye contact. Don't look to me for anything. If you act submissive to me, they won't respect you," she told him, ticking the points off on her fingers. She added more, this time pointing at him.

"And don't ask questions. If they take you in, follow everyone else's lead and do what they do. Don't take anything that looks like it belongs to anyone else, and don't let anyone take anything of yours either. Be prepared to fight, and fight dirty, for no reason at all. There are no rules. Keep your eyes open and your mouth shut.

"You got it?"

"Keep quiet, look down, don't take shit from you or anyone else, except that asshole Lobo guy. Got it. Anything else that I need to know, teach?" he asked, more sarcastic than he had intended.

"Fine, be an asshole. You're on your own, big man. Good luck," she grumbled, firing up her bike and drowning out any retort or apology.

Drew followed her onto the road, glaring at her back. That first day, when they met on the road outside Iowa Park, he actually thought that she might be something special, that his future wasn't as bleak as the curse made it seem. So much for that fantasy. Grimly, he wondered what was happening back home. He hoped his father was okay. He planned to call him once this meeting with the pack was over. At least the damn moon was done for now, and he had four weeks of "normality" in front of him.

They rode for just over an hour, stopping for gas outside Amarillo. They both knew that they would be encountering the rest of the Firar soon. They entered the attached McDonald's, and loaded themselves down with food.

As they were finishing their meal, Ramona cocked her head to the side. Drew froze in mid-bite as he, too, heard distant, heavy thrumming sounds, like building thunder. Ramona glanced once at Drew, eyes wide with fear. He stared back. It was time. The Fenris Firar had found them.

The parking lot was overwhelmed as twenty dirty hogs wheeled in, bearing leather clad bikers. Patrons nervously moved to the side, allowing the gang as much room as possible. People hurried to leave the store, in some cases abandoning food recently paid for, eager to put space between themselves and the bikers.

If they noticed the furor their arrival had caused, the bikers gave no sign. Their attention was directed at the two Sportsters parked off to the side. The Firar congregated around the bikes, drawing in tight, completely surrounding the white and orange Harleys.

As the thunder died away, the leader of the pack swung his leg over his bike, removed his sunglasses, and yelled, "Ramona!"

"Here, Lobo," came the response from the doorway to the McDonald's. Ramona and Drew stood just outside, facing the lycan gang. "We were on our way to meet you, like I promised. Didn't realize you were this close, or we would have just ridden straight to you."

"Of course you would, 'Mona," Lobo sneered. "Well, we're all here now, just one big happy family." He swept his arms over his gang. "A little public for conducting family business, though, don't you think? What if we don't like your little friend?" There were scattered laughs from the assembly.

"You met us, Lobo. We'll go wherever you want to."

"Yes, you will. Before we go, though, we should get some provisions. Caleb, Piggy: food. Be quick," he said, snapping his fingers at the two scouts. The pair hurried off, pulling out wallets thick with pilfered money.

Lobo turned back to Ramona and her companion. "Well, well, let's meet the new prospect, shall we?" Lobo smiled. "Come over; stand by your bike and introduce yourself," he instructed, waving Drew over to stand in front of the pack.

Drew was used to being watched by hundreds of people. He'd been scrutinized, adored, and occasionally vilified, by football fans for much of his young life. None of that prepared him for the stares of the Fenris Firar. The pack members studied him with expressionless faces, and there was a palpable aura of hostility and hunger in the air.

He resisted the urge to hunch his shoulders protectively as he walked past the Firar, slipping among the bikes to get to his ride. Despite the early morning sunshine, he felt cold. And pissed off. Feeling this defensive scared him, and made him want to lash out.

His posture must have been visible to the outlaw leader, because Lobo laughed again, and shouted, "Relax, nothing is gonna happen here. We just wanna see how pretty you are. There, that's nice. Hold that pose," he cooed, as once again the rest laughed.

Drew stood his ground, face burning, lip curling slightly. Ramona said, "Okay, Lobo, they're back, can we get this show on the road, or what? Let's get going; you can stare at the pretty boy more later if you want."

Lobo's gaze snapped over to Ramona. "Fuckin' bitch. Shut the hell up. You'll get what's coming to you soon enough. You shouldn't want to rush it. But if that's how you want it, let's get going," he sneered. "Piggy, you and Aardwolf, Caleb, and Wrench, all of you ride behind them and make sure that they stay with us. Let's ride."

Drew looked at Wrench, who met his glance with a grin and a fierce throat-cutting gesture. Then he motioned for Drew to get on his bike and precede him out of the lot. His smile for Ramona was full of evil intent as well. She flipped him off and took off after

Drew. The rear guard fell in behind them as the pack headed for a deserted area to conduct their 'business.'

It didn't take long for Lobo to find a suitable site. He pulled into an empty lot, then drove his bike to a small wooded area, out of sight from the road. He shut down his chopper and stepped to the center of the clearing. The others parked and circled him.

The Fenris Firar's leader held up his arms dramatically, calling the pack to order. Silence ensued, all eyes on the big man in the middle. Lobo smiled. He enjoyed these moments, when everyone was watching him, hanging on his every word.

"Members of the Firar, we have business to deal with today. One of our own has bitten a human," he began. "Ramona attacked a human last month, and left him alive. To make her mistake worse, she didn't tell us until after we had left the area, so that we couldn't finish him off cleanly." Jeers came from the pack, and hateful looks were directed at Ramona and Drew.

"Now this man has turned. He is one of our kind. Ramona has petitioned us to let him join our pack. This whelp—I really can't call him a man, wants to be one of the Fenris Firar; one of the chosen."

The weight of the gang's eyes fell on Drew, and he forced himself not to flinch or slouch.

"He has our curse. He has a ride," motioning towards Drew. "But does he have our blessing?" Lobo turned his hands palm up, asking the pack for their opinions. A discordant roar erupted. Loud voices overlapped each other, pack members vying with each other to be heard.

Lobo let it build for a time, then held up his hands again for silence. This time, it took longer for the members to fall quiet, with muted grumbling from several continuing on as Lobo resumed speaking.

"My people, it gets worse. Our faithful Wrench," he inclined his head towards the eager rider, "has determined that this kid, this child who wishes to join with us, has a father who set the police on our heels.

"Our little Ramona, who we brought in to our fold, and made one of us, has not only been *aware* of all of this, she *still* chose to bring him into *our* midst." He leveled an accusatory finger at Ramona. "She has given me no assurances he won't betray us, and bring the police. For all I know, they may be closing in on us as we speak," he added, as Ramona's eyes blazed at him with fury.

"And so, my good people, I leave it to you: kill him, or let him in?"

Loud shouts of "no chance" and "kill the bastard" were interspersed with cries for Ramona's head as well. Lobo grinned. It was going just the way he wanted it to. He looked at Ramona, saw her anger, and knew that she was going to speak. Perfect.

"Members of the pack: listen to me!" the raven-haired woman yelled. Eventually the gang quieted enough for her to be heard, but she was surrounded by hostile faces. She was angry enough right now to not care.

"I didn't ask for this 'gift.' This curse was forced on me, against my will, as it was for all the rest of you. Do you forget how you each came to be a member of this fucked up pack?"

Her accusations quieted some of the comments, as faces lost some of their hostility. "I didn't intend to bring anyone into this shitty existence, but it happened. I bit someone and he lived. Now he has this curse, too. He has the right to live out his life, the same as any of the rest of you. Do you deny that?

She rounded on the gang leader. "Lobo tries to scare you with stories of the police. It was his actions, and Wrench's, that brought the cops, not Drew's. If he is made a member of the pack, it would insure that he wouldn't bring in the cops. Why betray himself?"

The pack was silent, mulling over her words. Lobo let them think for a moment, and then spoke again.

"Pretty words, my Firar. Doesn't change a thing. The brat still doesn't belong here. Look at him—hasn't said a word in his defense. What, is he chicken? Or perhaps stupid? We don't need more of that; we already have Aardwolf," he said, to chuckles.

Drew spoke. Goaded by the big man in the vest, he couldn't keep quiet. His blood boiled, and he stepped forwards to confront the bigger man.

"Fuck. You," he snarled, fists clenched.

Lobo laughed uproariously, the gang joining in. Drew looked around, nonplussed. What was so funny about him insulting Lobo?

"Oh, little boy, that's good. That's real good. You wanna fight with me? Sorry, but only pack members can challenge for the right to lead. You're just a prospect. Or maybe just tomorrow's road kill… we haven't decided yet." He laughed mockingly. "Tell you what, maybe we should play with you a little, see if you're worth keeping around," Lobo said, pretending to wipe tears of laughter from his eyes.

Ramona shot Drew a hard look, then turned to face Lobo again. In a voice void of emotion, she said, "we invoke the right to trial by combat. If he wins, he rides with the pack. If he loses, he goes."

Silence descended over the pack. Lobo pretended to mull the challenge over. He had set this up carefully, and had a pretty good idea how it would play out. He pursed his lips, playing the game to its fullest extent.

"Fine. Little boy, you get to fight for your right…" he intoned. "Wrench, front and center. You're the idiot that allowed all this to happen, so here's your chance to make it right." Pointing at Drew, Lobo commanded, "Take out the trash."

Wrench growled and hurled himself at the teenager. Drew was caught off guard, things happening too fast for him to adjust to. Wrench hit him low and dumped him to the ground.

Blows rained down on Drew's head. Wrench was unloading on him, intent on inflicting as much damage as he could, as quickly as he could. Drew pulled his head up, into Wrench's chest, to protect himself. He wrapped the smaller man in a bear hug, pinning his arms so Wrench couldn't punch at him anymore.

The biker growled again and leaned down, trying to bite at Drew's ears. With a savage twist, Drew threw the man off of him and jumped back to his feet. He brought his hands up, fingers twisting into claws. His face reflected the savagery that was now lodged in his soul.

When the smaller man came at him again, Drew grabbed his right arm with his left, pulling him closer, and smashed his right forearm into Wrench's face. The man's nose shattered. He followed with a knee to the stomach, doubling the biker over.

Drew brought both forearms down on Wrench's back, driving him to his knees. Collins' mind was so full of rage that he was reacting more like an animal than as a thinking, rational human being.

It cost him. Wrench kicked out, driving his boot into the side of Drew's left knee, buckling his leg and dropping him to the dirt. The vicious biker came up with his own forearm, catching the younger man under the jaw and snapping his head back. Drew fell on his back.

Wrench regained his feet and stood over the fallen man. As Drew turned over and tried to get up, Wrench savagely kicked him in the ribs, dropping him back to the ground. Blood poured from Wrench's nose, but he looked triumphantly at Lobo. The pack leader held out his hand, thumb extended sideways, Roman emperor fashion, and turned it down, to the cheers of the pack.

"Go ahead, Wrench, kill the little fucker," Lobo called. "When you're done, you can go back to that shitty little town of his and kill his daddy, too." He cast a sideways glance at Ramona, grinning wickedly. "We'll take care of his bitch ourselves."

Wrench smiled and pulled out his namesake, the large wrench he often used to great effect. He held it up with a flourish, and the gathered bikers cheered him on.

Ramona was held back, just as she started to jump into the fight. Piggy grabbed her from behind and hissed, "No, no, no, bitch. Stay right here and watch. You're next."

Drew lay on the ground, ribs aching, jaw out of place, and knee throbbing. He'd never been hurt like this before. Dimly, he heard Lobo's voice calling to Wrench, telling the little man to kill him. His pulse accelerated. He heard the outlaw leader say that after he was dead, they would kill his father, too. Fresh hatred poured through his veins, and he rolled away from Wrench's first swing with the heavy tool.

Wrench missed his overhead smash, the young man rolling away from him. The biker swore and stepped up to swing again. Drew rose to his feet and faced the approaching man, eyes blazing with fury. Thoughts of his father being victimized by the demented psychopath in front of him brought a snarl to his lips.

As Wrench swung his weapon, Drew brought up his left arm, blocking against the inside of his opponent's wrist. He swept the arm down, and seized the wrist with his right hand. Shifting in behind Wrench's arm with his left side, Drew struck Wrench quickly on the side of the jaw and then in the front of the throat.

The outlaw gagged, shifting back slightly. Drew retained his grip on Wrench's right wrist, drawing him forwards. His left forearm pushed against his throat, forcing the biker's head back. Drew shoved harder, encircling Wrench's neck with his left arm, and arching the smaller man's back, so that he looked like he was trying to do the limbo.

Wrench's left arm flailed at Drew ineffectively. The young man growled and straightened up, violently yanking up with his tensed left arm. There was a loud crack, and the biker's body went limp. Drew dropped him to the ground with an oath. Contemptuously, he spit on the dead biker. "That was for my father, you piece of shit. And for Lucy."

He locked his reddened eyes onto Lobo's. His chest heaved, struggling to regain his breath, winded from both the fight and the stress. The pack was silent. Lobo smiled at the newest member of his gang.

"Well, well, the kiddie's got claws," he observed. "Welcome to the Fenris Firar, junior. I guess Ramona will show you around, introduce you to everybody. Ulric, you and Graybeard take care of our late, lamented Wrench, will you?"

The leader looked around at the assembly. "The rest of you assholes, be nice to the newbie. Who knows, he may be able to kill you, too. Violent little kid, it must be all the football," Lobo smirked. "Ulric, a word with you," he said, turning away for a whispered conversation with his lieutenant. The huge man nodded and followed his leader.

"Okay, break it up. Party's over!" Lobo yelled, startling the somewhat dazed group of bikers into motion. Most of them were still trying to deal with the suddenness of Wrench's demise, and Drew's acceptance into the pack. Soon, though, they started squabbling over Wrench's few possessions, and the women that were still without their own rides had a fight to determine who took over the panhead.

Piggy, fresh off her victory, spat a mouthful of blood at Ramona, smiled, and flipped the other woman off. "Someday soon, bitch, you'll get yours. Watch your back," she threatened, and stomped off to put her things on her newly acquired ride.

Ramona glared at the ugly woman's retreating back, wondering if she should try to take her out right now, while she could. Looking over at Drew, who was limping her way, holding his ribs, she decided to wait. He was hurt, likely shaken by his fight.

"Drew, you okay?" she asked, taking his arm as he reached her, the previous day's anger and distance forgotten.

Drew pulled his arm free and glared at her. He hadn't forgotten her treatment. The young man shook his head and walked off, trying his best not to limp and show weakness to the outlaws that openly stared at him. Finding a spot to himself, Drew sat down awkwardly and stared at the ground for a time. His body shook uncontrollably. Abruptly, he leaned forward and vomited. After heaving for several minutes, he shuddered and then sat back.

The knowledge he had just killed a man ate at him. Drew reflected bitterly on how his life had changed over the course of a month. He had gone from popular senior in high school, with aspirations of playing college football, and whose biggest worries consisted of term papers and whether or not he'd ever get past second base with a girl, to a man on the run from the law, guilty of killing his neighbor's dog, sexual assault on another teen, and now, murder.

The thoughts led to another bout of dry heaves, as his body tried to physically purge him of his guilt. It didn't work. Eventually he gave up, and he lay back on the grass, staring up at the sky.

"First time killin' someone, huh?"

Caught completely unaware, Drew twisted quickly around, gathering his feet under him, ready to defend against this surprise visitor. He heard a man laugh.

"Easy son, I'm not here to fight. Just wanted to see how you're doing. Most of our injuries heal quick on their own, but if something's out of place, it can hurt like hell. Let's take a look, okay?"

Drew relaxed. It was the older guy from the gang, Graybeard, or something like that. The guy looked like he was in his early fifties, like Drew's father, but had a harder edge. He stared at Drew appraisingly. "Never even been in a serious fight before, have ya, kid?"

Drew shook his head.

"Don't worry about it. It was self-defense. No one will blame you for Wrench. He was a vicious little fucker. Doubt anybody'll miss him much, except maybe for Lobo. Always liked stupid people who'll do anything for him." Looking around him, he motioned towards a few of the others. "Like Ulric. Aardwolf, too, I guess. Watch them, Collins. If they think Lobo wants you dead, they won't hesitate to try to take you out to advance themselves in his eyes."

The burly, bearded biker reached out and took Drew's chin in his hands, tilting his head from side to side, checking his jaw. "Hmm, looks okay. Have a helluva bruise tomorrow. How's your knee?"

Drew flexed his knee, wincing as he straightened and bent his leg. It hurt like hell. "It's okay, I think. Just hurts; nothing feels wrong." Getting to his feet, he shrugged his shoulders to loosen them up, and looked at the older man.

"Thanks. I'm okay now. Just feels weird, you know? I just killed a man with my bare hands, but I don't feel that bad about it," Drew said, shrugging. "I wanted to kill him ever since I found out he was the one that took Lucy." Drew sighed. "What happens now?"

Graybeard smiled. "Now you ride with us. It's a hard life, but it beats lying around, waiting for some farmer to shoot you during a full moon while you're out hunting."

Drew nodded. He flexed his knee once more, then followed the other biker back to the clearing. The rest of the pack were setting up camp for the night. The Firar were oddly quiet and subdued, considering their usual level of raucous activity. A few members called out a quiet, "hey, kid," as he entered the camp, but beyond that, he was ignored.

Ramona was setting out her stuff, and trading evil glares with the ugly biker chick they called "Piggy." As far as Drew could tell, she was well named. He didn't have any trouble believing that she was some cursed beast

Drew stopped beside Ramona, looking uncertainly around for his things. The young woman nodded to their left. She'd set his backpack on the ground next to her own. His bike had been moved to a spot just alongside her Hugger.

"Thanks," he mumbled, unsure of where to go. She was completely unreadable. He sat down heavily, favoring his injured knee.

"You're welcome. Do you want anything to eat? The rest of the pack ate while you were…sorting stuff out," she said, staring at the ground. Drew studied her. She seemed ill at ease herself. 'Good,' he thought. 'Why should I be the only one?'

Ramona stood quickly, turning away and swaying off to find him leftovers while offering him a stunning view of her backside. Drew caught his breath, staring despite his resentment. The silver-eyed siren glanced back at him over her shoulder, catching him staring. She smirked and resumed her search.

Drew sat, determined not to blush. So he was checking her out, big deal. After everything that he'd been through recently, looking at a girl's ass seemed pretty trivial. 'After all,' he told himself, 'it's not like we haven't been…' his thought process derailed. How did you describe what they'd done? Could they be lovers? Was he still a virgin? They had mated as wolves, but not so much as kissed as people.

'Shit,' he swore. If his life got any more complicated, he'd need Jones to explain it to him. As if that moron could make sense of anything. The guy could barely pass English, and that was his native tongue.

Memories of Doug made him suddenly homesick. He really hadn't thought about what Jones, nevermind his father, were doing in his absence. Odds were, Doug and Amy were frantic, waiting to hear from him. He had the cell phone that they'd purchased for him, insisting that he check in from time to time. Well, he definitely had news for them.

'Remember that guy that abducted Lucy Parsons,' he'd say. 'Yeah, well, I killed him, and joined a werewolf biker gang, running with the same chick that bit me.' Right. That story would go over great. They'd probably come after him with butterfly nets. He'd wait on the update.

Ramona came back with a paper plate covered with roast beef, bread, cheese, and hamburgers. She handed it to Drew along with a Big Slam of Mountain Dew. He wasn't sure that he wanted the caffeine, but all the carbohydrates looked really good. He dove into his food, pausing only to take an occasional swig of soda.

Once Drew cleaned the entire plate, he looked up at his companion, who hadn't moved the entire time, expressionless as she watched him. He suddenly felt self-conscious.

"Um, thanks, Ramona. Sorry, I was just so hungry. I forgot to thank you. And for putting my stuff out, and moving the bike." He looked back down at the plate in his hands. "So, what do we do now?"

"We just hang loose. Tomorrow we'll have to deal with Lobo more. He's not done with us, not by a long shot. And it's going to get worse," she finished, with a bitter edge.

"What do you mean, 'it's gonna get worse?' I thought this was how you wanted it to go. I fought that asshole, and joined the pack. You're safe, I'm safe, and my dad is safe. What's wrong with that?"

Ramona looked away. When she spoke, her voice was low and cold. "While you were off puking and getting your shit together, Lobo paid me a visit. Said my continued acceptance was now up to you. You own me, in the eyes of the Firar, and I'm your 'old lady.' It's my job to see that your every wish is fulfilled, and that you're taken care of."

Drew stared at her. "And that's so bad?"

"It's meant to be an insult to me, Drew. I'm supposed to be totally subservient to you, and have no rights in the pack at all. I'm just your property. Lobo meant it as punishment, and is trying to drive me out."

"I wouldn't ever do anything bad to you, Ramona," Drew insisted. "What do you mean, 'totally subservient,' anyway? Do all bikers talk like you?"

Ramona glared at him. "You stupid shit. I'm not an idiot. Not all bikers think and speak like Aardwolf. If I want to use words like 'subservient,' then I'm damn well going to use them. So fuck you," she spat. "*And* your limited redneck vocabulary!"

Drew sat back, at a loss. Before he could find a way to appease the angry woman, another presence announced itself with a disagreeable odor, poorly masked by an overabundance of cheap perfume. A heavy bundle was dropped on the ground near the couple's feet.

"Lobo wanted him to have this. Make sure you get the patch on it right away, 'Mona," Piggy leered, reveling in Ramona's new 'position.' The fat-faced biker turned up her nose at Drew and sauntered off.

Ramona shoved herself up from the ground, cursing. The young woman was incensed, muttering under her breath that she would kill the fat pig, and wear her ugly head as a hat. When Drew tried to speak with her, she snarled at him, telling him that her problems were, in fact, all his fault. He shook his head and turned to pick up what Piggy had thrown on the ground.

The bundle consisted of two items. The largest was a black leather jacket. It was an extra large in almost brand new condition, with a liner and removable sleeves so that it could be worn as a vest. The second was a dirty patch for the back, bearing the logo of the Fenris Firar. It was old and stained, and appeared to have been just recently torn off a different jacket.

Drew raised the patch to his nose and sniffed. Wrench. The patch used to be his. Collins threw it down in disgust. He picked up the jacket and inspected it. It bore the faint scent of an unfamiliar man.

"Well, slip it on, idiot," Ramona snapped. Obviously her mood hadn't improved while Drew was checking out Piggy's delivery. Impatient, she moved around him, adjusting the jacket around his shoulders, fussing with zippers and lacings, muttering under her breath.

Drew snarled at her, "Hey, it's not my fault that bitch hates you. Don't take it out on me. None of this was my idea, Ramona."

"Just shut up and give me the jacket. I'll get the fucking patch stitched on in a bit, and then you can be all official, the newest member of the kennel club," she sneered, snatching both jacket and patch from him, then stomping off to find a needle and thread.

Drew ground his teeth in frustration and looked around. Many of the Firar were sitting around, openly grinning at him. . Damn it. He felt like kicking someone's ass. Then he remembered earlier. A man was dead, and he was responsible. The thought drove all feelings of violence from his body, leaving him drained.

Sitting down, he opened up his backpack and started pulling things out. Halfway through, he stopped, puzzled. His favorite shirt was missing. He hadn't packed much, but he knew he had put his old practice shirt, emblazoned with his name and number, in here. Now it was gone. He looked around again, eyes narrowed.

No one looked suspicious, so he went back to sorting out his things. When Ramona returned, she dropped the jacket, with its newly sewn patch, next to him, and a dirty duffel bag in front of him.

"Wrench's stuff, belongs to you now," she said, before stalking over and sitting down amidst her own gear, silent. Evenly returning the stares of the other pack members, she was able to stare all of them down with the exception of Piggy, who just leered at her in obvious enjoyment of her rival's disgrace.

CHAPTER 33

Robert Parker had just entered his office, flanked by Deputy Becker, when Jeremiah Randall announced "Sheriff, we got a wire from the cops in Amarillo. They found a body this morning, matches the APB we put out on the guy from Bernie's. It just came across, Sheriff, so I haven't called them yet. Figgered you'd wanna do that yerself."

'Jesus,' Parker thought. 'At least let us come in the door.' The meatloaf they'd had for lunch at Albertson's was sitting heavy in his stomach, and Randall's immediate 'ambush' was enough to send him reaching for the antacid in his pocket.

"Show me what you've got, Jerry," Becker said, reaching for the page in the desk sergeant's hand. "We'll take a look."

The sergeant pulled it away from Ray's outstretched hand and put it behind his back. "This is for the Sheriff, not you, deputy," he said pompously.

"Damn it, Randall, what do you think he's gonna do with it? Run away and hide it from me? Give me the damn thing, then, and get the hell out of our way." Parker snatched the now crumpled piece of paper from his upset subordinate, and walked with Becker back to his office, pointedly slamming the door on the lingering sergeant.

Parker laid the sheet down on his desk so that both men could examine it. Under a grainy head shot of the deceased man was a description of the circumstances surrounding the discovery of the body. A man on his way to work had found it dumped on the side of the road. Preliminary cause of death appeared to be a broken neck, but were other indications of violence, consistent with a beating or fight.

As Parker and Becker were looking, Randall buzzed in. "Sheriff, line one is the State Police. They want to talk to you about the body."

Becker reached over and punched the speaker button, then line one. Parker nodded his thanks and leaned over his desk.

"Parker."

"Sheriff Parker, this is Sergeant Morris from the State Police. Want to talk to you about the stiff. You did get our fax?"

"Yeah, Morris, I'm looking at it right now," Parker answered. "Might be the guy we're looking for, but I need to take the picture to our witness first."

"Sheriff, we don't have an ID yet, but expect to within the hour. Looks like the guy's probably been dead almost twenty-four hours, neck's broken—probably what killed him, and was holding a big mechanic's wrench with dried blood on it. He was wearing a biker jacket with the membership patch ripped off."

"Okay, so maybe it was gang related. If it was our guy, the world is a better place without him," Parker said, as Becker shook his head reprovingly. Parker shrugged. It was the truth.

"Well, Sheriff, we may have a problem with that. You see, we found the wrench in his right hand, but he had a torn shirt in his left. Looks like he tore it off of the guy he was fighting with," came the voice from the speaker. "The shirt was a football practice jersey. It had the number twelve on it, and the last name Collins was on the back."

"Oh fuck. Shit on me," Parker breathed, reaching over to switch off the speaker. His world spun out of control. Drew couldn't be involved in this, there was no way. Even as his heart cried out, "No, it's impossible," his mind was putting together the timing and possible sequence of events.

"Sheriff Parker, are you still there? Hello?" his phone shrilled. Ray Becker picked up the handset and spoke quietly into it for a moment, then hung up.

Becker looked at his boss. "I told them that you needed to make a couple of calls, and that you'd get right back to them."

"Thanks, Ray," Parker said, sitting down at his desk. "Can you give me a minute?" His legs seemed to be having difficulty supporting him. "Now," he barked, as his deputy stood looking at him with concern.

"Sure, boss, whatever you say. I'll be out in the hall." Becker slipped out of the office and eased the door shut behind him. Parker heard voices almost immediately, glancing up long enough to see Ray cut off the sergeant, who was trying to get past the younger man and enter Parker's office.

Putting his head into its accustomed place, buried in his hands, he tried to think of what to do next. He didn't want to confront James, but he also knew there was no way he could pawn this off onto someone else. Wearily, he raised his head.

He stood up, put on his hat, and walked to the door. Becker was still standing just outside it, back to the office, arms folded across his chest, clearly standing guard. 'Good man, that Ray Becker. Deserves better than the way I treat him,' Parker thought. 'Kinda like my wife.' Lord knew she deserved better than how he'd been treating her lately, too.

Opening the door, he brushed Becker aside. "I'm going to visit Jim. Got to show him the picture and talk with him some about Drew. When the Staties call back, put them through to me, okay?"

"Sure thing, sheriff. Anything else?" Becker asked.

"No, just…thanks, Ray. I appreciate everything you do here. You're a good man," Parker mumbled, pushing past the startled deputy and striding out the door.

●●◖◯◗●●

James Collins was performing a 10,000 mile service on a newer Electra Glide Ultra Classic when Parker arrived.

"Jim. We need to talk. Can you take a break?"

Collins nodded his head at the bike. "Almost done. Can you give me a few minutes to finish up? The guy's already here waiting for it."

"Go ahead," Parker nodded, sitting in a chair by Collins' tools. James stared at him for a moment, then sighed and turned back to the Hog. He hadn't expected the sheriff to wait there with him.

Fifteen minutes later the bike was done, Parker surprisingly helping his friend with wiping the big blue machine down and polishing it up. The mechanic pulled it outside the service area and handed the ticket to the manager, then informed him he'd be taking his break.

Collins walked outside, and followed the sheriff to a nearby bench and sat. Neither spoke for a time. Finally, Parker cleared his throat and turned to his best friend.

"Jim, we got to talk about a couple of things." He pulled out the crumpled page and handed it over. "I need you to look at this picture, see if you recognize the guy."

James looked at the photo and stiffened. He'd never forget that face. Even as bad a picture as it was, it was easy to identify.

"Yeah," he grunted, not looking up. "It's him. The one that was in the shop. Looks dead. Is he?"

"Uh-huh. State Police found his body couple hundred miles away, near Amarillo. Neck's been broken. Looks like he tangled with the wrong guy."

Collins raised his head, staring straight at Parker. "Good. If he was the one that took Lucy, then I'm glad. They should give whoever did this a medal. Wish I could have been there."

Parker looked back at him. Without blinking, he fired back, "Is that really what you think? We got a suspect, James. It's Drew. His shirt was found in the dead guy's hand."

What little color James Collins had, vanished. He stared blankly across the parking lot, lips working soundlessly.

"Drew. How? Can...can...I mean...what happened? Do you really think he was involved?"

"Jim, no one will talk about what happened that night, but the reality is that Drew is gone, and we're pretty certain that he killed that dog, then took your Sportster and vanished. I know that you told people that he was just sick and staying home," Parker shot his friend a fast look, trying to catch something. "But he hasn't been around since that night, has he?"

Nothing. It was obvious Collins hadn't seen his son. Parker felt something inside him wither and die. His nephew was definitely involved.

"I haven't heard from him, Bob. Not a word," Collins said, softly.

"Didn't think so. Do you have any idea where he could be, maybe someone he told? Jim, do you have any idea who might? No one just leaves without telling someone."

Parker suddenly thought of Doug Jones, Drew's best friend. 'No one leaves without telling someone,' he said again in his head. Who else would know? Who better than his best friend? Doug was even there the night it happened.

"Jim, I gotta go see somebody. If anybody contacts you, asking questions, refer them to me—don't talk to anybody. I'll come by tonight and check on you, okay?"

Parker left his childhood friend sitting forlornly on the bench outside of Bernie's, staring at his hands without expression. He didn't look up as the sheriff left the parking lot in a hurry, tires squealing.

●●❨◗◉◖❩●●

Drew started his second day with the Fenris Firar with apprehension. Upon waking, he found Lobo and his henchmen, Ulric and Aardwolf, sitting on the ground in front of him, watching him intently.

"Mornin', sunshine," Lobo greeted him. "Sleep well?"

"Yeah, fine," Drew muttered, sitting up and facing them. He looked from face to face, trying to read what was going on. Ramona sat next to him. Whatever their problems between them, she at least knew where, and with who, her priorities were.

"Ah, the lovely Ramona. Nice of you to join us," Lobo greeted, with a smirk. "So, Collins, how is she? Used to be with me, you know. Come see me later and I can tell you more about what she likes. Right, "Mona?" he leered.

"Do you need something, Lobo?" Drew asked. He carefully controlled his anger, not wanting to start something that he wasn't ready to finish. Especially after yesterday.

"Yeah, kid. We got to go collectin' today. I figure since you deprived us of Wrench, and he was one of our scouts, you can do his job. Of course, maybe you ain't up to it, but let's give it a try, huh?"

"Lobo, this guy's a burn right now. He just left his hometown and they gotta be lookin' for him," Ramona said, scowling. "You make him go out and somebody'll see him for sure. You really want that trouble?"

His grin said what his words didn't. He was counting on Drew being seen, and picked up...or shot. "Why don't you let your old man decide that for himself, bitch? Stay in your place," Lobo growled back.

"Kid," he continued, turning back to Drew, "you got to learn to keep your old lady in line, or else someone might get angry. So, you wanna earn your keep or not?"

"Depends on what I have to do," Drew said carefully. "Don't want to do anything illegal."

The pack erupted in laughter. Lobo seemed delighted, his raucous laughter could be heard over everyone else's. He theatrically wiped away tears of merriment.

"Boy, our entire existence is against the laws of nature. Our very lives are illegal," he said, face devoid of any vestige of humor. "In order for us to survive, we are forced daily to break mankind's bullshit laws. Don't you ever whine to me again about illegal, you got that? Never again!"

Lobo rose to his feet, enraged. "Fuckin' little pussy," he spat. Turning away from Drew, he motioned to one of the other bikers in the crowd. "Red, take Wrench's place as scout. Pretty boy needs to grow some balls, I guess. Killed a man yesterday, now he's all worried about breaking the law."

The red-haired biker nodded and headed over to his hog. Following Caleb's lead, he pulled out and rode off, with Winnie trailing. Ramona stayed behind with Drew, despite being the fourth scout for the pack.

Drew stood, watching the departing scouts with a scowl on his face. Lobo had made a fool out of him, but there was more to it than that. The leader was trying to set him up for something worse. He glanced over at Ramona, to see if she, too, caught a sense that Lobo was playing him.

The woman was glaring at Lobo's back, hands curled into claws. 'If ever looks could kill...' Drew thought. The look she gave Lobo was murder. Drew decided he could talk with her later.

●● ◖◗●●

By the time the three scouts returned late that afternoon, Ramona was calm enough to explain some of the facts of life to Drew. Drawing him away from the lounging pack, she took him for a walk, so they could talk without being overheard.

"Scouts do more than just find decent locations to camp. Their job is to find neighborhoods ripe for burglary. Sometimes they find 'entertainment' also," she explained. "Almost every member of the pack has a specific job, you'll have to find something useful to contribute."

"Like what? There has to be more to what we do than steal from houses. How could twenty or so people live on just that?"

Ramona shrugged. "We roll drunks, waylay hitchhikers, fleece other biker gangs... anything to get what we need."

"Sounds delightful. It's not bad enough that we're werewolves, we have to be thugs and deadbeats too?" Drew asked, incredulous and outraged. "Jesus, Ramona, how do you live like this?"

It was the wrong tack. She spun on him, lashing out and slapping him across the face. "Fuck you, kid. I'm doing the best that I can to survive! If you have a better plan, Drew, I'm all ears. This is the only answer I have for you right now. It isn't my pack, so it's not my decision. You came looking for us, remember?"

Drew refused to back down. There was no way he could live life completely on the wrong side of the law. Stupid, arbitrary rules were practically made to be broken, but to live by hurting others was just unacceptable.

"Ramona, I'm not trying to judge you, I'm trying to figure out how to live my life. And there are certain things that I can't do. Hurting innocent people for gain is wrong, and I don't think that I can do it. I don't think it's how you want to live, either."

"Fine, Drew, draw some moral line in the sand. I agree with you: hurting innocent people is wrong. But how many people are innocent? And what exactly were my alternatives?" she asked, frowning. "Neither of us have a choice here, Drew. We can either be members of this pack, or die."

Drew was silent. 'I will not live by stealing from people, and hurting them for gain,' he told himself. 'No way.' His parents raised him better than that. His mother was dead because of someone who'd lived like the Firar. He'd be damned before he became the very thing that had destroyed his family.

His resolve must have shown through, because Ramona stopped walking and grabbed his arm. She turned him to face her, and looked long and hard into his eyes. As always, he felt as though he was losing himself in the depths of those mystical silver eyes of hers.

"Drew, don't do anything stupid," she urged, voice low and insistent. "I detest my life. I loathe myself for what I've become. But consider the alternatives. There are no other options available for us right now. Find another answer before you get us both killed."

Drew turned his head away, breaking eye contact before she could get him to agree to whatever she wanted. She was right, of course, and her safety was tied to his, but he wasn't going to make promises to her that he didn't know if he could keep.

He resumed walking. After a moment, she joined him. Neither spoke, but the silence this time was more comfortable. Theirs was now a shared cage, their fates intertwined. They retraced their steps, heading back towards the camp.

●●❨❨◯❩◗●●

The scouts had returned by the time Ramona and Drew got back. "Good news, Lobo" Caleb announced, almost leaping off of his bike. "We found an old farm with no one living there no more. The house is old, needs painting, but all the windows are intact, it has furniture, and the place has its own well, so it has running water. There's a barn and a big machine shed, too," he grinned, rubbing his hands in satisfaction. "We can park the bikes inside and still have room for everybody to bed down indoors. There's no neighbor close by, either, so no one should notice us, at least for a while."

"How far is it?" the big man asked.

"Shit, it's only twenty minutes or so from here. Red found it while Winnie and I was lookin' for a pawnshop. Wanna go now? I can take you, and let Red and Winnie get some food and meet us there," Caleb asked, eager to please.

"Mount up, Firar, we're out of here!" Lobo yelled. "Come on, dickless, you and your bitch get to go, too. Maybe once we're there, we can find something useful for you to do," he added, looking over at Drew.

The pack hurriedly threw their belongings on their bikes and lined up. The whole assemblage roared off.

After twenty minutes, the entourage pulled into the empty farm. The scouts had done well: the place was deserted and desolate. No other houses could be seen from the driveway, which meant no one else could see them, either.

Lobo immediately moved into the master bedroom and left the rest of the pack to squabble over living space. Drew stayed out of the pushing and shoving, finding a quiet corner in the hayloft and setting his backpack down, content to be away from the rest of the bikers. Ramona put her things down next to his and looked around.

"Nice digs, Drew. Don't suppose you could have tried for a bedroom at the house? You know, closer to the bathrooms?" She stared at him. "You know, importance in the pack is determined by dominance. Hiding isn't going to help us," she said.

"I'm not going to get into a fight over a room in a broken down old house with no electricity, just to improve my status in a gang that I want nothing to do with," Drew told her. "It's better to just stay out of the way until I can get things sorted out. I kinda thought that you wanted to stay out of the way, too. Why try to bait me into fighting?"

"I don't know. I just hate skulking around, acting like I'm afraid of everyone. One of these days, I'm just going to kill that fucking Piggy. Who cares if she's banging Lobo; it's not like he's picky. Bitch," she spat out.

"Relax, Ramona, it's not worth this much stress. We need to figure out what we're going to do. I thought being more isolated would make it easier for us to talk. And stay out of trouble." 'And out of Lobo's sight,' he added mentally. He wasn't exactly afraid of the big biker, but he was cautious. He also knew that the guy had an agenda concerning him, and until he knew what was going on, he wanted to sit back and observe.

The girl snorted, obviously not convinced. She turned away to sort out her things, ignoring her companion. Drew watched her for a few moments, then sighed and opened his own backpack.

He picked up the cell phone that Doug and Amy had given him, one of those pay-as-you-go numbers they'd activated for him. Out of curiosity, he turned it on. Once it had powered up, it showed him his number, then beeped.

Ramona looked over his shoulder. "What's that?"

"Cell phone. Friend of mine got it for me. I'm supposed to check in with him from time to time and let him know that I'm still alive," he said, turning it over in his hands. "Never had one before. Wonder why it beeps."

"You probably have a message" she replied, taking the phone from him.

"Message? But nobody has my number," he said, confused.

"I assume that your friend would know your number, since he got you the phone in the first place," Ramona said. "You really are a dumb jock, aren't you? Jesus, I thought you were smarter than this," she chastised, shaking her head. "Anyway, here, listen to your voice mail," she said, handing back his phone.

Drew held the phone to his ear, in time to hear Doug's voice start.

"Drew, it's Doug. Listen, man, there's big trouble. Sheriff Parker just left, and he's pissed as hell. I already called Amy to warn her, since he's goin' there next. I think that he knows we helped you.

"Drew, the cops found a body. It was that guy, the one that took Lucy Parsons. His neck was broken, and he had your practice jersey in his hand. The cops think that you killed him, Drew. Jesus, I hope that you're all right.

"Anyway, I wanted to give you a head's up. The cops are looking for you in a bad way now. Your dad told everyone that you were just home sick, and Megan never told anyone about what happened that Wednesday night, so none of that's bad.

"But this! God, Drew, what am I supposed to do? Call me, okay?" The voice ended with a click.

Drew sat back, mind and heart racing. So that's what had happened to his shirt: someone had taken it to plant on Wrench's body. Lobo'd probably told Ulric to leave it where it'd be found easily. That would be why Lobo had wanted Drew to play scout earlier, too.

It was all a set-up, a sham. Lobo assumed that Wrench would kill him, and they could dispose of his body at their leisure before going after his dad. If Drew won, they could set him up for Wrench's murder, and get rid of him that way. Either way, Lobo would get what he wanted.

"Ramona, I need to think for a bit. I'm going for a walk. Keep an eye on our stuff, okay?"

"What do you mean, 'keep an eye on our stuff' Drew? What's going on?" she demanded. "What was on that message?"

"The cops found Wrench. He had my shirt in his hand, complete with my name. Lobo set me up, Ramona, he took my shirt and planted it on Wrench's body. And I need to figure out what to do about it," he replied, trying to push past her.

"Hey, I'm involved in this, too. Come on, let's go for another walk, we'll talk. I'm serious. We'll find an answer. I just don't know what it is right now. Let me go with you, please?"

Drew looked down at her in surprise. She'd never struck him as the begging and pleading type, yet here she was, practically begging him to let her help. Again he was struck by how her fate was tied directly to his. He had no right to keep her out.

"Okay, let's go. Just give me a minute to get my bag; no sense giving anybody all of my cash and stuff," he said, sweeping his belongings back into the backpack and then slinging it over his shoulder. They spread out a blanket from Ramona's pack to mark their spot, and went outside to explore and mull over options.

•• ◖◗ •••

Matt Roth was on to something. Pieces of this story kept refusing to fit into the puzzle the police were trying to sell as a complete picture. He'd seen the photo and description of Steven Hemingway, the biker found dead on the side of the road by Amarillo. The picture matched the police sketch of the guy wanted in the abduction of Lucy Parsons the previous month in Iowa Park.

When he tried to talk with the local cops, though, they all stonewalled him. None of them had any idea who the dead guy was, or why Roth was interested in a dead vagrant found on the side of the road two hundred miles away. Beyond that, they had no comment.

Actually, one of the younger deputies had a comment for him, but it wasn't anything he'd be able to print. He'd followed up on the rumors that another wolf had attacked and killed a guard dog just behind Drew Collins' house, and then disappeared after reaching the hospital. The deputy, a black man named Winslow, had been a veritable gold mine of information until a sergeant, Ray Becker, caught him talking and threatened to have him reassigned to guard duty at the dump.

Roth at least learned that the cops had followed a blood trail all the way through town, until it ended abruptly in some bushes outside the emergency room. Lab work had confirmed the blood on the ground was lupine. However, the blood in the bushes had been mingled with human blood, too, and no one would address that bizarre problem.

His attempts to interview Drew Collins' father, James, also ended disastrously. He hadn't remembered that Sheriff Parker was his brother-in-law, until the cop showed up, lights blazing, skidding into the Collins driveway The seriously pissed off lawman threw the reporter into the grass, threatening to have the reporter arrested, or shot, if he didn't leave.

Roth knew better than to lodge a complaint. Small-town law enforcement in Texas was a mixed blessing. Getting on the bad side of the police could lead to unemployment, or worse. He merely collected his scattered notebook and pens, and left.

He'd already gotten what he needed, anyway. It was obvious that Drew Collins wasn't there, sick or otherwise. That story was an outright lie. Now he had to find out why, and what the kid's connection to the dead biker was.

The sober-for-almost-a-week reporter sat at his desk, fighting the urge to simply go have a scotch and forget about the story. No one else seemed to care. Shaking his head, he picked up a sheet of paper dropped on his desk by his editor. Supposedly, Larry Lee

Tate was seen again, ducking out of a convenience store just south of Wichita Falls. His editor wanted him to go and check it out.

Roth groaned. Tate sightings were a dime a dozen. The cops got at least a dozen calls a day from people who all claimed to see the escaped killer. One imaginative old lady even swore that he came into her home and spent the night with her. The toothless old bitty told Roth that he was "the best lay of my whole life—and I slept with two governors and a president; you know, the one from Arkansas." Roth had shuddered and printed her entire quote, much to the amusement of the community.

He rose to his feet, determined to get the interview over with as soon as possible, and then get back to the real story. Maybe he'd spend some time online tonight, searching for stuff about the biker gang. Deputy Winslow had called them the Fenris Firaw, or Fireraw, or something like that.

CHAPTER 34

Life at the farmhouse settled into a routine for the Fenris Firar. The bikers slept late, then rose and consumed prodigious amounts of food. After lazing around for several more hours, they divided into small groups to work.

One group worked on the bikes, cleaning them up, performing basic maintenance and inspections, to ensure that they were in decent working order. Another group worked on food preparation-cooking meals and setting aside the proper amounts of provisions. A third group ran errands, going into nearby towns to procure supplies and parts that the other two groups needed for their work.

The fourth group were the scouts. They rode off every day, scouring the surrounding countryside for paydays. Rich, empty houses were marked, as were businesses. Ranches were picked out too, because since the Firar were predators, they often craved fresh meat instead of cold, processed, and packaged prey.

Ramona had been a scout, but with the addition of Drew to the pack, and her demotion to being his mentor/slave, Piggy was given the task. And she was *not* happy about it, either. Scouting was a high risk position, and she'd set her sights on being Lobo's old lady, not being responsible for anything.

Because of this, and her long-standing feud with the silver-eyed beauty, Piggy never passed up an opportunity to put Ramona down. Her most recent insults had been directed at her prowess in bed, or lack apparent thereof.

"Yeah, Lobo was just saying last night, that he'd never had sex as good before in his life until now. What can I say; I'm just an animal in bed. Not like that dead-fuck Ramona," Piggy taunted. "Lobo said she was terrible. Looks hot, but can't get it done.

Figures that she'd take up with a little kid like Collins; he's probably don't know any better. Maybe I should teach *him* a thing or two, let him know what he's missing," she told the pack one morning.

Most of the Firar looked at each other and smirked. Over the years, they'd all had the "privilege" of having sex with Piggy; she was loud, sweaty, and definitely horrible. What she thought she knew about sex apparently had nothing at all to do with her proficiency at performing it.

Drew, for the most part, kept to himself. He was quiet and distant, but not aloof to the pack, and they bore him no dislike. Or like. At this point, he was mostly a nonentity. He stayed with Ramona, and the rest assumed it was to eventually "bag" her. And for that, they didn't blame him at all.

Drew was assigned to the mechanics, who were led by Graybeard. The bearded biker was a competent shade-tree mechanic, and knew his stuff. Drew actually knew more about motorcycle maintenance than the older man, but kept quiet and did the simple tasks that he was assigned.

One early evening, the pack decided it was time for another round of "Biker Olympics." Every contest had different events, and it was bad form to repeat the same game two times in a row. Lobo set out an obstacle course, with old tires to climb over, a barbed-wire fence to jump over, a rail to run down, and then, finally, the contestant had to evade Ulric, and knock a can off of the gate to the round pen.

The massive biker roared, pulling off his vest and hurling it to the side. He took up his station in front of the can, while Caleb was sent through the maze.

The small scout showed remarkable agility at running the tires, and dove over the barbed-wire fence, tucking into a somersault and coming back to his feet quickly. As the pack cheered, he leaped lightly onto the railing and ran down the length of it, jumping back down to the ground. Now only Ulric stood between him and the finish line.

Caleb feinted to his right and then dodged to his left, trying to avoid the giant. Ulric swept out his right arm, hooking the smaller man in a vicious collar, and slammed him to the ground. Ulric stood triumphant, holding his arms aloft, as Caleb shook his head, trying to clear the cobwebs.

"Next!" Lobo yelled. Amidst much pushing and shoving, mostly to back up, a new contestant lined up, prepared to make a run. The biker, a bigger, blond man with a straggly beard, slapped his hands together and rubbed them. He gave Lobo a big thumbs up, then flipped off Ulric, who snarled at him.

The man took off, not nearly as coordinated as Caleb had been, but still agile for someone his size. He took his time after jumping off of the railing, measuring Ulric and the distance he had to cover in order to reach the can. Suddenly, he bolted for the gate, rushing straight at the bigger biker. Ulric roared and charged to meet him. The two collided, and the blond was driven into the dirt by a crushing tackle.

He didn't get up.

Almost everyone laughed heartily. "Live stupid; die young," Lobo quipped, as a couple of other men dragged the unconscious biker out of the way. Once the path was clear, Lobo looked around, scanning faces, as if he were deliberating.

"Hey, kid. Get up there. Your turn," Lobo called, waving Drew over to the starting line. Collins wasn't surprised. He'd known this was a setup as soon as he'd seen Ulric take his place at the end of the obstacle course. 'Screw it,' he thought, reaching down and picking up a small object with his right hand.

Drew stepped to the line and crouched down. His arms flexed, and he smirked at Lobo. He raised an eyebrow at the leader, who glared at him, and growled, "Go!"

Collins shot off the line, racing through the tire drill, which he'd done in football practice regularly for almost ten years. He vaulted the barbed wire easily, and leapt up onto the railing. He ran down the length of it, and as he approached the end, leaped straight for the distant gate, and the waiting behemoth.

At the apex of his leap, Drew's right arm shot forwards, and the rock that he'd picked up left his hand in a blur. Collins landed on both feet, as the can sitting on top of the gate was catapulted into the air by the well-aimed stone.

Ulric stood next to the upended can, his face a study in confusion. His mouth hung open, and he kept looking from the can to Drew and back again. Finally, he looked slowly over to Lobo, to see what his leader would do.

Lobo cut off the scattered cheering with a vicious throat-cutting gesture. He stalked over to where Collins was standing. "What the hell do you think that you're doing? You asshole, that's cheating. I ought to tear your fucking head off, kid. Are you trying to make a mockery of our games, boy?" he yelled, incensed almost beyond words.

"What? No one said anything about how I was supposed to knock the can off of the gate. It just seemed to make sense to me. What's the big deal?" Drew replied, keeping himself just out of arm's reach of the infuriated big man.

"You fuckin' cheated. Do it again, and this time, no throwing shit. This is a man's game, not some little kid's. Go on, get over there and run it again. Ulric, you ready?" Lobo called. Ulric nodded, smashing his fist into his other hand.

By this time, the entire pack was paying close attention. It was obvious to everyone, even dense Aardwolf, that Lobo was angry and wanted Drew to fail. They shifted nervously, unsure how to react. Should they encourage the new guy and risk Lobo's wrath, or jeer him and mock his efforts?

The Firar elected to keep silent and let it play out. Drew took his place again; and when Lobo yelled at him to go, he blasted through the tires a second time, and then vaulted the wire. He took the railing at full speed, and caught Ulric off guard. The big man had thought he'd have some time to prepare for Drew's run at the can, but Drew was on him faster than he expected.

Drew swerved to his right at the last moment and, as Ulric shifted and reached out for him, stiff-armed him with his left hand. The big man lost his balance and fell back, his hands closing on empty air, while Collins ran past him and stopped in front of the can. Looking back at Lobo, the young man insolently thwacked the can off of the gate with his finger.

"Was that okay?"

This time the Firar erupted in applause. Drew's audacity and skill won their approval. Consequences be damned, they were tired of being roughed up by Ulric, and were ecstatic almost to a man to see someone finally beat him. The fact that Drew had done it twice just made it better.

Lobo snarled and stalked out to the gate. Upon reaching the two men, he roughly slapped Ulric in the face. "Idiot," he snapped.

"Fucking idiot," he amended, hitting the huge man again. Ulric growled. He was humiliated and angry, and Lobo was approaching the point of going too far.

Despite his fury, Lobo was savvy enough to know that he was at the point of pushing his massive lieutenant over the edge. He backed off. He needed another way to try to put the cocky kid back in his place.

Lobo raised his arms for silence. The Firar hushed up, watching him closely. They, too, were curious to see what would happen next.

"Okay, the kid's hot stuff at obstacle courses. Let's see how he is at coming up with our games," he said, turning to the young man.. "Everyone in the pack contributes to the Olympics, it's your turn to give us an event, kid, so what will it be? Can you think of anything fun for us?"

Drew thought for a moment. He knew a lot of drills from years of football practice and PE classes; both Coach Stanton and Mr. Rew were big on contests and agility drills. He smiled and nodded.

"Yeah, it just so happens, I do."

Collins looked around, measuring distances. Stepping to his right, he drew a line in the dirt with his boot, about thirty feet across. He hopped to the other side of the line and turned to face the watching pack.

"Okay, this is called a chicken race—your partner rides your back. This," he said, pointing to the line with his boot, "is the starting line. And the finish line. You start behind this, with a partner.. Anything goes; you can kick or push or trip other pairs, or try to tip them over. If you come off your ride, you have to stop and get back on before you continue.

"See that light pole over there," he said, pointing ahead a hundred yards past the house, to a utility pole with a yard light. "That's the halfway point. Once you get to that spot, you change jobs and come back. First pair to cross the line wins. Clear enough?" Drew asked, looking around.

The Firar grinned and began pairing up. Initially, many picked smaller partners to carry, before lining up. As they looked out at the yard light and thought it through, realizing they needed to be carried back by their smaller partners, they stepped back to regroup.

Lobo and Ulric partnered off, as did Winnie and Piggy. Drew turned to Ramona and asked, "Can you carry me? I weigh about two hundred pounds. You look more than strong enough for this."

The woman stared at him. She shook her head. "You're nuts. Yeah, I can carry you that far, but it won't be fast. Won't matter anyway; Lobo and Ulric will make sure they win."

"Don't worry so much about this. It's just a game, and anyway, we'll be fine. Come on, let's get to the line," he said, ushering her over to the starting point, where most of the others were already assembled.

"Okay, boost me up," she said.

"No. I ride first," Drew responded, surprising her. "This way we get the slow part done first. People will mostly leave us alone, because we'll be way back. After we switch, and you're on top, use your legs to hold on, and use your hands. Push people, grab them, pull them off balance. I'm going to crash into people, too, especially the bigger ones. If they're carrying big people, they're easy to separate. Got it?"

Ramona looked at him. He was calm. He had to know that even if this was just a game, the Firar used these contests to determine pecking order in the pack. It was a dangerous game he was playing here.

She watched him study the pairs, eyes lingering on Lobo and Ulric, who were wheeling around, shoving others and promising to bring death and destruction. She saw his face tighten momentarily and understood: Drew knew exactly what was going on. He was using this to strengthen his position in the pack, and try to weaken Lobo's hold over his future.

The raven-haired biker turned to face the pole and crouched. Drew moved behind her and put his hands on her shoulders. "Ready?" he whispered in her ear. She flushed; their proximity and position had distracted her, making her think of other things.

"Yeah," she replied, returning her attention to the game. He hopped up onto her back, wrapping his legs around her waist. Her legs gave, then steadied, as she took his weight, arms under his knees to support him. He put one arm around her neck lightly, and tapped her on the shoulder with his free hand.

"Okay, GO!" Lobo shouted, and bolted, carrying Ulric as fast as he could. The two massive bikers moved into an early lead, due in part to getting the jump on everyone else on the starting signal. It helped to be in charge.

The other pairs hustled after them, growling and bumping into each other. Several laughing bikers fell heavily to the ground, rolling apart and getting up to try again. One or two kicked out their feet, trying to trip those coming after them.

Ramona staggered around them, navigating as best she could while carrying a two hundred pound man on her back. She didn't feel like she was making much progress, but Drew seemed fine with their performance. She thought maybe he just wanted a reason to be this close to her.

"Okay, as the other groups start coming back, head right for them," he told her. "We're going to slow them down."

Lobo and Ulric had already rounded the corner, switched places, and started back. Caleb and Red were right behind them, the two smaller men making up for their lack of size with quickness.

As the leading pair got close, Drew reached out and snagged Piggy by her hair. He hauled back on her, and then pushed hard on her shoulder. Over balanced, Winnie tripped and fell, spilling her ugly teammate onto the ground right under Ulric's feet. The huge man went down like a bowling pin, dropping Lobo into the dirt.

"Fuck!" the outlaw leader shouted. "Get up, you idiot," he yelled at Ulric, as Ramona and Drew continued on to the halfway point. The other biker jumped back to his feet and set himself. Lobo jumped back on, but their momentum had been lost.

At the pole, Drew slid off of Ramona's back. "Turn around," he said. He took a knee, and as she stepped up close to his back, he scooped her legs and stood up, easily taking her weight.

Once she tapped his shoulder, he took off. She was light, and he was strong and coordinated enough to run with her. They flew past the other pairs, weaving in and around the other groups before they could even think to interfere.

Lobo turned in his place, looking over his shoulder to see the competition. Drew was coming up fast, leaving the others far behind. It was down to just the two of them. He hit Ulric on the head, exhorting him to hurry up. The big man growled and dug in, trying for more speed.

Drew caught him right at the line. Just before they crossed, Drew came up alongside the bigger pair and suddenly cut over, crashing into Lobo and Ulric as hard as he could. Both pairs stumbled. Ulric threw out his hands in an effort to keep his balance, and Lobo slid down his back, feet touching the ground.

Ramona and Drew staggered and recovered. While Lobo jumped back up onto his lieutenant's back, Drew high-stepped over the line. Dropping Ramona, he turned and grabbed her face in his hands. In full view of everyone, he kissed her hard on the mouth.

Before she could pull away or hit him, he broke the kiss and took her hand. He raised their arms in celebration. Some of the others cheered. Others looked at Lobo to see his reaction.

Lobo glared at Drew in disgust and rage. He wanted to kill the little fucker on the spot. He also knew that he couldn't, the pack wouldn't tolerate it. The miserable brat had won again, in full view of his followers. Something needed done.

"Yeah, yeah, very good," he said, mockingly clapping his hands. "You're really good at chicken-shit games, kid. Still haven't found anything useful for you to do, though, have we? Not real helpful so far, kid," he sneered, spitting to the side. "Enjoy it, though. Soon enough, you'll have to be a grownup and do some *real* work. Come on, Ulric, let's figure out where our next meal is coming from," he finished, turning away from the more sober Firar.

Drew turned to Ramona and smiled. "That went well," he said. "Nice guy. We should really invite him to dinner some time."

"It's not funny, Drew. He may just show up for '*dinner*' at your father's house some day," she scolded. "This isn't a game. This isn't some playground, where you and your jock buddies can push everyone around with no real consequences," she growled, angry with him for acting like a schoolboy.

"Hey, fuck you. I know it's not a game—I killed a man last week. Some game, murder. I'm trying to find some answers and so far all you can do is criticize everything that I do. At some point, it might be nice if *you* actually came up with an idea or two of your own," he shot back.

"Speaking of ideas, I don't remember discussing the whole kissing me at the end of the race thing. What's up with that, Drew?"

Caught off-balance, he laughed, flushing slightly. "I thought that it would piss Lobo off. And...well, I really wanted to. You're awesome, by the way," he said, grinning.

"Yeah, well, kissing isn't all I'm good at," she retorted, walking away and leaving Drew open-mouthed and staring.

The young biker spent the rest of the day watching her, trying to gauge her seriousness. Was there an offer there, or was it just a joke, something designed to keep him off balance?

Chapter 35

Pressure had become Parker's new companion. The State Police were hounding him daily, wanting updates on the investigations at Iowa Park. They called his brother-in-law regularly, asking for information about Drew.

James claimed to have no idea about Drew's whereabouts. Parker had personally screamed and threatened Doug Jones, and got nowhere. He *knew* that the boy knew more than he was telling, but also that he wouldn't give up anything unless Drew told him to. His nephew had that effect on people. He inspired loyalty. Even as a little kid, Drew's friends wouldn't give him up. Doug was solidly behind Drew, even if it was possible that he was a killer.

Even that damn nurse, Amy Bishop, was somehow involved, and refused to tell him anything. It was almost as though there was a conspiracy going on, designed to cover up something so bizarre or heinous, that no one wanted to see it brought to light. That was what frightened Parker most. He was certain now that he knew what was actually happening. He was also certain that he didn't want to prove it.

What he needed was a way to get the Staties, and that damn reporter, Matt Roth, off of him and his department. Roth puzzled him greatly. He'd known the guy for years, he was a lush. Not a bad reporter, but seriously uninspired. Now, for some reason, he'd gotten ambitious and aggressive.

Roth was asking questions that Parker didn't want to answer. Unfortunately, at least one of his deputies wanted those answers, too, and was asking the same questions. The sheriff would have bet his job Winslow had shared his file on the Fenris Firar with the reporter.

His phone rang. Wearily, he picked it up. "Parker."

"Uncle Bob? It's Drew."

Parker sat up in his chair, staring at the phone in shock. He looked around, noting that his door was closed and no one was close by. He brought the receiver back up near his ear.

"Drew? Where the hell are you?" he demanded.

"Listen, Uncle Bob. I don't have much time. I'm okay. I'm with the Firar for now," he stated. "You probably heard all about Wrench. He's the one that took Lucy" Drew cleared his throat, Parker could almost hear the guilt in his voice. "He attacked me, Uncle Bob, was gonna kill me. It was self-defense. I was set up," Drew insisted. "The leader of the Firar is out to get me. He staged everything: the fight, the body, he even stole my shirt to leave with Wrench."

"I'm working on what to do, Uncle Bob. Tell dad that I'm all right, okay? Look, I gotta go, but I wanted you to know what's going on."

"Drew, wait. Don't go yet. We gotta talk. I need to know… Drew? Damn it, don't you hang up on me!" Parker yelled at his now absent nephew. He slammed the phone down in anger. "Shit!"

"Everything okay, Bob?" Lem asked, sticking his head in the office.

"Damn it, I thought that I left that door closed! What the hell are you doing in here?" He glared.

"Sorry, boss, I thought that maybe you needed me." Lem rotated his toothpick and grinned. "You were a little loud, boss. Wanna tell me anything?"

Parker, about to lash out again at his senior deputy and closest friend, reigned in his temper. Lem was only trying to help. Not that he could. Or anyone could, for that matter.

"Sorry, Lem, just having a bad day. Give me a minute, will you? I need to sort a couple of things out," he said, making a show of moving papers around on his desk. The redheaded deputy watched him closely for a few seconds, then nodded and stepped out, pulling the door closed behind him.

Alone once more, Parker sat and sipped his coffee. He at least needed to delay the State Police, and throw Roth off for a time. Frowning, he picked up his phone again, and dialed.

"Bernie? Sheriff Parker. Let me speak to Jim, would you? Thanks," he said. A couple of minutes later, he thoughtfully replaced the receiver and called Lem into the office.

••（◉）••

Drew discovered, much to his surprise, that the majority of the pack enjoyed his performance at the 'Olympics.' This sudden popularity, however, was tempered by the pack's knowledge that Lobo hated him, and was out to get him.

Ulric, as expected, treated Drew as poorly as possible, constantly trying to goad the younger man into a fight. Drew, knowing the score, and being a bit smarter than the hulking biker, refused to be baited.

Ramona, however, was a different story. The fiery woman had to be forcibly restrained from throwing herself at Piggy, who delighted at baiting her. At one point, Drew caught her in mid-leap, after Piggy questioned her parentage, and how she'd gotten her silver eyes.

As Ramona thrashed and struggled, her porcine tormentor laughing, Drew said to her over his shoulder, "Maybe you shouldn't laugh. If I let her go, she'd kill you. You shouldn't trust me that much; after all, remember what happened to Wrench."

Piggy shut up immediately. She stared at the powerfully built young man, trying to get a sense of how serious he was. Ramona stopped struggling as well. After Piggy walked off, she turned on Drew.

"So why stop me? Let me end this shit now. I can take her," Ramona insisted. "I'm tired of her shit. It's been going on for three years now. Or was that just a bluff, to get her off my back?"

"It's just a bluff, Ramona. Jesus, what do you think, I'd want you to kill someone just because they're annoying? Get real. We just need the rest of them to think that maybe I'd do that, so they leave us alone," Drew explained, shaking his head.

"Well, at some point we'll need a better answer than that, because we're just putting off the inevitable," she said.

"Believe me, I know," he griped. "But we don't have a better answer yet. Playing for time is all we've got right now."

"It'll get worse, Drew. Soon. We're coming up on the next full moon, and Lobo gets nuts around then. Very soon, he's gonna put you in a spot that you can't just think or stall your way out of."

He looked at her sourly. "I know. We'll cross that bridge when we come to it."

"Hey, pretty boy! Come here," Lobo called. Drew and Ramona looked over towards the house, where Lobo stood. "Come on, get your ass over here, now!" he said, waving his arm.

Drew sighed and walked over. The games were getting ridiculous. Sooner or later, he was going to lose his temper, and the hirsute biker knew it. He was counting on it.

Lobo smiled widely as Drew approached. He pointed at his bike. Drew obediently looked down at it. Aside from being intolerably filthy, it seemed fine. He shrugged.

"What, you don't see it? Sounds funny, pretty boy. Graybeard says you're hot shit with the tools, so I want you to fix it," Lobo said, smirking.

"Now, mind that you don't clean it. It's a rat bike, the dirt is part of my image," he continued.

Under his breath, Drew muttered, "Clearly."

"What? What did you say?" Lobo demanded.

"I said, 'clearly.' The dirt is part of your image, Lobo. I was agreeing with you," he added, as some of the Firar laughed openly. Behind him, Ramona smiled and turned away so that Lobo couldn't see her.

"Yeah, well, some dirt might just help your image, too. Right now you seem the sort that was popular in prison; all clean cut and spiffy," Lobo mocked, holding out his hand limply.

"Sounds like you know all about it," Drew said off-handedly, as he crouched down to look at the hog.

Lobo's face darkened. "Just fix the bike, smart ass. If you can," he said and stalked off.

Graybeard joined Drew in looking the bike over. "You see it, don'tcha?" Drew nodded. The exhaust was cracked, just where the pipe swept down and back from the engine.

"Ain't nuthin' we can do with it, kid. Needs replaced," the elder biker stated, spitting off to the side.

"I know. Needs fixed, too. Cracked that close to the manifold, it'll be hard on the engine. Suppose Lobo knew that already, and just wanted to make me look bad?"

Graybeard looked at Drew. "Does it matter? Seems like you need to just try your best to stay out of his way for now. Survival over pride, young man."

Drew thought about it. It made sense; he was just hoping for a more definite commitment from Graybeard as an ally. It seemed that he was a pragmatist. Probably kept him alive.

"Okay, let me tell Lobo about the bike. He can come to you for a second opinion if he really wants to humiliate me," Drew said.

The older man nodded. He watched Drew walk away. Very slowly, the gray-haired biker smiled. Lobo was going to have to find some other way to get under this kid's skin.

Only a handful of reporters were present for the Iowa Park Sheriff Department's hastily called press conference. That was intentional. Parker didn't want to face a large number of eager newsmen with pointed questions. A couple of locals wouldn't be nearly as bad.

Except Matt Roth was out there. Parker could see him standing there, sort of huddled in his light jacket. He carried himself smaller than he actually was, and had always seemed mousy and non-threatening. His newfound passion for uncovering the truth behind this story, though, made him seem like the devil incarnate.

The sheriff pushed that thought from his mind. He needed to be clear and undistracted to pull this off. He reviewed his speech. It was simple and short, with just enough truth to it, he hoped. Mentally crossing himself, he stepped up to the microphone. Lem and Becker took up positions flanking him.

All six television and newspaper reporters hushed up and looked at him expectantly. The two cameras were rolling.

"Ladies and gentlemen," Parker began, "my name is Robert Parker and I am the sheriff of Iowa Park. I have an update for you all. After I'm done, I will take a few questions.

"Almost two months ago there was a body discovered in the park. A young man from Longview, Scott Thomas, was attacked and killed by a pack of wolves. A young woman who had been with him was a witness to the attack, but was unharmed.

"Shortly thereafter, an employee of Bernie's Harley-Davidson named Lucy Parsons was abducted by a member of an outlaw biker gang known as the Fenris Firar. Her body was discovered at an abandoned lot, burned and apparently partially eaten by wild dogs or wolves.

"That same weekend, a high school student was attacked on a camping trip by what appeared to be a large wolf. He received non-life threatening injuries and was released from the hospital after a brief stay.

"The boy and his father were also at that time victimized by the same type of break-in that occurred at several residences in the community, including the one where Bill Jameson was assaulted. Various items were stolen from the home.

"A couple of days ago, the Texas State Police found the body of the biker wanted in connection to the Lucy Parsons abduction and murder. He had been killed, apparently in a dispute over the stolen goods from Iowa Park's community. Several small items were found at the scene, and will be returned to their rightful owners after due process.

"There is no connection between the animal attacks and the rash of violent crimes perpetrated by the outlaw gang, nor is there any reason to suspect anything other than a falling out among the biker gang being responsible for the death of the suspect up in Amarillo.

"While the case remains open in Amarillo, the investigation into the robberies, and the kidnapping, along with the murder of Lucy Parsons, has been satisfactorily closed.

"Thank you for your time," Parker concluded, looking out at the assembled newsmen for the first time since beginning his speech. The men, who'd been listening intently, showed a variety of expressions, ranging from bored, to puzzled, to outright upset.

Matt Roth's face belonged in the latter category. He smelled a snow job. There was something rotten in this story. He raised his hand, before the sheriff could leave the podium.

"Sheriff Parker, I have a question," he called. Parker turned at looked at him wearily.

"Yes, Mr. Roth, what is it?"

"Sheriff, if the Collins' house was burglarized as well, why was there no report? Other homes made it into the report, but there was no mention of their house." He crossed his arms and stared.

"Mr. Collins came to me privately to report it. He didn't wish to call attention to himself, and said that beyond some property damage, that nothing of substantial value had been taken."

"Property damage? Like what? None of the other homes had any," Roth countered.

Parker fixed the rumpled-looking man a withering stare. "Mr. Roth, since your paper ran the story on the break-ins, I would expect you to have better possession of the facts. All of the homes that had been broken into suffered serious vandalism. The Jameson home had over fifteen thousand dollars damage done to it. In the case of the Collins house, a rear window was destroyed, along with structural damage to the wall. The Menard's in Wichita Falls got a bonanza from our little town, I can tell you.

"Now," he said, looking over the others, "is there anyone that maybe did their homework beforehand that has any questions?"

Roth put up his hand again and started to blurt out another question. Parker cut him off immediately. "Not you, Roth. I haven't got time for half-assed journalism. Get your facts straight and then come talk to me. Don't waste my time. Anyone else?"

The others shifted. Parker stared intently at them, almost daring them to ask a question. Aside from Roth, who still kept trying to ask questions, only to be continually waved aside by Parker, no one raised their hands.

"Thank you," the sheriff grumbled and stepped away. Roth followed after him, tugging on his arm.

"Sheriff Parker, do you really expect us to buy that load of crap? C'mon, what about the Collins kid? Where is he? Why did his shirt end up in the dead man's hand?"

Parker grabbed the man's wrist and pulled his hand off of his arm. He twisted it up and in painfully, glaring at the smaller man. "Roth, keep your damn hands to yourself. I told you to go away, now get!" He shoved him away and turned his back.

Roth wasn't about to be put off. He shook his wrist, grimacing, and then headed back towards the lawman. Two deputies smoothly took his arms and guided him aside.

"Now, Mr. Roth, let's not go getting' the sheriff mad or nuthin'," the tall redhead drawled. "Why don't ya ask us yer question? We love being in the paper, don't we Ray?"

The dark haired, serious looking deputy nodded. "Certainly. Mr. Roth, if you have any questions for us, we would be happy to oblige. Remembering of course, that some things are privileged information, and we can't share everything with you. But, anything that we can do to help you out, you just let us know," he said, slipping open the reporter's car door and easing the still protesting man into his car.

"Thanks, friend, we'll talk more later," Becker said, shutting the car door and walking away with Lem.

Roth stared after them for a time, then drove off. He had pushed enough for one day; but there was no way he was going to let this one drop. This story stunk.

The two deputies paused before entering the sheriff's office. Ray glanced around before quietly stating, "Roth was right, you know. There's something wrong here. It was all I could do to keep a straight face while Bob was talking. What's going on?"

"What makes you think that I know? Ah'll bet the Staties don't know about his press conference, either."

Becker shook his head. "Swell."

"Could be worse," Lem stated.

"Yeah? How could it be worse?"

"Could be raining," the redhead said, walking into the sheriff's office, grinning. He'd just watched 'Young Frankenstein' the previous night with his wife and loved using lines from the Mel Brooks classic.

Becker groaned and followed his fellow deputy into his bosses' room, closing the door behind him. He turned his attention to the sheriff, who sat at his desk, chin propped in his hands.

"What do you guys want?" he asked. Parker had expected them to come in and try to grill him about the conference.

"Sheriff, what was all that about? We know that there was no break in at the Collins house. Your nephew disappeared, and is implicated in that biker's death. What gives?" Becker asked.

Parker stared ahead, giving no indication that he'd heard. Lem gently nudged his arm. The sheriff twitched and looked at his deputies.

Softly, in his gruff voice, he told them about Drew's phone call, and his fears. He held nothing back. He pulled out Winslow's file on the Fenris Firar and dropped it on his desk. After five minutes, he fell silent.

Parker looked wearily at his men. They were smart, loyal, and competent. They also had every right to think that he was insane. Part of him wouldn't blame them if they did.

Lem spoke first. Parker's longtime friend put his hand on the sheriff's shoulder. "Bob, this hasn't been an easy fall. We got shit that hasn't happened around here ever. We're all worried about Drew, and James. But seriously, Bob... werewolves?"

Becker took over. "Sheriff, look. We can put off Matt Roth and his stupid column, and deal with the Jameson's lawsuit. We just have to keep our cool, and find the truth. It'll work out, boss. I promise."

Parker snorted. Becker was so predictable. Of course he'd advocate staying the course, being calm, and letting things settle out. If only logic and simply staying calm would make everything right.

"I don't care at this point what you two think. As long as I am the Sheriff at Iowa Park, we do things the way that I say. Now, if you don't mind, I have some calls to make, so beat it."

CHAPTER 36

Drew's Sportster thundered down the Texas back road. Bungeed to the back of his bike were the new parts for Lobo's hog. He'd gone into town himself for them, needing to get away from the pack. The moon would be full the following night, and the entire pack was getting edgy.

The young man was feeling more and more violent as the moon swelled, Lobo's taunts becoming harder to resist. Thus the need to get away from everyone, and just feel the wind in his face as he rode. He goosed the throttle, sending the orange bike hurtling forwards. Drew grinned.

The Firar were drifting towards the barn when he finally returned. He shut off his Harley and followed. Inside, he could hear raised voices. Ramona was yelling at Lobo, who responded with laughter, and informing her she had no say in the matter. Drew could also hear something or someone thrashing around.

The young man pushed his way to the front. Lobo stood, arms crossed, grinning, while Piggy and Aardwolf were picking up Drew and Ramona's belongings. On the floor, at Lobo's feet, was a young girl, with her arms and legs bound, and a gag in her mouth.

"Welcome back, pretty boy," Lobo mocked. "We were just relocating you and your bitch. We have entertainment for this evening and next, and need to appropriate your spot. Don't worry, though, you can still join in the fun. Sloppy seconds are better than nothing, you know."

His grin as he towered over the girl turned Drew's stomach. "Anyway, get your shit out of here," he commanded, as Aardwolf tossed him his half-open backpack.

Drew caught his pack out of reflex, staring at the girl on the ground. It was hard to tell, since she was crying and writhing around, but she seemed young, maybe fifteen or so. Memories of Lucy Parsons, the college girl that had worked with his father, flashed through his mind.

"No. No way," he said, looking up at Lobo. "This isn't happening. Not here, not now, not ever." He drew himself up to his full height and scowled. "No way," he repeated.

"You don't question me, you little shit," Lobo roared, lashing out and knocking Drew off his feet. "This is my pack, and my decision. Join in or die, I don't care which one."

Drew sprang to his feet with a growl. He was about to launch himself at the leader of the Firar when a mountain fell on him from behind. Ulric tackled him, and held him face down on the floor. Piggy and Caleb held Ramona, who was cursing and trying to get to Drew's side.

Lobo laughed. The pack echoed him, albeit a bit subdued. The head of the pack took notice, and looked around at his 'family.' His face turned ugly. "What's the matter with you? The moon is almost full and I found us some fun, like always. We're predators; we prey on the weak. It's the way of the world. This thing," he said, reaching down to scoop up the teen-age girl, "is just a fucking sheep. Her existence is to provide sport and sustenance for the hunters. And we are the hunters; the Fenris Firar."

Lobo's voice rose higher as his passion and bloodlust soared. "We hunt, we kill, we take from the sheep what we want. This is our place, it's in our very blood. You can feel it. Can't you?" he asked, holding an arm aloft, poised over the struggling body of the girl that he held with his other hand. "Don't deny who you are."

The Firar responded. Many cheered or howled. Others growled and stomped their feet, reaching out their hands towards the bounty that Lobo held. The pack leader smiled. He had them back in his corner. They would partake of the feast.

"God damn it, no!" Drew cried, slipping out from under Ulric. He surged back to his feet and spun to face the other pack members. "We don't have to live like this. We're predators, but not criminals. Not rapists and murderers."

"Boy, you're really starting to piss me off," Lobo growled, clubbing Drew on the back of the head. "Get him out of here," he commanded. Ulric and Red grabbed him again.

"Now, where were we?" he crooned, leering at his hostage. He stroked her hair gently. "It's okay, my little sheep. You'll be fine. Trust me," he said as he turned and winked at the rest of the pack. There were a couple of snickers.

Outside the barn, Drew and Ramona were unceremoniously dumped onto the ground. Their belongings were thrown down as well, things scattering around the yard.

Piggy spit at Ramona. "Piece of shit. I don't know why we can't just kill you now and be done with it. Fuckin' princess," she sneered, and turned away. The others joined her, anxious to get back to join in the festivities.

"I am not letting this happen. That girl doesn't deserve this," Drew kept repeating.

"What are you going to do about it, Drew? You can't change the whole pack. We're fucking cursed, you realize that? Don't you feel the pull, the urge to go back in and participate? I do. That's why I ran last time. It was the combination of hating them for doing it, and loathing myself for wanting to be a part of it."

"I feel… the lust, I guess. I want violence. But not at her expense. She's a victim. We may be cursed, but we're not fucking animals. We're human, too," he said, starting back towards the barn. "And I am not going to let her die."

"Wait," Ramona said, taking hold of his arm. "You can't fight the whole pack. You'll just be killed, and they'll kill her anyway."

"I don't have to fight the whole pack. The majority of them are just followers, Ramona, they'll do what they're told or forced to do. I just need to stop Lobo, and that fucking giant Ulric. And Piggy, I guess. And probably Caleb. And maybe Red," he trailed off, seeing his problem.

"If you're really serious, there is a way. You need to challenge Lobo directly, as leader of the pack. He has to fight you by himself. But he's bigger, stronger, and he's been killing people for a lot longer than you've been alive," Ramona pointed out.

"He is not going to kill that girl," Drew said, gritting his teeth. He could hear loud cries and cheers from inside the barn. "I can't take much more of this."

"Okay, let's set up the bikes in a circle, headlights facing in. It'll be dark in a few minutes; we need the pack to see the fight clearly. Once they're arranged, we'll turn on the lights, and go call out Lobo."

Drew nodded and they went to work, wheeling the motorcycles into a large circle in the yard. Drew hurried, his mind stubbornly refusing to think about the consequences of what he was about to do, and what would happen if he failed.

As dusk was gathering, their preparations came to an end. Ramona told Drew to wait by his Sportster and get himself ready for the fight, while she went in and brought out the pack. He nodded and began shaking out his arms and doing leg stretches; his expression bleak.

Ramona went in. The scene that greeted her was what she had expected. Many of the Firar already had their clothes off, and the entire pack was congregated in a tight circle around Lobo and the runaway.

"There is a challenge!" she cried out in her loudest voice. "Lobo, your right to lead this pack is being challenged. Right here, right now," she continued, as the pack's attention was diverted to her. All eyes swiveled towards her, some wide in surprise.

"What do you say, Lobo? Will you meet this challenge, or do you yield your rights as leader of the Fenris Firar this night?" Ramona mocked, taunting him. She had to make the challenge real enough that they would leave off their gang rape. She decided to twist the knife a little further.

"Lobo, there's a young man outside that thinks he's more man than you. I can tell you for a fact that he is," the beauty said, licking her lips. "I think that he's much better...equipped, to lead us than you are, if you know what I mean."

Lobo roared in anger. He snatched up his pants, dropping the sobbing girl back to the floor, where she curled into a ball and lay still. The rest of the pack piled outside, seeing the lights of the bikes come on suddenly.

When Lobo stepped out of the barn, he was greeting by the entire pack. They were silently standing next to their machines, in a huge circle, with the headlights illuminating a central clearing, where one person stood. It was Drew. The lights played off his muscular chest and shoulders.

"Lobo, I'm calling you out. I don't think that you're the best leader for this pack," he called out, loud enough to be heard over the bikes.

Lobo sneered, not impressed, nor intimidated, by the young man's obvious strength or presence. "Pretty boy, you don't have the right to challenge me. Only pack members can do that. You're just a probie."

"Actually, Lobo, you made him a member when you gave him Wrench's patch," Graybeard pointed out. "According to our laws, he has the right to fight for leadership."

"This is ridiculous," Lobo growled. "He's just a fucking kid. I'm not taking this seriously. Come on, let's get back to our party."

The Firar murmured their disapproval. Not a one of them moved. Even Ulric and Piggy held their ground. A challenge had been made, and it had to be met.

Lobo sensed it. He was in danger of losing his pack again to this upstart. The kid needed to be put in his place, and if that place was six feet under, that was fine with him. He'd planned on killing him anyway, after he'd had some more fun tormenting him.

"Fine, then. Let's get this over with; I've got a date waiting for me in the barn," he said, circling the younger man in a crouch. "You realize I'm going to kill you, don't you?"

Drew matched him, his teeth bared in a snarl. The watching Firar thrilled. This close to the full moon, their hormones were on overload, and the sight of two alpha males sizing each other up, shirtless and squaring off to fight for dominance, was enticing. They started cheering and yelling. Many cheered for Collins.

It threw Lobo off balance. He hadn't actually thought that any of the pack would support the kid. He paused and looked around. Drew noticed his discomfiture and laughed.

"What is it, Fletcher? Worried you're not the popular one now?" Drew taunted him. "Maybe you should just run back to Canada, eh?"

Lobo froze. He hadn't heard his real name in years. How did this kid know that? No one here knew his real name, or where he was from.

Drew took advantage of Lobo's surprise to step in and hit the bigger man with a jab and cross combination that rocked Lobo back several feet. Blood trickled down the leader's nose, as the Firar roared and howled at the sight of first blood.

Lobo grimaced and spit at Drew. The bloody phlegm missed by two or three feet, but distracted Drew long enough for Lobo to grab his leg and dump him onto the ground.

The two men rolled around, neither able to seize the advantage. They rolled apart and came back to their feet, chests heaving with exertion. Almost without pause they threw themselves forwards, locking up and each trying to take the other back down to the ground.

Drew slammed a knee into Lobo's stomach. The burly man grunted with the impact and doubled over. Drew pivoted, dumping the man to the ground, and viciously kicked at his head. Lobo covered up and rolled away, coming back up out of range.

So far the younger man had the advantage, much to the surprise of not only the pack, but Lobo as well. He needed to change that. The leader of the Fenris Firar reached down into a side pocket of his leather pants, and pulled out a nasty looking eight-inch, double-edged knife, with serrations down one side.

The Firar roared with excitement as Drew pulled his belt free of his pants and looped an end in each hand. Lobo stalked him with the knife, waving it around in the air, searching for an opening.

Drew kept his weight forwards, and moved his hands opposite of his opponent's. If Lobo's knife was high, his hands with the belt in them were low. When the knife went low, his hands went high. He stayed just out of the older man's reach.

Lobo, seeing an opening, lunged and plunged the knife low, attempting to drive the blade into Drew's stomach or groin. Drew blocked downwards with the belt, pushing Lobo's hand lower than intended, and slipped past the thrust. The belt swept up to Lobo's neck, and then around it as Drew spun, looping his hands on either side of the leader's throat.

Drew crossed his hands behind Lobo's neck, twisting and setting his back against the bigger man's. He exerted all of his force into the choke, straightening Lobo up, overbalancing him backwards.

Glancing back over his shoulder, Drew saw Lobo's right arm rise up high, and watched the older man reverse his grip on the blade, now holding it point down. He started to swing his arm downwards.

Knowing that he couldn't do anything to prevent the stroke, Drew abandoned his choke, releasing the belt and back-stepping quickly out of the way. The killing thrust missed, but Lobo turned to follow up quickly, hurling the belt from his neck.

Lobo raised up the knife again, lunging forward and bringing the point violently down just inside Drew's collar bone. At least, that was his intention. Drew passed the knife with his left hand, shifting in deeper so that the knife went past him and slightly above his shoulder.

Drew's left arm slipped around Lobo's back, his right arm circled under the pack leader's own right arm, and hooked around his neck. His hands locked against the side of Lobo's neck and he squeezed his arms, drawing them in like a boa constrictor wrapped around its prey.

Lobo was caught securely in a standing version of the triangle choke. Drew pulled tighter, tucking his head against the bigger man's shoulder and turning him over, so that he fell heavily to the ground. Collins maintained his hold; keeping enough pressure that Lobo could neither use his knife, nor get any air. After a minute, Lobo went limp.

Drew let go and pushed at his enemy. He didn't move. Collins kicked the knife away and stood up. He looked down at the unconscious man without expression, and then raised his eyes to the silent Firar.

The fight was over. The Fenris Firar had a new leader, and Drew wasted no time in asserting his authority.

"Someone go get that girl. Dress her and run her to the nearest hospital. Drop her off and get back here," he said, panting. No one moved. "Now!"

"You didn't kill him. It's not over," Graybeard explained.

"I'm not going to kill him. I beat him, that's enough. Now go help that girl and get her to the hospital. Graybeard, you're in charge of that."

"Yes, sir. Come on, Winnie, you can help her get dressed." The older man turned back to Drew on his way to the barn. "It won't be over for Lobo, though. Not as long as he's alive. You may lead some of the pack, but your problems aren't over."

"No kidding. Still a werewolf, still wanted for murder, still a member of this bunch. I got it, Graybeard. Thanks," he grumbled. He looked around for Ramona. She was standing off to the side, holding his belt that Lobo had discarded. Her eyes were huge.

"Well, now what?" he asked, with a half-smile. Aside from keeping the Firar from raping and killing their latest hostage, he didn't have a long-term plan past challenging Lobo.

Ramona shook herself, seeming to come out of a trance. She looked down at the leather belt in her hands, and then at Drew.

"Come on, let's go to the house," she told him, walking off without bothering to see if he followed or not.

Ramona swept into the farmhouse, going directly to the room that Lobo claimed as his own. She laid the belt down on the bed, and grabbed Lobo's belongings. Pushing past Drew, who entered the room behind her, she threw the stuff into the hall.

She bumped into Drew again, as she spun to re-enter the room, and pushed him against a wall. She held up a hand to keep him there. Once more, she collected an armload of stuff, and threw it into the hallway, this time hitting Piggy, who had come in to get her things.

"Hey, you bitch, what do you think you're doing?" the ugly woman had demanded. She aggressively thrust her face into the room.

Ramona slammed the door without warning, catching Piggy solidly. The fat biker fell back, bouncing off of the wall and sliding to the floor, dazed. Ramona yanked the door open again, glaring down at her.

"Get out of this house, Piggy. Take your ugly, bleeding face, and your disgusting, smelly things, and get them out of this house. Now, before I kill you." She glared down at her hated rival.

Piggy got slowly to her feet, and then bent over and collected her possessions. As she grabbed the last item, Ramona kicked her in the butt. Piggy growled, but took her punishment, walking away without so much as a backwards glance.

Ramona shut the door again, facing Drew and leaning back against the door. Her hands went to her vest. She untied the front, slowly, keeping her eyes locked onto Drew's. Once it was unlaced, she opened the vest, uncovering her breasts. She shrugged out of the garment, letting it drop to the floor.

The raven-haired woman stood motionless in front of Drew for several long moments, and he took full advantage, staring in fascination at her full, ripe breasts. Drew started to reach for her, but she held up her hand, holding him in place.

Expressionless, Ramona turned and picked up the belt from the bed. She stepped up to Drew, close enough that her chest brushed his. Her taut nipples traced lines of fire down his torso as she sank to her knees, still maintaining eye contact with him.

Drew groaned, wanting to put his hands on her, but afraid to break the spell. Once again, her silver eyes held him captive, and now she was using her body to further draw him in. He felt her hands gently unbutton and unzip his pants. He broke eye contact with her then, glancing in embarrassment at his erection.

Ramona felt no such embarrassment. With a small groan of her own, she pulled his pants and underwear down, freeing him. "Mmm, yes," she murmured, her warm breath caressing his shaft.

She leaned back, causing Drew to sigh in disappointment. Ramona looked back up at him and smiled. She quickly looped his belt around her neck and drew it snug. The free end she held in her right hand.

Reaching up, she found Drew's left hand, and pressed the belt into it. The kneeling woman then pushed their joined hands back, drawing her head towards his groin.

Her lips parted and she took him into her mouth. Drew trembled, his nerve endings on fire; the feeling beyond anything he'd ever experienced. He could feel her tongue on the underside of his cock, pressing upwards gently as she slid him in.

Ramona kept pushing his hand back, pulling her head further towards him. She took him all the way in, down into her throat, and her nose pressed against his rock hard stomach.

"Jesus!" Drew cried, looking down at her in shock. He had only heard wild mostly made up stories about anything like this.

He grabbed her soft breast with his right hand and cupped it, reveling in its firmness and size. She was bigger than she seemed when clothed. Her figure was trim and athletic, but very well developed. Her hard nipple grew and pressed against his palm.

Ramona's gag reflex took over, and she choked on his length, her eyes watering. Drew dropped the belt in shock, letting her go. Her mouth came off him, and she coughed.

"God, Ramona, I'm sorry. I'm really sorry," Collins was saying when she slapped him hard across the face. Roughly, she shoved the free end of the belt back into his hand. She licked the end of his cock and looked back up at him; then pointedly looked at the belt in his hand.

Nervously, he pulled slightly on the belt, and she took him back into her warm mouth. He pulled further, and she swallowed him again. This time he relaxed the belt, and she slid back off slightly, and avoided gagging.

It felt too good to stop. Drew pulled the belt again, and again Ramona deep throated him, taking him all the way down. His hips began to buck as he set a rhythm, moving her up and down his cock.

The sensation was overwhelming. Within two minutes, he lost control of himself. Crying out, he exploded. Ramona, sensing his climax, thrust him all the way down, feeling him spurt repeatedly down her throat. Drew dropped the belt and grabbed her head in both hands, holding her in place as he came.

Finishing, Drew let go. Ramona slowly slid her lips off of him, inch-by-inch, and then sucked on just the tip, getting the last drop of cum. Drew shuddered, gently caressing her hair as she looked up at him with those marvelous eyes.

"Well, what do you think?" She asked.

"Oh my God," he moaned, still stunned.

"Yeah. But what do you think?" Ramona demanded, rising up to stand in front of him once again.

"What do I think? I think that you may have some serious dominance issues," Drew responded, at a loss.

She slapped him again. "Do you want to psychoanalyze me or get laid? Don't think that you're done yet, boy."

Drew stared at her as she peeled out of her leather pants and underwear. His mouth went dry as he realized that she was serious.

"Umm, we can put off the therapy session for now, if you'd like," he stammered.

Ramona climbed onto the bed and said smugly, "bring the belt, Drew. This time it goes on you."

Outside their window, a pair of eyes glared at them. By the time the young lovers exhausted themselves and fell asleep, the eyes were gone, their owner slinking off to plot revenge.

CHAPTER 37

When Drew awoke, he didn't know where he was. Sunlight streamed through a nearby window, causing him to blink and raise a hand to shield his eyes. His movement triggered a soft groan from the soft body next to him.

Memories flooded his brain as he looked over in surprise at the young woman lying beside him. Ramona lay on her side, the blankets pulled up to her neck. In repose, her face lost the hard edge that she cultivated in order to survive. She looked almost angelic, Drew thought.

He began recalling the things they'd done the previous night, and grinned. So much for being an angel. Amazing. Best night of his entire life. Staring at her sleeping form, he knew he was in love with her, and probably had been since before their wild evening.

Thoughts of their evening led inevitably to what had triggered their passion, and his smile faded. The life or death fight with Lobo for leadership of the Fenris Firar had happened almost too quickly for it to affect him. There hadn't been time then to be nervous or frightened.

He had left Lobo alive. Presumably he was gone, at least for now. Odds were, though, he would have to deal with him again.

Drew's stomach soured at the thought. Despite the amazing feeling of waking up next to Ramona, he felt sick. He realized that if he did have to deal with Lobo again, he would have to be ready to kill him.

Carefully, he slipped out from under the covers and found his clothes. They were scattered around the room, causing him to smile once more at the recollections of passion.

Drew opened the bedroom door and walked out into the hallway. It was midmorning, and several members of the Firar were lounging around the living room when he walked in. Several smiled widely at him, having been able to hear a good portion of his late night antics.

He blushed and dropped his head, which resulted in uproarious laughter. His features tightened angrily, and his fists clenched, until he realized that they weren't mocking him. They were genuinely amused, happy for him, and enjoying his embarrassment.

Drew laughed with his pack. "Was I that obvious?"

"You mean loud?" one called, to the accompaniment of more laughter. "Or do you mean, 'was it that obvious I was a virgin?' Because the answer to both is yes." More guffaws.

"Bite me," Drew retorted, still grinning.

"I think she took care of that," Winnie got out between fits of giggles. One of the men slapped her shoulder and she fell off of the couch. "Hey, watch it, asshole," she snapped, kicking at the prone man.

Her sudden ire brought the room to a more serious mien. The moon would be full that night, and they would be under Drew's unproven leadership. It was now his responsibility to keep the pack safe during the times they were in lupine form.

The looks directed at him grew more speculative and measuring, as each member contemplated that fact. No one had liked Lobo, but everyone knew that he'd provided for, and took care of, the pack.

Drew nodded at the unspoken questions. They were right to wonder. "Let's get everyone together for a quick meeting. We've got plenty of time before nightfall, but we need to go over the plan. Let's meet in the yard in five minutes, okay?"

He turned away before anyone could answer, giving the impression that he wasn't really asking. It was a technique that he'd watched his uncle use for years, and always seemed to work for him. It must have been effective this time, because the Firar broke up and headed out to round up the rest of the pack without any grumbling.

Drew went back to his room to find Ramona awake and finishing getting dressed. Drew felt a brief surge of disappointment; he'd really wanted to see her naked again before going outside to lead the meeting.

Ramona must have seen something of that in his face, since she smirked and shook her head. "You haven't got time for that, lover boy; we've got work to do. Maybe later. You know, round two. Or three, or whatever round we're up to," she added.

She kissed him quickly on the cheek as she brushed by. "Come on, Drew, let's not keep your new pack waiting. They get impatient easy, and they're gonna be a little anxious with a full moon tonight."

Drew reached for her, and she slapped his hands away, laughing. "Later, now come on." She grabbed his hand and pulled him out of the room with her, leading him down the hall and out the door.

Standing outside in the yard were sixteen people. They didn't look happy.

"Lobo's gone. Took his bike and gear," Graybeard said, stepping forward. "He took Ulric, Piggy, Red, Aardwolf, and Caleb with him, along with most of the cash and food," he finished, looking expectantly at Drew.

Shit. First day and he'd already been screwed over. And now they were all looking to him for answers. He didn't want to be in charge; he just didn't have a choice—it was take over or let that little girl die. Speaking of which...

"Graybeard, did you take care of that girl? Did she get dropped off at a hospital?"

"I took her myself, Drew. She's a tough kid; she'll be fine. Nobody did nuthin' but scare her a little. I think I was seen leaving, but nobody got a good look. Just a guy on a bike, dropping a runaway off at the ER."

Drew nodded. "Okay, that's the most important thing for right now. We are not a bunch of murdering rapists. Not anymore," he growled. 'And never again,' he swore mentally, looking around at each member in turn. All nodded.

"Now, as for Lobo and his assholes. They couldn't take anything that we really need. We travel light and live off the land, so as long as we have our bikes and the road, we'll be just fine. I have some money that should tide us over for a while; we can run into town soon and get supplies.

"Winnie, get a list together of what we need to get through today, tonight, and tomorrow morning, too. Take someone with you to pick it up. I'll give you the cash you'll need once we have our list," he instructed the woman. She nodded and moved off, motioning for a young man whose name Drew couldn't remember to accompany her.

"Graybeard, I don't trust Lobo any farther than I could throw the bastard. What are the odds that he'll either give up our location to the cops, or come back to cause us more problems?"

"I'd put it at about fifty-fifty, Drew," Graybeard said after considering it briefly. "My bet would be that Lobo might set a trap for you, but probably wouldn't fuck us all over. Still, to be safe, maybe we should relocate."

"Kinda what I was thinking, Graybeard. You want to take charge of that? Find us a place to hide out for tonight at least?" The older biker nodded and turned to leave. Drew called as he turned away, "By the way, what's your name? Your actual name," he added.

The man turned back to look at him. After a moment's hesitation, he quietly replied, "Morris Turner." He turned again and walked off. Drew looked after him, frowning.

"Where do I know that name?" he muttered.

Ramona spoke unexpectedly from behind him. "Morris Turner is wanted for killing his wife and children, Drew. He slaughtered them one full moon about ten years ago. He joined up with Lobo soon after. Supposedly Lobo was going to help him find the person that bit him, so that he could get his revenge, but we all think it was Lobo that bit him in the first place."

Drew vaguely remembered hearing the same story when he was seven or eight, when he'd overhead his parents and uncle talking about the case. It was a sensational crime, and had led to a nation-wide man hunt for a man who supposedly butchered his wife and children with 'animal savagery.' Now Drew knew the reality: Turner had been bitten and turned for the first time. Surrounded by his family, he had attacked them.

"Jesus," he breathed. He could easily imagine having done the same thing to Doug and Megan, if he hadn't managed to escape the house.

"Okay," he said, more briskly as he recovered his mental balance. 'Note to self: call him Graybeard.' "The rest of you, let's pack up and get ready to move. Make sure to police the grounds after you're done—we want to leave as little evidence of our stay as possible."

Drew paused, having a dark thought flitter across his consciousness, then vanish before he could see it clearly. Something was bugging him... Oh well, it'd come to him.

"Ramona, can you pack up our stuff? I need to get money for Winnie and see to our cleanup."

The beautiful woman tossed her hair angrily. "What am I, your maid?"

"Damn it, now's not the time to be a pain in the ass. Just pack up our stuff, like you were any other productive member of the pack, and get it on our bikes. There's something I need to be thinking of..." he trailed off, looking past her, trying to capture the elusive thought.

"Fine," she huffed, stalking off to the house. "I'll bring your money out for you, too. Be just a minute." He nodded vaguely, still distracted.

After about an hour, the Firar were ready to break camp. Winnie and the other rider weren't back yet, and since Graybeard wasn't either with their new destination, they sat and waited. The full moon would rise in nine or ten hours, and the bikers were on edge. Two or three arguments broke out among the easily bored bikers, leading Drew to think that perhaps they needed to take a ride, give themselves something to do. He signaled for them to mount up.

"C'mon guys, we're going for a cruise," he yelled, firing up his orange monster. Their reactions were drowned out by the powerful

Sportster's exhaust. Looking over, he signaled to Ramona that she was to remain behind, to meet up with Winnie and Graybeard.

She signaled her displeasure by scowling and flipping him off. Drew grinned and nodded, mouthing, "later," and pulling out. The others followed, revving their engines and jostling for position.

Two hours, and one gas station visit, later, the Fenris Firar found themselves back at the farmhouse, Ramona greeting them as they pulled off the road, sarcastically ushering them in with her arms and bowing.

Drew stepped off his bike and took off his sunglasses. He raised his eyebrows. "So? Everyone back?"

"Yeah. Around the side of the barn. I didn't know when you'd get back, so we didn't set out food yet," she said, walking beside him. Apparently she'd gotten over her displeasure at having to stay behind.

"Good. Hey, Graybeard," Drew called, seeing the older man leaning against the old building. "Did you find us a new nest?"

"I think so," the older man nodded. "It's about an hour away, no facilities, but it has lots of cover, and it's isolated. We should be fine for tonight at least."

"Good. Let's go now," Drew said, turning on his heel and facing back towards the bikes. His pronouncement was met by a chorus of groans and mutterings of "lunch first, asshole."

Drew straightened and barked, "We are leaving now. Lobo and his goons have been gone for hours, and we are not staying here any longer than we have to. Mount up," he commanded. Grudgingly, they followed him back to their hogs.

"Graybeard, you got point. Williams, take rear," he instructed, pointing the blond who'd been knocked out by Ulric earlier to the last spot. It would be his responsibility to see that the pack stayed all together, and that nothing fell and got lost. The straggly-bearded man nodded and gave him a thumbs up.

As Graybeard led off, Drew and Ramona took up leadership positions side by side and just behind him. They looked over at each other and grinned. Ramona revved her bike, mocking his earlier antics on his dirt bike. That seemed like a lifetime ago. And in many ways, it was.

Shortly after two in the afternoon, the Firar arrived at the pasture Graybeard had found for them. It was rough and remote, but offered a hiding spot for the bikes, and shelter for the pack. They stowed the bikes and sprawled out in a loose semi-circle.

Winnie and Ramona brought out the food and drink, and they ravenously dug in, knowing their bodies would need the extra calories for the upcoming transformation. The amount of food consumed was prodigious; no one would believe that a group in the kind of physical shape the Firar appeared to be in could be so gluttonous.

Graybeard leaned back, belching contentedly. Lazily, he waved his hand in the air. "Mr. Boss Man, if you'd care to go over the hill and to the left, there's a creek with running water. I managed to snag a couple of sheep from a nearby herd, and they're tethered down by the water. Figured we'd use them later, since you made me return our last one," he dug, baiting Drew to guage his reaction.

Drew stiffened momentarily, then relaxed, realizing the test. He put on a thoughtful expression and stroked his chin. "Hmm, well, yeah, that's probably a good idea. Maybe you should go first, but be sure to gag them—I hate to listen to sheep getting screwed by horny old men. Or did you just mean to eat the little critters?"

The Firar guffawed. Graybeard smirked. "Hey, boy, bestiality is what we're all about, remember? Them were some interestin' animal sounds coming from your room last night, as I remember," he teased.

Drew flushed as the pack laughed again. Ramona even blushed as Drew threw a quick look her way. "Did you have animals in our room after I fell asleep? Damn, there was a party, and I missed it," he grinned. "Just Ramona and a few hundred of her closest friends."

Winnie joined in. "Uh, no, sounded like Ramona and her one CLOSEST friend, as in so close that you can't tell where one ends and the other begins!"

Ramona glared at her. "Okay, enough," she huffed, much to the amusement of the group.

"Is that what he said?" Winnie asked, pointing at Drew. Huge laughter, even from Drew, who recognized that his fiery girlfriend was on the verge of attacking the smaller, somewhat mousy woman.

Drew waved his hands. "All right, let's go over plans for tonight," he said, still smiling, but bringing everyone back to a more serious tack. "We have the bikes secured out of the way; we have food and water for after the change, thanks to Graybeard, and we have food for the morning, too." There was still something nagging at him, lurking in the back of his mind. "Is there anything that we've overlooked?"

All afternoon, he'd been distracted by images of the previous night with Ramona (he'd never look at his belt the same way again), and the fight with Lobo. Something about what Graybeard had said about not turning on all the Firar, but getting even with Drew alone...

"Shit!" Drew swore, leaping to his feet. "How fucking stupid am I?" He grabbed his backpack and furiously dug through it, scattering clothing and personal effects onto the ground. He pulled out his cell phone and turned it on, walking away from his curious followers so that he could hear better.

He had a message. Drew listened to Doug's panicked voice, his heart sinking. He should have known.

"Drew, it's me, Doug. You need to get this message fast, buddy. It's about 4:30 in the afternoon, and the shit's hit the fan. Those bikers are back. Amy called me just a few minutes ago, Drew. An ambulance just brought in a body, and it was a cop. Amy said he'd been beaten to death. Guess he tried to pull over the bikers and it didn't work out very well.

"The whole town is on alert. Cops are everywhere, and pissed as hell. Haven't seen your uncle yet, but I'll bet he's looking to settle with that Lobo guy or whatever his name is. Call me, huh?"

Drew looked at the phone in his hand. It was just shy of six pm. Being late October, it would be dark in a little over two hours. He wasn't the most experienced at this, but he figured that the change would happen fairly soon after dark.

It was going to be close.

He threw the phone at his backpack. "How far are we from Iowa Park? Come on, how many miles?" He snapped at Graybeard, pulling the key to the Sportster out of his pocket.

"About a hundred and fifty, I think. Are we going back there?" Graybeard asked.

"You're not. Your job is to stay here and keep tabs on the pack while I'm gone," Drew said, panic in his voice. "Lobo is making a run at my father. I fucking should have known. I'm going back. If it works out, I'll be back tomorrow afternoon. If I'm not, assume the worst and get the hell away. Go out east where nobody knows about us. The heat around here will be too intense after this—they killed a cop.

"I gotta go. Take care of them!" he shouted, climbing on his bike. Ramona was right beside him, standing her Hugger up and preparing to start it.

"What do you think you're doing? I need you here," Drew yelled.

"Screw you, Drew. I'll be damned if I stay behind and let you just ride off to get yourself killed," she snapped, firing up her bike.

Drew stared at her for a moment, trying to think of an argument that would keep her out of harm's way, but coming up short. Instead, he found himself mouthing the words, "I love you," at her.

Ramona, still looking at him, mouthed back, "I know." She took the lead, exploding out of the dirt driveway and onto the road, Drew's orange Harley right behind her.

CHAPTER 38

It was a two hour race against the setting sun. Drew and Ramona blasted along the road at breakneck speeds, hitting and maintaining a hundred and twenty miles an hour on straightaways. Curves and turns were taken faster than they could be safely handled, but despite several near-miss disasters, both riders kept the pace.

After an hour, they screamed into a gas station to refuel. Drew tossed money at Ramona, who raced inside to pay, while Drew furiously pumped gas into both tanks, slopping over the sides of each one. Ramona ran out of the service station, chugging a bottle of Gatorade. She passed it to Drew as she jumped onto her bike, gasping, "Drink. You'll need the water."

Drew slammed it down without comment, pitching the empty at the garbage bin. "Let's go," he grunted, wiping his mouth.

"Drew, we're not going to make it, are we? Even if we beat nightfall, what can we hope to accomplish before we turn? What if Lobo's already killed him?" she asked, eyes filled with fear.

"He's alive. Lobo will wait until he changes to kill him. He gets off on torturing and terrifying his victims. He'll keep my dad alive until after he changes. I know it," Drew growled, as much to convince himself as her. "I'm going to stop him."

The pair roared back onto the road, blowing past a local cop so quickly that he couldn't register who or what they were before they were beyond him. The cop, a twenty-five year veteran who was due to go off shift, just shrugged the incident off and continued on his way. Drew didn't even notice.

As they got close to Wichita Falls, Drew recognized where they were. He whipped in front of Ramona and opened it up even more. Despite her best efforts, the she couldn't keep up with him. The bored-out Sportster was just too much.

The pair was losing the race. The sun was falling faster than they could fly across the surface of west Texas. All too soon, Drew and Ramona were using the headlights to track other vehicles, rather than the vehicles themselves.

Five minutes out of Iowa Park, Drew felt his first twitch. The feeling of wrongness hit him, and he felt a shiver down his spine. He ignored it and kept the throttle wide open, desperate to get back to his father's house. Ramona wasn't even in his rearview mirror.

Another jolt, this time stronger. Drew screamed in anger and frustration. He was *not* going to fall short; he refused to lose the most important race of his life. His spine arched in agony as he fought off the urge to change.

Three more blocks went by in a blur. Drew was almost in sight of the house when he finally lost the battle against the pull of his curse. He put the bike down in a barely controlled slide, tearing up someone's yard, and tumbling to a stop. He tore at his clothes. His time as a human being had ended. With a howl, the wolf burst forth.

•• (◐) ••

Deputy Winslow was frustrated. All of his life, he'd wanted to do something that mattered; something relevant. He'd thought that becoming a cop would lead to great things, but once the novelty wore off, he realized that most police work, especially in a small town like Iowa Park, was tedious.

Earlier this fall, he'd thought that his big chance had finally come. Outlaw bikers blasted through his quiet town, bringing with them a pestilence of violence and mayhem. There were rumors of wild wolves, attack dogs working with the bikers, and even the bizarre occult twist of werewolves.

He'd been assigned to put together a file on the bikers, known as the Fenris Firar, by the sheriff himself. Eagerly, he'd thrown himself into the task, compiling an immense amount of information, and drawing some truly frightening conclusions.

To his immense disappointment, the sheriff hadn't followed up on any of it. He wasn't even grateful. Whenever Winslow had brought up the subject of the Firar, Parker brusquely cut him off. No one was allowed to talk about it, not even a month ago when the biker suspected of abducting Lucy Parsons was found dead.

On top of that, Winslow was almost suspended for talking with the reporter, Matt Roth, as well. Actually, he'd been afraid that Parker was going to shoot him for that one. Luckily, a severe tongue-lashing was all he'd gotten.

So here he was, on the afternoon of another full moon, cruising around and muttering to himself about life. He wished that he could listen to the radio, but he was on duty, and Becker had made it clear that any rap while on duty was strictly forbidden.

With the radio silent, he heard what initially seemed like distant thunder. He cocked his head to the side and listened. With Bernie's being one of the largest Harley dealers in the state, lots of bikers came through Iowa Park. But he couldn't help but think of the Fenris Firar.

His eyes widened alarmingly when they swept into view. Six hogs cruised down the street, each one bearing a biker wearing familiar colors. It was the Firar, or at least some of them. The one in the lead was clearly Fletcher Burroughs, known as Lobo.

Their sudden appearance caught him off guard. Whatever their intentions, it couldn't be good. He snatched up his mike and radioed it in. Without waiting for instructions, or even a confirmation, he flipped his lights on and cut across the oncoming Firar, parking diagonally across their lane of traffic.

He jumped out of the car, hand unsnapping his holster and loosening the gun it held. Deputy Winslow swallowed nervously; this was the chance he'd long envisioned, but the bikers were huge, and menacing. Plus, they had him outnumbered six to one.

'Still,' he reminded himself, 'it was broad daylight, in the middle of town. Nothing really bad would go down right here and now.'

"Okay, let's see some hands. Shut off the bikes and remain where you are," he shouted, drawing his weapon.

The leader of the pack, Lobo, smirked and held up his hands. "Easy, little man. We ain't gonna hurt ya. We're just riding through. We enjoyed your town so much last time we were here; we just thought we'd pay y'all another visit. Right, guys?"

The other five bikers stepped off their bikes and rested them against the kickstands. Winslow shifted his stance, bringing the gun to bear on them instead. Their faces, in contrast to Lobo's, were blank. The deputy wasn't fooled for an instant; there was menace in every movement that they made.

"Don't move," he repeated. "You guys should have known better than to come back here. We've been looking for you," Winslow said, feeling better with the bikers at the other end of his gun. "I said don't move!"

"Well, lucky you, Deputy...Winslow," Lobo mocked, leaning in to read his nametag. "Because you found us. All...by...yourself," he growled, seeming to grow in size and sheer ferocity by the second as he glared at the lawman.

Winslow stood frozen, his eyes captured by the bloodshot gaze of the big biker. As if rehearsed, Caleb leapt forward while he was distracted and snatched the gun out of his hand. At the same time, Red dove low, tackling the deputy around the knees.

Jimmy cried out in shock as he was disarmed and slammed to the pavement. He struggled to get back to his feet, but the red-haired biker had a firm hold of his legs. He reached down, trying to pry the man off of him, when he felt a large shadow looming.

Ulric raised his boot high, and smashed it down onto the struggling deputy's arm. Winslow's right arm broke with a sickening crack that brought a fresh scream from the lawman, and a coarse laugh from the bikers.

An ugly woman stepped up and drove her boot into his side, cracking ribs. Red let go and scrambled back to his feet in time to join in, as all five began stomping the deputy. Lobo remained on his bike, looking on in satisfaction.

After a short time, the bikers stepped back. On the ground was a sprawled, bloody wreck that was once an Iowa Park Sheriff's Deputy. The bikers climbed back on their hogs and thundered off, rapidly disappearing, despite the large gathering crowd.

Within seconds, other squad cars shrieked to a stop, officers spilling out with guns in hand, frantically looking for the perpetrators of this outrage. An ambulance arrived at the same time that Sheriff Parker did. By that time, Winslow's body was covered by his coat, the cops first on the scene having ascertained he was beyond medical help.

Parker did what he could to keep a leash on his men's emotions. They were all furious, scared, and spoiling for payback. An APB was issued, and everyone, on duty or off, was sent out into the streets to find the bikers. It was a small town, they couldn't be hard to find.

It turned out though, that they were. In fact, the six members of the outlaw gang had vanished. No one could find them. Even after making multiple passes through Albertson's and Wal-Mart, and stopping at Bernie's, no trace of Lobo and his followers remained.

●●❰❪◯❫❱●●

James Collins pulled in to his garage, lost in thought. After closing the door, he glanced at the Honda still parked in its normal spot, now with a light coating of dust. Next to it was the empty space where his Sportster used to be. He hoped that Drew was taking good care of the bike. Shaking his head at the irrelevance of the thought, he walked into his quiet house, and straight into the arms of the six people lurking there.

"Well, hello, Mr. Collins. Nice to finally meet you," one of them greeted him. "We let ourselves in," he said, waving to the broken rear window. It was the same one that Drew shattered going out last month.

"We got some things to discuss, you and I," the big, hairy man continued, sitting down in James' chair and motioning to the couch. Two of the bikers shoved him down onto the cushions and remained standing over him.

"James, you don't mind if I call you James, do you?" he said, as Collins sat stoically, "We have to talk about your son. Little Drew has become a huge pain in the ass for me. He stole my gang from me, the little fucker. I started that gang; I populated it. It's my family, and he just took it away because he didn't like what we were doing.

"And since he took my family away," Lobo leaned towards him, "I'm going to return the favor. Tonight, I'm going to take his family away from him." The large man grinned wickedly, sending a chill down James' spine. "This is what we're going to do: first, you're going to call your buddy the sheriff, and tell him to come over here; just him, all by his lonesome, and then the three of us will get this whole thing all worked out."

He yelled at the one of his bikers. "Aardwolf, get the man his telephone!" The scarred biker looked around, located the elusive device, and shoved it into the elder Collins' lap, growling.

"Well, now that we've got that taken care of, let's just dial up that pesky sheriff, shall we? Remember, James, tell him to come alone, and come right in; the front door is open. Nothing more, okay?"

James Collins looked slowly from the biker to phone in his lap. He picked up the receiver and dialed.

"Parker."

"Bob, it's Jim. The bikers are here."

"I know that, Jim. They killed one of my deputies," Parker shouted into the phone, his nerves frayed.

"No, Bob, you don't understand," Collins said, quietly. "They're *here*, at the house. They want you to come over. Just you, by yourself. Come in the front door, it's unlocked."

"How many are there? Do they have Drew?" Parker asked.

Lobo gave a sign to Ulric, who yanked the cord from the wall. The line went dead.

"Good, Jimmy boy, that was just fine. Now, we'll just make ourselves comfy while we wait. Piggy, Ardie; keep an eye out, will you?" he asked, waving his hand in the air. The ugly woman and the scarred man went out the back door to keep watch.

The gang leader looked back at Collins and smiled happily. It was starting to get dark. Soon, very soon, the party would get interesting.

●● ◖◯◗ ●●

Matt Roth stood up from his desk suddenly, cursing like a sailor whose leave had been canceled. He reached down and slapped the top of his laptop closed. He absolutely could not bring himself to type up the story that his editor had asked him to do. He knew that it was crap. The whole thing stunk, and he refused to help cover the truth with this load of fertilizer.

He looked around the office: most everyone else was gone for the day. The reporter took his jacket off the back of his chair and pulled out his keys. 'Screw this,' he told himself. He was after the truth.

He went outside and got into his car. After a moment's reflection, he started it up and drove off. James Collins knew more about what was going on than anyone else that wasn't a cop. Time to turn up the heat. If necessary, he'd camp out on his step, and force Sheriff Parker to arrest him, if it came to that.

●●◖◯◗●●

Parker pulled into James Collins' driveway and shut off his car. The lengthening shadows seemed to contain hidden menace. His gun was already out, safety off, and sitting on the seat next to him. He was boiling over; rage over Winslow's brutal murder, and fear for his brother-in-law mixing together to form a whirlwind of emotion.

Right now, he'd like nothing better than to shoot every biker he saw. But as he drove up, there were none in sight. No hogs on the pavement, no bikers lurking around corners, and no wolves crouching in the shadows. He spared a glance up at the sky- if his nightmare were coming true, there wouldn't be any wolves yet. It wasn't dark enough.

Deciding that there was no threat to be found outside, he cautiously went up to the front door. Electing against knocking, he threw open the door and stepped in, gun held aggressively in front of him.

"Hello, Bob," James said quietly from his chair. The fading light showed him to be sitting with his arms and legs duct-taped in front of him.

The muzzle of Winslow's 9mm was shoved against his right temple. The biker holding the gun smirked at him, as another reached over from the left to relieve him of his weapon.

"Okay, Lobo, all clear," Caleb called, still pressing the dead deputy's service weapon tightly against the sheriff's head.

The former leader of the Fenris Firar came out from around the corner and smiled hard at the sheriff, a feral grin that promised death and mayhem. Looking in the biker's eyes, Parker had no doubt he planned to kill them.

"Where's my nephew?" Parker demanded. It was the wrong opening.

Lobo's face flushed, and he snarled. He clubbed James in the back of the head as he went by, glaring at the lawman. Parker heard the biker next to him hiss in anger.

"Fuck you, cop. 'Where's my nephew?' Who gives a fuck? Your nephew is the reason we're here, asshole. That little prick took over my gang. He took away my family, so now I'm here to take away his," Lobo sneered, enjoying Parker's look of anger.

"Oh, yeah, and we stomped that little black cop of yours, too. That one was free; we did that for the fun of it. No, no need to thank us," he added. Parker lunged forward. The red-haired biker tripped him, and the sheriff crashed heavily onto the floor.

Lobo reached down and snatched him up. Despite the man's size and bulk, the outlaw biker handled him like a child. "Have a seat, cop," he hissed, throwing him easily into the second easy chair in the room.

A biker that was even bigger than Lobo swiftly taped his arms and legs together, leaving him relatively helpless. He wasn't gagged, however.

"So what's this all about, then? Just revenge on us because Drew took over your gang? How'd he do that, anyway? Was he smarter, or just plain better than you, huh?" Parker mocked.

Ulric rocked him hard, slamming an open hand into the side of his head and causing him to see stars. It was almost worth it, seeing the look on Lobo's face. As soon as his head cleared, he started in again.

"So what's the big deal, anyway? A bunch of losers like that can't be that big a deal to a tough guy like you, Fletcher. Just go find a new group of morons to have follow you around and think that you're the shit," he spat, ducking Ulric's backhand.

Lobo held up his hand, forestalling his lieutenant's next blow. The big biker smiled again at the cop, moving to stand just in front of him.

"Oh, but my dear sheriff, those 'loser bikers' as you call them are so much more than just losers on motorcycles. Oh, much more. But I think you already know that, don't you sheriff," he said, eyes narrowing. "Yeah, I think you've got a pretty good idea just who and what we are, don't you, sheriff? That's what worries you so much about your precious nephew, isn't it? Afraid that he's one of us?" Lobo taunted, taking pleasure in Parker's changing expression. "Well, guess what—he is! He's taken to his new life in a way that scares even me. Kid's fucking psycho," Lobo stated, enjoying Parker and Collins' horrified reaction to his words.

"Kinda fitting, that his daddy and uncle get to die at the hands of what they fear most," he crowed, stretching luxuriously, basking in the two humans' hatred. "I'm going to enjoy this."

A sudden commotion at the back door distracted him. Aardwolf and Piggy appeared, dragging with them a medium-sized man in disheveled condition.

"Lobo, we caught this guy sneaking around the back yard. Says he's a reporter, demands to talk to Collins. Thought you'd like to meet him. If you want, he can wait outside with us," Piggy said, licking the side of the unfortunate man's face, and leering.

"No, that's okay, Piggy, we'll just make room for one more guest here in the living room," Lobo said, smiling at the man's shudder. "Park him here on the couch, Piggy. Tape him up, too, Ulric, we'd hate to have our guest leave halfway through the party. That'd be rude."

"So," he said, looking at the newcomer curiously, "a reporter, huh? What brings you here tonight? An interview with James, here? Did you have an appointment that you didn't tell me about?" he asked, turning to Collins.

James shook his head. He looked at Parker. "Bob, what's going on? Are these guys nuts? They act like they believe the same stuff that you told me earlier. You know it can't be true," he said. He looked at Lobo. "There's no such thing as werewolves."

Roth jerked, flinching at the word. "What? What are you talking about?"

Lobo laughed. "That's what you came to find out, isn't it? What the deep, dark secret was; what was being covered up? Well, little man, tonight's your lucky night. You get to witness first hand an unbelievable story. Sadly, you won't have the chance to write about it, since you're going to become dinner. Nice of you to drop in, by the way," he laughed, pleased by Roth's horrified expression.

Lobo's face seemed to ripple, almost like a wave had passed through him. He grinned. "And so it begins. Gentlemen, enjoy the show." He growled out the last, flinching as the second shot of pain hit him.

"Look, little men," he snarled, holding up a hand that had sprouted long black claws and hairs along the back. He flexed it, opening and closing the distended fingers in front of their shocked faces. "Get a good look, sheep," he managed to gasp out, while tearing off his clothes.

Suddenly, lights shown through the window as a car slid sideways in the drive, lights flashing. A sheriff's car slammed to a stop, two deputies piling out.

"Deal with it," Lobo growled, his voice barely human. Five hideously snarling wolves bolted out the back door, rushing around the corners of the house at the cops.

CHAPTER 39

Becker and Lem had been canvassing the town with the other deputies, furiously searching side streets in their cars, when they stopped at Albertson's. They both got out and stood, surveying the mostly empty parking lot.

"They couldn't have just disappeared," Becker grunted, staring around at the neighborhood.

"Naw," Lem, drawled. Becker glanced at his fellow deputy. His body language was tense, but his voice was normal, sounding almost bored. Ray himself was a wreck. One of their own had just been brutally killed, and those responsible were out there somewhere, waiting for them.

Soon, he knew, the time that he had nightmares about would be upon him: the life-or-death struggle, where his weakness would finally be exposed for all to see, and he would fail.

If Lem felt that way, he gave no sign. The red-haired man merely looked eager to find the bikers that had killed Jimmy. He'd been in almost constant contact with Parker at the beginning of the search, sharing information and locations.

Lem started to switch the toothpick that was his regular companion over to the other side of his mouth, and then stopped. It occurred to him that he hadn't heard from the sheriff in over twenty minutes.

"Ray, y'all heard from Parker lately? Don't remember hearin' his voice for a while," he asked.

Becker frowned. "No, not for about a half hour. Why? What are you thinking? Do you think he went somewhere on his own, without telling us? " he asked, suddenly stiffening as he thought it through. "Why would he do that?"

A thought struck him. "Lem, he went to Collins' house. I'll bet you anything! That's where the bikers would go, too. That's the witness. I'll bet they came back to eliminate him, and Jimmy tried to pull them over.

"C'mon, let's go. Ride with me, it'll be faster to take one car," he snapped, jumping behind the wheel and starting the Charger. Becker turned on the lights, flipped the siren, and stomped on the gas. Tires shrieking in protest, the car tore out of the parking lot.

"Do we call it in?" Lem wondered. "Have them meet us at the house?"

"We don't know that they're there, yet, Lem. It's just a guess," he replied.

"It's not just a guess, Ray. You and I both know that that's where Parker is. Those bikers went there, too, and you know it. If you want to get there first, and then call it in, that's fine."

The two men looked at each other. Both nodded. They would get there first and see what was going on, then call it in if they needed to. They wanted to help Parker, and it was just possible that involving the rest of the department could hurt the situation. They would check it out first.

●●◖◯◗●●

Becker and Lem raced up the front walk towards James Collins' door. Both men spun, one each way, drawing their guns as they heard the vicious growls coming from either side of them. Wolves burst from around the dark corners of the house. Not just any wolves, like Lem had seen at the zoo as a child, but nightmarish monsters, with eyes that glittered with rage, and snapping teeth that flung drool and slobber off of them, as if rabid.

Toothpick dropping out of his slack mouth, Lem recoiled in terror as the largest of the creatures threw itself into the air, launching its open jaws at his throat. His finger tightened on the trigger of his Smith & Wesson, sending a bullet into the ground beside him.

Monstrous jaws snapped shut on Lem's neck, as the huge wolf slammed into him, driving him to the ground. He felt a horrible ripping sensation at his throat, and then a gush of boiling warmth, almost like he was drowning. He attempted to scream, but what came out was a barely audible gurgling.

The giant wolf dipped again, biting down and shaking its massive head from side to side, and Lem felt nothing else. His head, almost severed, flopped to one side, his legs twitching spasmodically.

Becker brought his gun up reflexively, firing point-blank at the nearest wolf. It tumbled to a stop as the deputy shifted to fire at the animal behind the first one. That wolf, too, sprawled to a dead stop as he shot it twice in the head. There was a third creature right behind that one, and Becker fired right into its open mouth, blowing out the back of its skull.

Ray didn't blink as he swiveled to shoot the big wolf standing over Lem three times in the body. It was almost like things were happening in slow motion. He watched that wolf shudder with the repeated impacts and start to fall over.

Too late he realized there was one more. The last of the wolves leapt over both its fallen pack mate and Lem's body, soaring in feral majesty at the stunned deputy. It reached out, jaws extending to close on the man who had shot four of its mates.

Its flight was arrested by a black-furred streak that shot past Becker's shoulder, crashing full speed into his attacker. Two wolves hit the ground, snarling and tearing at each other with primitive fury. The black wolf howled with rage, its silver eyes promising death to the other. Its adversary growled low, seeking desperately to find a killing grip.

Becker stood, pointing his gun at the two combatants, at a loss for what to do. He felt, more than saw, a rush of movement from behind him and spun, whipping his gun around. Another wolf, this one gray with a black mane, raced past him and hurled itself without pause at the living room window.

●●◗◯◖●●●

The three men watched in terror as Lobo made the transformation from human to wolf. He'd made sure to stay in plain sight of them, so they could see every unearthly twist and shift that his body went through.

Roth screamed more than once, unprepared for what was going on around him. He'd known that there was more to the story than what Parker was letting on, but in his most fevered nightmares, he couldn't have expected this.

Parker was concerned for Roth, afraid that the younger man might just snap, but also partly hoping that he would. Going insane might be a mercy. But he was more concerned for James. The man deserved better than to go out like this. He'd been through too much already.

His final concern was for his wife. She had been with him through so much, seldom complaining, always supportive, and always worrying about him. This would be too much for her to deal with. The injustice spurred him to motion.

As Lobo fell to the floor, his spine shifting, Parker rocked upwards, managing to get to his feet. Unable to balance because of the duct tape holding his legs together, he toppled over, landing on the floor right next to the transforming biker.

Horrified, he stared as Lobo's jaws stretched and split, teeth extending and jutting forwards, only inches away from his face. He squirmed, trying to get further away from the monster.

With a triumphant howl, the shaggy wolf regained its feet. It stood over Parker; lips pulled back, teeth bared. Saliva dripped onto the prone sheriff, who looked up defiantly at the huge wolf.

"Fuck you," Parker whispered, as the beast drew back and opened its mouth wider.

With a spectacular crash, the living room window exploded inwards, showering the room with flying glass. A gigantic gray and black shape landed on all fours in the middle of the room, teeth bared in a horrible snarl, and a deep, rumbling growl issuing from its massive chest.

Lobo, instinctively ducking the flying object that crashed through the window, straightened back up and looked at the newcomer in shock. He recognized the scent: Drew Collins. The bastard had followed him, and was now trying to keep him from his revenge.

The monstrous wolf growled, curling its lips away from outsized canines. Fur bristled between its shoulder blades as it faced the younger wolf. Hatred filled Lobo's heart as he glared at Drew. The two nightmare creatures stood inches apart in the crowded living room, covered in glass shards, teeth bared, tails low, ears back. For a moment, nothing moved or made a sound.

Then, so quickly that all three humans flinched in surprise and fear, the wolves threw themselves at each other. Teeth snapped, and throats issued horrifying challenges, as almost five hundred pounds of seething fur and fury fought madly.

Lobo had an advantage in both weight and experience. Drew, still new to lycanthropy, wasn't used to fighting as an animal. He was, however, fighting to protect his father and uncle from a hated enemy.

The wolves slammed into the couch, pushing and shoving against each other hard enough that it tipped over backwards, spilling Matt Roth onto the floor behind. The terrified man sat up just as Lobo succeeded in throwing Drew over the top of the couch.

Drew's two hundred pound form crashed into the bound reporter, pinning him on the floor. He yelped in terror and pain as the huge wolf pushed off of him and leaped back over the couch to knock Lobo sideways.

Lobo hesitated. He wanted to kill Drew, but causing him anguish by making him watch his family die would be ideal. So instead of pursuing Drew over the furniture as he knocked him aside again, he turned and attacked the nearest human on the floor beside him.

Parker kicked at the giant muzzle as the wolf reached out to bite him, cursing loudly and trying to scramble further out of the way. The shaggy monster flinched away from the kick and snapped its mammoth jaws, missing the sheriff's feet by millimeters.

And then Drew was back, knocking the bigger wolf away from his uncle. Even in wolf form, he knew that these humans were his to protect, and that he must keep them safe from Lobo at all costs.

Deliberately, the gray wolf shifted, placing himself squarely between Parker and Lobo. Blood and saliva dripped slowly from his mouth. He lowered his head in anticipation of Lobo's next charge.

It came quickly. Lobo leapt at his foe, jaws open. Drew growled and sprang, coming in under Lobo's extended lower jaw, and trying to fasten his teeth on the larger wolf's throat. They crashed together in midair and fell in a struggling heap.

●● ◖◖◯◗◗ ●●

Outside, the black wolf was fighting for her life as well. She had blocked her rival's attack on the police officer, and opened up a gash on Piggy's neck, but wasn't able to do any serious damage despite her surprise strike. Piggy had recovered quickly, and threw herself at her enemy with a savage snarl. The bitter rivals tore into each other with a vengeance.

Becker was in a quandary. He kept his gun trained on the two wolves on the ground in front of him, but was keenly aware that there was action going on inside the house, too. He'd seen the huge gray wolf go through the window, and heard the sounds of heavy combat coming from the living room. The lawman knew that his responsibility was to Parker and the citizens of Iowa Park at risk in the house. He should shoot both wolves and move inside. He knew that he could kill them both as they struggled on the lawn.

The Sheriff's deputy brought his gun up. The movement caught the attention of the black wolf, and it glanced up at him. Silver eyes stared into Becker's, and he froze in shock. He'd seen those eyes before, at Albertson's grocery store. Only then they belonged to a beautiful young woman with ebony black hair and a biker jacket.

Ramona's distraction cost her. Piggy surged up from under Ramona and seized her by the throat. Massive fangs bit deep, seeking the jugular. The black wolf growled and tried to twist away.

Becker adjusted his aim, firing more out of instinct than reason. The bullet struck the stocky wolf in the shoulder, causing it to release its death grip on the silver-eyed one. The ugly wolf roared in pain and anger, snapping its teeth at the lawman, promising death for the interfering human.

Ramona leapt away from Piggy, then back in so fast that Becker couldn't begin to follow the movements. In less than a heartbeat, the black wolf struck. Piggy had just enough time to realize that she'd somehow lost before her eyes glazed over and she fell over in a spreading pool of blood.

●● ◖◉◗ ●●

Drew and Lobo were both covered in masses of cuts. Blood flowed freely over their coats, and tufts of fur were floating in the air, torn free by snapping jaws and clawed feet. But neither wolf was able to claim an advantage.

Lobo roared in fury, his eyes gleaming insanely as he glared at the upstart that was ruining his life. Dimly, it registered in his lupine brain that the longer this went on, the more likely it was he would be killed.

From outside another gunshot rang out. A howl sounded, angry and hurt, followed by another wolf's roar of triumph. Both wolves paused, attention diverted for a moment.

Parker took advantage, and made a move for the gun Lobo had dropped on the floor. The wolf looked back and saw the sheriff crawling for the corner of the room. In an instant, he leapt onto the man, smashing him flat to the floor. Parker felt the wolf's weight crushing him, and the hot fetid breath from its mouth as it leaned in to kill him. Desperately, he tried to roll and throw the monster off.

Lobo growled as his intended victim struggled. The rocking motion of the man under him threw off his balance, and made him shift to retain his position. For just an instant, he paused.

Drew hit Lobo at full speed, driving the bigger wolf over backwards, off of Parker. The sheriff rolled away from the wolves as best he could, the gun temporarily forgotten as he sought to escape the carnage.

The gray and black wolf was now on top, snapping at the bigger wolf's throat, trying to penetrate the other's guard. Lobo brought up his rear paws, trying to kick Drew off him, but the younger lycan would have none of it. Drew twisted his body to keep Lobo pinned beneath him, avoiding his rear paws. Ignoring Lobo's horrid growls, he viciously attacked his foe. Blood and fur flew from the combatants, splattering the room, and the three humans that bore witness to the titanic struggle.

Lobo caught Drew's front leg in his jaws. The new werewolf was attempting to use his leg to push Lobo's head to the side, and the wily older wolf swept his own head around, seizing the paw in his teeth. Lobo bit down hard, and Drew howled in pain.

If Lobo thought that Drew would back off, he was wrong. Drew was lost in his blood lust, and simply kept pushing. The damaged front leg wedged in Lobo's mouth gave Drew the leverage he needed. Lobo's head was forced to the side, and Drew shot in, jaws clamping on his enemy's throat. Lobo released his grip on the front leg, attempting to squirm away. Drew savagely bit down, and wrenched his head to the side, tearing Lobo's throat wide open.

Blood sprayed. Drew howled in victory. The huge wolf under him kicked and struggled. Lobo's eyes rolled as he felt his life pouring away. Drew kept him pinned, as Lobo's movements become more frantic.

The older wolf's legs stopped kicking. The large gray wolf staggered upright, and froze. Standing in front of him, with one arm worked free from the tape, was Sheriff Parker. Clutched in his hand was Winslow's gun, pointed directly at the wolf's face.

Neither moved. It was a stand off. Parker raised the gun slightly, sighting down it. His finger tightened on the trigger.

"Bobby, no!" James cried out. "Don't shoot. It's Drew. You know it is."

Parker's hand began to shake, and he lowered the gun. "Yeah, I guess it is."

Roth, still not sure what was going on, yelled, "Shoot it, sheriff! It may go after us next."

"No it won't, Mr. Roth. He came back here to save us. I can't very well shoot him for saving our lives, can I?" Carefully, Parker put the gun on the floor and fumbled with the duct tape binding his legs.

After freeing himself, he turned to help his brother-in-law, who remained in his chair, staring in horror at what his son had become. The wolf also remained still, eyes locked with his father.

Once all three men were freed, they gingerly moved toward the shattered front window. All of them had heard the gunshots just prior to Drew's dramatic entrance, but had no idea what it had meant, or who was out there. Roth peeked out at the front lawn, while Parker and Collins went out the front door instead. The large wolf raised its head, looking over the sill with the reporter.

On the grass, five huge wolves lay bloodied and unmoving. One deputy also was on the ground, his throat a ruin, head at an unnatural angle. Standing over the deputy was another man in uniform, in the classic Weaver shooting stance, holding a final wolf at bay. This one was all black, with silver eyes sparkling with intelligence. The eyes flicked to the window, and took in the sight of the large gray, peering over the sill at her. Her tail waved once, slowly.

"Becker!" Parker rasped, coming out the door at a stumbling run. The man holding the gun never flinched. His eyes remained steady on the wolf.

"Ray. What happened? Is that…oh, God, it's Lem," Parker said, dropping to his knees beside the body. "What happened, Ray? Who killed Lem? Was it that black wolf?" the sheriff growled, raising up the pistol he had brought outside with him. "That's the one that bit Drew, I think. He said it had silver eyes."

The wolf in the window growled once and leaped out onto the grass. He limped to stand with the other wolf, briefly touching noses and then turning to face the lawmen. They kept their weapons trained on the wolves.

James Collins stared at the animals. He knew that Drew was one of them, and that he was protecting the other. Slowly, he stepped in front of his brother-in-law, turning to face him, and in the process turning his back on the wolves.

"No," he said. "Not them. Let them go."

Parker wasn't convinced. Another of his deputies was dead, this one a long-time friend. He tightened his grip on the automatic, and said, grimly, "Move, James. This damn wolf killed Lem. I won't shoot Drew, but Lem needs to be avenged. Get out of the way."

Surprisingly, it was Becker who spoke up. "Wasn't the black one, boss. It was that big fucker to the left. The black one saved my ass. The last one from the house would have got me; it jumped me too fast, and got past my gun, when the black one tackled it. I couldn't bring myself to shoot this one, since it saved my life. We've been standing here since, kinda stuck."

"Let them go, Bob. You heard him; the black one didn't hurt anyone," James repeated, his voice stronger. "It saved Ray. Shooting her won't help Lem. Or Jimmy. Let them go."

"Her? How the hell do you know it's a her?" Parker demanded, still holding his gun.

"I saw her, Bob. She came into Bernie's with the guy that took Lucy. No mistaking those eyes." James shuddered, horrified despite his resolve. "It's her, it has to be. Let them go, Bob, please?" he said, this time stepping forward and reaching out for the gun.

Parker grimaced. He put the safety on the gun and stuck it in his holster. Becker lowered his weapon. All three men shared a long look with the two wolves.

The sheriff moved back to Lem's side and knelt down. Becker joined him, and James looked down at them momentarily. When he looked back up, the wolves were gone.

•••◖◗◗•••

Matt Roth watched everything from the window. He saw the pair bolt off, exploding into motion and vanishing. Silent, leaving no trace. He shuddered and turned around to pick his way out of the living room, joining the others outside. His eyes widened as he looked at the floor. The huge wolf was gone. A thick trail of blood led to the back door and vanished out into the yard.

Roth stared out the back door, and went the other way. He got into his car and slumped behind the wheel, trembling. Reaching into the glove compartment, he pulled out a flask filled with whiskey. He hadn't touched it, or any other booze, for almost a month.

He considered the flask, and what it contained. The escape from what he just witnessed and gone through. Then he considered the price of crawling back into the bottle; what it would do to his soul.

The reporter poured out the flask onto the driveway and drove off, trying to figure out what he'd write about this night. If he wrote anything. Who'd believe any of it, anyway? He was a reporter, after all, not a writer of fiction.

CHAPTER 40

Late the next morning, Drew and Ramona walked into the Parker home. His Aunt Mary met them at the door, and gave Drew a big hug. She looked nervously at Ramona, but nevertheless shook her hand and invited them in. Waiting inside, were Drew's father, his uncle, Doug Jones, and Amy Bishop.

Nurse Bishop cleaned and dressed both Drew and Ramona's injuries from the previous night. While she tended to them, Drew asked questions.

"What are you two doing here, Doug? Not that I'm not glad to see you, but I'm a little confused. No one was supposed to know we were here."

"Thank your uncle, Drew. He called Amy to come and check you over, make sure you were okay. She called me, and here we are," the teen said, staring at Ramona.

"Okay, but why call Amy? I kind of thought you two didn't like each other," Drew asked his uncle.

"Doesn't matter who likes who, kid. I knew that she helped you the last time; you did, Bishop, no sense in denying it now," Parker grunted, when the nurse turned to protest. "So, I figured this way you could get medical treatment without expanding the circle of people who know what's really going on."

"So now what?" Drew wanted to know. Things had happened very quickly, and the fallout from the previous night would likely be severe.

"Dude, you are still a burn," Doug said. "I think that the sheriff and your dad have most of it worked out, though. Reads kinda like a sci-fi book, though, I think. If I tried to turn in a paper like this, I'd get chewed out for sure."

He looked again at Ramona, who had been silent the entire time. His face slowly shifted into a huge grin. "So, Collins, this is her, huh? Damn. Makes everyone in this town look like a dog by comparison."

The stupidity of what he had said sunk in, and everyone at the table turned to glare at him. His face flushed crimson. "I mean, she's really hot, Drew. She is *totally* hotter than anyone around here." Amy looked up from cleaning one of Drew's cuts and raised an eyebrow.

"Uh, I mean, shit," he muttered, sitting back. The others laughed quietly at his discomfort. It wasn't much, but for a group that had been through what they had, it was a start.

"Bitch," Drew said, shaking his head in mock severity.

"Jerk," Jones snapped back, causing Ramona to stare from one to the other in puzzlement.

"It's from a TV show," Drew explained. "One about demons, and vampires, and werewolves and unbelievable shit like that." He grinned. "Not like the real world at all."

"What's next for you?" Parker asked.

"We need to go," Drew said. "The rest of the pack is holed up, waiting for us. I can't just leave them; I'm responsible for them. Anyway, there's no way we could stay here, being what we are."

"What about their crimes, Drew? Are we supposed to just let them skate on murder, robbery, and all the rest?"

"The ones on the lawn did most or all of that stuff. Wrench took Lucy, and he's dead too. The Firar aren't much better or worse than anyone else, we just have this fucking curse, and have to live with it," Drew said, shaking his head. "Our days of stealing and hurting people to get by are over. We're going to find a better way." He paused and looked at his mate. "You have my word. Ramona and I are going to lead them down a different path."

He stood up and pulled his shirt back on. "What about you? How are you going to deal with this?"

Parker sat, staring at the floor. After a few moments, he looked up at his nephew, who seemed so much bigger and older than he had just two short months ago. He sighed.

"Got home this morning and talked it over with Mary. I'm resigning, Drew. It's been coming for a while. There's no way I can come clean with this, and I can't be the sheriff here and cover it all up, either. So we're gonna move," he said, sighing. "Mary has family in North Carolina, and Bernie is going to help me get a job at the Harley dealership in that town. Says they need a good sales manager, and he knows the owner.

"Becker is going to be the new sheriff. He'll do a great job. Coolest customer I ever met. Shot four of those fuckers as they came at him last night. Wish Lem coulda made it, though." For a moment, Parker's eyes glistened, and he almost lost it. He struggled for control, fighting back the tears.

"Roth quit his job this morning, too. I hear he wants to move up north, get a fresh start in some big city with no animals running loose. Hope he stays clean. Not a bad guy if he can stay off the sauce.

Parker's voice became brisker as he regained control. "So, I understand Becker is putting out an APB on the six bikers that killed Jimmy, and plans to hold them responsible for all of the killings and robberies that happened here. You and the girl should be okay.

"Wish it didn't all have to be like this, Drew. You keep in touch with your old man, you got it?" Parker said gruffly.

"Yeah, uncle Bob, I got it. Speaking of which, uh, dad, can we talk?"

James, who had been sitting on a chair the entire time without speaking, slowly made eye contact with his son. He nodded. The others looked at each other and got up.

"Come on, gang, let's go outside for a bit. Let them talk," Mary said, shooing them towards the door. "Ramona, let me tell you all about Drew's favorite foods, and how he likes them prepared."

Ramona looked at her, startled. Mary Parker smirked at her, and the younger woman relaxed. She was being teased, not domesticated. Smiling back, she stepped outside with the sheriff's wife.

Drew and his father sat silently at the table. Now that they were alone, neither knew how to start, or what to say. The younger

Collins knew from experience that he'd have to find a way to initiate.

"Sorry about taking the bike, dad. I didn't think I'd be able to catch up to the gang on the Honda. Too much open road. Runs amazing, though. About threw me right off the back the first time I opened it up," he started.

James grunted. "Yeah, gotta watch the takeoff, especially out of first or second. Once you're rolling good, it doesn't jerk so much."

Drew bit his lip. "Dad, I'm sorry. For everything. For leaving, for running out without saying anything, for putting you in this mess."

"Drew, there's nothing to apologize for. Wasn't your fault, none of it. You saved our lives, coming back like you did. A lot of men wouldn't have done that, just woulda kept running away."

Drew felt himself starting to choke up. He forced a smile onto his face. "I don't suppose you'd let me make payments on the bike, would you? It'll be hard keeping the respect of the gang, riding on a dirt bike. Probably get my ass kicked every day, by the women."

"Keep it. It's yours. Paid for already. Just treat it good, son. It's a serious machine," James said. The elder Collins tried to hold back his emotions, though his eyes gave them away. "Always meant for you to have it someday anyway."

"But what about you? What are you going to do, dad? That bike was your baby," Drew asked.

For the first time in a long while, Drew saw a smile creep across his father's face. He almost looked young again, like a teenager getting his first car. "Remember the XR1200, Drew? Released only in Europe? Well, we just got them in yesterday at the shop. Bernie told me that I can have one, my choice of color. I was thinking about black, this time. Already done the orange.

"'Course, it's gonna need a lot of work. The air flow on the stock version is all wrong, and it should really have the Buell heads from the Firebolt, but I think I can get it all straightened out," he said, eyes gleaming as he considered tinkering with his new toy.

Drew smiled. His father would be happy, kept busy for weeks tricking out the new Harley super bike. "Sounds great, dad." He glanced around. "Well, I suppose we should probably take off. We've got a ways to go before it gets dark again."

He rose. So did his father. Impulsively, they hugged. Father and son stood for a time, feeling closer than they had in three years, despite the vast gulf between their lives.

When they rejoined the others outside, both men had tears in their eyes. Mary looked closely at both of them, and smiled. She put her arms around them and squeezed.

"Drew Collins, you stay out of trouble, now. I have Ramona's word that she's going to stay very close to you, and watch you like a hawk." Behind her, Ramona smirked. Drew flushed, knowing what her idea of 'staying close' to him meant.

Parker came up and shook his hand. "You take care, Drew. Once I get settled, I'll call your cell and leave you my number. You need anything, you call us."

Drew nodded.

Finally, Doug and Amy stepped up. Awkwardly, Doug hit his best friend on the arm. "Well, so long. Don't do anything that we wouldn't do...I hope," he mumbled, looking at Amy wistfully.

"You truly are a moron, Jones," Drew said. "Take care. Amy, thanks a bunch. I can never repay you, but, thank you."

Bishop smiled at him. "I still owe you, Drew. You saved my little brother. That debt can never be repaid. However, it might help if you stop showing up at all hours, bleeding profusely. Then we could call it even."

Drew and Ramona walked out to the driveway where their Sportsters sat. With a final wave, they fired them up and drove off. As they watched the two ride away, Amy slipped her hand into Doug's.

"Don't do anything we wouldn't do?" she echoed, softly. Doug's surprised look gave way to an immense foolish grin. There had to be a God. And He, too, must have a thing for nurses.

EPILOGUE

Larry Lee Tate cursed as he stumbled. Just the night before, he'd taken refuge under the overpass, chasing off some old bum, who'd actually created a cozy place to bed down. Now, after more than a month of being on the run, he was still in Texas, and still flat broke. Those runaways and bums that he'd caught were penniless, having nothing of value.

Some of them he killed, just because they pissed him off. Some he killed because he was angry. Some got away, and some just didn't interest him at the time, so he let them scurry off.

Now, however, it was dark, and he was hungry. *And* it looked like some asshole freeloader had taken up residence in his spot. He'd have to make an example of this shit head, whoever he was. Or she. That thought brought a twisted smile to his cruel lips.

Maybe some fun before dinner, he thought, looking down at the shapeless mass huddled under his blanket.

"Hey, bitch, wake up. You're in my spot. Hey, asshole," he raised his voice, prodding at the person. He poked again, this time harder. "Hey, buddy, I'm talking to you," he growled, yanking the blanket back.

A huge wolf lay under the ratty blanket, shivering and covered in blood. Some of it looked dried, while fresh blood smeared his blanket and the ground under the animal. It was obviously in terrible shape.

"What the fuck?" he asked, dropping the blanket in surprise. "What the fuck are you doing here, wolfie? This here is my spot. Get out," he said, prodding the giant animal with his boot. "Fucking thing. Get out!" he yelled, kicking harder at the unresponsive beast.

The wolf reacted, suddenly lashing out and fastening its monstrous teeth onto his leg. Growling horribly, the injured wolf bit down, savaging the escaped convict's lower leg.

Larry Lee Tate howled in agony. He bent over and tried to pry the wolf's jaws off of his leg. When that failed he began beating the animals head with his fists. The pain made him lose it. A familiar red haze descended over his eyes, and he lost track of where he was, and what he was doing.

When he came to, the wolf was lying dead on the ground, and his hands were covered in fresh blood. His leg was torn open, pants ruined, and his own blood was soaking into his boot.

"God damn it!" he screamed. God hated him. The whole world hated him. That was fine; he hated them back. Furiously, he kicked the dead wolf again. And again. He ignored the pain in his mangled leg; it didn't matter. What mattered was that he was hurt, and that somebody had to pay for it.

His entire life was that way. And it wasn't over yet. More would pay before he was through. Lots more. Giggling, he licked blood from off his fingers.

Please Turn This Page
For A Preview Of

ABOMINATION

By Dan Coglan

ABOMINATION

INTRODUCTION

The RV rocked, heavy impact causing the thirty-nine foot camper's suspension to groan. Six-year old Chrissie Watts shrieked in fear. Her mother swept her up in her arms, holding her tightly.

"Hush, Chrissie, it's okay. It's just the wind. There's a nasty storm outside, but we're fine in here," Connie said, looking at her husband over the top of her child's head. Her eyes were wide with terror. Despite her soothing assurances to her daughter, she knew it wasn't a storm that had moved the camper.

Hoarse breathing was heard from just outside the door. The doorknob began to turn. The door was locked; the knob halted after only a partial rotation. A low growl of frustration sounded clearly, and the entire side of the RV rattled as something powerful slammed against it.

This time both Chrissie and her mother screamed. Christopher (Chris to his friends) Watts, entrepreneur and self-made millionaire, grabbed a golf club and stepped in front of his wife and daughter. Whatever was out there was smart enough to open doors. And it wanted in.

Watts pivoted, facing the front of his 2006 Fleetway, as he heard footsteps heading around the nose of his vehicle. He couldn't see anything, since his family had long since closed the curtains for the night.

Quickly, he threw back the curtains and flipped on the headlights. There was nothing in sight. The New Mexican campground looked much the same as it had earlier in the day

371

when his family and their guest had pulled in and hooked up water and electrical lines. Only a couple of other campers were visible, and there were no lights on in either one.

"Corey, you and Randy check the back bedroom. Be careful, and don't do anything to antagonize whatever it is, okay?" Corey was a responsible nineteen-year old, but way too eager to prove that he was as tough as his old man.

"Right, dad. We're on it," the husky young man answered, waving at his smaller friend to follow him. The narrow-faced, intense looking kid grudgingly followed his best friend towards the rear of the large RV.

They stepped past the bathroom, and gingerly opened the door to the surprisingly plush bedroom. It was empty. The curtains were drawn, and the bed was made. The Watts hadn't turned in yet, since the family vacation trip called for group activities like card games and movies.

Corey moved the curtain behind the bed aside and looked out. He thought he saw a shape dart away. "Hey, asshole, come back," he shouted, pounding on the glass.

"Corey, go easy, man. If somebody's out there, we don't want to piss him off," the timid boy warned.

"Geez, Randy, grow some balls, would you? There's somebody out there, messin' with us. It pisses me off. He's scaring mom and Chrissie." He turned back to the window and opened it a crack.

"Jerkoff, get back here. I got something for you," he called. The response was immediate.

A tremendous impact literally tore the corner of the bedroom off. It was a slide-out, so that the room could be enlarged when parked. There was a ripping, crashing sound, punctuated by a hideous roar as the back left end of the camper was peeled open.

Both young men staggered, thrown off balance by the concussion. Leaping through the opening at them was a figure from a nightmare. A large, man-shaped creature, covered in fur, mouth filled with fangs, and eyes blazing with insane fury, hurtled forwards and landed on the two.

Randy pulled away from the monster, curling into the fetal position beneath it, trying to make himself as small as possible. It didn't help: the creature leaned down and savagely bit into the cowering boy's neck. He cried out in agony.

Corey twisted, trying to free himself from the thing's leg. He punched at the hairy appendage, cursing at the top of his lungs. The vaguely lupine face whipped up from its first victim and snarled, blood dripping from massive canines. A tremendously muscled arm shot out, huge black claws extending out of what should have been fingers.

Corey staggered backwards, looking down in shock at the ruin that had been his chest and torso. As he crashed against the cabinet that had been built into the wall, he noticed idly that his intestines were spilling out onto the ground, looping on top of his splayed legs. Then his vision went dark.

The creature leaped up and charged down the short hallway, blasting Christopher Watt backwards and off his feet. Connie Watt turned away from the monster, shielding her screaming six-year old. It didn't matter.

The horribly growling man-thing ripped Connie's head completely off of her body, causing a brief geyser of blood, and then reached down and snatched up the child.

Christopher, bloody but back on his feet, swung the nine iron as hard as he could, bringing it down savagely on the creature's back. The monster merely grunted, and ripped its hands in opposite directions, silencing Chrissie's high-pitched shrieks by tearing her in half.

Her father screamed in outrage, swinging the club again. This time the beast reacted. It reached out, snatching the club out of the man's hands in mid swing. Roaring directly into Christopher's face, it snapped the club in half, throwing the pieces to either side, and then closing its hands around the man's head.

The monster wrenched its outsized claws down and slightly outwards, ripping the human's face open, and shredding into the chest cavity and then exiting down past the groin. The man collapsed like a marionette with its strings cut.

Howling triumphantly, the creature stood in the center of its bloodshed and carnage. Distantly, sirens could be heard. The upright beast looked around, spotted the locked door, and ripped it off its hinges on its way out of the RV. Shaking itself like a dog after a bath, the creature sent blood spraying everywhere and then raced off into the darkness.

CPSIA information can be obtained
at www.ICGtesting.com
Printed in the USA
FFOW04n2236310315
12304FF